BATTLETECH

BLOOD WILL RISE

BY TOM LEVEEN

BATTLETECH: BLOOD WILL RISE
By Tom Leveen
Cover art by Tan Ho Sim
Interior art by Chris Daranouvong, Dale Eadeh, Brent Evans, Stephen Huda, Harri
    Kallio, Matt Plog, and Anthony Scroggins
Cover design by David Kerber

Printed in USA.

Published by Catalyst Game Labs,
an imprint of InMediaRes Productions, LLC
5003 Main St. #110 • Tacoma, Washington 98407

PROLOGUE

CELESTIAL PALACE
CHANG-AN
LIAO
CAPELLAN CONFEDERATION
18 OCTOBER 3149

In Guanken's mind, he gave his left eye for the people.

The slender, quiet man, now in his seventies, had been born into a hard-working commonality caste family, and raised to be grateful for such a gift. He retained that gratitude through his education, which, while sufficient, showed that Guanken was not a particularly apt scholar.

The fierce gratitude instilled in him by his parents carried Guanken to the gates of one of the Capellan Confederation's great MechWarrior schools, where he hoped to qualify for the *janshi* caste, but dimmed when he washed out early. Guanken followed explicit orders very well, but lacked creativity and imagination, two things a good MechWarrior needed to succeed on the battlefield. He operated a BattleMech simulator well enough, but seemed unable to apply tactical thought in his simulations. To this very day, he had never sat in the cockpit of an actual 'Mech.

Undeterred, Guanken sought next to join the Capellan Confederation Armed Forces infantry. He survived his initial training, but in the first week of his operational training, an explosive charge went off too early and cost him the left side of his face, including his entire left eye.

During his recuperation in a military hospital, Guanken had been visited by a pair of smartly dressed women who identified themselves as Maskirovka—the espionage branch of the Capellan Confederation Armed Forces. They expressed sorrow for his condition on behalf of the entire CCAF, which would have made Guanken weep had he not been so heavily drugged. He adored "the Mask" as much as he, and all other Capellans, feared them.

The Mask agents went on to say they had read his records and, as he fit a particular profile they found intriguing, and would he be interested in serving the state in a new capacity? And by the way, this new job would bring with it a cybernetic eye allowing him to see and record everything his gaze fell upon for the rest of his life.

Guanken readily accepted the offer. Anything to serve the beloved state!

The ocular surgery, always a dicey proposition, went exceptionally well, so well that the cybernetic eye was indistinguishable from his natural one. So too did his facial reconstruction, a cosmetic operation not widely available to rank-and-file Capellans. Guanken bore a scar from the crown of his head down to his chin, but over time it had paled and softened, so that a person had to be facing his exact profile to see it.

Once back on his feet and with the cybernetic eye in full working order, Guanken went for further training on Sian, capital world of the Confederation. This training was unlike any he'd received to date: to become the perfect servant to the Celestial Wisdom himself, Chancellor Daoshen Liao.

Guanken still remembered how his heart had soared when his mission had been made clear. His life's work was now to serve at the pleasure of Daoshen, beloved leader of all Capellan space. He would clean, he would serve tea, he would lick the very soles of Daoshen's boots if so asked.

All he had to do to keep the job, his handlers said, was to keep his mouth shut and eyes open.

Literally.

This, it turned out, was the easiest part of the job. For more than twenty years now, he had been a part of the Chancellor's direct support staff, the army of commonality members and trustworthy servitors who kept buildings clean, cared for clothing and bedding, prepared food and drink, served it, and generally made life comfortable for the Celestial Wisdom so he could focus on the great responsibility of leading and protecting his people.

Such work was less glamorous than being a MechWarrior, but Guanken didn't mind. He served Daoshen personally!

Guanken and a handful of others like him had perfected the art of invisibility. They were furniture until it was time to act, and then they acted with silent, smooth efficiency. He had ascended the ranks of the servantry to become one of the few personal assistants granted intimate access to Daoshen. He brought tea when summoned, and made the empty dishes disappear silently and unobtrusively. He aided Daoshen in dressing in his ceremonial robes. He served the state.

Guanken also recorded hours, days, and years of footage for the Maskirovka.

"To protect the Chancellor," according to his handlers.

"For the good of the state," they'd tell him.

Yes, Guanken would think as he nodded. *For the good of the state.*

PART 1

CHAPTER 1

DRONANE
LIBERTY
CARVER SYSTEM
TIKONOV COMMONALITY
CAPELLAN CONFEDERATION
19 OCTOBER 3149

Danai Centrella-Liao sharpened her knife by hand.

She found the slight grinding of the whetstone against the blade eased her into a tranquil flow state, where she could freely associate and connect some of the eight million random thoughts occurring to her every minute.

As *sang-shao* of the Second McCarron's Armored Cavalry who had recently defeated two insurgencies, Danai needed every moment of tranquility she could muster.

Her calmness broke as someone knocked on the door to her quarters, a chilly home office appointed in pale, glaring wood.

"Come," Danai called, and winced. Her voice had been prone to giving out lately, growing as worn and scratched as the controls on her former BattleMech. She sat up straight, pulling the long, black hair of her hasty ponytail off her shoulders to hang down her back.

The heavily polished door opened. An exhausted smirk crossed Danai's face at the difference between the height of the top frame and the short stature of the man who walked in.

Wu Feng, standing 1.7 meters tall, but broad-shouldered, strutted into the office and closed the door behind him. Like Danai, he wore his green House Liao utility uniform, and Danai noticed gray concrete dust on his dark boots. She didn't care that some of the dust shook off on the silk carpets spread across the office floor. She didn't own the place; she'd appropriated this house weeks ago after putting down the insurgency here, in and around the bay city of Dronane. The house was well-decorated, having belonged to a Republic of the Sphere politician who now justly labored to rebuild the city as part of the Capellan servitor caste.

Such was the fate of any who sought to harm House Liao and its protectorate. With work and luck, he could become a Capellan citizen.

"*Zhong-shao* Wu," Danai said, greeting her executive officer by his rank, the equivalent of a lieutenant colonel in the Free Worlds League. She did not rise from her plush tan leather chair, sitting behind a broad oak desk that matched the door, window frames, and beams in the ceiling. Nor did she set down the combat knife, one of two Ceres Arms Slasher blades she normally wore in sheaths on her calves while in her BattleMech coolant suit. The second blade sat in its leather sheath beside a dark green blotter.

"*Sang-shao,*" Wu said with a nod, using Danai's military rank of colonel rather than her royal title, duchess. The MAC had a longstanding tradition of not saluting.

Danai scraped the blade with her stone a final time before using the tip to gesture at Wu's dusty boots. "I take it the rebuilding efforts continue to go well."

Wu Feng grinned. He gestured to one of the two padded chairs in front of Danai's desk, and the *sang-shao* nodded.

"Well enough," Wu said, sitting opposite her. Small clouds of dust puffed from his sleeves. "I was going to send Noah to give you an update, but he had a bit of an accident."

Danai tensed, her bronze skin flexing over her knuckles as her grip tightened on the knife. She considered *Sang-wei* Noah Capshaw the closest remaining thing to a friend a colonel and duchess could ever have. "Is he hurt?"

Wu's grin became a smile. "Only his pride. Face-down in wet cement."

He clapped his hands together vertically to illustrate.

Involuntarily, Danai jumped.

Quickly she dropped the blade onto the desk blotter and covered her eyes, hoping the amusing image of Noah Capshaw faceplanting into wet cement would elicit at least a chuckle from her—and conceal her surprised twitch.

No chuckle arrived. She hadn't laughed in ages. Or smiled.

As she set the whetstone down and reached over to put the knife back in its sheath, Wu's smile faded. "Noah did want to give you an update after getting cleaned up, *sang-shao*, but after hearing his report, I thought I'd come in his stead."

Danai slid the knife home and placed it beside its twin. "You don't look happy about that."

Wu shifted in the leather chair. His brown eyes peered at his commanding officer with something that, to Danai, resembled suspicion.

"As far as things here on Liberty go, we're tip-top," he said. He set his weight on the arms of the chair, leaning forward and casually lacing his fingers. "No snipers, no other insurgent activity. A few dust-ups in the local bars, nothing out of the ordinary. We've been taking it easy on the locals and going hard on our people, per your orders."

Danai nodded. Her current rules of engagement for the Second McCarron's mandated military combat not take place in cities and urban areas. Sometimes, leniency converted the conquered. Her rules allowed for military targets within a city as needed; otherwise, the MAC was to go easy on civilian territory. She based much of these engagement rules on the long-dead Ares Conventions, modeling how she wished to conduct campaigns.

In an ideal world, at any rate.

She hoped this care with civilian areas would help earn the hearts of the conquered to the Capellan cause, the welcoming them into the protection of the CCAF. Soon enough she would have to crack down on the local population if they continued to cause "dust-ups," but for the time being, Danai saw no reason to flex the might of the Inner Sphere's most powerful army.

To her way of thinking, the locals were themselves Capellans now, part of a long and proud legacy in which everyone worked for the betterment of everyone else. House Liao maintained a perfect—if hundreds-of-billions strong—family.

Whether these same locals accepted their new roles in Capellan society was another matter, one Danai hadn't the strength to enforce quite yet. She could, however, show them that a person in uniform was not above the law, hence her order for strict discipline among the Capellan ranks on the ground. She hoped it would send a proper message to the liberated populace.

"But Noah has other concerns, *Sang-shao*," Wu continued.

"Yes?"

"About you, ma'am."

Danai blinked. On guard now—a feeling she disliked in general, and particularly when with a trusted person like her XO—she sat back in her chair. "Me?"

Wu gently cleared his throat. "I appreciate the extra work you've been giving Noah. He's a good man, with a lot of potential, and he's rising to every occasion. Stumbling into wet concrete notwithstanding."

Neither of them smiled.

"So he's been spending more time in here with you," Wu said, scanning the office as if to illustrate the point. "He's seen you more often than I have since the Republic insurgency ended. And, to be frank, *Sang-shao*..."

"Be frank, indeed, *Zhong-shao*," Danai said. Her eyes narrowed. She did not like where this conversation was headed.

Wu plunged ahead, his forehead wrinkling. "He says you've been drifting. Losing focus. You're not as sharp as you were before."

Despite herself, Danai felt her eyes glazing over even as he spoke. "Before what?"

She knew the answer before he said it:

"Mina, Your Grace."

Even the use of Danai's royal title as Duchess of Castrovia did nothing to soften the stab of pain in her chest at the mention of Wilhemina Liao—also known as Mina.

Despite recent twin victories here on Liberty as well as the world of Hall, Danai felt the weight of leadership like a heavy winter cloak. The sensation seemed to restrict her movement and make her uncomfortably warm. She'd lost too much in both campaigns. She tried to tell herself it was all part of the life of a MechWarrior, never mind a *sang-shao* in charge of a regiment of hundreds of soldiers.

The losses incurred on Hall, in particular, had been more personal than usual.

Her thoughts darkened anew as memories of Mina, her royal mentor, came to the fore. Danai had spent too many hours these past months pushing away her memory and attendant grief. This ploy of ignoring her feelings had worked fine, as far as she was concerned; it left room for nothing but rage.

Thinking of Mina now, though, with Wu Feng's probing gaze upon her, Danai felt the dam of her emotions crumbling.

Capellan Chancellor Daoshen Liao, also known as The Celestial Wisdom, among other titles, had assigned Wilhelmina "Mina" Liao to be Danai's aide when he'd named her as Duchess of Castrovia. The lovely woman had stayed by Danai's side throughout the campaign on Hall, guiding and advising. Their relationship had been tenuous at the beginning, but as the days of war rolled on, Danai found Mina's quiet resolve and easy wisdom a winning combination.

Friends? Perhaps, perhaps not. *Sang-shaos* and duchesses were rarely afforded the luxury of having actual friendships, and Danai held both titles. Nevertheless, ultimately, Danai came to love Mina as a true and worthy friend. That, she could say in full truth.

Mina's death by an insurgent roadside bomb had ignited in Danai an unholy fury the likes of which she'd not felt in many years.

Fury...and a colossal sense of exhaustion.

"Mina," Danai said quietly, echoing Wu.

"If I may, Your Grace?"

Danai shook herself to clear her vision and set her gaze on Wu.

"We have Liberty well in hand," he said. "Fifth MAC is en route to take over for the Second. They'll be here in a week, maybe less. There's nothing pressing here for you to do, but you also can't relax. Not with people like me and Noah barging in with our reports on concrete mixing and water treatments. Maybe...a break is in order, ma'am."

Danai barely grasped the suggestion. "You want me to leave Liberty?"

"I want you to be your best for the Second MAC," Wu replied firmly, with no insubordination in his tone. The Second was Danai's regiment; Wu was her second in command. "If I was in a position to give you orders, which I am very, very not...I'd get you off this world and onto someplace nice for a while to..."

Here, Wu's words seemed to escape him. Danai waited for him to finish, but the XO only unlaced his fingers and made a gesture of uncertainty.

Danai understood. There wasn't more to be said. His point was well-taken.

And maybe even exactly right. Just hearing the suggestion of a break made that weighty, invisible winter cloak of despair feel just a shade lighter.

All the same...

"A *sang-shao* can't just up and hail a DropShip like a taxi," Danai said, sitting up straight. "I appreciate the suggestion, and I appreciate Noah being forthright with you about his concerns, but I'm fine."

Wu sighed and stood. He tugged his tunic straight and began dusting his palms together. Tiny plumes of concrete dust burst around his fingers.

"All due respect, ma'am—"

He clapped once, a sharp, explosive sound.

Danai tensed and jerked.

Wu met her eyes carefully.

"No, you are not."

CHAPTER 2

The various affairs of state that came with overseeing Liberty's reconstruction and education of the populace kept Danai from seeing Noah until the day after her conversation with Wu.

Having just finished an hour-long meeting with two local leaders and three of her own subordinates, Danai was sweaty and uncomfortable, and needed to get outside. She stalked out of the house and marched toward an area being rebuilt after the insurgency campaign, where she found *Sang-wei* Noah Capshaw directing a crew of Capellan servitors.

"*Sang-wei!*" Danai called as she walked toward him.

Capshaw spun, and braced his body immediately upon seeing who'd called his rank. The construction team scurried away at her approach. "*Sang-shao!*" he replied briskly.

Danai could see his nervousness. It almost amused her, and on the spur of the moment she decided to lean into it. Maybe it would rouse a smile. "I've not had a report from you in three days, *sang-wei*. Why?"

Sang-wei Capshaw had aged tremendously in the two and half years Danai had known him, and not for the better. She regretted the toll recent battles—victories and losses alike—had exacted on the young man's features. His once-bright white hair had taken a yellowish tone, and the bags beneath his eyes had grown heavier.

His salute-like brace was crisp as ever, though, Danai was pleased to note. Her own forty-first birthday had recently passed—quietly, and without fanfare, the way she preferred it—and she'd noticed slight aches and pains that hadn't existed even as recently as her first meeting with Capshaw, when he'd joined her command lance of the Second MAC two years ago.

War wreaked havoc on the human body, even when that body was busy winning battles across multiple worlds in the Inner Sphere. Danai had recently started gerontological treatments when she felt those aches persisting for longer than they should have.

"I beg your pardon, *Sang-shao*!" Noah said. "I felt my presence was needed at some of these construction sites. Per your orders, the buildings are being replicated in—"

Danai was too exhausted to keep up the pretense. Lowering her voice from a trainer's shout, she said, "At ease, Noah. I'm giving you a hard time. Walk with me."

With a relieved look, Noah relaxed his body. "Yes, *Sang-shao*."

She led them away from the noise of construction. IndustrialMechs moved laboriously through and around a decimated five-story building, repairing the foundation and gathering broken ferrocrete for disposal. Danai turned her head to watch the workers until they had passed the ruined building.

"Wu told me about your encounter with the wet cement," she said, now facing forward as they followed a sidewalk deeper into Dronane's downtown.

"Not something I'd care to do again, *Sang-shao*," Noah replied.

From the corner of her eye, Danai saw him blush.

"*Zhong-shao* Wu also shared your worries about me."

Noah sucked in an audible breath. "I am sorry, Your Grace, I didn't feel that—"

"It's all right. I'm glad you said something. In the future, I want you to know you have full permission to bring such concerns to me directly."

"Yes, Your Grace."

Danai crossed her arms, slowing their pace to allow a green-painted Capellan *Buster* IndustrialMech pass by at the upcoming intersection, its tracked feet rumbling and grinding across the road and sending vague tremors through her boots. Another WorkMech, a yellow *Carbine* with a cargolifter and backhoe for hands, followed close behind it.

She watched the 'Mechs trundle past. "You're a fascinating person, Noah. You've shown yourself adept on the battlefield, but you keep a warm heart. That's rare in our business. I hope you can maintain it. It may serve you well."

Noah's blush deepened. "Thank you, Your Grace."

The WorkMechs having passed, Danai continued their walk. "I want you to know I've given thought to what you and *Zhong-shao* Wu have now brought to my attention, and I have decided you are right. I may need a break."

Noah smiled, his blush receding. "I think that's wonderful, Your Grace!"

"So," Danai went on, "I have decided that when time permits, I will take a leave on Castrovia. It is 'my' world, after all, isn't it?"

She was unable to keep a certain tang of bitterness from her voice. Daoshen had named her Duchess of Castrovia, a title normally reserved for the next in line of the Chancellor's office, a position she did not covet. Plus, she'd already been named successor to her "sister" Ilsa's nation of the Magistracy of Canopus. Danai was replete with titles, and didn't want any more.

Which, she admitted privately and not without some antipathy toward her "brother" Daoshen, may well have been a factor in Daoshen's calculations. He did nothing without thought; granting her the title over Castrovia had some political benefit, else he wouldn't have done it.

Becoming the Duchess of Castrovia, though, was what had brought Mina into her life. The jagged memory of her murder cast a pall over any joy Danai might wring from being the ruler of an entire world. These last few days, as she'd reacquainted herself with the planet via holovids and books, she'd come to the conclusion—or perhaps acceptance—that she was, in fact, a duchess, and that perhaps such a title came with benefits she may as well enjoy.

And, with luck, help heal the loss she felt for Mina and so many other colleagues lost in the recent insurgencies.

"It won't be today," Danai clarified, trying to free her mind from emotions as they bubbled up. "I'll have to spend some time offloading my responsibilities here on Liberty to the Fifth MAC, and then, of course, hope there are no more invasions or insurgencies forthcoming in Capellan space."

Noah chuckled softly. "Well, I have heard Sheratan come up in recent briefings..."

Danai smirked. "Sheratan? Naturally. They've been rebelling against any flag within eyeshot for a thousand years. What's going on now?"

"Nothing of worry, Your Grace. I'm sure the local Liao militia will run any insurgents into the ground. But by the sound of it, the Sheratans are...tenacious?"

"For certain," Danai said. "Sheratan's reputation precedes itself." The temperate agricultural and mining world had traded hands over several centuries, most recently belonging to the Republic of the Sphere—until the Sheratans had booted them out. House Liao had moved to reclaim the world, which it had previously held almost continuously for centuries.

Every time a House tried to bring Sheratan into its fold, the Sheratans fought back.

They always lost, but they always fought. Danai could admire that.

She paused and turned to the younger man. "Noah, when I depart for Castrovia, whenever that may be, you will accompany me."

His eyes widened. "Me, Your Grace?"

"We really must do something about this humility of yours. Yes, you. Look." She gestured to another crew of workers and WorkMechs fixing a damaged wall in a commercial building. "This is your doing. You fight well, but you can also rebuild. You have good instincts. You will not be a *sang-wei* forever. One day, a regiment will be yours. Maybe even Second MAC, if you can wrest it from Wu when I'm finished here."

Noah ducked his head to cover a pleased grin.

"But to do that, there are other lessons to learn," Danai said. "Politics. Navigating Court intrigue. How to be served, as well as to serve. So, you will join me and start to learn these lessons."

Noah's grin slid to a frown. "But...shouldn't a higher rank accompany you, like *Zhong-shao* Wu? I don't want to step on anyone's—"

"Wu will be in charge here. Hell, he can run Second MAC entirely. No, I want you there."

"Yes, Your Grace."

They stopped as down the street, a Capellan worker got into a shouting match with a local businessman. The Capellan shoved the suited worker.

"I believe duty calls," Danai said. "We'll speak more later."

"Thank you, Your Grace," Noah said, but he was already turning away to rush over to the fracas.

Danai watched him go, envying his youth. But yes, she'd made the right choice to bring him along to Castrovia.

She returned to her office and began making plans to depart Liberty immediately.

CHAPTER 3

MAIN BUILDING OFFICE
NORTH PORT
QUANTICO ISLAND
LIBERTY
CAPELLAN CONFEDERATION
30 OCTOBER 3149

Sang-shao Gwendolyn Vaughan stood in her office overlooking Quantico's northernmost port with arms crossed and a grim smirk on her face. Through large picture windows, she watched one of several hammerhead cranes move cargo containers of spare parts around the large blue-water shipping terminal.

About damn time, she thought.

Gwen Vaughan was a tall woman, sporting close-shorn black hair and wearing Big MAC utilities with boots polished to a mirror shine. The boots weren't easy to get this way, not while working so close to an ocean.

That being said, she'd started to enjoy the salt air now that the MAC had booted the Republic Armed Forces off Liberty. There was no time for R&R, of course; tossing the RAF off-world had come at heavy costs. Gwen's Fifth MAC was in desperate need of repairs and parts.

The crates being unloaded now, primarily for BattleMechs and ground vehicles according to the receiving list, needed to get offloaded to warehouses ASAP. Gwen knew these replenishments were far from enough to get the Fifth back up to full capacity.

She'd take what she could get.

A knock on her office door jarred her. She turned and bellowed, "Come in!"

A short, lower-ranking soldier scurried inside with a noteputer. Vaughan thought his first name might be Stephen, but wasn't sure. His name tape read *Salzwedel.* "*San-ben-bing* Salzwedel," she said with a nod, reaching for the noteputer.

"Message, *sang-shao*," Salzwedel said in a worried tone. "The *Perkins* has missed two check-ins this morning."

Vaughan frowned at the screen. The *Perkins* was a submarine, full crew of 137, patrolling the waters around Quantico.

Salzwedel went on before she could ask any questions. "And the far sonar nets north of here are down."

"Down?" Vaughan barked. "Why?"

"Ma'am, that's the same area the *Perkins* was set to patrol today."

A worm of unease unspooled in Vaughan's stomach. "And our other ships?"

"Reporting anomalies in that part of the water."

Anomalies, Vaughan thought. *Just like that new tech the RAF threw at us, maybe?*

She didn't bother waiting for the worm of unease to grow any larger. Sometimes, instinct was the better part of defense. And her instincts were on fire.

"All hands," she ordered. "Battle stations. Now!"

Salzwedel asked no questions. He darted from the room. Vaughan heard him shouting the order as he raced down the hallway and through the building.

No, no, no! Vaughan thought. *It cannot be those RAF bastards, not already—*

In the dockyard, a ship blew apart in a blazing red and yellow fireball. Vaughan's building was close enough, she could feel the tremor in the floor.

She took a stunned step backward as multiple *Phoenix Hawk* BattleMechs emerged from the water. *The sea*, she thought dimly. *They came from the sea. Like the pirates they are...*

Even as she raced from the office to reach the command center, Vaughan thought she understood the details of the attack flashing through her brain in nanoseconds.

The RAF had re-grouped off-world and used a pirate jump point to return to Liberty. How in the hell they'd disrupted or destroyed the sonar nets in the ocean protecting the shipyard, Vaughan couldn't guess; she only knew in her gut they had. Maybe it was some ECM gizmo that had failed land tests but worked well enough in the water, or maybe it was some bit of *lostech* yanked from mothballs, or maybe it was RAF special forces working with exceptionally camouflaged battlesuits. She remembered clearly the advanced camo battlesuits the RAF had used this past summer; maybe that was how they'd disabled CCAF early warning systems in the ocean...

Doesn't matter, don't care, Vaughan thought as she ran. The reality of a dozen *Phoenix Hawk*s making short work of the thin hulls of the blue-water navy in the shipyard were all the facts she needed right now.

She reached the top floor of the office, lungs pumping hard. "Report!"

The makeshift command center she'd established for Quantico buzzed as angrily as a nest of hornets. Professionals that they were, the Fifth MAC wasn't panicking—but Vaughan tasted it in the air.

Instead of offering an immediate answer to her request, one of her subordinates, a young woman named Kesh, raced to Vaughan and gestured to the doorway the *sang-shao* had just come through. "Ma'am," she said breathlessly, her short, white hair glistening in the overhead lights, "we need to get you back to Bellacqu."

"Not bloody likely," Vaughan snapped. "I said report."

Kesh shot a worried glance at the command center's holotank. The three-dimensional projections showed the entire north wharfs being overrun by RAF *Phoenix Hawk*s. Only now were Third MAC forces scrambling to intercept. On the relatively calm ocean surface, dozens of RAF Cizin and Scapha hovercraft skimmed toward the docks.

"We've identified them as Fifth Fides," Kesh replied. "They somehow shut down the sonar nets and took out at least one of our subs, maybe more. Half a dozen of our ships have stopped responding."

Vaughan stared at the holograms as Kesh spoke. Half or more of her 'Mechs and other ground forces were in repair bays, and another quarter of those fit for duty were low on ammo or suffering an armor shortage.

Her military brain scanned all available information about their position. The CCAF had reoccupied the crumbling Quantico Marine Fortification ruins and begun restoring its defenses, but if the Fifth Fides was at full strength or the RAF had additional forces ready to deploy, Vaughan wasn't convinced the fortifications would hold. Not in the Fifth MAC's current state of readiness.

Reality sank in quickly. "We have to hold them here," she said. "Because if we don't..."

Kesh nodded, and Vaughan could see metaphorical dominos toppling in the younger woman's eyes. If the RAF established a beachhead here, within days—maybe less—they could potentially march across the entire island and take it back from the Capellans.

"We just took this goddamn planet," Vaughan seethed. "I'm not about to hand it back." She shouted over the command center: "All hands! Eyes on me! Comms, you stay at your posts and be ready to coordinate a tactical withdrawal on my mark. Otherwise, if you are ambulatory and can fire a weapon, get down to the docks! Move!"

She rushed from the command center without waiting for acknowledgement. This was Fifth MAC—they'd do their jobs.

The *sang-shao* took her own order as well, running hard for her BattleMech to join the fray unfolding on the wharf.

Sang-shao Vaughan was belted into the cockpit of her *Marauder II* in mere minutes. And mere minutes later, she was moving the massive war machine out of its repair bay and directly into the fight with the Fifth Fides assault force bouncing from the water onto the beaches around the wharf.

The *Phoenix Hawk*s were supplemented by additional units, Vaughan saw immediately; even as her HUD lit up with enemy targets, she noted a *Warhammer*, *Kheper*, and *Berserker* among the ranks of the RAF, strafing boats and Fifth MAC units alike.

Crisscrossing laser beams turned the air into a latticework of glowing horror. *Sang-shao* Vaughan marched straight into the middle of it, sending azure blasts of PPC fire into every painted target within reach. Her warrior mind achieved a sort of quiet calm, as if watching the battle from above. Here came a *Kheper*, firing deadly Gauss rounds; Vaughan retaliated with two shots from her medium lasers.

Like many of the Fifth MAC units, her *Marauder II* was empty of ammo for her autocannon. Vaughan paid the fact no heed. As long as the cannons in her 'Mech's arms held up, she'd stay in the fight.

Three enemy BattleMechs converged on her position, firing at will. The *Marauder II* suffered multiple hits across the front of its body, melting slag or pinging off armor. On instinct, Vaughan fired her jump jets and landed behind the approaching *Warhammer*. Even as the ground still trembled from her landing, the *sang-shao* fired both PPCs at the rear flank of her target.

The *Warhammer* spun to evade, but took both shots in its side. The *Kheper* and *Berserker* both hurried to adjust their fire as well, but held back momentarily; Vaughan's jump had put their comrade in the line of fire.

Vaughan jumped again, this time backward, pointing her massive BattleMech at a cluster of hovercraft racing toward the main building. An infantry battle raged outside its doors, the MAC taking cover behind decorative pillars while the hovercraft unleashed a torrent of lasers and slug throwers.

She timed her jump well, landing 100 tons of destruction on the front end of one hovercraft that hadn't been able to slip out of the way. With the machine at a standstill, Vaughan pointed one arm at the top of the craft and blew it apart with a blast from her PPC.

The other hovercraft laid on their accelerators, darting and weaving between enemy and friendly units alike to help prevent their buddy's fate. Watching them while she retreated away from the three 'Mechs still pursuing her, Vaughan took a brief moment to assess the battlespace outside her cockpit window.

All around the wharf, the grayscale paint schemes of her beloved Fifth MAC BattleMechs were scored and scarred with laser marks. Chunks of armor were missing from torsos, legs, and arms. A MAC *Dola* on her right stumbled and fell facedown as two *Phoenix Hawk*s blasted its left foot out from under it.

The Fifth Fides swarmed like ants over the wharf. In the water, several ships were clearly sinking. But the invaders were taking care not to target the fuel depot or other critical infrastructure.

They meant to stick around.

Vaughan pivoted and fired back at the three 'Mechs closing in on her again. Her heart ached with realization even as she managed to stop the pursuing *Berserker* in its tracks with a well-placed PPC shot to its right hip.

"All units," she said into her comm. "This is Vaughan. Retreat. I say again, retreat. It's over. Fall back to rendezvous Bravo."

She fired her jump jets, sailing the hundred-tonner over a fuel truck, which her pursuers again avoided firing upon. Vaughan pushed her *Marauder II* hard to the south, away from the carnage on the wharf, aiming for the MAC's predetermined fallback position.

Still ensconced in her cockpit, where no one needed to see, she wept bitterly.

CHAPTER 4

RAINSPIRE
SHERATAN V
TIKONOV COMMONALITY
CAPELLAN CONFEDERATION
15 NOVEMBER 3149

Jack Cade recalled a story from long ago, a tale told by his dearly departed father about a little village struggling amid a terrible drought. The village came together to pool a portion of each family's meager water ration to tend a sapling planted in the town square. This was their resistance, their resilience; their way of telling the drought itself that they would never give up fighting it, never surrender.

Ultimately, the village succumbed.

But the tree remained, nourished by their most precious resource until it could survive on its own. According to the parable, that tree still stood, testament to humankind's will in the face of certain destruction.

Jack thought a lot about that tree.

It had been on his mind the past few months in particular, and it loomed large in his mind now as he sat at a round table at the Hacker, his favorite local pub since he'd first become a MechWarrior.

Goddamn, that was a long time ago, he thought, only half-listening to one of his buddies growling and pissing about the dirty Caps. Jack extended his fingers and studied the tan color he'd inherited from his father, and the rough callouses he'd earned from combat.

"So let's mount up and kick these ratsuckers out!" Hemitt was saying by the time Jack tuned back in. "We've done it before. It's our right, it's our *heritage*!"

For the past six weeks, the town of Rainspire had been making life tough on the Capellan garrison. The Caps had recently lost three people to improvised explosives tossed into their hangouts, and the townspeople had held the line against giving up any information they had on which Sheratans might be responsible. As word of these attacks spread, other parts of Sheratan were starting to follow suit. Even the larger cities had turned to Rainspire as inspiration. Those cities weren't violent yet, but they'd get there, so long as Rainspire continued to lead the charge.

Jack inhaled deeply through his nose, taking in the scent of earthy pipe smoke and spilled beer. The plank floor of the Hacker was redolent with both, never mind the fresh pipes being lit or the newly poured beers being spilled. This bitter, rich combination never failed to soothe his mind. This was home.

He interrupted Hemitt as the other man was about to begin another tirade. "Your 'heritage' is gonna get blown off with the rest of your dainty bits if you field what we have against what the Caps will send," Jack said. He sipped his blackberry mead, savoring the rich alcohol, fermented locally with Sheratan honey. Delicious.

The others at the table turned in unison to look at him. He hadn't spoken in thirty minutes.

"All right, Jack," Hemitt said through gritted teeth. "What's your plan, eh? Roadside IEDs? Snipers? Bake sale with poisoned cookies? Eh? What?"

Jack shook his head with a little smile hidden behind his graying beard. "You're starting from the wrong place, Hem. Start at the goal and work backward."

Hemitt slammed a fist on the table, rattling the glasses atop it. No one flinched; such behavior was the norm for the man. "Dammit, I am! The goal is to make every Capellan on this world pay for being here and taking our independence!"

Jack raised his glass and swirled the ruby red liquid. "Is it?" he asked. "Ought it be? I'm not sure."

He took a sip, finishing the flute, and set it down. With a contented sigh, he laced his fingers across his ample belly and sat back in his chair.

"Sometimes," he said, "all you gotta do is plant a tree."

CHAPTER 5

CELESTIAL PALACE
CHANG-AN
LIAO
TIKONOV COMMONALITY
CAPELLAN CONFEDERATION
16 NOVEMBER 3149

The Celestial Wisdom, Chancellor Daoshen, ordered an invasion early in the morning. Guanken saw and heard it all. So did his cybernetic eye.

The Celestial Wisdom gave the order to a room full of his top *jiang-jun*—generals and other military advisors known as the Strategios.

Meeting in one of the massive conference rooms in Daoshen's palace in the resplendent city of Chang-an, the Strategios sat around a circular redwood table centered beneath a frosted, domed skylight. The smooth, pale walls formed a circle, with one double-doored entrance for guests and a smaller, nearly concealed portal for servants like Guanken. Four massive crimson pillars, 8 meters tall, held up the ceiling. Glistening black tiles paved the floor in nearly seamless 2-meter squares.

Guanken and three other servants had already prepared and served green tea in delicate white cups, which now dotted the table. The cups were empty; the meeting had carried on for thirty minutes.

Guanken and his confederates stood against the curved wall, eyes slightly averted to the floor, trusting their highly attuned peripheral vision to alert them to any needs of the Strategios.

The generals had fussed and argued amongst themselves for most of the half-hour, and most of their ramblings left Guanken a bit dizzy. He hadn't spent nearly enough time in the military to fully appreciate their jargon, so he tuned it out and kept his focus on Daoshen, attentive to any slight shift in his mood or demeanor that Guanken could address.

"The future of Liao lies coreward," said the Celestial Wisdom.

Guanken concealed a shudder of joy beneath his loose red silk uniform. He adored the Celestial Wisdom's voice—smooth, articulate, gentle. Yet also commanding, unyielding, confident.

For that voice, Guanken would die if so ordered.

Most of the attending generals, he saw, grew still before nodding their agreement. The few outliers who did not nod sat motionless; their faces utterly expressionless.

Daoshen issued this pronouncement from a throne at the far side of the table. The enormous seat was carved with hissing dragons belching cherrywood fire. The Chancellor's white robes stood out upon it like a photo-negative pupil.

"Danai's recent gains and other victories permit us to move more assets coreward," Daoshen went on, his divine voice echoing gently between the pillars. "Forces of the Republic of the Sphere fall daily. Their resistance is token at best. Therefore, now is the time to take Keid. For a start."

None of the Strategios moved.

Automatically, Guanken's meager education conjured a mental Capellan system map and identified Keid. In its early history, the planet had been known for its agriculture and valuable minerals. Once a Capellan holding, the world had fallen to a succession of invaders, most recently the Republic of the Sphere. To Guanken's knowledge, the RotS or "Rotters" still held the planet and its vast industries. His mouth nearly puckered at the thought, and he fought an urge to spit.

The Celestial Wisdom's next words echoed Guanken's personal belief: "Keid belongs to the Capellan people. It must be returned to them, and their subjugated populace welcomed back into the family of Liao. It is so ordered."

Guanken noted an ever so slight hesitation before the Strategios stood—and applauded. He had to force himself not to clap along with them, overwhelmed by the Celestial Wisdom's love for his people.

"What of Sirius, Chancellor?" asked one of the Strategios. "We have drawn up battle plans."

"Commit nothing to Sirius for the moment," Daoshen replied with a dismissive wave of his fingers. "But be prepared. The battlespace will change rapidly."

The Strategio nodded his understanding, while the others quickly wrote notes on electronic tablets or pads of cream-colored paper.

Another general, a tall woman with heavy black eyebrows and trim, dark-red hair, placed an open palm against her chest and bowed to Daoshen. Guanken did not know her name, but many combat awards gleamed on her uniform. "We will begin preparations immediately for the taking of Keid, Celestial Wisdom. We will deliver the planet back to the people with all haste."

Daoshen stood from his throne. Guanken marveled at his grace.

"Good," Daoshen said with a faint smile. "We shall make an official visit next year, if not sooner."

Guanken detected movement among the Strategios; a shift in the atmosphere.

"Visit, Your Grace?" a short, somewhat rotund man asked. Guanken could not see his rank.

"By next year?" asked another, a bald man whose pate shone beneath the skylight.

Daoshen slipped his hands into the wide sleeves of his robe. Guanken's heart soared to watch his poise as the Celestial Wisdom stepped away from his throne and walked a slow circle around his Strategios.

Guanken took pride in noting how the Celestial Wisdom stood just slightly taller than anyone else in the room, even the woman with red hair. The Celestial Wisdom's robes draped to the floor, concealing his feet. No one—*no one!*—would ever know how many centimeters were added to the heels of Daoshen's soft boots, which Guanken polished himself each morning.

"The Capellan Confederation is the greatest military force in the Inner Sphere," Daoshen said as he paced a circle around the others. "Even the Clans tremble at our might. Yet despite our overwhelming strength, it is not always raw power that serves us best. It is the imposition of will, the breaking of our enemy's confidence, that wins wars."

Daoshen finished his circumnavigation and ended beside his throne. "When the Chancellor of Capellan space sits enthroned on Keid, a world rightfully our own, the Inner Sphere will hear clearly our intent and see plainly our power. In this way, the greatest liberation of all will have begun, and the enslaved people of our enemies will gladly welcome our confederation."

The greatest liberation of all? The Celestial Wisdom meant Terra, birthplace of humanity.

Guanken nearly wept.

He waited anxiously for the assembled generals to applaud once more. When the applause did not rise, Guanken frowned—though no one observing him would have seen it. He and the other highly placed servants could express all sorts of emotion without moving a single muscle.

"While I agree that we will take Keid with all haste," said the bald officer, "We...may need more time to properly take and hold it."

Daoshen turned his head slightly to let his wise gaze fall upon the man. Power shone from his eyes. "There is nothing to stop us, *Jiang-jun*."

The officer swallowed and dipped his head. "Of course, Your Grace. Our preparation will begin immediately."

Daoshen blinked slowly and recentered his head. "That is all."

The assembly bowed in unison and walked toward the double doors. Two of Guanken's fellow servants were there long before the doors were reached, and opened them for the officers. As Guanken's duty at the moment was to attend the refreshments, he stayed at his post and waited for the Celestial Wisdom to exit or else issue some other order.

One man stayed behind, however. Guanken recognized him as Kamer, a member of Daoshen's immediate bodyguard detail, and loyal member of the Maskirovka. Kamer's long blond hair shone brightly in the conference room, as if made from golden steel. The man showed few wrinkles, but his dark skin appeared dry and even cracked in places, like an old statue.

He offered a shallow bow to Daoshen. "Your Grace, if I may have a moment?"

"Kamer," Daoshen replied.

Guanken knew little of Kamer personally, but appreciated how relaxed Daoshen looked in his presence. Ensuring the Celestial Wisdom's peace of mind was chief among Guanken's priorities. Kamer had been on the Chancellor's detail for many years.

"My heart is heavy, Your Grace, but the time has come for me to retire from my position, with Your Grace's permission."

Daoshen smiled, showing no teeth. "Well-earned, Kamer. Go and enjoy the fruits of your labor for the people."

"Thank you, Your Grace. I'll be departing soon to fetch my replacement. We will both join you here for a transition period. You should know I have overseen her recruitment, training, and selection myself. She is one of our finest. You will find her a good match for your security detail. I trust her implicitly."

"If she comes with your approval, say nothing more. What is her age, Kamer?"

"Her birthday was yesterday, she just turned twenty-one, Your Grace."

"I shall look forward to meeting her. Perhaps one day..." Daoshen added, "she and her descendants will have the privilege of celebrating a birthday experienced on Terra."

Kamer returned a knowing smile. "With all haste, Your Grace. Have you a need for anything else?"

"No, Kamer. Go and fetch your protégé. We are anxious to meet the youngster."

Kamer offered another shallow bow before turning and marching to the exit, with the two doors still held open by Guanken's fellow servants.

A birthday on Terra, Guanken thought, trembling. *What a gift that would make!*

CHAPTER 6

LAW ENFORCEMENT OFFICE A/3
COMMERCIAL DISTRICT
RAINSPIRE
SHERATAN
TIKONOV COMMONALITY
CAPELLAN CONFEDERATION
30 NOVEMBER 3149

"That is *it*!"

Sang-wei Ori Juang slammed the flat of her hand against her desk. Her subordinate, *San-ben-bing* Antony Hayes, twitched.

Juang pointed a finger at Hayes as if he was personally responsible for the report on her desk. "Double the SecurityMech presence across the city. No, triple it! The very instant anyone on these streets steps out of line, take them into custody or gun them down!"

Hayes considered his next words very carefully. *Sang-wei* Juang was known to her subordinates to be a 100-percent type of person; the type who, in her good moods, would buy rounds of drinks and whoop it up with others half her age.

The counterpoint was moments like this: unfettered fury.

On the other hand, Hayes and his security crew knew such anger was never misplaced. Juang loved her security team, and not a one of them doubted her commitment to their safety. Woe to those who harmed "her kids."

And some rebel in Rainspire had done exactly that. Again.

His eyes dipped briefly to the noteputer on Juang's desk. On the screen, the most recent casualty report still glowed white. Daniel Teye, a *si-ben-bing* in the security brigade, was the latest victim of a seemingly random crime that took his life. A mugging, the report claimed—but Hayes knew as well as Juang that this was merely code for an assassination by a growing rebellion. Teye had been the equivalent of a beat cop, with no useful intel to insurgents, which meant he'd just been the wrong Capellan in the wrong place at the wrong time.

It could have easily been me, he thought. *It still may be some day.*

"I can put more people on the schedule, *Sang-wei*," he said after only the barest hesitation. "But we cannot double or triple the 'Mech presence because we don't have double or triple the 'Mechs. There's a few busted ones in the motor pool we could maybe get running again. Barely. But that's it."

"Do it. I want armor on those streets, even if it's just for show."

"Yes, ma'am."

Juang sat back down in her office chair, fist clenched. "Let's not bullshit this, Hayes. Are we actually going to find the sonofabitch who did this?"

Hayes wanted to lie, but Juang needed honesty. "I doubt it. Crowded space, nighttime. A public that's either in bed with the rebels or turning a blind eye to them. Teye's killer is a ghost."

"A ghost still out there, just waiting for another opportunity," Juang growled.

"Agreed, *Sang-wei*."

Juang lifted her gaze to him, but her expression had softened. "What am I going to tell his daughter? The same bull I've told the other partners and children, I guess. Dammit!"

Hayes knew Teye had been a single father. The mother of his child had been killed years before in a pitched 'Mech battle off-world. His daughter was now ten.

He said nothing.

Juang opened her mouth to issue either another rant or an order, but was interrupted by a cry from the front office.

Both officers ran from the room, Hayes in the lead to protect his senior if necessary. But the ruckus came from an unusual source: a girl of maybe twelve years old, standing near the double doors of the police station main office, weeping—

And bloody.

"My god," Hayes muttered and raced closer.

The girl, with fine features and long, blond hair, held up her left forearm. Her skin glistened wetly with fresh blood.

"What happened?" Hayes snapped as he approached through the rows of officers' desks. Most of the people here had already gotten up to help. They parted for Hayes when he reached the crowd.

"Outside!" the girl wailed. "A man with a knife!"

"Just now?" Hayes demanded. His fingers traced the handle of his pistol.

The girl nodded quickly, her expression a blend of terror and pain.

Her nod was all the impetus Hayes and the others needed. Drawing their weapons, the team rushed from the building, out to the city street.

Their building sat on a street corner, and Hayes blinked at the realization that the crossroads were unusually vacant for mid-morning. Nor did any of the usual foot traffic clog up the sidewalk.

When his gaze snapped to a white trash can he didn't recall having seen before, the scenario became clear.

"Back!" he cried—but too late.

The trash can burst apart in an explosion of shrapnel. Searing bits of metal blazed into Hayes' face, chest, and groin. He saw several of his fellow officers clutching their faces, falling down, bleeding, screaming.

He landed hard on the concrete. Gray smoke obscured his vision, for which he was grateful—he was alive and could see, anyway. For the moment.

Instinctively, Hayes lifted his head to scan for his boss. He saw Juang hurtling out the station doors, headed straight for him.

Wait, the girl, he thought groggily, and tried to form the words as Juang began assessing him. *Where is the girl?* Sangwei, *it was her, it was a setup, she wasn't injured at all...*

But the girl had vanished.

Also, he found that he could not speak, for he had no jaw.

CHAPTER 7

LUNG WANG-CLASS DROPSHIP GLADIATOR
CASTROVIA SYSTEM
SIAN COMMONALITY
CAPELLAN CONFEDERATION
25 DECEMBER 3149

Merry Christmas, Danai thought, tapping the flat of one of her knives against her bare palm.

Her accommodations on the DropShip—like all military transports—were anything but merry. As a *sang-shao*, never mind being Duchess of Castrovia, Danai was afforded luxuries aboard the ship others were not. A private bunk, for one, although she shared a head with the ship's captain. This private room measured long enough to accommodate her thin bed, with another half-meter allowance for the doorway; no more. In width, it measured scant centimeters beyond Danai's outstretched arms.

Ah, the plush life of a duchess, she thought wryly, even as she appreciated the passing of stars outside her room's single porthole window.

The DropShip was mere hours from touching down on Castrovia, yet Danai felt compelled to continue working. *If by "working," one means "fretting,"* she thought, and slapped the blade against her palm again.

In this particular moment, she stared at the noteputer screen strapped to her laughably miniature desk, charting the movements of the Capellan Confederation Armed Forces as a headache pounded her temples.

She winced and rubbed the left side of her head with her fingers. Her brother the Chancellor was no fool, but Danai wondered at his thinking. Daoshen had reduced his plans for Phase Two of Operation Tiamat. Rather than reclaiming both Sirius and Keid, he had opted to focus solely on Keid. According to her latest briefing, Keid was fully in Capellan hands, having experienced resistance only from local militia, which had crumbled quickly.

Taking Keid is a good victory, Danai thought, *but it leaves the obvious question: Where are the Republic Armed Forces?* Despite the relative ease of taking Keid, in her professional opinion, House Liao risked fighting too many wars on too many fronts.

The Federated Suns, also known as House Davion, had not attacked them—yet. The Chancellor's recent incendiary speech to the Confederation, in which he directly countermanded Danai's own negotiated truce with Julian Davion, had lit a fuse with the Capellan public, which was Daoshen's precise intention. At the time of her non-aggression agreement with Davion, Danai had considered it a diplomatic—and, frankly, military—victory. Then Daoshen had spent half an hour last year announcing to the entire Confederation that the CCAF was *at war* with Davion, that House Liao would do everything to protect its beloved citizens.

Trash. All of it. Total garbage.

In practice, the treaty Danai brokered with Julian Davion still held, but the rhetoric on both sides spoke of nothing but war. Danai clearly recalled Mina's explanation of Daoshen's purpose: keep the people focused on a bogeyman they already hated while the Chancellor plunged onward toward Terra. The ploy had worked, and all too well; Maskirovka intelligence from Davion space indicated no immediate threat, but centuries of warfare with the other Great House meant the peace could shatter at any moment.

So the Davions were one piece on the game board Daoshen had to consider.

Then there were Clans. The damned, damned Clans.

After the defeat of Stefan Amaris and the fall of the Star League in the 28th century, General Aleksandr Kerensky led his Star League Defense Force into deep space to escape the coming civil war and preserve their ideals. Decades later, his son Nicholas forged a new society from the fractured remnants—a warrior-led civilization known as the Clans. The Clans' very existence was predicated on the claiming of Terra, and short of their utter destruction, the Clans would never stop pursuing their goal of possessing humanity's homeworld. And they had the technology and numbers to do it.

The Solaris gladiator in Danai would have relished a BattleMech confrontation with MechWarriors from Clan Jade Falcon or Clan Wolf, the two leading candidates to reach and conquer Terra. Her trigger fingers itched to have some good old-fashioned toe-to-toe slugfests with them.

But the veteran regiment commander in her knew better than to pick a fight with them just for the sake of the fight. The CCAF was currently the heavyweight in the ring of the Inner Sphere, and the Inner Sphere knew it. So too must the Clans. If Daoshen continued his race for Terra, however, conflict with at least two Clans, the Wolves and the Jade Falcons, was inevitable. Ultimately, Danai wasn't keen on the idea of fighting either, much less both at the same time.

No. For the foreseeable future, war with the Clans was a fool's errand.

And what of our "good friends," the Draconis Combine? she mused. By treaty, they and the Capellans had left one another alone recently, so both could press their goals abroad without fear of the other. That alliance had been shaky to begin with, and Danai wasn't entirely sure where the agreement lay at the moment. Certainly the Combine had its own designs on Terra, and Daoshen would never share humanity's homeworld with another House. Danai believed the Combine had its hands too full on other borders to risk a strike against the Capellans, but that didn't mean they weren't a piece of this giant, bloody puzzle.

And finally: if Daoshen Liao really did press forward the goal of conquering Terra, not only were the Clans baying at the door, but the remnants of the Republic of the Sphere had almost certainly marshaled all available resources to Terra as well. That would help explain why resistance on Keid had been so light thus far.

Once, not long ago, the Strategios and Daoshen himself had been certain a Rotter incursion into Capellan space was forthcoming. That incursion had not materialized. So where was the RAF? Only a few months ago, Danai herself had witnessed DropShips tearing into the sky off Liberty, doubtless full of RAF personnel and materiel. They had to have gone *somewhere*.

Smart money was back to Terra.

Danai bristled at the thought of a potential five-way war for Terra among the Confederation, Jade Falcon, Clan Wolf, the Draconis Combine, and the RAF. Never mind if Davion got into the mix again on the Capellan flank, or made some kind of half-assed gambit for Terra. She understood Daoshen's intent to open a direct corridor of worlds coreward toward Terra; such maneuvering would allow a clear path for weapons and equipment to marshal nearer to the world than Sian or Liao. But the taking—and holding—of humanity's homeworld would require every single resource House Liao could muster coreward, leaving many gaps in their defenses behind them as they went.

"Foolish," Danai whispered, then thought, *All of us are*.

She slipped her knife into its sheath and rubbed her head between both hands. Squeezing her eyes shut, she tried to order her brain to stop spinning. When it didn't, Danai opened her eyes and reached for the comm to request hot tea—but her voice escaped her as Castrovia slipped into view in the porthole window.

Mouth hanging open, Danai unbuckled herself from her seat and floated away from the desk, pulling herself toward the window. Placing her hands on the cold bulkhead, she nearly pressed her face to the safety glass like a child at an aquarium.

Danai had never been to Castrovia before. She'd heard reports of its beauty, and as a veteran of many years of interstellar combat, she'd seen a great many beautiful worlds from space.

Castrovia left them all behind.

More than ten years ago, Danai had traveled to Terra to attend the funeral of Victor Steiner-Davion. Approaching the bright blue world had left her somewhat awestruck, but Terra had the weight of reputation, history, and legend behind it.

As the DropShip sank into an approach orbit around Castrovia, Danai caught herself thinking: *This is mine?*

Far past the planet but still visible to her naked eye, a dense orange and blue stellar nursery nebula hung suspended in the cosmos. Danai wondered what it must look like at night from Castrovia. A faint blue ring surrounded the planet. Barely visible, a tiny and shockingly fast moon—a captured asteroid, perhaps—raced along the ring's perimeter like a dog on a track. The small moon itself gleamed white, leaving her to guess blindly at its composition.

Castrovia's sun burned cool, causing the planet's upper atmosphere to have a greenish cast not seen while approaching Terra. Dozens of white clouds whorled and spun on this side of the world like little whirlpools over one of the planet's oceans.

"Little," of course, was relative. On the planet's surface, each one of those whirls must be a colossal storm.

It's beautiful... she thought, and something tight in her chest loosened, a tightness she hadn't realized—until it vanished—she'd been carrying for many months. She smiled, and only noticed because the small muscles in her face complained briefly. It had been so long, the muscles seemed to have atrophied.

She backed away from the porthole and groped behind her for the intercom, not wanting to miss a moment of the planet's passing. She called for Noah.

"Noah," she said, trying not to sound breathless. "How soon 'til we land?"

Her aide, as she now thought of him for the duration of their stay, replied less than a minute later. "About an hour, Your Grace."

"Have you seen it?"

"Seen what, Your Grace?"

"Castrovia. Go, look."

The comm fell silent for a few moments before Noah returned. "It's amazing!"

"Yes," Danai said. "It is." Stunned at the wonder in her own voice, she blinked and added, "I'll meet you in the disembarkation lounge after touchdown."

"Copy that, Your Grace."

Danai hung the small transmitter back in its cradle and returned to the porthole to watch the world—*her* world—drift past.

She no longer had a headache.

CHAPTER 8

MIRNY SPACEPORT
LIANGRAD
CASTROVIA
SIAN COMMONALITY
CAPELLAN CONFEDERATION
26 DEC 3149

Danai was accustomed to stepping out of a DropShip in a BattleMech, walking down a boarding ramp to an unfamiliar world and environment. Jungles, deserts, icy plains—every combat drop was different, with different sets of tactical needs she had to address on the fly.

Disembarking on Castrovia was an entirely different experience. The gravity here was ever so slightly less than on most of the worlds Danai had traversed, and she felt the difference as soon as the DropShip touched down. She and Noah followed a ramp out of the ship to take their first breaths of Castrovian air on their way to a wheeled transport.

As Danai's boots clacked on the cold, hard steel ramp, her step had an undeniable skip that, to her horror, made her want to giggle. She kept it locked tight behind her lips. Giggling was not proper for a duchess, much less a *sang-shao*. Yet as she walked with Noah alongside her, she felt the weight of her military title begin to slip away.

The pair were escorted by vehicle to the terminal buildings. Stepping out onto a sidewalk leading to a short suspension bridge over a shallow gorge, Danai got the same exhilarated thrill she'd experienced seeing the planet from her DropShip window.

"Noah...have you ever seen the like?"

Capshaw stood beside her, looking out the opposite direction. "Never, ma'am." Based on the breathless quality of his voice, Danai believed him.

The immediate flora surrounding this particular area of the terminals consisted of enormous white-barked trees topped with narrow branches bearing crimson petals. These trees, Danai supposed, were responsible for the cherry-cinnamon aroma drifting beneath her nose as she took a deep, cleansing breath. The trees stood as tall as BattleMechs, and reminded her of cherry blossoms grown in vast orchards on Liao for replanting and decoration on as many Capellan worlds as would support them.

Beneath the bridge, perhaps 10 meters down, a wide, slow-moving river carried native ducks with shiny green feathers to unknown destinations. Danai thought she could hear them quacking at one another over the various hisses and creaks of the DropShip behind her as it cooled. Looking further out, she saw the spaceport had been designed to exist in harmony with its environment: reflective silver buildings were trimmed with green creeping vines which supported bright orange fruits, and more of the cherry blossom-like trees provided shade over open-air arcades and walkways.

Ahead, two glass doors swished silently open. Danai turned her attention to the entourage sliding out to greet her.

Four large men in dark green boxy uniforms marched out first, splitting with military precision to form a protective tunnel at the doorway. Danai noted their sidearms on thigh-rigs, but also slim, gleaming, ceremonial hatchets hanging from wide black leather belts. Each of the men wore a forked beard with two small jade beads woven into the tips.

Once these guards were in place, a fifth man—of much slighter build—stepped out to meet her. He looked older than the bodyguards, with thinning black hair swept backward in a shiny lacquer. He wore a uniform of similar color to the bodyguards, but embroidered with silver whirlwind designs that reminded Danai of the storms she'd seen in Castrovia's atmosphere from her window.

"Your Grace," this man said, stopping and offering a deep bow with his right hand pressed against his chest. "Welcome to Castrovia. I am Yunhai, your escort and chief-of-staff."

Beside Yunhai, a young boy stood at attention like a proper soldier, wearing a uniform similar to Yunhai's, but in light pink. Yunhai gestured to him. "May I introduce Tiko, who joins me as a student of the duchy. He is in training, Your Grace, and with your permission, he shall accompany me on most daily business, when appropriate to his age and station."

Danai smiled at Tiko. "Thank you, Yunhai. It is an honor to meet you, Tiko."

The little boy bowed—stiffly, but Danai saw his heart was in the right place. "Your Grace!" the child said with evident pride.

Danai judged him to be perhaps eight. Tiko's tan skin gleamed, and faint roses dappled his cheeks. Danai decided she could live with his presence. If he became a distraction, she could always ask Yunhai to dismiss him.

She nodded back to Yunhai, and introduced Capshaw. "Noah will be my personal aide during my stay. Please keep him apprised of all scheduling and other necessities."

"Of course, Your Grace," Yunhai said. "Though at present, as per your request, your schedule is completely open. I would be happy to make suggestions that may be beneficial for you as the new duchess at your leisure."

"Thank you, Yunhai."

The escort turned to Tiko and raised a thin, sculpted eyebrow. The boy squeezed his eyes shut for a moment as if trying to recall some great fact. Then at last, in a long burst of breath, he said, "May I escort you to your car and take you to your lodging?"

Tiko smiled big, as if proud he'd remembered what to say. Yunhai made a tiny clucking noise. Tiko frowned, thought for a moment, then shouted: "Your Grace!"

Danai laughed.

Danai *laughed*.

The sound startled her, and it seemed to startle Noah as well, who glanced at her as if expecting her to have been wounded.

"Yes," Danai said, "I would like that very much. After you, Sir Tiko."

The little boy looked as though she had handed him the world's greatest toy. He spun on one foot and marched past the bodyguards, back into the spaceport.

Yunhai faced Danai, an unspoken question on his face: *Do you mind him?*

And Danai, still grinning from her laugh, waved him off. *No, not at all.*

The three adults entered the spaceport, Yunhai in the lead, followed by Danai and then Capshaw. The bodyguards closed ranks around the group as soon as the doors were sealed behind them.

Minutes later, and much to her surprise, Danai realized she was still smiling.

Danai and her entourage took a short walk to broad, slow-moving escalators, which brought them down to the ground floor and out a private door to two awaiting vehicles. The sidewalk here, like everything she'd seen of the spaceport thus far, blended into the natural surroundings. Made from white pavers, it wove between strips of grass that seemed to be mowed taller than other lawns she'd seen.

Unable to help herself, Danai stepped to the edge of the pavers and crouched to run the tips of her fingers over the tall grass. The leaves, perhaps 5 centimeters high, had been trimmed to an exact, flat plane. They felt like velvet against her skin.

"Oh," Noah said, sounding both surprised at something he'd seen and surprised he'd let himself react aloud.

Danai stood and followed his gaze. She squinted west as the moon, a pale white crescent, appeared over the horizon. Fascinated, she stared as it sped upward, even as she watched. From her perspective, the moon appeared to rise another arc-minute every ten seconds or so, a wildly enormous visible speed for any moon she'd seen.

The bodyguards had already opened a passenger door for Danai in the long black vehicle. Yunhai stood at the front passenger door, ready to get in, when he saw her and Noah's intrigue.

"That is Sairo," he said. "Quite a sight after sunset. You can also see the Hara Nebula in the east after dark."

"Your world is extraordinary," Noah said quietly to Danai.

She only nodded lightly, wonderstruck at Sairo's fast movement higher into the afternoon sky.

Danai felt Noah's hand gently take her elbow. "Your Grace?"

She shook herself and climbed into the waiting car. Noah followed, and one of the bodyguards closed the door. Danai recognized the dull *thump* of a well-armored vehicle designed to merely look like a luxury car on the outside. Her entourage knew well who their passenger was.

Danai noticed little Tiko was not in the car with them. To Yunhai, who sat in a seat facing her, she said, "Tell me about my youngest aide. Where does he come from?"

"Born into it," her chief-of-staff said as the vehicles rolled away from the spaceport. He has spent his entire life on Castrovia, watching his mother and father both attend to the needs of the duchy. Of course, we haven't had an actual duke or duchess on-world for some time. His parents were anxious for him to see our duchess first-hand."

Based on Yunhai's expression, he was anxious himself.

Danai nodded, then turned to watch the city go by through her window, wondering if she could ever live up to the expectations of her people.

CHAPTER 9

"...and your personal offices," Yunhai said as Tiko raced ahead to push open one of two massive wooden doors decorated with ornate scrolling.

Despite the door's size compared to Tiko's diminutive stature, it opened oily smooth, with not so much as the faintest creak. Danai smiled at the boy as he stood at attention, holding the door open for her. She stepped into her new office and put her hands on her hips, surveying its wondrous detail.

The walls were dark wood with a ceiling soaring a full two stories high. A 2-meter diameter circular window pierced the far wall, behind an enormous metallic desk. Intricate latticework created a border around the pane. The pane itself, made from a single sheet of glass, was tinted a soft blue. Sunlight pouring through it cast the office in a dim glow.

Danai paced slowly toward the desk, swinging her head left and right. Bookshelves stretched the lengths of the side walls, all the way to the ceiling. A single wrought iron ladder rolled on a brass railing encircling the entire office to grant access to the old tomes lining the shelves. The desk itself stood bare except for two short lamps on either side. While the floor of the office was smooth, dark wood slats, the desk sat upon a polished, white marble slab 12 centimeters thick.

She stopped before the desk and turned to face Noah, Yunhai, and Tiko. Her new bodyguards had stayed behind in the short hallway connecting Capshaw's new office with her own; no guests could enter Danai's office without first passing Noah.

"Well," Danai said airily, "it'll do for now."

Noah was first to catch the humor in her tone, and grinned. This cued Yunhai to do the same, while young Tiko only allowed a quick glance her direction before facing forward again at his position beside the open door.

Yunhai crossed to Danai's right, gesturing to a door she hadn't noted on her first pass through the room. "Through here, a private office and ensuite," the escort said, "as well as closets for your formal attire as needed."

He switched arms to gesture back toward the main doors. "Security is never more than a heartbeat away at all times via a panic button on your desk. All your personal servants and guardians are fully vetted by the Maskirovka. On a daily basis, your detail will include..."

Danai barely heard him, turning instead to walk to the circular window and look out at her new world. The city of Liangrad spread out before her like a living map. Her office was on the tenth floor of this civic building, and proved to be the tallest in eyesight; other buildings within view peaked at five or six stories.

Only after a long period of silence did Danai realize Yunhai had ceased speaking. She turned in a hurry and nearly apologized. "Yunhai," she said abruptly, "I was...please, continue."

Her chief-of-staff smiled and dipped his chin. "There is nothing more that cannot wait for another time, Your Grace. Shall we go to your palace?"

Danai took another slow look around the office, wondering what sort of work a duchess might be required to do. Whatever it might entail, at least it would be done in beauty.

"Yes," she answered at last. "Unless there is anything pressing." She crossed to Yunhai, admiring the white marble tablet as she went.

"Not pressing," he said. "The separatists have waited this long, another day or so won't—"

Danai reached out and gripped Yunhai's arm.

"Separatists?"

DANAI CENTRELLA-LIAO'S PERSONAL QUARTERS
PALACE OF THE DUCHESS
LIANGRAD
CASTROVIA
26 DECEMBER 3149

Danai had spent her childhood in luxury, primarily raised by her Aunt Erde Centrella on the rather hedonistic world of Canopus IV. Thanks to being the sister—or so the public believed—of Chancellor Daoshen, she had extravagant living quarters on Sian as well.

Her apartment in Liangrad, however, counted among the more luxurious places she'd lived, though its decorations were more spartan than she'd expected. Regardless, as she relaxed in it during her second day on-planet, Danai discovered she appreciated the furnishings. Rather than being rich and lavish to show off her wealth, the rooms were focused upon ease, comfort, and practicality.

Her main apartment consisted of several suites of rooms taking up the entire fifth floor of a building not far from her office. At present, she and Noah Capshaw sat alone in a sitting room furnished with sturdy wood furniture and silk trappings.

The luxury of her living quarters was lost on Danai at the moment, however, as she and Noah both held computer tablets in their hands, scowling at them in tandem.

"Separatists," she growled.

Noah said nothing, but his frown deepened.

"I thought we'd finished with this sort of thing on Liberty and Hall," Danai said. "This is not why I came here."

"The good news," Noah said, "is that they don't appear to be violent."

"Yet."

"I was trying to be positive."

Danai tossed the tablet onto the table between them. "I'm a duchess, Noah, I don't have time for positivity." She pressed the heels of her palms to her eyes. "Dammit, I didn't come all the way to Castrovia to get into a street fight."

Noah, too, set his tablet down on the table, though more gently than his boss. "I'm not sure you need to, Your Grace. Castrovia has been the domain of Chancellor Daoshen for a very long time, and to my knowledge he never spent time here. He has no relationship to these people. Look at how your escort and the others treated you yesterday."

"They treated me like the royal I am," Danai said with thinly veiled disgust. She was a MechWarrior, damn it all. The luxury here was lovely, but the same could be bought on a dozen different worlds. She didn't feel royal.

"Yes, they did," Noah said, and Danai heard the caution in his voice, "and you are. But few, if any, of them, have been in the presence of a royal. They are...overwhelmed by you."

Danai cocked an eyebrow, encouraging him to continue.

Noah shifted in his chair. "What I mean is—if I may, Your Grace—your being here is not just an honor to them. It is a dream. You represent everything they believe about being Capellan. Like what Yunhai said in the car yesterday about Tiko's parents. They've longed for the day when their leader would come and be with them, to allow them to serve. I wouldn't be surprised to find the people behind this separatist movement feel the same, in that they, too, would be overwhelmed by your very presence here in Liangrad." Capshaw returned her raised eyebrow with one of his own. "That is a powerful weapon that has nothing to do with charged particles or focused energy beams."

Danai considered Noah's words for a moment. He had a point.

"I'm glad you're here," she said. "I might have otherwise sent a few BattleMech lances to hunt these separatists down."

She stood and stretched her arms overhead. Across her body, several joints crackled.

"Bring me their leader," she declared, then grinned. "Did that sound imperious enough?"

Noah grinned back. "Indeed it did, Your Grace. I'll start working on it now and have an answer for you by—"

Danai waved, cutting him off. "No, no. Not now. Go rest. We haven't even been on-world for a full day. We'll tackle this fresh in the morning."

"Yes, Your Grace." He stood, gathering his tablet between his hands, and turned to go.

"Noah."

He faced her, bracing slightly.

"I really am glad it's you here with me."

Noah's cheeks reddened briefly. To her words he merely murmured, "Your Grace," and quickly retreated from the suite.

OFFICE OF THE DIRECTOR OF THE CHANCELLOR'S SWORD
CELESTIAL PALACE
CHANG-AN
LIAO
27 DECEMBER 3149

Dmitry Minghua had many names, many faces, and many jobs. This one, as the head of the Maskirovka's *Zang shu jian*, or Chancellor's Sword, had become his least favorite in the last five minutes.

As he stared at the report and captured images emanating from a small, secure holovid projector, Dmitry had to recall his breath training from his younger days in the military to get his heart rate down.

One word kept running through his mind as he looked at the images and read their attendant notes.

No.

No, no, no...

He mashed the projector off and stood up from behind his desk, running a palm across his mouth. The office, draped in heavy black and crimson curtains, blocked all sunlight from Liao's star.

If the details in the report were accurate, and Dmitry had no reason to suspect they were not, then he must report it to the Directorate—the office of the director of the Maskirovka, second only to the Chancellor himself as it pertained to all things espionage.

Dmitry paced the length and breadth of his office, fingers curling and uncurling into dense fists. His tall boots made no sound on the plush black carpet.

If you tell the Director, Dmitry addressed himself, *you risk exposing your agent. He'll need to know everything, and that will take my agent out of play, when I need her in place now more than ever.*

One did not ascend to the Office of the Director of the Chancellor's Sword without having redundancies upon redundancies; private spies within the spy agency itself. One of these, a middle-aged woman whom Dmitry had come to count upon for her rare but always accurate observations on military comings and goings, was known only to him. To the rest of the world, she was a laborer in one of Liao's many military shipyards, nothing more.

But laborers saw things. Heard things. And on those rare occasions she brought intelligence to Dmitry over the years, he paid attention. Most often, her insights were related to missions he already knew about, and was able to dismiss her reports, grateful to know that some secret had leaked, and he could address it.

But this—

She has made a mistake, Dmitry reprimanded himself. *That must be it. This report cannot be right.*

Yet if it is, he countered himself, *then...*

"Then the Confederation could be destroyed," he whispered.

Angry, confused, and angry all over again at the mix of emotions, Dmitry threw himself back into his chair and formed a fist with his right hand, his left cupping it tightly.

Kamer, he thought. *Kamer is the one who must know first. While there's still time.*

"There is only ever one," they say. *That one may now be needed.*

He lunged for the hardwired comm on his desk.

CHAPTER 10

CAFÉ MORPHEUS
CHANG-AN
LIAO
TIKONOV COMMONALITY
CAPELLAN CONFEDERATION
7 JANUARY 3150

The air outside Café Morpheus was pungent with oolong, jasmine, and chamomile. The little shop catered to the business crowd, white-collar managers who snuck out for a quick sip of espresso or, as was more frequent in the Capellan Confederation, tea. Most of the populace in this corner of Chang-an consisted of members of the Commonality caste— skilled and unskilled laborers—who preferred taverns to the semi-swanky white marble balustrades and columns of the cafe.

The heavy odor of teas swirling out of the café and onto its stone patio made Roberta Anjing's nose wrinkle. Her body ran on little more than thick espresso shots, energy drinks, and loyalty to her oath to defend the Confederation.

The older man sitting across from her smiled faintly and took a delicate sip of his mint tea from a white china cup. His hands moved with the precision of a doctor. "Relax, Robie. You look like a spy."

Robie sniffed and tried to make herself look casual. "Whatever," she mumbled.

Maxim Kamer's smile grew, revealing white teeth like boulders. "Excellent. Your performance is on point."

Robie sat up, abandoning the persona of a put-upon teen. She gave herself a taste of her espresso as a reward. "Thank you."

They sat quietly and sipped. Robie marked three separate tables on the patio where potential enemies sat enjoying a mid-morning snack. Or pretending to. That old woman with her print book of number games? Possibly a Davion. The pair of suited men beyond her? Maybe RAF, capturing intel like whales cruising silently for krill. That mother and child opposite could easily be elements of the Watch of the Jade Falcon Clan.

Or perhaps each was precisely what they appeared to be. Still, it paid to be wary.

"I will ask for a final time: you understand the critical nature of this assignment?" Kamer said.

"I do," Robie replied. Her blue eyes scanned behind her longtime instructor and mentor for potential threats or espionage. She saw none, but marked two men and one woman exhibiting certain signs she'd been trained to look out for.

Kamer toyed with his cup as if it were a ball of modeling clay. "And that it may cost your life?"

"I give it gladly."

Kamer nodded, his expression as inscrutable as the Celestial Wisdom. Robie knew Kamer dyed his long, lanky hair blond, but changes to one's appearance were a normal part of Maskirovka agents. Tomorrow he might be be red-haired, or black-haired, or bald.

"The loss of your young life is not an outcome I hope for," Kamer said. His voice was unusually kind. Her training had not been gentle this past decade. "There are great things in store for you, Robie."

"Thank you. I will not fail."

Kamer gathered his hair as if preparing to put it into a ponytail, but let it go again to drape across his shoulders. Robie, in automatic response, ran a palm over her bristle-brush red flat-top, wondering idly if she ought to let it grow out for this assignment. She figured it would depend on what her new boss wanted. She only knew him from photos and holovids.

"There is only ever one, Robie," Kamer said softly. His expression seemed pained, not one she was accustomed to seeing. "Only one with your training and your responsibility. It is a great and terrible honor."

Robie's heart lurched in her chest. This assignment could—*would*—be her last if she made even the smallest error. The margin between success and failure was a matter of mere breaths.

She nodded at her mentor.

"There has always been one of us in this position, but this is the first time in ages that the office has been without the Death Commandos near at hand," Kamer continued. Robie noted how clandestinely he scanned the area for problems, as she had. "That is entirely the doing of our commander, sending more and more bodies into the fray coreward. But it means that you will now assume nearly sole protectorship of him, just as I have for the past several years."

Robie gave her mentor the smallest possible nod of understanding, such that only he would see it.

"From this point forward," Kamer said, squaring his shoulders, "you are on your assignment. Fulfill it. There is nothing else. If you require anything, bring the request directly to me and me alone. Otherwise, you are free to carry out the mission in whatever manner you deem fit. You shoulder an immense burden."

Robie understood. With both the Red Lancers and Death Commandos forward-deployed toward Terra, her role beside Daoshen Liao was more critical than ever.

Kamer stood and straightened his black suit jacket. Robie kept her seat on her padded wicker chair; to stand would indicate to any observers that she was a subordinate of someone with power. While true, no reason existed to broadcast the fact.

Maskirovka agents, after all, dealt in deception.

"The office must be protected at all costs for the benefit and protection of the people. You, Roberta Anjing, are now tasked with that sacred duty."

"I understand." *For the good of the state.*

Kamer offered a deep bow, a rare professional courtesy among the Mask. Robie was young, but understood the symbolism: it was offered to the deceased in private funeral ceremonies.

She'd offered them herself not long ago, as her friends and comrades in the Maskirovka were shipped off Hall in metal caskets.

Robie accepted the bow with a short nod. Kamer buttoned his coat and let himself out of the café patio, leaving Robie to contemplate her next actions and her fate.

She stayed in her seat, sipping the espresso for another twenty minutes. Her gaze wandered; the three people she'd marked earlier had moved along before Kamer's exit, and Robie spotted no new potential threats.

She finished her drink and slung on a plain brown faux-leather coat. Hands stuffed into its pockets, Robie walked briskly down chiseled stone sidewalks to her hotel. She was scheduled to report to the palace in three hours, and she wanted to be ready.

CHAPTER 11

Yunhai appeared visibly disturbed as Danai's three-car motorcade wove through the wide streets of Liangrad. She watched, amused, as his fingers fidgeted in his lap. "Nervous?"

He blinked. "Forgive me, Your Grace. This is not the sort of detail I am accustomed to."

"Hence your being here. Young Tiko and his family had never seen a real duchess before, and so are having him learn how to conduct himself now. The same ought to be true for the duchess' escort, yes?"

"O-Of course, Your Grace," Yunhai said, stammering a bit. "It's just, this is a military interdiction and—"

"Not quite yet, it isn't," Danai interrupted. "We'll take stock after this meeting and see where we stand. According to all the intelligence you've given me so far, the White Moon has made no physical assaults."

Yunhai pursed his lips. "Some shoving at protests. Three have been arrested for other physical altercations. If you allude to anything on a greater scale..."

"I do."

"Then I must admit, no. I would not call the White Moon peaceful, but in the interest of honesty, I will admit they've made no overt *military* gestures."

"Then this is not yet a military interdiction," Danai said. She surprised herself with the tone of her voice. Normally such a phrase would contain an edge meant to put an end to further discussion with a subordinate. Here, in the cool confines of the motorcade's middle vehicle, sinking into supple leather cushions, Danai realized her tone was less formal.

Am I being too relaxed? She made a mental note to ask Noah about it later.

Her *sang-wei*, for his part, kept his eyes on them both until they stopped speaking, then turned to look out his window. "So many green spaces," he remarked. "I've counted three parks just since the palace."

Yunhai brightened, presumably at the change in topic to something more civic-minded. "Yes. We have made it a point to create them within walking distance of any urban center. We encourage children and families to be outside and exercise. *Wèile guójiā.*"

Danai smiled in agreement. For the good of the nation, it made sense for its people to be healthy, and to enjoy their lives.

"Tiko," she said abruptly as she followed Noah's gaze outside.

"Ah, yes," Yunhai said, leaning over a bit in his seat. "Today he has off. He loves football."

The motorcade drove slowly enough that Danai could watch the boy kicking a black and white ball with a number of other children around his age. Even from the car, through the tinted safety glass, she could see the joy on his face.

"Quite a child," she said softly.

Twenty minutes later, the motorcade rolled to a halt before Liangrad's enormous arts complex. Danai reached for the door handle, but pulled her hand away as one of her bodyguards appeared outside and opened it for her.

I should be used to this, she thought, and stepped out. It was as though her combat duty had erased her memory of times she'd been to Liao and Sian, where she'd been treated as royalty rather than military.

She'd elected to wear a form-fitting uniform in forest green, not exactly military, but not exactly informal. She kept her hair pulled back in an inornate black clasp, and wore no visible armament. Her retinue of armed guards carried plenty, and Danai knew without asking that her entire route from the car, through the lobby, and into a gallery had been pre-selected and secured by her protective detail.

It wasn't the cockpit of her *Black Knight*, but it was the next safest thing.

"I do wish we had arranged to meet at the palace," Yunhai fretted as Danai, Noah, and the security guards walked briskly toward a side entrance.

"Her Grace did not wish to use her private residence to convey superiority," Noah answered. "For the time being, she deemed a neutral ground appropriate."

Danai didn't bother adding to his explanation. It was right, and it was enough.

The off-white public arts structure stood in a field of purple flowers, with its main auditorium building towering three stories higher than the four cube-shaped buildings surrounding it. Each of the cubes housed different galleries and performance spaces, and Danai had chosen one particular fine art gallery for the meeting.

What she did not remind Yunhai was that as a public building, the Capellan government already had full control of the space. In theory, the arts complex belonged to the people, to be used by them for their artistic expressions. In practice, the Capellan government owned and operated the place, making it far easier to create security guarantees for the duchess.

Plus the optics were better here. Every separatist or citizen with separatist sympathies was watching her today to see how she treated the leader of the White Moon movement in a public space.

Truth be told, Danai was curious to find out herself.

She'd done her homework on Aria Skyelar, and come away intrigued but unimpressed. The woman was fifty years old, came from an arts background, and had no children. Her husband had been a civilian technician on IndustrialMechs with a penchant for watercoloring before his sudden death five years prior. Aria Skyelar, according to Danai's brief, blamed House Liao for his death, insisting long hours and unforgiving working conditions had directly led to his demise.

Danai's bodyguards guided her and the others into a brightly lit hallway, down its length, and into a long, white-walled art gallery. Iridescent paintings hung on the walls, spotlit from above. A table covered in red velvet sat in the middle of the gallery, with two armchairs on opposing sides. A carafe of slightly sweating clear water and two glasses stood in the middle of the tablecloth.

Danai took the seat facing the door through which Aria Skyelar would arrive. She wanted to see the woman walk.

"Is there anything else?" Noah asked as Danai sat.

"No, this is all fine. I'd like you to be in the room, but keep the bodyguards outside. I don't want them to be a distraction to Ms. Skyelar."

"As you wish, Your Grace. Good luck." Noah briefly touched her shoulder and stepped back several paces, standing at parade rest.

Danai didn't have to wait long. Before she had finished pouring herself a glass of water, the door opened again, and Aria Skyelar marched inside.

The woman wore a slim, tight, knee-length white skirt, topped by a yellow blouse and white jacket. She wore low heels, which clacked loudly on the tile floor of the gallery. Her hair, an electric blue shade, was pulled smooth across her head and ended in a tight bun. She carried no bag, no notebook, no computer.

All right, Danai thought as she rose. *Here we go*.

Danai extended a hand over the table. Aria Skyelar reached her seat and shook hands. Hers was warm and uncalloused.

"Ms. Skyelar," Danai said, taking back her seat. "I am so glad you agreed to meet."

Skyelar sat, placing folded hands on the table top. She did not reach for water.

"Your Grace," she said, and nothing more.

Closer up now, Danai could see her lips lined in dark red, and wrinkled at the corners. "Well," she said, "shall we—"

"We want you off this planet." Skyelar's dark eyes flashed with the words.

Danai appraised her coolly, letting silence build before answering. "I see. I'm afraid that is not an option at this time."

"No," Skyelar said, lips tight. "You are not afraid, Your Grace. Not yet."

Danai wanted to laugh, and thought better of it. "Indeed?"

"I will call for a general strike. I will shut this world down."

"Then I would summon SecurityMechs to encourage the workers back to their places," Danai replied.

One corner of Skyelar's mouth turned up. "Of course you would, which would only reinforce the point. We are not free here. We labor under the heel of Daoshen Liao, and for what? Insufficient health care?"

"I've read about your husband," Danai offered, keeping her tone respectful. "I am sorry."

"Your sorrow will not solve this issue. *Your Grace.*"

Danai sat back. "No, I suppose it won't."

"Shall we commence with the threats?"

Danai blinked. "I'm sorry?"

"That's why I'm here, isn't it? We've sat here less than a minute and you've already mentioned your security BattleMechs. What other means of 'cooperation' are you going to throw at us when we refuse your orders?"

Danai shook her head slowly, eyeing a droplet of condensation on her glass as it dripped toward the tablecloth. "None. Your followers have thus far eschewed violence, and so then will I. You say the White Moon movement desires freedom, which, according to you, is not a state you currently enjoy."

Aria Skyelar lifted her chin in agreement and defiance.

"Then your freedom I grant you," Danai said.

The other woman's defiant expression melted a bit. "What do you—"

"There is a particular area of state land a hundred kilometers south of Liangrad," Danai said. "I grant it to you and the White Moon movement. It is currently unlogged, unmined, and has a source of freshwater. You do not like living here amongst Capellans on Castrovia, and you clearly won't leave and seek your fortune with, perhaps, the Davions, or perhaps the Regulans, both of whom would no doubt welcome Castrovian refugees with a warm embrace."

Aria Skyelar's eyes widened slightly.

"You want your freedom, Ms. Skyelar, away from the *clear* meddling of the Confederation into your private affairs. Then go. Craft a new life for yourself and your followers. But you will be stripped of your Capellan citizenship. You will not be permitted a standing army. You will be free to engage in trade with other communities on Castrovia or with visiting offworld merchants, but not with any enemy of the state. You and your people will leave this very afternoon, and I wish you all the best."

Danai made a show of scraping her chair legs against the tile floor as she stood.

"But, no!" Skyelar said abruptly. "You can't just—we, we cannot—"

"Indeed you can," Danai said. "You will be glorious pioneers, fleeing the intrusive and wicked boot heel of House Liao. Just... as...you...*wished*."

Aria Skyelar's defiance utterly vanished. She opened and closed her mouth, her eyes darting side to side. Danai imagined the other woman quickly calculating how cozy her home in Liangrad was compared to the log cabin—at best—she might have in the woods.

"To be honest," Danai said into the silence, "I am not exactly sure why you took this meeting, Ms. Skyelar. You had some endgame in mind. I assure you this is mine. Take your people and go, and leave my city in peace. *Or.*"

Skyelar met her eyes. Hers searched Danai's for reprieve.

"Or," Danai repeated, "you can stay in Liangrad, call off your followers, end your demonstrations and protests, and file formal grievances through the office of the planetary refrector as you see fit. But the very instant I hear your name or that of the White Moon associated with so much as a hand-slap against another Capellan, I will have you removed from the city."

"I...can't control *everyone*," Skyelar said.

Danai placed her palms on the tablecloth and leaned over the water pitcher.

"Oh," she said quietly, "but I believe you'll learn how."

She let the words hang in heavy in the space between them for a long moment before straightening.

"If I can aid you in your endeavor in any way, please reach out to my staff. They will contact me immediately and I will do my utmost to help. Goodbye, Ms. Skyelar."

Danai stepped around the table and marched toward the doors. Her detail opened them upon her approach as if hearing her footsteps nearing.

Once in the hall, Yunhai skittered nearer to keep up with Danai's brisk pace. "How did it go?"

"We'll soon see," Danai said. "Is the Mask in place?"

"Yes, deeply embedded in the White Moon. They've been the source of our intelligence."

"Good. The very instant there is so much as a whisper of military-style action, I want to be notified. Wake me up, interrupt my high tea, whatever."

Yunhai nodded. "Yes, Your Grace."

In moments, Danai and Noah were whisked into the middle vehicle of their caravan. Yunhai scurried into the follow car, talking quickly on a comm. This left Danai and Noah alone in the back of the vehicle.

"That was an education," he said as the motorcade got underway.

"You think she learned something? I doubt it."

"I meant me," Noah said. "The way you handled that..."

Unconsciously, Danai patted his hand. "You're doing fine, Noah." She looked out her window and asked, "What else is on my agenda today?"

Noah fumbled with his personal computer before answering. "Ah, nothing. Nothing, really. A dinner this evening with the military council."

"That park we passed earlier, where we saw Tiko. I want to go there."

"Um—yes, Your Grace, of course." He thumbed the interior comm and gave the instruction to the driver, who replied in the affirmative.

"May I ask?" Noah said.
Danai sighed silently. "Just...some research."

CHAPTER 12

CELESTIAL PALACE
CHANG-AN
LIAO
19 JANUARY 3150

Robie and Kamer met Daoshen Liao in his private study, attended by a single servant with a long but slight scar down the left side of his face. This man stood near a far corner, head slightly bowed, as stationary as furniture.

Chancellor Daoshen Liao sat at an enormous desk, polished to a gleaming crimson hue. A holovid played in the center. In the holo, Robie recognized Keid from her studies, and noted three-dimensional DropShips, highlighted in blue, circling the planet.

The Chancellor looked up as Robie and Kamer entered this inner sanctum, with its marble panels and bright chandeliers. The room had no windows.

"Chancellor," Kamer said with a slight bow. "May I introduce Roberta Anjing, also called Robie."

"Celestial Wisdom," Robie said, and bowed. Lower than Kamer.

When she lifted her head, she saw the Chancellor smiling faintly. "Robie. Welcome. Kamer tells me you are a top student."

"Yes, Your Grace." No need to embellish. Her job was to shut up, watch, listen, and act only when and if it was time to do so.

"And, happy birthday," Daoshen continued.

"Thank you, Your Grace."

Daoshen's smile widened perhaps a centimeter.

"Qu," he said.

The servant in the corner yanked a dagger from his sleeve and lunged at the Chancellor.

PINE PARK
RAINSPIRE
SHERATAN
19 JANUARY 3150

Jack smoked a thick cigar as he gazed up at the tall conifer planted in a crossroads downtown. The tree had been there for as far back as he could remember. A short red brick wall surrounded the tree, and fresh woodchip mulch covered the ground around it. He almost hated to ruin the aroma from the green needles with the smoke from his cigar.

Almost.

He'd smelled so many different kinds of smoke over the past five decades, the cigar was like an aromatic candle to his old nose.

Not so long ago, this crossroads would have been filled with morning traffic. Now it was virtually silent, apart from the mutterings and shufflings of Rainspire pedestrians hurrying to get to their assigned jobs. Jobs assigned by Capellans, who knew—they said—how to best serve the state.

Jack felt someone's presence appear beside him, stealthy but not secretive. From the corner of his eye, he recognized Tai, an older man with skin and hair as dark and gray as Jack's cigar ash. Tai wore a knitted black watch cap, and his hands were slung casually in the hip pockets of a blue coverall. He'd been a 'Mech tech since he was old enough to lift a wrench, and beat Jack's age by ten.

"Some tree," Tai said. He didn't turn to face Jack any more than Jack turned to face him; both men merely stood looking up at the conifer.

Jack blew out smoke in a thin stream, and nodded. "Yep. How's the new job?"

Tai chuckled. "Oh, you know. We're all one big, happy family."

"Mmm."

They stood together silently while life went on around them. Mostly pedestrians these days; the collapse of the economy had halted imports of critical parts, and Capellan economic policies had disrupted the supply chains. As a result, cars had to be scavenged for parts to keep other vehicles running, and traffic was way down. Everyone looked hungry. No one smiled, no one said hello.

The RAF hadn't been a joyride, but this?

"Hear you're looking to plant a tree yourself," Tai said. "You an arborist now?"

"Might be."

Tai chuckled again. "Why don't you come by work later tonight, if you can stomach it. I may have something you can plant."

Jack drew heavily on his cigar, making sure to keep his lips dry on the end. He blew out the smoke and inhaled its fine scent before holding the cigar vertical and passing it to Tai. "I'll be there."

"Thanks for this," Tai said. He took a short puff and meandered away.

Only after Tai had cleared the tree did Jack let his gaze settle on the older man's back, the blue coverall stained with BattleMech lubricants and grease.

He smiled. Sometimes, even now, there were things that brought joy.

CELESTIAL PALACE
CHANG-AN
LIAO
19 JANUARY 3150

Robie vaulted the desk before the scarred servant made a full step toward the Chancellor. The servant cried out as she snapped bones in his wrist and disarmed him, the dagger ending up in her left hand, his arm in her right.

They landed in a tangle on the floor near Daoshen's feet. The servant groaned piteously as Robie pressed a knee into his sternum.

Daoshen clapped his hands lightly.

"Excellent," he said softly. "You may release Guanken. He was only following my orders. He has served me in the office for decades, and is trusted implicitly. Thank you, Guanken, for your suffering to ensure our new bodyguard is prepared for any contingency."

Robie took a moment to digest her leader's words before carefully climbing to her feet and stepping back, prepared to drive the dagger into the servant's throat if he made a wrong move. She glanced at Kamer, whose face remained impassive. If he was impressed with her or upset with the Celestial Wisdom, his expression showed no sign.

"Guanken," Daoshen said as the servant worked himself slowly into an upright position. "Kamer will take you to the medics to see to any injury. Robie—you are impressive indeed. Stay with me awhile while we get to know one another."

Robie tilted her chin down in deference as Kamer helped Guanken from the office. To her surprise, the servant offered her a smile as if in thanks. Pain interwove between the expression, yes, but his gratitude was evident.

Grateful for what? Robie thought. *That I didn't kill him? Or—*

Or that he was pleased to have served, even knowing the possibly fatal outcome?

Robie had studied such servants during her training. The Celestial Wisdom didn't need mere butlers and stewards; such positions could be easily filled. To serve the Chancellor personally as an aide, as this man Guanken did, required a level of commitment rivaling that of any MechWarrior or Maskirovka.

Fanatical devotion.

By the time Robie had reached this conclusion, he and Kamer were past the threshold. Kamer gave her the slightest glance over his shoulder as he closed the door, and mouthed words meant strictly for the young Maskirovka agent:

"Good luck."

Then they were gone.

Daoshen slid closer to Robie. He reached out a single finger and brushed it along the side of her shaved head. Robie felt the red bristle snap back into place in the wake of his touch.

"You are quite young to be in the Maskirovka," Daoshen said. His voice was smooth. Quiet. Controlled.

"Thank you, Chancellor. I was raised in it."

His fingertip stayed on her, letting it drift down her neck to her shoulder. "Oh?"

"My parents were killed in battle on Styk. It was their wish that I serve the state close to home, but they'd insisted to friends that I not fight on any front lines."

Daoshen hummed, acknowledging the comment, as his finger traced down her bicep, then elbow. "Then you understand your place in the state."

It wasn't a question. "I do, Chancellor."

"To serve the state is every Capellan's purpose," Daoshen said. He was whispering now.

"Yes, Chancellor."

His hand reached her own. "At all times. In all things. With all heart."

"Yes, Chancellor."

"Good," Daoshen said, moving closer. "Very good."

He squeezed her hand.

CHAPTER 13

As a mercenary MechWarrior, Jack had been at war most of his life. He could pilot basically any bipedal machine a crew could throw at him, though his favorite tended to be the medium-weight 'Mechs for the balance of speed and power. That said, he'd seen some incredible destruction wrought by lighter machines when a competent MechWarrior was on the stick.

What he saw now nearly took his breath away.

Without turning to Tai, he near-whispered, "Who else knows about this?"

"Just me, far as I know."

Jack faced him, letting his paranoia be his guide. "How long have you known about these?"

Tai shrugged. "A year, roundabout. Stumbled into 'em looking for a part."

"You've known these were down here for a *year*, and you're just telling me *now*? Why?"

Tai, as grizzled as any war vet Jack had ever known, meet Jack's eyes with steel in his own. "Merta's gone."

Jack's stomach dropped. *"What?"*

Tai nodded, his face somber. "Yesterday. Caps came and got her. Said she had a necessary skillset to serve the good of the state."

"She makes wedding dresses."

Tai met his gaze again. "Or uniforms."

Jack wanted to swear, wanted to spit. Neither would have had any impact. "You know where?"

"No idea. Said they'd let me know. Yeah. We'll see about that. Maybe all the way to Sian for all the difference it makes."

"I'm sorry, Tai."

"Me, too, Jack. Me, too. Anyway..." He gestured at the enormous underground hangar. "I thought these might help you with your tree-planting."

Jack walked away from his friend, deeper into the hangar, mind spinning with possibilities.

The hangar was filled with BattleMechs.

At a rough estimate, Jack figured at least thirty or forty combat 'Mechs, plus another few dozen non-combat machines: miners, AgroMechs, and other Industrials. On each machine, the emblem of the Republic of the Sphere shone on armored torsos. Not a single machine looked to have ever seen combat, as if they'd been walked here right from the factory.

"You have my attention," he said, turning to Tai. "Now tell me how these all got here."

"Near as I can tell, the RAF just didn't have the crew or space to bring 'em with. Not enough MechWarriors to go around, and they won't exactly be needing a bunch of corn-pickers where they're headed."

"And where's that?"

Tai laughed—a low, unhappy sound. "Where everyone's going these days, old friend."

Jack smirked as he went to examine a *Locust*. "Not me. I'm staying put. You really think they just left them behind?"

"The records show them being delivered here, and that's about it. Nobody came for these when they cleared out the other depot back in '35."

"If there's records, why don't the Caps know that?"

"Because the Caps don't keep the records. I do."

Jack grinned. "And maybe those records are missing from the system."

Tai shrugged. "Maybe they are."

"What about munitions? Spare parts?"

"Well, that's another story." Tai dipped his head to invite Jack off to one side. He followed readily, his heart pounding. *This many machines...*

Tai took him to a warehousing section of the hangar, where four dusty forklifts stood parked and ready to unload pallets from tall metal shelving.

"This is what was left," Tai said, slapping a military-wrapped pallet of boxes. "Plenty of these, but not much in the way of ammunition for the autocannons."

Jack hunkered and wiped dust from the plastic. "How many of these? What sizes?"

"Took an inventory about a week ago," Tai said, gesturing down the row of weaponry. "Seven hundred fifty-three, all together, various sizes."

Jack stood. His knees popped. "Seven hundred fifty-three mines," he repeated. "That's a lot."

"Isn't it, though." Hands in his pockets again, Tai nodded toward the end of the hangar. "You might have noticed these BattleMechs didn't come through that tiny door upstairs. Let me show you something else."

Jack fell into step beside him as he walked down the center aisle created by the parked BattleMechs. He recognized *Locusts*, *Stingers*, *Wasps*; up ahead, a couple *Javelins*; a row behind that, a *Vixen, Blade,* and *Cougar.* And others.

Enough BattleMechs for an entire battalion. If he could muster one.

After the combat machines came the IndustrialMechs, designed for agriculture, mining, and construction for the most part. These, too, looked brand new, if a bit dusty. Then multiple rows of hovertanks.

"What, no aircraft? Artillery?"

"Sorry, Jack. Guess you'll have to make do."

The two friends traded grins.

They reached the far end of the hangar and came to three rolling loading-bay doors large enough to admit the tallest of BattleMechs. Between each was a standard 2-meter door. Tai opened one of these, stepped into darkness, and turned on a light.

Jack walked in behind him as rows of industrial scoop lights popped on in sequence, one after the other, down a very long corridor wide and tall enough to allow two 'Mechs of any size to walk side by side.

"So this is how they got them down here," he said, "but where's the entrance?"

Tai pointed down the tunnel. "About 10 kilometers thataway."

"Ten!"

Tai nodded. "And a few other tunnels like this one that aren't wired for lighting and never got finished. Who knows what the Rotters planned to do with those."

"You've been to the entrance? Where's it empty out?"

"Carlisle Woods. Deep in them. Not the kind of place you'd stumble onto by accident. Good cover, not easy to spot. This whole bunker was meant to do one thing: crawl up somebody's ass."

"Ten K," Jack mused. "That'd put us, what, no more than another thirty or less from Daggaknott."

"Uh-huh. And less than five from the crater."

Jack whistled. "Good to know."

The crater dated back several millennia, carved out by an asteroid long before humans stepped foot on Sheratan. From the sky, it looked like an enormous gray blemish in a field of green trees. Little grew in the infill but grass. Further out, much of the woods closer to Rainspire had been cleared for agriculture, with endless kilometers of alfalfa and other grasses and grains stretching almost from the shallow crater's rim to the edge of Rainspire itself.

"Come on," Tai said. "Let's head back up."

Tai shut the lights off and led the way past the 'Mechs and up the staircase back to the ground level, making sure the proper doors were locked and concealed behind them.

He walked Jack back to the vehicle Jack had borrowed, one of the precious few still in use around town. "So if you want to plant some trees, Jack, they're all yours."

Jack put a hand on his friend's shoulder. "I'll take 'em. Thank you, Tai."

"One thing."

Jack removed his hand. "What?"

"Do me a favor. Tell the major to stay out of trouble."

Jack grunted. "The major does what the major does, I can't help that."

"Sure you can. She listens to you, Jack. I know she's been busy. I hate seeing her in the middle of all this."

Jack sucked a breath in through his nose, something akin to a sniffle. "Explain that to her dad."

"I'm explaining it to you. You know I'm right."

"I'll let her know you said so."

"It's all I ask." Tai thumped him once on the back and turned to leave.

Jack's voice stopped him. "You know none of this will bring Merta back."

Tai paused, not turning around. "I know. But that ain't why we're doing it, is it?"

"No," Jack said after a moment. "It's really not."

"Keep me posted," Tai said, resuming his walk back to the bay.

Jack didn't bother to reply. He climbed into the vehicle and drove for his friend's home in Uptown to return it, his warrior's mind on fire with possibilities.

OUTSKIRTS OF RAINSPIRE
SHERATAN
22 JANUARY 3150

Sang-wei Ori Juang wanted blood.

In the two months since the deaths of *Si-ben-bing* Daniel Teye and *San-ben-bing* Antony Hayes at the hands of insurgents, her rage hadn't cooled in the slightest. Following additional attacks on Capellan property and personnel throughout the city, her desperate need for vengeance had intensified to levels that worried her subordinates.

Not long after their deaths, Juang had begun taking one of her security force's *Guard* SecurityMechs out on patrol herself—after her shifts. This went against protocol, but no one seemed of a mind to point it out to the *sang-wei*.

Her patrols had not gone well. She'd wanted to catch someone in the act of some act of sabotage or other crimes against the state. So far, she'd told some kids to go home after curfew and called in foot patrols to arrest a pair of drug dealers. Not much else.

Not nearly enough, she thought.

Tonight, Juang piloted her *Guard* through the commercial district and out to the surrounding residential areas. All was quiet; locals would peer out from windows and some dared to flash rude hand gestures, but nothing more.

Dammit, she wanted a fight!

Scowling alone in her cockpit, Juang headed into the farmland. So far, her own and other Capellan forces had come up empty-handed when it came to where the insurgents gathered to plan their attacks; perhaps they waited until late and used farm houses, counting on their remoteness and wide swaths of flat land to alert them to incoming patrols...

Her HUD flashed red.

Juang blinked. BattleMech contact? Nearly eight weeks of constant failure had dulled her reactions.

She swung the four-legged 'Mech in the direction of the enemy transponder. A *Locust*.

"Hi there," she snarled. "You're not one of my kids. What're you up to?"

The *Locust* had taken a few jaunty steps from the forest line about two hundred meters away. Just as Juang turned the *Guard* that way, heedless of the crops crushed underfoot, the *Locust* pilot seemed to spot her as well.

The other 'Mech turned and crashed back into the woods.

"Oh, like hell you run away from me!" Juang shouted, and throttled forward.

She knew the errand was foolish, if not fatal. The *Locust*, while only outweighing the *Guard* by five tons, had nearly twice everything else: speed, armament, armor. In the hands of a good MechWarrior, the *Locust* would prove more than a match for the smaller *Guard*, with its twin machine guns and armor designed merely for urban riot control.

But they don't have a score to settle, Juang thought grimly, marching as fast as she could through a field of greens. *That's the difference.*

Also, the *Locust* was clearly spooked. Juang tracked it with relative ease as it maneuvered between the trees.

Juang sent the *Guard* crashing into the tree line. While the canopy was dense, blocking moonlight from penetrating to the forest floor, her SecurityMech's stable low center of gravity let her shove through low-hanging branches and thick bushes like they were cobwebs.

The nimble *Locust* darted in a zig-zag pattern, weaving through gaps too narrow for Juang to easily follow, but the forest thickened up ahead. The distance between the two 'Mechs dwindled.

Anxious at possibly losing her prey, Juang briefly squeezed the triggers on her twin machine guns, sending a short hail of tracers through the woods. She'd ordered the usual rubber bullets replaced by standard shells after what had happened to Hayes and Teye. No mercy, as far as she was concerned, until someone of a higher rank told her otherwise.

Muzzle flashes illuminated the darkness in bursts, and she caught a brief glimpse of the *Locust*'s back—its most vulnerable area.

Too far. The rounds flew harmlessly through the trees.

Cursing violently, Juang pushed the *Guard* ahead as the *Locust* tried to find a quick path away. The terrain became uneven, the ground rising and falling across a dry creek bed and lumpy, tangled roots as Juang continued her chase.

"Come on, *come on*!" she chanted. "Turn around!"

Abruptly, the insurgent *Locust* burst into a clearing. The flat space appeared to be a dried-up pond, its banks steep.

The *Locust* pilot hesitated as if decided whether or not to engage. Juang lined up another burst from her machine guns, but before she could fire, the *Locust* surged forward. The bipedal 'Mech scrambled up the opposite side of the clearing, its clawed feet digging deep gouges into the loose dirt as it climbed.

Nearing the clearing, Juang fired carelessly, her rounds chewing up the embankment and clipping the *Locust*'s left leg.

The fleeing 'Mech slipped, but managed to haul itself over the lip of the embankment and disappear into the trees.

"No!" Juang forced the *Guard* forward. The steep incline was easy for it, the quadruped handling the obstacle with ease.

An alarm blared in the cockpit as Juang crested the rise. In less than a heartbeat, she realized: the *Locust* had stopped running and turned to face her.

Twin medium lasers lanced out, their emerald beams illuminating the dark. One shot went wide, burning a smoking scar into a nearby tree. The other hit the *Guard*'s right foreleg, searing armor and superheating the myomer underneath. More alarms buzzed in the cockpit, warning of imminent catastrophic problems.

Gritting her teeth, Juang scuttled the *Guard* to the left and returned fire. Her machine guns roared, bullets hammering into the *Locust*'s boxy body and right leg. The other 'Mech reeled under the impacts, stumbling backward.

"Hayes! Teye!" Juang bellowed. "That's for them!"

The *Locust* pilot was either easily startled or utterly unskilled; the pilot didn't return fire. Instead, the insurgent turned and bolted, as if remembering its superior speed and trying to put distance between them again.

Juang snarled and followed, but lost ground quickly; the trees thinned here. It would take the *Locust* only a few moments to get out of range.

She fired again, this time using controlled short bursts, hoping to clip a leg again, force a stumble—something. Juang caught the *Locust*'s left leg, blowing off a bit of armor plating to expose the delicate workings of the 'Mech's ankle, but the pilot raced on.

Ahead, Juang realized the *Locust* pilot's goal: open farmland.

"No, no, *no!*" she cried, and emptied her bins.

The *Locust* dashed past the tree line even as the *Guard*'s machine guns peppered its back. A few wisps of smoke billowed from the wounds and were whipped away in a light breeze.

By the time Juang reached the tree line, the *Locust* was in an all-out sprint. Too far away to shoot. Too far away to catch.

As the enemy 'Mech vanished into the night, Juang beat her hands against the console and screamed.

CHAPTER 14

DANAI CENTRELLA-LIAO'S PERSONAL QUARTERS
PALACE OF THE DUCHESS
LIANGRAD
CASTROVIA
1 FEBRUARY 3150

Danai enjoyed breakfast on the balcony outside her sitting room in the palace apartment. She wore forest-green silks, her hair loose, as she sipped mint and green tea from a delicate cup and gazed at the sunrise. The Hara Nebula faded slowly from view as the sun rose. Sairo, Castrovia's absurdly fast moon, fell again toward the horizon, shining white.

She'd seen a thousand moons from a hundred worlds. Beautiful sunsets and sunrises, moonsets and moonrises. Yet something about seeing this particular moon moving so quickly made the Duchess of Castrovia pause and consider her place in the universe. Watching it made her feel small, diametrically opposite to how she felt piloting her *Black Knight* or her old BattleMech, *Yen-Lo-Wang*.

A new feeling, yes, but not a particularly bad one.

Having been up for two hours already to get some private exercise time in the palace's gymnasium, she'd already called for Noah to get an early start on the day. He rang the bell to her personal apartment just as the sun became a full circle in the eastern sky.

"Come," Danai called. The door, operating on her voice command, swung open silently, admitting Noah inside.

Since arriving on Castrovia, Noah seemed to have taken a cue from Danai, wearing pressed civilian suits, which she only recently realized he must have purchased for himself. Upon the realization, she'd immediately ordered an expense account for him from her seemingly limitless financial resources.

Today, he wore dark blue. Danai admired the cut of the suit, and that *Zhong-shao* Wu's recent weight training with him had helped the creases sit splendidly on his frame.

"Good morning, Your Grace," Noah said, entering onto the balcony. "Beautiful day."

"It is. Have a seat. Tell me how this beautiful day is going to go."

Noah sat upon a wrought-iron chair, plentifully padded with light green cushions. He raised his tablet, sat back, and crossed his legs. In that moment, Danai saw the future leader he was fast becoming.

"Good news from the Maskirovka," he said with a bit of a grin. "The White Moon is organizing itself to make a run to lead the Artist caste."

Danai echoed his grin. "Of course. With Aria Skyelar as its first candidate."

"Yep," Noah said, smiling now. "It seems Ms. Skyelar has *separated* herself from the more reactionary separatists—no pun intended."

Danai laughed.

Noah tapped his screen. "But in a related development, one of her closer associates has asked for a meeting with you to discuss your land offer."

Danai's eyes widened. "Really? Didn't see that coming."

Noah nodded. "A man named Don Fraser is heading it up. Seems he has several families interested in making a go of it."

Danai sipped, considering the request. While she'd been fully committed to making the land available to Skyelar—idle threats were not in her toolkit—she'd believed Skyelar would pass. Which, of course, she had. That there might be pioneering souls on Castrovia willing to take up the risk had not occurred to her. She had to admire them.

"Set up a meeting with Fraser," she decided. "As well as whatever meetings need to take place to get the gears in motion to grant them land."

"Consider it done, Your Grace."

"What else?"

Noah's expression soured as he tapped his tablet again. "Nothing overwhelming. The Third Capellan Chargers have been dispatched to Sheratan."

"Sheratan still? What's going on over there?"

"Something of an escalation," he replied. "Some fire bombs and more frequent assaults on the Capellan garrison. One 'Mech on 'Mech battle, but rumors of more on the way."

"Third Chargers... *Sang-shao* Stefano Rossetti?"

"Yes, Your Grace."

"Hmm. He's competent. Should be an easy fix. What's next?"

Noah uncrossed his legs and shifted in the chair. "Since we've taken Keid, the Chancellor intends to visit there early next year."

Danai sat up and set her cup down. "Why would he leave Liao?"

"No messages, Your Grace, so no one is quite sure. That information comes from our Mask liaison."

Danai stood and tied the belt around her waist tighter with a quick jerk of the ends. "Keid," she repeated. "That's far too close to the front. That *is* the front. There is no reason for Daoshen to go there."

Or not tell me, she thought, but did not add.

Noah stood. "Shall I send a message, Your Grace?"

Danai fumed silently for a time, eyes darting across the beautiful landscape of Liangrad. The city was coming to life below: lights popping on in windows, traffic increasing. Somewhere far off, she heard music.

Keid, she thought. *What are you doing, Daoshen? Just putting yourself in danger. But you don't do things off the cuff, do you "brother"? You're up to something.*

"Send an official congratulations about Keid from the duchy," Danai said at last. "That's all."

"Yes, Your Grace."

Dammit, she didn't want to think about this the rest of the day. Or week. Or longer. Daoshen Liao was Chancellor, and would do as he pleased. He would speak to her when he had something to say, and not before.

"Since I doubt any will be forthcoming from Liao," Noah ventured, tucking the tablet against his hip in preparation to go, "may I congratulate you on the White Moon situation? It was a remarkable thing to see, Your Grace."

Bless you, Noah, Danai thought. "Accepted," she said. "With thanks. Have you eaten? Can I have some breakfast sent up for you?"

"Thank you, Your Grace, I'm fine. I'm meeting Yunhai in an hour."

"Very well. Thank you."

He offered a shallow bow. "Of course, Your Grace."

"And, come to think of it...from time to time, Noah, 'Danai' wouldn't kill either of us. At least while we're here on Castrovia."

Noah took a deep breath, eyes skittering for anywhere to look other than the Duchess of Castrovia, his *sang-shao* in battle, sister to the Celestial Wisdom. Danai rather enjoyed seeing him struggle to figure out how to respond.

"I will try, Your Grace," he said as he blushed. After a beat, he added, "Danai."

Danai bent and lifted her cup, tipping it toward him. "See? Not so bad."

Blushing, Noah reached for his leather satchel. "One last thing, Your Grace," he said, retrieving a holovid cube. "It's from Nikol Marik."

"Nikol!" Danai exclaimed happily. "Yes, please."

Danai had befriended Nikol Marik seventeen years prior on Terra, at a party held by—of all things—the Republic of the Sphere. They had remained as close as was possible even without the aid of HPGs for instantaneous interstellar communication. Danai's departed Aunt Erde and Nikol were the only people in the Inner Sphere who knew about the assault she'd suffered from Caleb Davion.

Noah handed her the cube and quietly retreated as Danai activated it. It was good to see her friend's face. It had been too long—a fact Nikol addressed immediately.

"Danai," Nikol's recorded image said with a smile. *"We've lost too much time, my friend. You are in Castrovia now! It must be so beautiful. I insist you send me a holovid of your own making right away. Do I take this as a vacation, or perhaps a permanent move? How is the life of a duchess treating you? Luxuriously, I hope! But I also better hear of you piloting a BattleMech. Don't get rusty on me!"*

Nikol's expression in the three-dimensional image shifted.

"But now, tell me, Danai...how are you really? No beating around the bush, my friend. I expect a prompt response and I expect it to be detailed. How are you?"

Nikol hesitated. *"Danai, you know I'm not really superstitious. I know you're not, either. But I do want to hear from you, and I would appreciate your instincts on how things are going in your part of the universe. I can't shake a bad feeling lately. Not that I think you are in any particular danger, or that I am either, for that matter. Just something in the wind, I guess. What do you think? Have I lost my mind?"*

Danai's trusted friend chuckled and rubbed her forehead.

"Maybe we're just getting old! Anyway. I don't want to leave you with that. Send me an update as soon as you can. I could use your kind face and comforting words. Let me know how things are. Okay? I miss you, my friend. Please let's find a way to connect in person again soon. Otherwise I'll have to hijack a JumpShip straight to Castrovia!"

She smiled again. *"Be well, Danai. 'Bye."*

The holovid faded out, and Danai found grateful tears in her eyes as she smiled at Nikol's message. She hastened to brush the tears away as she prepared a holovid of her own.

"Nikol! It is so good to hear from you!"

CHAPTER 15

Castrovia's sun seemed to stand still directly overhead. Its direct light warmed Danai's skin even as a gentle breeze cooled her body and sent stray hairs whispering across her face.

Her opponent was skilled, but Danai stood unfazed. The stakes for this battle were too high to let fear get the best of her.

"Are you certain this is a good idea, Your Grace?" Yunhai asked quietly, nervously, from her left side.

Danai grinned at him. "I'd get off the field if I was you. That, or suit up and help me win this."

Her chief-of-staff had asked such troubled questions more than once over the past couple of months, and to a certain extent, Danai had taken delight in seeing what mischief she could get into that would make Yunhai's mouth turn down or his forehead wrinkle in concern.

Today was no exception.

She waved at the man on the side of the playing field, who blew a whistle.

The game was on.

Danai charged across the field, wearing her battledress long pants and a thin jersey top. She supposed some kind of padding would have been helpful, and certainly Yunhai had recommended it, but based on the opposition racing toward her, Danai felt her warrior's body would be sufficient to take any abuse.

Across the field, Tiko was in the lead of a group of children. Danai thrilled to see the little boy's determined expression. She'd told him not to take it easy on her, and like any dedicated servant, he was taking the order to heart. And like any dedicated child, he furthermore was taking the order at face value.

Tiko handled the soccer ball with near-expert precision as Danai bore down on him. He shuffled left, then right, juggling the ball between his feet as she tried to slip in to knock the ball away. No luck; the little boy juked around her and tore down the field toward the goal.

Danai shouted her surprise and mock-anger, turning quickly to chase him down. Tiko was fast, but smaller, and Danai put on a burst of speed to catch up, her spiked shoes drilling into the manicured turf.

She reached him before he could rear back for a kick toward the goal. Tiko responded quickly, altering his path. Danai laughed at his skill. But she wasn't about to simply stand aside and hand him a victory. It went completely against everything she'd ever known as a MechWarrior.

On the sidelines, people cheered. Danai could not tell for whom the observers shouted, nor did she care. If anything, she hoped the rallying cries were for Tiko, not the Duchess of Castrovia.

Her body sent her ongoing reports of minor twinges and pains, which Danai ignored. She kept up with her physical training just fine—she knew she could get called into her BattleMech on some far-flung world at any time. But football with an eight-year-old? That was an entirely different sort of workout.

"Oh, no you don't!" she cried as she and Tiko got tangled in a foot battle near the goal. Her feet lost the battle. Without warning, the youngster's legs got caught around her ankles, and Danai fell abruptly to the ground, face-first.

The unexpected blow coughed the breath out of her. She smelled grass, and tasted blood. Miniature stars twinkled in the darkness of her closed eyes.

"Your Grace!" she dimly heard Yunhai's terrified cry from the sideline.

Before she could even think to move herself, what felt like dozens of hands were on her limbs, turning her over and helping her into a seated position on the field. Opening her eyes, Danai first saw the terrified face of Tiko standing at her feet, his expression a mixture of open horror that he'd hurt someone with the growing realization that this person was his boss, and the boss of his entire world, among other titles.

She saw one of her bodyguards standing near Tiko, flexed and ready to spring.

She saw a man and a woman further back, clutching one another in mortal fear; she recognized them as Tiko's parents.

She saw Yunhai gripping his face with both hands, could see him calculating just how much trouble he was going to be in for this terrible event.

Danai Centrella-Liao, Duchess of Castrovia, just laughed.

"I'm *fine*," she said, shaking away the hands of her bodyguards.

They backed away, their expressions showing uncertainty on whether or not to believe her.

She pointed in Tiko's face. "You!"

The boy sucked in a breath. Danai noticed his knees were stained with grass. She roared and leaped at him, taking Tiko to the ground, where she dug her fingertips into the boy's ribs.

Tiko released a burst of unabashed laughter at her tickle and tried to roll away. Danai didn't let him. Together they laughed, until the other adults on the scene breathed sighs of relief and even joined in the laughter.

After finally releasing Tiko from his torment, Danai assured everyone in attendance that she was unharmed. She sent Tiko back to his pick-up game with a dozen other children, and spent several minutes with his parents to calm them.

"He has been wonderful," she said to them. "You should be very proud."

Indeed, her youngest servant's training was coming along excellently, according to her and Yunhai alike. Months ago, Danai thought she would have bristled at the idea of a youngster around. Now she found Tiko's determined attempts to do well in his job rather relaxing. And when memories of war and loss intruded, as they often did, she turned to the boy's antics to push them away for another moment.

She spent several minutes with the public who'd gathered nearby to catch a glimpse of their duchess. She shook hands, accepted bows, smiled, and extended thanks. Only after the guards finally shooed everyone away did Noah approach.

"Well," he said, sitting beside her on a sideline bench intended for players while she rubbed a soft towel over her sweaty face. "It's good to know you have a backup career if this whole MechWarrior-Duchess thing doesn't work out."

She threw the towel over her head like a hood and grinned at him. "Right, thanks."

Noah handed her his computer tablet. "Thought you should see this. It's Sheratan."

Danai took the computer and squinted at the report on it. "More attacks?"

He nodded and pointed at the screen. "Five deaths. Several ground vehicles ruined. It's getting worse, Danai."

"But not as bad as Liberty or Hall," she pointed out, handing him back the tablet.

"Agreed," Noah said. "But given the Chancellor's recent drive coreward, it does make me a little nervous. That's eight 'Mechs and five pilots out of whatever bigger fight is coming next, somewhere other than Sheratan. Can we afford that?"

Danai scowled, but hid it behind her towel. "There's no such thing as affording death and loss of 'Mechs. And you're right. That's particularly true right now."

Daoshen's push to create a corridor pointing toward Terra seemed to be working, but even victory came with a cost, a concept Danai remained unconvinced Daoshen fully appreciated. Yes, his plans had yielded victories for the Capellan Confederation, Liberty and Hall among them, where she and Noah had fought, but also worlds like Keid, New Home, and Procyon—worlds governed previously by the Republic of the Sphere, and now firmly in Capellan hands as of this past October, just after she and Noah had left Liberty.

Sheratan, too, counted among these newly reacquired systems. Daoshen's plots had been successful time and time again recently, but as leader of the entire Confederation, he could understandably only see the larger picture. He lived a life of maps stretching light years and astronomical units, not neighborhoods and streets.

Or ball fields and playgrounds, Danai thought suddenly, her gaze settling on Tiko in the distance as he scored a goal against the other team. When he turned her direction as if to see if she was watching, she forced a smile and waved to him. Tiko's face bloomed.

"There's more," Noah said. "But I'm sorry, maybe I should have waited for you to return to the palace."

Danai gestured his worry away. "It's good to be outside. What is it?"

"Liberty."

Danai blinked at the word, having just thought it herself. "What about it?"

Noah rubbed a hand over his chin, which Danai just then noticed had a pepper of black stubble. "We lost it."

Shock drove Danai to her feet. "Lost it? Where is *Zhongshao* Wu? What's happened to the Second MAC?"

Noah immediately rose to meet her as adults in the area turned to look at them. Danai didn't care. "They left not long after we did, on schedule," he said quickly. "Second MAC is on Hall. It was the Fifth MAC who lost Liberty to an RAF counterattack."

"When?"

"October. Danai—Your Grace—it was barely a week after we left the system. Days, really."

Danai paced a circle, hands on her hips, heedless of the watchful eye of Yunhai and the other adults nearby. The children went on playing, and she envied them.

"Then we should go take it back," she said, stopping her pace and looking at Noah.

"We haven't been ordered to," he answered quietly.

"Ordered," Danai repeated, and kicked at the grass. "Ordered...what are Wu and the Second doing on Hall?"

Noah checked his tablet. "Nothing of note. Most likely just...*keeping* it."

"The Second MAC has better things to do than garrison a beaten world."

Noah nodded, apparently thinking it wise to not add words as Danai's mood darkened.

Danai resumed her pacing. Dammit, she'd lost too much for the system to simply fall back into Republic hands again. What had been the point? Was Hall next? What had Mina died for?

"Liberty..." she whispered. "God*dammit.*"

Without warning, Danai stalked toward the motorcade. Noah and her entourage hurried to catch up.

"Back to my office," she barked at everyone in general. "I'm sending a message to my brother."

In seconds, everyone was loaded into the waiting cars and vanishing from the playground.

CHAPTER 16

**COMBAT INFORMATION CENTER
CELESTIAL PALACE
CHANG-AN
LIAO
20 APRIL 3150**

Robie stood apart from Daoshen in the Combat Information Center, close enough to act if need be, but the room was filled with Strategios, who posed no threat. All the same, she kept her gaze roving, knowing where every person's hands were while they stood or sat before holovids.

Tensions were high; Robie felt it in the manner of their speech. Even the normally taciturn Chancellor seemed uptight in his white robes as the room awaited long-sought military results.

"Relay coming in now," said a tech sitting at a console.

The low chatter in the room, lit principally by monitors and low lamps, ended abruptly. All eyes focused on the central holovid as an image resolved, forwarded from a DropShip now nearing Liao.

Someone gasped. Robie marked the noise and let her gaze flit across the projected image.

She might have gasped herself if not for her training. She'd never seen anything like it.

Daoshen's chin tilted up, as if he had suddenly smelled a foul odor. One of the Strategios cursed under his breath. One man grabbed the arm of the person next to him.

The image showed what had once been a Capellan JumpShip. Robie recognized what little remained of the fore end of an *Invader*-class JumpShip, but the mangled wreckage behind it looked like crumpled tinfoil. The entire ship appeared to have been crushed between some vengeful deity's fists.

The tech spoke again, her voice quavering. "Report confirms all souls aboard lost. Incoming message from the *jiang-jun* on Procyon... 'The Wall around Terra is still up.'"

Following this announcement, Robie expected there to be a flurry of activity—generals making pronouncements and shouting orders, perhaps. House Liao currently fielded the largest army in the Inner Sphere, but no military could shrug off the loss of a JumpShip.

Instead of a flutter of recriminations or orders, though, everyone but the techs turned silently to look at Daoshen.

The Chancellor stood very still, eyes unblinking as the three-dimensional image of the *Invader* ship slowly rotated. He then took a step closer to the image, as if his mere gaze could undo the horrific damage.

Daoshen abruptly swept his robes aside and lurched from the operations room. Robie leaped to follow. Only then did the officers left behind begin shouting at one another.

Robie said nothing as the Chancellor and a handful of aides walked with him through the palace halls, two in front to clear a path, the rest trailing behind. Except for the forward guards barking orders at other passersby to get out of the way, no one spoke.

They reached Daoshen's private office. The secretary on duty stood quickly as the Chancellor approached, and a servant whisked open the office door. The aide nearest Daoshen took a step to follow, but the Chancellor waved him off. The servant closed the door, ensconcing the Chancellor alone in the office and leaving his retinue casting glances between themselves in the reception area.

From behind Daoshen's door, a crash sounded.

Robie shoved others out of the way to reach the door. Someone grabbed her shoulder.

"I wouldn't," one of the guards warned quietly.

Robie shrugged him off and flung open the office door.

A delicate white vase lay smashed on the floor. The Chancellor himself stood nearby, shoulders pulled back, fingers curled into claws, lips drawn away from his teeth.

Robie quickly slid inside and closed the door behind her to prevent any further observation by the staff in the reception area. She kept her back pressed against the door.

Daoshen whirled on her, snarling.

Robie stood motionless, face impassive, eyes open and ready to accept any punishment the Chancellor felt appropriate to deliver with her breach in etiquette.

The punishment did not arrive. As he glared at her, Daoshen's rage slowly cooled. He took his time to straighten up, tug his robes into place, and resume the placid expression Robie had become accustomed to.

"That was a terrible loss."

Robie nodded, thinking it wise to not add her own thoughts on the matter. She knew the JumpShip had left Procyon with a skeleton crew in an attempt to breach the notorious invisible wall somehow erected around Terra by the Republic of the Sphere. The Fortress Wall, as it was known, prevented unauthorized ships from entering the Terran system. Those that tried either disappeared, never to be seen again, or were bounced back to their launch points...practically unrecognizable.

Robie waited silently for orders.

Daoshen gestured mildly to the wrecked vase. "Have someone attend to this. I will be in my private quarters."

"Yes, Chancellor," Robie said quietly, and slipped back out of the room.

Most of the staff had scattered. Only the on-duty secretary and two servants remained, though Robie could see the bodyguards in the hall outside the reception area.

She turned to Guanken, who had appeared while she was in the office with Daoshen. The man still wore a plastic brace on his wrist where Robie had injured him.

"There is a mess in the Chancellor's office," she told him. "Have it attended to. The Chancellor will be in his private quarters until further notice."

Guanken dipped his head in understanding. Robie lit out for Daoshen's residence, accessible by him through a hall attached to the office, to await his needs there.

CHAPTER 17

CELESTIAL PALACE
CHANG-AN
LIAO
30 MAY 3150

Sang-shao Rell Curtis rubbed his palms together as he waited for his subordinate, *Zhong-shao* Hao Jie, senior commander of the Rao DropShip attached to the Third Sian Dragoons. Curtis had dedicated his life to the Confederation, to protecting and expanding its borders, a fact he took great pride in. The rest of the Inner Sphere, even the Clans, hadn't half the honor of House Liao.

And now, for the first time in his sixty-six years, Curtis wondered if it wasn't all for nothing.

He scraped his hands over his graying crew-cut hair, thinking those salt-and-pepper patches would be fully silver by the time his grim business was complete.

Curtis kept his seat as a knock sounded on the wooden door of his office. "Come," he called in a baritone that his mother, rest her soul, had insisted he train for singing. Over his career in the CCAF, Curtis had come to realize she'd been right. Sometimes a low word could accomplish what a shout could not.

The door opened, and *Zhong-shao* Hao Jie entered. He closed the door and braced his body. "Sir."

"At ease. Come have a seat, Bent."

Jie relaxed and stepped over to Curtis' desk, sitting in one of the two cushioned chairs facing his superior. Though it did not show beneath his dress uniform, the *zhong-shao*'s left arm had a curious divot mid-forearm from a brush with death in his early career before rising to command the DropShip *Gold Swan*. This divot had earned him the nickname "Bent."

"How are you?" Curtis asked. The words were short, clipped; not meant to elicit a long reply.

Bent understood, and nodded. "Well, sir, thank you."

Curtis nodded, eyes darting across his desktop. "I'm going to make this brief, *Zhong-shao*."

"Yes, sir?"

"I need a captain and a skeleton crew. Someone who follows orders. A combined-arms commander who knows his shit. Are you that commander?"

Bent gave a tiny smirk of pride. He had been a loyal and decorated officer for decades. "I'll stand by my record."

"That's not going to cut it right now. I need a 'yes, sir' or 'no, sir' from you."

Bent's demeanor instantly shifted. All traces of his well-earned pride vanished from his expression. "Then yes, sir. Absolutely and of course."

Curtis slid over a red folder, knowing it was odd. Paper wasn't exactly in high use. "The contents of the report in this document could get a lot of people killed. Including you. Including me. You'll read it—"

He tossed a commemorative butane lighter atop the folder, a trinket from some *sang-shao's* wedding party years ago.

"—then burn it. Accept the offer inside, and you'll be fast-tracked to ranks you didn't even know existed in this military."

Bent kept his hands in his lap, eyeing the red folder. "And if I don't accept it, sir?"

"I'm trusting in your record to keep your mouth shut."

"Sir, as a regimental commander, I do have clearance for—"

Curtis felt his face go stoney. "Not for this. No one's got clearance for this. Just my boss. *His* boss. And me."

He watched Bent's jaw working, debating with himself. Curtis didn't blame him. But, as Curtis suspected, Bent's loyalty and curiosity won the moment, and he reached for the folder.

Curtis leaned back in his black leather chair. He watched Bent's face carefully as the grizzled man scanned the report.

When Bent looked up, his eyes were wide. "Sir—"

"Yes or no, Bent. It's that simple."

Bent worked his lips and tongue like he desperately needed water. "This comes from the Celestial Wisdom?"

"*Directly* from."

Bent uncharacteristically let his head droop as if his body had deflated. "You know I and my officers are the best ones for the job."

"I do."

"I cannot say no."

"You *can*," Curtis offered with a forced generous tone. "But."

Bent nodded. One did not say no to the Celestial Wisdom and go on to enjoy life thereafter.

Curtis let the silence between them grow. He needed Bent to come to terms with the mission in his own time.

It took less time than Curtis had thought, which served to underscore his choice. Bent was the right commander for the job.

"You can count on us, *Sang-shao*," Bent said, closing the folder and sitting up straight in his chair.

"Good," Curtis said softly, and did not try to hide the pain he knew shone in his eyes. "If it's any consolation, Bent, I'll be right there with you in hell."

Bent replied with a slight bow of his head. "I understand."

"Read the full report. Any questions, you come to me. *Only* me. When the *Autumn Rain* is ready, tell me. I'll send the official order."

Bent rose and braced. "Understood, sir. We'll get it done."

"I know you will. If you feel so compelled, you can offer the crew my apologies."

"No, thank you, sir. They'll do their duty as always."

Curtis grunted a sick laugh. "Which is why I tapped you. Good luck, Bent."

"Thank you, sir."

Bent braced again, and let himself out of the office, closing the door softly.

Curtis ran a palm over his lips, hoping the gesture would somehow ease the sick taste in his mouth. He'd done his part. Now it was up to Bent's handpicked crew to do the rest. He knew the younger man even now, walking the halls back to his office, was mentally selecting the handful of crew he'd need to get this job done.

Curtis swore quietly to himself.

"Getting this job done" was going to change a great many things.

CHAPTER 18

Danai fumed. She paced. She cursed. She wanted badly to get into the cockpit of her *Black Knight* and unleash hell.

On her brother.

"You will soon have other responsibilities," Daoshen's message went—no matter how many times Danai watched it. *"Enjoy your time on Castrovia. You will reunite with your unit shortly."*

That was it. That was the extent of Daoshen's response to her request to take the Second McCarron's Armored Cavalry back to Liberty.

She sat down at her desk in huff, grateful to be alone. She'd ordered Noah to wait outside, in his own office, while she listened to the Chancellor's reply.

Meanwhile, on Liberty, Wilhelmina Liao's death grew ever more senseless.

What's the point of being a duchess and sang-shao *of the Second MAC if I can't use it?*

Danai leaned her head back on her chair and closed her eyes. For the first time since arriving, she began to regret her decision to come here. Money, power, influence...all of it useless with a mere wave of Daoshen's hand.

She debated a caustic response, but talked herself out of it. What would be the point? Better to remain on Castrovia as instructed.

"Noah," Danai called.

He appeared immediately. "Yes, ma'am?"

"Find me the closest proving ground or training center and get my *Black Knight* there as soon as possible. I need to blow up a few things."

"May I join you, ma'am?"

Danai cracked a forlorn grin. "Yes. I'd rather enjoy that."

Noah nodded, and disappeared to make the necessary calls. Danai sat back in her chair again, hoping a few hours in her *Black Knight* would quell the anger bubbling inside her chest.

MAGISTRACY ADMINISTRATION OFFICE
CRIMSON
CANOPUS IV
MAGISTRACY OF CANOPUS
1 JUNE 3150

Ilsa Centrella-Liao made her decision unilaterally, alone in her private office, near midnight. The words she was about to speak were not meant for anyone other than her brother.

She also held little hope of those words having the desired effect. All the same, the words mattered. All words mattered; she knew this as the Magestrix. What one said and how one said it could make the difference between life and death. Between war and peace.

Between love and hate.

And she hated Chancellor Daoshen Liao.

But this private, secure message would not convey that hate. Even if Daoshen knew of her true regard of him, he likely did not care one bit. The man had far greater things on his mind.

Far greater ambition.

Which is why this is a message that must be sent, Ilsa thought. *Future generations will find it on the record as needed.*

Danai will find it. She above all will need to know I made every effort to curb Daoshen's hubris.

Her private office was lit by yellow lights embedded in the floor. This cast a soft, sunlit glow throughout the room. Ilsa adjusted herself on her ornate chair, centered the camera to her preference—the lens would capture her head-on, with no inferior nor superior angle. Daoshen would notice such details.

Pulling on her most calm, warm smile, one she had perfected over many years as Magestrix, Ilsa began the recording. She used no script; she had no need.

"My dear brother, and Celestial Wisdom...with all humility before the wisdom of the Chancellor, I implore you to reconsider what appears to be your current course of action as it pertains to the claiming of humanity's homeworld, Terra.

"Of course, I am not privy to the military workings of the Capellan Confederation. I am content to lead my small Magistracy close to the protection offered by my Capellan sisters and brothers."

This last bit was an ego stroke, and Daoshen would likely realize it. Canopus had a perfectly functional military, and ever since her marriage to the Duke of Andurien, Ilsa's military might had roughly doubled. Knowing the CCAF would not invade her nation made it possible to keep her own troops on more far-flung worlds to defend against other invaders. She believed, though, that this acknowledgement of Capellan strength would please her brother.

"The day will arrive when it is right and good to approach the integration of Terra into the Capellan Confederation, where it so rightly belongs. However, I do wonder, brother, if perhaps this illustrious victory is best reserved for our sibling, Danai."

Ilsa's practice referring to Danai as their sibling rather than child paid off well; she could tell neither her face nor her voice betrayed the disgust she held Daoshen in for having forced her to bring Danai to term.

On the other hand, she often reasoned with herself, Danai had shown herself quite intelligent and skilled. And useful. Erde Liao, an ancient woman now and Ilsa's regent, had raised her well.

"Danai has proven herself time and again across various campaigns of liberating worlds from the Republic of the Sphere. She is loyal, honest, and, to be frank, one of the greatest MechWarriors in the Confederation. I am sure I need not remind the Celestial Wisdom that I have named Danai as my successor here in the Magistracy. This is a most suitable title for her; she has more than earned this rank and privilege. For this reason I suggest, humbly, that the taking of Terra be left to her excellent skills and warcraft.

"Please accept this idea with my gratitude, Chancellor. My own military advisors, coupled with my personal experience in such matters, suggests that House Liao is not quite in a position to push forward to Terra, and that continuing to do so imperils the entire Confederation. And what imperils the Confederation imperils both the Magistracy of Canopus and the Duchy of Andurien. It is true you possess a vast army, dear brother, but even your resources are not infinite. I urge you to reconsider your current course.

"With all blessing to the Celestial Wisdom,

"I remain yours, Ilsa Centrella-Liao, Magestrix of Canopus."

Ilsa turned off the recorder. She played it back, decided it was sufficient, and set its security protocols before summoning a servant to ensure it got to Daoshen as soon as possible.

He will listen, she thought, turning to other responsibilities of the day. *He must. The Capellan Confederation stands to become the one great stabilizing force in the Inner Sphere.*

Or become the thing that damned them all.

CELESTIAL PALACE
CHANG-AN
LIAO
13 SEPTEMBER 3150

Robie watched Daoshen watching his sister speak.

"...to reconsider your current course. With all blessing to the Celestial Wisdom, I remain yours, Ilsa Centrella-Liao, Magestrix of Canopus."

Robie flicked her eyes to the holographic image as it faded. Ilsa's last words seemed to hover in an echo above the desk.

She waited patiently.

Daoshen stared, unblinking, at the holocube containing the message. He steepled his fingers before his lips and, for a moment, appeared to cease breathing.

At last he roused himself, sitting up on the throne. Still staring at the cube, he addressed Robie, "I will send a response now."

"Your Grace," Robie murmured, and hurried to bring a holo-recorder to his desktop from a closet of such supplies in the next room. She set it on the desk, facing the Chancellor, and adjusted it to present him the best angle and light. "Ready, Your Grace?"

Daoshen nodded. His expression had softened to include a peaceful smile.

Robie activated the recorder.

"To Ilsa Centrella-Liao, Magestrix of Canopus."

Daoshen's head tilted ever so slightly to the side, like a bird of prey.

"I am the lord your god."

Then he sat back in his throne, and nodded vaguely to Robie. She turned off the recorder and picked it up in both hands.

"Send it immediately," Daoshen said, examining the decorated fingernails of his left hand.

"Your Grace," Robie said quietly, and quickly stepped from the office.

CHAPTER 19

MAGISTRACY ADMINISTRATION OFFICE
CRIMSON
CANOPUS IV
2 NOVEMBER 3150

In the months that passed since Ilsa Centrella reached out to Daoshen, she'd convinced herself that he would see reason.

She now called herself a thousand kinds of fool for believing it.

Ilsa felt the individual muscles in her abdomen cinch tight, one by one. The tightness spread to her limbs like slow-flowing magma, burning everything in its path.

She sat quite still for several minutes, unblinking at the three-dimensional image of her brother the Chancellor.

"I am the lord your god."

Moment by moment, Ilsa controlled her breathing, willing the rage in her body to cool.

I am the lord your god.

She knew she ought not be surprised at Daoshen's response. What had she expected, after all? Capitulation? Tacit agreement? "Yes, Ilsa my love, I'll stop the invasions right away, per your wise counsel?"

Her calming exercise took a bit longer than usual, but eventually worked its magic. When she was fully in possession of her emotions again, Ilsa touched a button to open a private link to her security chief.

"Thao speaking."

"Zandra," Ilsa said in smooth tones. "Would you be so kind as to join me in my private office as soon as possible?"

"Right away, Magestrix."

"Thank you."

Ilsa switched off the comm and sat back in her chair. A persistent pain in her left hip twinged, but the old warrior ignored it. Her gaze drifted to one wall, where a small reproduction of one of her favorite photos hung: herself at age sixteen, standing proudly with three Red Heart Guards atop a *Men Shen*.

Her eyes weren't what they used to be, but Ilsa readily saw the proud defiance in her younger self. She remembered the day clearly and fondly, when the Red Lancers—of whom she'd been named honorary *sang-shao*—staged a full military parade to celebrate her sixteenth birthday.

Watching the might of one of Capella's elite warrior forces march in formation for her, Ilsa recalled a sense of power overwhelming her. She had been primed for leadership her entire life by her parents. As royalty, she'd had grown accustomed to having servants attend to her every wish.

Watching the army salute her, however, was an altogether different sense of power. *I could order them to open fire*, she remembered thinking. *I could make them kill everyone I see.*

The thought had at first made her giddy, almost high. Within moments, however, the giddiness was replaced by a realization of powerful responsibility.

And potential.

Indeed, it was a heady realization for any person to realize they held the power of life and death in their mere words. What Ilsa realized that day was that true power would come not from vulgar displays of violent action, but from wielding power quietly and carefully.

From that day, she paid closer attention to the politics of court, the politics of the Capellan Confederation, and the politics of the Inner Sphere. Her intelligence gathering network nearly rivaled the great Maskirovka, giving her the most recent updates from across the Inner Sphere several times a day. She learned how those in power wielded it well, or poorly.

And upon being removed from the line of succession many years ago after her little brother Daoshen was born, Ilsa began to make plans.

A quiet chime sounded, indicating a presence outside her office door. Smiling more fully now as her nostalgia cheered her, Ilsa said, "Come in."

Her trusted military aide, Zandra Thao, entered, closing the door behind her. Thao approached Ilsa's desk and stood at attention. "How may I serve you, Magestrix?"

"At ease, Zandra. Have a seat."

Thao wore an extraordinarily long black braid, the tip reaching well past her hips. This braid she scooped up in her left hand as she sat, as smooth and natural as one might brush hair off one's neck.

"I asked my dear brother to reconsider his designs on Terra," Ilsa said, rocking slightly in her chair to distract herself from the pain in her hip. "This was his response."

She played the holovid.

"I am the lord your god."

Thao's dark eyes widened as Ilsa snapped off the recording. "Does he mean it? Does the Chancellor believe he is being quite literal, Magestrix?"

"I'd like to think not," Ilsa replied. "However, knowing Daoshen as I do..."

She let the thought hang to assess Thao's reaction. Her thin sneer of disgust was precisely the response Ilsa wanted. And expected. The two of them went back a long time. Ilsa's trust in the younger woman was implicit.

Thao sat back in her seat and toyed with her braid as it lay across the lap of her utility uniform. The way she ran a thumb over each twist in the braid, Ilsa was reminded of counting prayer beads. "Well, I assume you did not call your military advisor in for tea," Thao finally said.

"Perhaps this afternoon, old friend," Ilsa said with a smile. "For now, I think it may be time to activate our green teams."

Thao raised an eyebrow. "I can put out the order immediately. It will reach them in a few days, some a few weeks. I should remind you, without the HPGs functioning, it would likewise take some time to recall such an order."

"I am aware, Zandra."

"I just want to be clear, Magestrix," Thao said. "This is the sort of operation that once launched, cannot easily be ended. And if Daoshen finds out it was you—"

"Daoshen fights more wars right now than he can possibly win. There is no limit to which of his enemies might strike in this manner. He won't think to blame me, at least not right away. And if he does, well, I welcome what remains of his over-extended armed forces any time."

"Several key Canopian units are still in the field fighting Capellan wars. He could elect to retaliate against them."

"Mmm. Yes. Have them prepare for such retaliation from their 'comrades in arms,' but have them do so quietly."

Ilsa was pleased to see the pride in Thao's expression. "I understand, Magestrix. Is there anything else?"

"No. But let's schedule that tea. I'd like to hear how your children are."

Thao stood, smiling. "Always happy to tell their tales. I will coordinate our schedules." She paused, then added: "Magestrix...I do have one question, if I may."

Ilsa gestured for her to continue.

"I just wonder...why? I'm only a soldier, and I like taking orders. I like to think I have served you to the best of my ability these past years."

"Indeed you have, Zandra."

"Then why the green teams? What is your end goal, ma'am? You're going to hurt Daoshen with this operation, but you won't cripple him. If you wanted to pick a fight with the Confederation, there are many other ways to do so, so that's not it, either. So why?"

Ilsa nodded as she spoke. From anyone else she'd be unlikely to tolerate the question. Not so from Zandra.

"In short, it is for Danai. As you say, this operation will not cripple Daoshen, but it will slow him, make him more cautious. With luck, that will be enough to blunt his ambitions long enough for Danai to assume the Chancellorship. If Daoshen is not stopped, Danai will have no Confederation to rule. She is young. She is battle-tested. She is smart. She will, in due time and with my help, come to lead all the Inner Sphere. Daoshen's ambitions are too fast, too big for that."

A new expression crossed Thao's face. The pride remained, but something like awe now blended with it. "Understood, Magestrix. Thank you. I'll activate the green teams now."

"Thank you. Send me a report as soon as possible on which worlds are impacted. Dismissed."

Thao offered a small bow and left the office. Only after the door was closed did Ilsa allow a simmering grimace to reach her face. Her hip hurt more now than ever, but she didn't want her physicians to know. Not yet, anyway. Perhaps later, if the pain impacted her ability to think.

As for Daoshen's message, Ilsa gathered the holocube into her aging hands, set it on the floor, and stomped on it until nothing but shattered fragments remained.

It helped.

CHAPTER 20

"Good morning, Your Grace," Noah said, joining Danai at her breakfast table.

"Good morning, Noah. You're not smiling."

"A message just came in, military courier priority," he replied. "It's from *Sang-shao* Stefano Rossetti."

"On Sheratan?" Danai asked, bringing up the message on her screen. These days, with Daoshen's constant warpath and the lack of HPG communication, it was almost impossible to keep track of CCAF troop movements.

"Yes. I thought you'd want to see it immediately."

Danai tapped a button and a three-dimensional rendering of *Sang-shao* Rossetti buzzed to life on her holovid.

"Sang-shao," Ross said, giving a short bow. *"I am not pleased to be approaching you in this manner, but I felt it best to contact you directly before alerting others. Of course, I understand if you feel otherwise and will take your advice immediately."*

Danai and Noah traded a glance.

"Sang-shao Cappelletti fell critically ill within days of our landing, and was evacuated back to Liao. I was

promoted in his place, and find myself...less prepared than I would prefer. I've studied everything I could about your recent liberation campaigns on Liberty and Hall, and how you handled a fledgling insurgency on Castrovia. Because of this, I wonder if I may request your direct help in the situation here on Sheratan."

The image of Ross visibly sighed.

"I am ashamed of coming to you like this, Sang-shao. *I can assure you the Confederation is at no risk for losing the system, but I have not been able to quell this rebellion. I'm deeply sorry for my failure here, and take full responsibility."*

Rossetti paused before straightening his tunic.

"If you would consider joining me here on Sheratan for a time, I would be most grateful. But again, of course, if you think it best to alert someone of a higher rank, I understand. But..."

Here, Rossetti seemed to squirm. Danai wanted to interrupt him, tell him she understood.

Because she did. Of course it would be right and proper for Ross to send for reinforcements from the Strategios, but doing so would bring attention to whatever failure he was experiencing on Sheratan. Asking a comrade of his same rank to come and offer guidance? Well, that was just a favor, and not something their superiors would have to note.

"It would mean a great deal to me," Ross' recording went on finally, *"if you would consider joining me here to advise. I await your response. Thank you,* Sang-shao.*"*

The message ended.

Danai slapped a palm on her desk. "The Strategios were foolish to send the Third Chargers in to put down a rebellion. This is the difference between war rooms and boots on the ground, Noah. The Third has a history as raiders. They are inexperienced with conducting anti-insurgency actions or acting as a garrison. The Strategios should know that."

If, she mentally added, *the Strategios are even the ones moving these pieces on the board right now. Maybe it's my dear brother alone. A man who has never served in a forward position. All he sees all day and night are maps, and that his colored markers moves the way he wants them to.*

"It should have been us," she said. "The Second MAC. Ross is asking me for this because he knows it's what we've been doing. For that matter, Second MAC should have stayed on Liberty. We'd still hold it if we'd stayed."

"Yes, ma'am," Noah said, but added, "Is there any possibility the Strategios wanted the Chargers to get more experience with an insurgency?"

Danai took that idea in and wrestled with it. Such a concept wasn't entirely out of place, she had to admit. Sheratan, long known for wanting to be an independent world regardless of which government controlled it, might be just the sort of low-level conflict needed to sharpen the Third for upcoming engagements. She did not really agree with this tactic, if it were true—but it also didn't matter in the immediate moment.

She shook her head. "Possibly, but it's not important. We have to deal with what's in front of us. Tell Ross we'll be on our way as soon as possible, and that I will keep it between us for the time being."

"Yes, ma'am."

"And tell Wu—where is the Second right now?"

"Hall, unless something has changed recently. With communication being as slow as it is without the HPGs, it's hard to say."

"Find out where the Second is for certain, and tell Wu to spin up the machine. I want the Second in reserve for this Sheratan nonsense."

Noah, oddly, did not immediately leave. Danai tilted her head. "What?"

"Do you think it will come to that, Your Grace?"

Danai glowered. "No. But sometimes an additional show of force is all that's needed."

Noah's expression softened slightly into a knowing look at his superior. "You're ready to be back in the saddle."

Danai's glower remained—then vanished as she nodded. "You know what, Noah? I am. Insightful as always."

Noah offered a short bow. "I'll get everything set up right now, and have Yunhai make preparations."

"No," Danai barked, waving. "I don't want a ceremony, no pageants. Ross needs help, and there's too much for me to do to be ready for it. We'll slip out, you and I. In the dark, if need be. Make sure Yunhai understands that."

"Right away."

Noah walked briskly from her quarters, closing the door behind him. Danai brought up all available intel on Sheratan, and started reading it closely, wondering what exactly Ross' main problem was on the surface.

And tried not to get distracted by the thought of taking the field again.

MIRNY SPACEPORT
LIANGRAD
CASTROVIA
6 NOVEMBER 3150

It hurt Danai's heart to see Tiko's brave face.

The little guy stood by the door leading to the ramp into Danai's DropShip. Tiko was adorned in his dress uniform, lovely red silks with white trim and a pillbox hat with a single tassel tickling near his chin. The boy shed no tears, but Danai could plainly see he was struggling with his feelings.

Eyebrows knitting together, Danai paused her procession to take a knee beside him. "You've been a tremendous help to me this past year, Tiko," she said, meaning the words in a way the young man could not yet understand, she was sure. It wasn't that he performed some act of service above and beyond his station by the manner in which he poured tea. Rather, his simple presence had calmed her, given her joy. They'd gone back to the football field on many occasions, and he'd grown much taller. Danai credited him as being what she had needed most after Liberty and Hall.

Now that she was moments away from boarding a ship to quell another insurgency, Danai found her feelings for Tiko rising in her throat. She swallowed them down. Never had she considered having children—her own family history prevented such a notion—and the boy hadn't changed her thoughts.

Still, Danai could now appreciate why people would want to conceive.

Tiko looked up at Yunhai, who stood half a pace behind Danai. Danai glanced back, and saw her chief-of-staff nod to the boy. "Tiko would like to present you with a gift, Your Grace," he said as the boy rummaged in his pocket. "With your permission."

"Of course," Danai said, facing Tiko again. "That is kind and thoughtful of you."

Tiko finally pulled a fist from beneath his long tunic and held a small object out to Danai. The duchess lifted her hand and took it.

A clay figurine. Danai turned it over in her hands. The figure was about the size of her palm, clay-red and kiln-fired. Shaped like a triangle, the human figure seemed to wear the approximation of a flowing gown.

"A queen," Yunhai said. "He made it himself, during his classes. Tiko thinks you should be queen of all Capellan space."

Danai pressed her lips together tightly for a moment before putting a hand on Tiko's shoulder. "Thank you," she whispered, and stood.

Two guards whisked the doors open. Cool air blew across Danai's skin. She was grateful for the excuse to blink her eyes against it.

Yunhai bowed. "It has been an honor, Your Grace. I hope you can return again soon."

She cleared her throat. "Thank you, Yunhai. That would be wonderful. We will certainly try." She tapped Tiko on the top of his hat. "Watch out for this one for me."

"Gladly, Your Grace."

Taking a deep breath, Danai stepped onto the ramp. She heard Noah behind her exchanging brief gratitude with Yunhai and the rest of the entourage.

Danai reached the opening to the DropShip and stepped inside, turning on her heel to face the others just as Noah stepped in.

As the guards and attendants bowed her direction, Danai impulsively waved at Tiko, keeping her hand low by her leg, and winked.

The boy's return smile shone brighter than the Castrovian sun.

PART 2

CHAPTER 21

A year ago, Danai had been behind the wire on Liberty to end a different insurgency. Having liberated that world and Hall, she had initially looked forward to giving her Second MAC a well-deserved break. Rebuilding towns on Liberty hurt by combat with the insurgents wasn't most soldiers' idea of a good time, but it also helped give them focus while allowing their bodies and minds to recover.

She'd enjoyed her time on Castrovia, though her emotions had tugged her in opposite directions during her stay. The world had been beautiful, the people warm. She missed her little assistant, Tiko. While she'd spent a lot of time just relaxing and recovering, Danai had also stopped an insurgency before it began, and she took pride in that.

Beelining for Sheratan now, Danai felt strong and... itchy. She felt her limbs and veins aching to be back in her BattleMech, even if she didn't see direct combat.

You can put the MechWarrior in a duchy, but you can't take the MechWarrior out of the duchess, she thought, and grinned in her cramped cabin.

Someone knocked on her hatch. She called, "Enter."

The door cycled open. A brief gust of cool, recycled air scented with the acrid aroma of ozone drifted inside her relatively luxurious accommodations aboard the *Gladiator.*

Sang-wei Noah Capshaw grinned wryly on the other side of the doorway. His newly close-shorn white hair gleamed under a bright hallway light. He wore comfortable green Capellan fatigues like Danai's own, the sort best suited to extended space travel. "You wanted to see me? I hoped to find you resting."

"I rested enough on Castrovia," Danai said, keeping things informal while she still could. Once they landed, their relationship would need to resume more formality. "Come in."

He stepped into her quarters, lavish compared to the others on board the ship: as *sang-shao*, or colonel, Danai was afforded a space measuring 2 by 3 meters with a small, fold-down desk, a tiny chair, a small bookshelf, and her narrow bed—all bolted to the floor. At this moment, research material on their destination—the warm, heavily forested world of Sheratan—lit her noteputer.

"Have a seat, Noah."

He sat and buckled himself onto the green upholstered bed opposite Danai's desk. His fatigue pants nearly camouflaged his legs to invisibility.

Danai used the hem of her blouse to polish one of her knives. "How's the travel been treating you?"

"Fine, ma'am."

"You're up to speed on everything planetside?"

"Yes, ma'am, I believe so."

"Good." Danai held the blade up to the overhead light, inspecting its glow. "What do you think about the situation on Sheratan?"

Noah shifted on the bunk and frowned. "*Think*, ma'am? That's above my pay grade."

Danai appreciated the humor. Such levity was both fleeting and necessary in a BattleMech regiment, particularly one about to drop into armed combat. While this trip consisted exclusively of herself and Noah, Danai knew bringing her entire Second MAC was still an option, and one she wouldn't hesitate to employ if necessary.

Chuckling, she replied, "Yes, think. Your most recent thoughts, your impressions. What are we getting into?"

Noah frowned.

"I mean it," Danai said. "I want your unvarnished input on what's going on down there on Sheratan, and how we ought to help Ross with it." Danai slid her knife into its black leather sheath on her calf and leaned back in her chair. The headrest banged into the bulkhead. The cockpit of her BattleMech seemed roomier.

Her *sang-wei* repositioned himself on the bunk. "Well, ma'am, for one thing, I'm still a little surprised the Third Chargers are having such trouble."

"What's surprising you about that?"

"I remember what you said about the Third specializing as raiders, but nevertheless, Ross should know what he's doing," Noah said, as if trying out the informal use of *Sang-shao* Stefano Rossetti's nickname among the rank-and-file. Danai noted it and let it pass. "He's young, but should have all the resources necessary to put a stop to an insurgency, and yet…" He seemed to struggle for words.

Danai nodded once and echoed him. "And yet."

Noah's frown deepened. "I also think it must be because this rebellion in Rainspire seems so widespread and so widely supported. We have Maskirovka agents on the ground, as always, but they've had no luck pinpointing the insurgent command structure. The entire city seems to be in on it, which is unusual. At the same time, the attacks on the Third Chargers and Capellan law enforcement are clearly coordinated efforts. This is not a free-for-all. And while the nearest large city, Daggaknott, hasn't seemed to engage so far, if things keep going this way, it's only a matter of time before they do. In my opinion."

Danai agreed with all of it. The insurgencies on Hall and Liberty had been comprised largely of former military, and behaved as such. The general public on those two worlds, while perhaps uncertain about their new roles in Capellan social structure, had not caused problems. On Sheratan, in the small city of Rainspire, intelligence suggested no citizen could be trusted. Several kilometers away, the large agricultural-industrial center of Daggaknott seemed to be choosing to stay out of the fray...for now.

Danai knew successful insurgencies had a way of quickly infecting neighbors. If Daggaknott turned on the Capellans too, things would escalate very quickly. She laced her fingers over her stomach. "And based on this intelligence, what is your conclusion?"

"Sheratan has a long history of insurgency against its ruling houses. Some of those movements were funded by the Confederation when we were not in possession of the world."

"And we don't know if we're fighting one faction or fifteen, or what its ultimate goals are."

"Exactly. In my view, it's a cult of personality. Someone's shown up, or just spoken up, who the people love. On Hall, we had Mayor Olatunde working for us—" Noah paused, glancing at his CO. Mayor Olatunde had been a good ally before insurgents—in some respect, his own people—murdered him on the street with an explosive device.

Olatunde, of course, was not the only loss that day. He'd been killed in the same roadside blast that took Mina Liao's life. While her time on Castrovia had allowed Danai to process her grief over Mina, the woman's ghost still haunted her. It was as though Danai's brain and heart had seized on Mina to be the avatar for all the friends she'd lost during Daoshen's endless campaign.

Danai winced and forced herself to refocus on Noah, gesturing for him to continue.

"—and the insurgents were primarily current or former Republic military. That doesn't seem to be the case on Sheratan. They have military assets, but their tactics are guerrilla. Yet they are doing a good enough job to force Ross back to his LZ as a safe zone. Ross hasn't been able to secure a foothold anywhere in Rainspire like we did on our last two deployments. Not without taking casualties. He's running at maybe 50 percent strength by now."

Danai allowed Noah to see her scowl. She agreed with his assessment. Even at the height of hostilities on Hall, she had controlled the levers of local government from the governor's office in the city of Harney. The insurgents there had sown chaos and uncertainty in the town limits, and taken their share of Capellan lives, but they'd come nowhere close to chasing Danai's regiment out of the city.

"*Sang-shao?*"

Danai blinked at his voice. "Yes. Sorry, Noah. Maybe you were right, I should get some rest while I can. Let's wrap this up. In your estimation, what are our options on the surface?"

"You don't have a plan, *Sang-shao?*"

"I have many plans. I want to know yours."

Noah took a moment before saying, "If I'm being honest, ma'am?"

"If you were anything but, you wouldn't be in this room."

He beamed momentarily. "I think we should fight a personality with a personality."

Danai arched an eyebrow. "Go on."

"I've met Ross once or twice at various functions, and he strikes me as a competent soldier. But to defeat a cult of personality, the opponent should be met with a personality."

Noah paused to eye her carefully, as if to see if she was following. He straightened his emerald tunic. "You are *sang-shao* of the Second MAC, one of the most respected and feared regiments in the Capellan Confederation, if not the Inner Sphere. You're a well-known Solaris championship contender. You also happen to be the Duchess of Castrovia, sister to the Magestrix of Canopus, and sister to the Celestial Wisdom himself, Chancellor of all Capellan space. You stand to inherit three interstellar nations, and potentially head the grandest super-state of thirty-second century."

Danai nodded vaguely at all that. She knew. She might try not to think about it very often...but she knew. And she knew where Noah was headed with all this.

Some days, Danai didn't know which title suited her best—she'd accumulated too many of late. As colonel of the Second MAC, she commanded a veteran regiment of troops. As Duchess of Castrovia, she essentially ruled an entire world. As sister—of a sort—to Daoshen Liao, Chancellor of House Liao, she commanded respect across hundreds of other worlds.

After her stay in Castrovia, though, a small and secret place within her longed to be just Danai again. No; MechWarrior Danai Centrella-Liao. That was the title that suited her best.

"In other words, ma'am," Noah continued, "not to diminish Ross, but your pedigree runs much deeper and farther. You achieved a bloodless victory against the White Moon insurgents on Castrovia when we first arrived,. I think it's possible that a negotiation with you on Sheratan may succeed where one with Ross is doomed to failure."

"Assuming we can even find the leader of this uprising to negotiate with," Danai pointed out.

"I think once they find out you've arrived, they'll be more than happy to take that meeting."

Danai chuckled humorlessly. "You flatter me, Noah."

"Begging your pardon, ma'am," he said earnestly, "but no. I don't."

Danai smiled again, this time with more candor. She enjoyed her chats with Noah, and had ever since he joined her command lance in the winter of 3147. She got along well with and trusted her XO, *Zhong-shao* Wu, but he was a grizzled old campaigner. Noah had some of the audacity of youth, an audacity Danai sometimes coveted. Further, he'd proven himself both discreet and loyal. Not to mention a fine MechWarrior, a skill that might come into play on Sheratan.

She stretched her arms over her head. "Thank you, Noah. That will be all. I'll take that rest now. When we land, make sure my *Black Knight* is ready to roll out. I want to see what Ross has been dealing with for myself."

Noah looked uncomfortable. "Are you sure you should be getting into fights, Your Grace?"

Danai smirked at his election to revert to using her royal title, doubtless to emphasize her prominent role in Capellan society. It was an astute move, if a bit clumsy. *He might make a decent politician yet.* Even as the thought crossed her mind, Danai hoped politics would not be his fate. Noah deserved better. She would only wish politics on her worst enemies.

"Don't worry, I'm not getting into any fights. I need to see what life looks like on the ground, from Ross' point of view."

"Yes, Your Grace, I'll make sure your *Black Knight* is ready."

"Thank you. And, Noah?"

"Yes, Your Grace?"

Danai loathed speaking down to her subordinates. She had to ensure, however, that her *sang-wei*—and the rest of the regiment—understood the stakes of their mission.

She lowered her register. "About the Chancellor's designs on Terra."

Noah let his gaze drift away from her as he nodded briefly. Chancellor Daoshen's interplanetary troop movements of late were clear to any first-year military cadet: he intended to assault Terra and claim it as Capellan territory for the first time in Capellan history. Danai, in fact, knew this for certain, having spoken to her "brother" about the plot. It was not yet public knowledge, but if Daoshen kept up his current pace of taking or re-taking worlds, he would have to publicly take ownership of the endgame sooner or later.

Terra, however, would not be easily taken. Others had tried over the past several centuries. Few succeeded. But passion for the Capellan nation ran high in its citizens and troops. If the Celestial Wisdom—Chancellor Daoshen—wanted Terra, then the people would sacrifice all to give it to him.

"I cannot speak to the Chancellor's specific plans," Danai said, trying to keep a sour note out of her voice. "But I do know that any such assault requires a clear and unfettered path from Liao to Terra. Brushfires like this nonsense on Sheratan are distracting from consolidating our recent gains. If it keeps up, if the Chancellor must continue to pull front-line units like the Third Chargers or MAC to put down insurgencies, his goals may not be realized."

"Yes, ma'am."

"I don't anticipate a hard fight in Rainspire, but it must be kept short so we can get on with the business of stabilizing the Confederation."

"Understood, ma'am."

"Good. And one last thing: nice job in here today."

Noah visibly resisted a big grin. "Thank you, ma'am!"

He braced his body rigid for a moment, the Second MAC version of a salute, before letting himself out of her quarters.

Danai moved to recline upon her bunk and snapped off the overhead light.

She snapped it back on within five minutes of realizing she wouldn't sleep and opened *Victories of Sheratan*, a history of the planet's various regional fighting forces.

This would make her third reading.

Everything she'd said to Noah about the taking of Terra was true. What she didn't say was how much she opposed Daoshen's idea at the present time.

An attack on Terra any time soon could cripple or kill the Capellan Confederation.

And Danai Centrella-Liao would not let Daoshen destroy House Liao.

CHAPTER 22

Danai walked down a narrow ramp, flanked a step behind by *Sang-wei* Capshaw. Both wore sharply presented fatigues suitable for infantry, but not for the cockpit of a BattleMech. In the event of such combat, each would don cooling accoutrements instead. For now, however, Danai wanted to show the Third Capellan Chargers she was ready to go into hand-to-hand combat at their side if need be.

They took a transport outside the drop zone. Danai kept her face neutral as she stepped out onto the rich soil of Sheratan V. She could *smell* the soil, and a light breeze carried the aroma of growing corn and alfalfa. The dark earth, packed down by countless Third Capellan Chargers boots, extended in a roughly 6-kilometer circle. The soil, Danai had learned, was runoff from surrounding woods, but did not reach far down. Beneath them lay scorched rock left behind from a meteor impact many millennia ago. This shallow crater provided the only decently flat surface near Rainspire, making it the most convenient landing zone for *Sang-shao* Rossetti's Third Chargers.

Danai scanned Ross' LZ, counting two *Overlord*-, two *Union*-, and four *Leopard*-class DropShips within eyeshot. In the distance, she picked out two *Hercules*-class DropShips as well, for the Third's tanks and infantry. The DropShips sat cool and motionless under the setting sun. To Danai's right, the north, beyond the LZ's perimeter, an immense stretch of agricultural land extended as far she could see. A vast conifer forest surrounded the crater LZ to the east, south, and west.

From her maps, she knew Rainspire—estimated population of 100,000—lay northeast of Rossetti's forward operating base here in the crater. Much of the land north and northeast was agriculture, with paved and dirt roads crisscrossing the landscape in even grids.

Danai rapidly calculated the job Stefano Rossetti had done with this FOB. Light BattleMechs ringed the perimeter, and Dannert-style concertina wire encircled the area like a glittering silver bracelet. Armored vehicles formed a makeshift gate to the west, with sandbag barricades and foxholes prepared to stop any unauthorized infantry.

"Dammit," she whispered. The FOB was as ready for defense as any she'd ever visited...which underscored the problem. The FOB looked all too permanent for a world that only needed the ending of a local insurrection. The Third had been here for three months now, and the whole base reeked of it. Personnel walked with heads down, shoulders hunched. People moved slowly. The DropShips seemed dusty and disused, unaccustomed to such long stints on the ground. The machines looked sad to Danai; like a MechWarrior wanted to be in the cockpit, a DropShip wanted to be flying through space.

From the direction of the makeshift gate, three Third Chargers approached. Danai and Capshaw walked briskly to meet them, boots sinking a centimeter into the packed but still-soft earth.

Sang-shao Stefano Rossetti was not only one of the youngest colonels in Third Chargers history, he looked the part. The young man wore his black hair in a short, flat cap against his skull, as if the hairstyle joined seamlessly with his tan-colored skin. His eyes were deep set and piercing, with long eyebrows creating a formidable visage.

"Your Grace," Ross said, squaring back his shoulders and staring at a point just past Danai's head. His two companions did the same.

"At ease, Ross," Danai said. "We are equals here, *sang-shao* to *sang-shao*."

If Ross' ramrod stance loosened at all, Danai could not detect it. "Indeed we are not, Your Grace," he replied, unblinking.

Danai waited for an explanation. When none came, the duchess gave the younger man a brief nod; Ross was right, and there was no further point in arguing it. They held the same rank on the battlefield, but none could deny Danai's duchy, nor her relationship to the Celestial Wisdom.

"Very well," she said. "Nevertheless..." She extended a hand. Ross relaxed, followed by his two companions, and accepted the handshake. Danai noted the tell-tale callouses of a MechWarrior.

She introduced Noah. Ross introduced his XO and a *sao-shao*, Aliana and Lubov. The four traded handshakes and brief pleasantries.

Lubov had the look and bearing of a man just past his prime, but fighting it every step of the way. His skin had the appearance of brown leather. His short black hair showed no gray. A lock of it, though, continually fell from what was otherwise lacquered in place, brushing the edge of his eyebrow. As a result, Lubov constantly raised a hand to brush it back in place. Aliana was made of more fragile stuff, with pale skin and large blue eyes, but Danai detected a strength of will in her stance and demeanor.

"I'm sorry I felt the need to bring you all the way out here," Ross began. "It's embarrassing, *Sang-shao*, to say the least."

"Not at all," Danai said, putting her hands behind her back and scanning the FOB again. Tents and bivouacs intended for short-term use had the look of permanent structures, with laundry drying on cords and chairs gathered around fire pits.

She tilted her head back. "No air reported, is that still true?"

"Yes," Ross said, matching her gaze to the darkening sky. No clouds blotted the slowly appearing stars. "Fast, light 'Mechs. Some RetroTech vehicles closer to Rainspire. Plus all the street-level garbage in the city—Molotov cocktails and such. But no sign of air forces. Not even a random helicopter. That's the good news."

"Tactics?"

Ross pointed toward the gate. "They mostly come straight at us from the north. I keep a few 'Mechs in the woods to make sure they don't sneak up on us through the trees, but they haven't tried that yet. They run in fast, fire long-range weapons, and run back out while we muster a response. We've tried tracking them back to their base, but they disappear like ghosts."

"How about prisoners?"

"We take out a 'Mech here and there with Gauss rifles, at a distance, but the pilots are either dead or die not long after. No actionable intel."

Danai frowned, assessing the area beyond the gate. "Are your remote sensors not working?"

"They were when we set them up," Ross said, grimacing. "Sappers took them out one by one until we were depleted."

"Mines?"

"Again—"

"Enough," Danai said. She turned to Noah. "*Sang-wei*, work with Aliana and Lubov here to patch our comms, make sure we're all on the same frequency. Then get me a list of what gear and personnel is up and running in the Third. And bring me the very first and the most recent after-action reports." To Ross, she said, "I assume your lists are up to date?"

She saw Ross clenching his teeth behind closed lips. "They are."

"Good. Capshaw, off you go. *Sang-shao* Rossetti...walk with me."

The other three soldiers braced in response, holding the pose until Danai and Ross had turned away.

With Ross at her side, Danai strode away from her DropShip and toward the perimeter of the camp. She spoke in low tones. "You've been in this LZ since you arrived in September?"

"Yes, ma'am."

"No outpost in the city? Why?"

"I know what happened on Hall and Liberty," Ross said. "It didn't seem prudent to lodge my people there. Also..."

Danai's anger flared at the reference to Hall and Liberty, but it cooled quickly as she saw Ross meant no insult.

Insurgencies on both worlds had cost her dearly, and though young, Ross was a vet. He knew loss.

"Also?" she prompted.

"When we got here, they were beating the crap out of the Liao militia and police in town. Molotov cocktails, bombs, assassinations. Danai, the whole damn town is in on it, but it's not like they're wearing uniforms. We—beg your pardon, *I*—tried to take over a civic building, for instance. They...gassed us out."

"Gas?"

"Homemade. These are farmers, mostly, and they can whip up some pretty awful chemicals. For what it's worth, they've never actually breached our perimeter." Ross swung a hand in half-circle to indicate the wire as they walked.

"Have they tried?" Danai asked.

Rossetti scowled. "Well. No."

"Tell me more about their tactics and machinery."

"They make raids with *Blades*, *Cougars*, and *Vixens*. We go out and return fire, try to hunt them down. But they've got home field advantage, and disappear." Here, Ross allowed something like an expression: disappointment. "Once the chase is on, they veer for the forest. They know these woods, and they use them well."

"What's your casualty ratio?"

The slight disappointment on Ross' face turned to ice. "Approximately two to one. For every one of theirs, we're losing two assets. BattleMechs, warriors, infantry—any mix."

Danai stopped and faced him. "Dammit, *what* is going on down here, Ross? You and your Chargers should be holding something more important than this, if not part of the tip of the spear."

"Your Grace," Ross said, "to be frank—"

"To be frank, you've had *months*!" Danai cut in. "There's no known formal military on the whole surface, RAF or otherwise. Yet an entire regiment of the CCAF has failed to secure the planet. To secure one *city*. To what, exactly, do you attribute this failure?"

While Ross' body gave no indication of having shifted, Danai nevertheless detected a change in the air, almost like the literal temperature.

She'd hit a nerve. Or several.

Good. She wanted to know what Stefano Rossetti was made of before charging into battle with him. Needed to know how this relationship was going to unfold.

Ross' gaze drifted to the gate, and Danai followed it. Six armed guards loitered near the armored vehicles and artillery there. They were alert; a good start. Portable spotlights turned on automatically as twilight descended, casting harsh beams to the north.

The sentries also kept an eye on Danai and Ross. As Danai casually scanned the immediate vicinity, she realized everyone with a Third Chargers patch was watching them while doing a poor job of pretending not to. She imagined she could read their thoughts: *The Duchess of Castrovia is here! The sister of the Celestial Wisdom has arrived!*

Hey, Duchess, she thought. *Like it or not, Noah was right about who you are and how people see you. Better start putting it to use if you want to get off this rock and keep Daoshen from doing something we can't undo.*

Ross' head suddenly centered, and he set his dark eyes on hers. "May I speak freely with you, *Sang-shao?*"

"Always, Ross. When we are alone, yes, please do."

"This bulk of the insurgency is contained to Rainspire. Daggaknott's not sending 'Mechs in to assault our position, anyway. If I could go in and take out Rainspire, this would be over. That's where this thing is centered."

Danai, unable to resist her body's natural impulse, crossed her arms over her chest. "You want to wipe out a town of *farmers?*"

Ross' jaw worked furiously.

"That option is off the table. I have specific rules of engagement," Danai went on. "You will abide by them."

"Begging your pardon, but your rules are not practical. They read like the Ares Conventions!"

"Because they are based in part upon them."

The Conventions hadn't been in official use in more than 700 years, but Danai had come to appreciate their spirit—that the destruction of civilian infrastructure and civilians themselves was best avoided in wartime. The treaty had originally been proposed by then-Capellan Chancellor Aleisha Liao. Danai took that ancestry to heart.

"*Sang-shao* Rossetti," she said, lowering her chin so as to glare down at the shorter colonel. "I will not have your regiment or mine dishonor the principle of preserving civilian life. The Second MAC ended two insurgencies on two different worlds without attacking those populations or infrastructure, and those enemy combatants were armed with Republic Armed Forces 'Mechs and personnel. Surely a little uprising can be quelled by this regiment."

"What's left of it!" Rossetti snapped.

Danai raised an eyebrow, but Ross didn't seem to care any longer about any difference in their social ranks.

"We're raiders, dammit," he said, his voice heated but kept low. "That's what we're good at. Being kicked around by insurgents and sabotage, it's demoralizing. Our supplies are dwindling, and raids into Rainspire to replenish get us killed by traps and ambushes. My warriors have no fight in them. I'm down an entire BattleMech *battalion*, Danai. I have to report that back to the Strategios. My next one's due in two weeks, and when they get it, I am finished here. I didn't beg you to come here for the laughs, I need serious help. Frankly, I wouldn't mind Second MAC dropping in and helping me take Rainspire apart brick by brick."

Danai kept her mouth closed, doing her best to balance Ross' obvious anger with her own outrage at his appalling tone.

You're not a duchess down here, she told herself. *He's a peer. And he's been through hell. Take it easy.*

Danai glanced across the FOB again. Having cleared her DropShip, she had a less obstructed view now of more of the camp. Two enormous *Pillager*s stood near one of the perimeter; the setting sun outlined their silhouettes, which Danai recognized instantly. The *Pillager*s were among the biggest and baddest machines ever fielded. At 100 tons each, the model bristled with weaponry and carried a staggering amount of armor. Not the fastest assault 'Mechs ever built, but one of the few with jump capability. *Pillager*s were built to decimate urban centers, and did so extremely well.

As she looked at the two *Pillager*s, Danai realized they likely served as nothing but guard towers. Like aircraft carriers of ancient days, they wouldn't go out alone—they'd be part of a lance of support 'Mechs. As with any MechWarrior, she was always glad to have a few assault-class Mechs around for the firepower, but in reality, they'd be next to useless in this type of campaign. Far too slow. So too would any heavies Ross had in stock.

Continuing her appraisal, Danai saw tanks and artillery pieces parked at intervals along the perimeter as well. Perfect for lobbing shells at distant clusters of enemies; merely decorative against spry light 'Mechs making hit-and-run raids.

She nodded at the artillery. "What about those pieces?"

Ross cleared his throat. "We blew through our FASCAM rounds early on. And down to the dregs for Gauss rounds. Re-supply has been—"

Danai waved him off. The Capellan war machine was doubtless focusing supply lines to Daoshen's race for Terra. Sheratan was a crucial stepping stone in that endeavor, but not currently at risk of invasion. They had only these damn insurgents to deal with.

Noah was right, she thought. *The Third was never outfitted or prepared for a campaign like this.*

"I understand, Ross," Danai allowed after a long pause. "Let's both keep our bearings, shall we?"

Ross lowered his eyes. "Of course, *Sang-shao*."

"What about the Maskirovka? Has money been tried, offers of land or title?"

Ross snorted. "The Mask reports yes. But their first approach was to strong-arm the populace, using intimidation instead of bribes. They're too late to try playing nice, so now no one will flip for them. They're trying to prep some people from Daggaknott to infiltrate, but that's not going smoothly or quickly either. I think Daggaknott's in on it, even if they're not directly involved. Honestly I think the whole damn planet's in on it. They just can't be bought."

Danai considered this. That was a new wrinkle. On Hall and Liberty, and most worlds for that matter, there were always a few who could be turned. For the Mask to fail at turning even a single Sheratan spoke volumes of this insurgency's strength that had nothing to do with firepower.

Put it all together, she thought, *and no wonder Ross is having a hard go of it.*

"Listen," Danai said gently, "you and yours have a good record. I don't contest that. I'm sorry the Mask's efforts aren't amounting to anything. Which is shocking to me, but—we are not attacking Rainspire. We're going to root out the insurgents one by one if need be, get this place under control, then go join the real fight."

"Terra," he said, meeting her eyes.

Danai smirked. "Let's not get ahead of ourselves. But both our regiments are certainly needed elsewhere, yes. Agreed?"

"Agreed, *Sang-shao*." He looked at her with appreciation.

"I'm on your side in all this. This time last year, I was fighting a similar insurgency. And I lost good people. Friends. Here I am seeing the same damn thing all over again. So let me be honest with *you*, now: I'm tired of it. Personally, I want a stand-up fight, I want to go toe-to-toe with real MechWarriors, not these overzealous fools who don't know when they're—"

Crimson lasers from the west pierced the darkness, landing against the bulkhead of Danai's DropShip and scattering light.

Danai winced as bits of melted slab dripped from the ship and hit the black ground with a dull *thump*. Ross' ships instantly began returning fire. The crew of her ship would be springing to their battle stations, awaiting the order to shoot back.

Ross lifted his eyes with a wry smirk. "That's them now."

Danai squinted into the darkness, seeking the source of the attack. "'Mechs?"

Ross remained unruffled as more lasers sailed through the air and blew off more armor from the parked ships. With the perfect equanimity of a soldier used to incoming fire, he said, "Indeed, *Sang-shao*. They've degraded our defenses such that they can run up nice and close enough for long-range weapons. We're still trying to figure out where the hell the insurgents got the 'Mechs. Maybe your DropShip could lend us a hand returning fire?"

She didn't like his tone, but didn't bother to argue as Noah raced up to her. "*Sang-shao*—!"

"Fire at will," she interrupted him. "But don't bother wasting any ammunition. Tell the captains to take the lead from Ross' men. And get our 'Mechs out in the field."

Danai glanced up and to her right. A hundred meters away, her *Black Knight* stood ready.

Despite her automatic anger at the attack, the rush of adrenaline felt good in her limbs.

"All right, Ross. Let's go say hello."

CHAPTER 23

The *Black Knight*, which Danai had decided to call *Julian*, was not as comfortable as her venerable *Yen-Lo-Wang*, but at the moment, she didn't mind. What mattered was finally getting kitted out in her cooling suit and dropping into the cockpit of a BattleMech.

The command couch had not yet quite conformed to her body the way her old 'Mech had, but it was getting there. A seam in the couch behind her right knee had finally softened, causing less irritation.

Serial number FS1010-031X, the notorious *Yen-Lo-Wang*, a *Centurion* BattleMech, had served her well for many years. Danai still missed the old warhorse, but this heavy 'Mech grew on her with their every outing.

A sigh hissed out of her as she sank into the command couch, and she discovered she was...perhaps not smiling, but nevertheless content. If Ross was to be believed, the next few minutes were not likely to be life-or-death, which made for a nice reintroduction to her war machine. She'd kept sharp on simulators during her stay on Castrovia, and the occasional outing on training grounds outside Liangrad, but even the best sims could only come so close to real combat.

Just don't get cocky, Danai reminded herself as she voice-activated the 'Mech. *Stay sharp, Duchess. Don't embarrass yourself out there. Imagine they get a lucky shot. Stay. Sharp.*

Lasers continued cutting through the darkening sky as she followed three lances of Ross' MechWarriors in medium and heavy BattleMechs toward the gate.

Noah brought up the rear in his heavy *Sojourner*. "Comm check," he said over the radio.

"Copy," Danai said. "I'm curious to see what—"

A beam of crimson burned into her *Black Knight*'s left shoulder. Danai blinked as the machine reported the hit. It was a glancing blow, resulting in little more than scorched blue paint.

"...Okay," she said. "So that's how it is." She put on a little speed to catch up with Ross' lance.

Danai's heads-up display quickly relayed sensor information, identifying a group of light 'Mechs as a *Blade, Vixen*, and three *Cougars*. Joining them were four other 'Mechs, but these were Industrial MODs. Danai's computer identified their profile as various AgroMechs, built for farm work. All of them, Battle and Agro alike, were light weight classes. Faster, for sure, nearly twice as fast as her *Black Knight* on open ground. And the AgroMechs, while as slow as her *Black Knight*, had stayed further away from the battle, launching a few volleys of LRM-5 missiles from crudely attached systems. None of the 'Mechs were designed for a stand-up slugfest.

Cruising through the gate behind the Third Chargers lance, Danai noted Ross had not set up a secondary perimeter to protect the FOB from enemy artillery—a potentially vital need she'd learned on her last deployment. Presumably, per his report, the insurgents on Sheratan did not have access to artillery; she had not seen the telltale craters in the FOB, and none of the intel she'd been given thus far indicated such long-range weaponry in possession of the enemy.

Then again, anyone within a hundred kilometers of the Chargers' LZ knew the Third were here the moment Ross' DropShips touched down. If the insurgency did have access to artillery, it might be they were just waiting to bring them out en masse. Ross' reliance on assumptions and best-available intel to set his perimeters was understandable for a man used to far-ranging run-and-gun fighting where victory relied on split-second adaptability, but perilous in a static, long-term defensive setting.

Either way, Danai thought, *an extended line of defense would be optimal*.

She thought these things even as lasers lit the dark sky around her and a handful of LRMs exploded against Ross' machines. She and Capshaw stayed back from the main fray, though it quickly became clear there was no real fray to speak of. Their opponents had moved in quickly in fast, light 'Mechs, launched attacks from a distance, and almost immediately skipped back the way they'd come, firing at random as they retreated.

Still. The loss of so many BattleMechs this past couple of months wasn't nothing. The insurgent 'Mechs were winning by attrition.

Danai watched as three lances of Ross' BattleMechs gave chase, but squinted one eye at his choice of 'Mechs. Of the fifteen on the field, only three 'Mechs were light enough to keep up with the insurgents, the others far too slow to stay in optimal range for long. To their credit, the MechWarriors fired everything they had at the fleeing insurgents, but the insurgents' speed and nimble piloting kept the light 'Mechs safe.

"Noah," she said into her comm. "Do you have that list of Ross' assets?"

"Yes, ma'am."

"Send it to me."

One of her monitors blinked a moment later, filling with an itemized list of all the Third Chargers BattleMechs and armor. Still moving her *Black Knight* forward at an even pace to keep an eye on the combat, Danai quickly sorted the list by which assets were field-worthy and operational.

Half the list went dark.

Danai swore. *Half? Fifty percent* of the Chargers' biggest, baddest weaponry was off the battlefield? When Ross said he'd "lost" a battalion, he meant *scrapped*. A lot more of his machinery was down for critical repairs, and parts were running low or non-existent. Had sabotage and other guerrilla tactics from Rainspire really caused so much damage? Perhaps Ross' adherence to Danai's rules of engagement had been a bit overzealous after all.

"Damn it, Ross," Danai muttered. She understood the *sang-shao*'s fear of reporting his losses to the Strategios, but his fear of taking action was costing him his entire regiment, one piece of equipment at a time. *And the insurgents know it.*

Danai accelerated, ready to add fire to the salvos being sent by the Third lances, but not really anticipating the need or value in doing so. She watched carefully as the insurgent 'Mechs sprinted down roads at full speed, taking tight corners with expert precision.

Those are veterans, Danai thought. *From the Republic of the Sphere, though? Or some other House? Mercenaries, maybe?*

She wasn't sure it mattered.

Danai ran her BattleMech as quickly as it would go, electing to follow roads and dirt paths to avoid ruining fields of crops. The Third lances tried mightily to blast their opponents in the weak rear armor. She could tell the battle was already over, but the Third Chargers MechWarriors didn't seem to agree. She appreciated their tenacity, but made a note to ask Ross about it later. Endlessly chasing these potshotters wasn't the best plan.

Danai slowed her 'Mech as the enemy vanished into nearby woods. She expected Ross' soldiers to not follow, but they crashed in behind the insurgents.

"Give it up," she said aloud, though not broadcasting over her comm. "Can't you see how they drive? They'll pull you in and blow you apart."

Rossetti's Third Chargers had a longstanding reputation of not retreating or surrendering, Danai knew. In fact, maybe that was the reason they'd been tapped for this job, despite their inexperience with insurgencies. Yet another factor working against them in this scenario.

Danai listened to the crosstalk over her comm. As she'd guessed, Ross' MechWarriors were now being assaulted from all sides, by the sounds of it.

"Sang-shao?" Noah broke in. "Should we follow them in?"

"They'll be out shortly, I imagine," Danai said.

And indeed, the lances stumbled out of the forest almost before she'd finished speaking. Smoke rose from holes in their armor, scorch marks seared across their torsos. All fifteen were accounted for, but each machine had suffered wounds.

"Splendid," Danai said, then added into her comm: "I don't suppose any of you all dropped one of those light 'Mechs?"

A captain responded, none too happily, "Uh, no. No, *Sang-shao*."

Right, Danai thought. "All units return to base. Let's get you cleaned up and figure out our next steps."

She turned *Julian* around and marched back to the FOB, with Capshaw beside her. "I think," she said only to him over the radio, "we've just seen a replay of what's been happening here on Sheratan."

"Agreed, ma'am."

"So it's time to try something new."

"Agreed again, ma'am."

Danai appreciated the smile in Noah's voice.

They entered the FOB together and brought their BattleMechs back into their DropShip bays. Techs quickly brought ladders and scaffolding to the cockpits.

"That was exciting," Capshaw said, climbing out of his *Sojourner*. Once on the ground, he looked up at the damage his machine had taken. "Not bad for a bunch of non-military insurgents."

"They're military," Danai said, even as she grasped Noah's slight sarcasm. "They might not play by military rules, but they definitely know what they're doing."

Noah wagged his head free of sweat accumulated during the fight. "Ross goes out every single time they bait him. He falls for it every time, and makes no progress."

"I agree. He and the Third are used to picking up and repositioning when a zone gets too hot. Dance, parry, riposte. He doesn't like standing still, and is moving just to feel like he's doing something."

"Did you learn anything from this little excursion, *Sang-shao?*"

"Perhaps," Danai said, closing her eyes and letting a breeze from the open bay doors dry her surrendering hair. "They had a certain attitude."

Noah grinned. "Yes! That's the word I was looking for the entire time. Attitude. Almost like..."

"Kids?"

"Exactly. Like they were throwing pebbles at the feral cats in the junkyard."

She raised an eyebrow, making Noah blanch. "I mean, *I* never did anything like that as a kid," he said quickly.

Danai chuckled, and Noah followed suit. "You're right, though. Like they were pestering instead of trying to kill anyone outright."

"With those 'Mechs versus what Ross can bring to bear, it might be the most they can do."

"No...Ross' AAR and casualty reports don't support that. Tonight might have been a skirmish, but sometimes they do serious damage, coming in close to the FOB. We can't dismiss that. Especially in Rainspire itself, even if they're not using 'Mechs there."

Noah nodded. "You think all the damage Ross has taken is the result of lucky shots?"

Danai crossed her arms, glaring out at the darkness where the farmland, undisturbed by either the insurgents or Ross' MechWarriors, sent rich aromas into the air. "Let's go back over those after-action reports. Maybe there's a pattern Ross didn't catch."

They turned in tandem to head for her quarters higher up in the DropShip.

"AgroMechs," Danai said thoughtfully as they walked. "Why AgroMechs?"

Noah shrugged. "Daggaknott is known for Hollingsworth Agrifoods. I'm not surprised they're refitting Agros."

"Agro MODs and military BattleMechs," Danai said. "So then, where are the industrials? SecurityMechs and the like?"

"Not as much use for them out here, I'd guess."

They reached a lift and stepped inside. Danai frowned and mentally scanned the surrounding forest. "But think about all these natural resources. They should be logging the absolute hell out of this forest. The Agros we saw tonight weren't outfitted for logging."

"Then again," Noah offered, "like Ross said, they know these woods. The last thing they'd want to do is cut down natural defenses."

"Mmm," Danai allowed, unconvinced.

Something was wrong here. The hell of it, she knew from experience, was that it could mean the insurgents were up to some longer game plan...or else they were simply too inexperienced to know how to run an effective campaign. The former could be dealt with militarily. The latter was harder— with no long-term plan or goal, they were wild cards, capable of absolutely anything, any time. That made them more dangerous.

"Tara Campbell is said to have raided all available arma- ments on-world almost fifteen years ago," Noah said. "I'm wondering where they got these lights and mediums."

"In other words, were they left behind and discovered, or are they being supplied."

"Yep. Republic?"

Danai considered. "No. The Rotters are pulling everything they've got toward Terra to get ready for Daoshen's big move. If they left something behind, it's because they didn't have either time or space. I can't imagine another House bothering to expend so many 'Mechs for a small insurgency... this is a found cache. And it's limited. That's why they're not committing to a stand-up fight. They have to conserve their resources."

They ascended the DropShip, stepping out of the lift together on the level where Danai's quarters were located.

"What's that mean for us?" Noah asked.

Her confidence surging as she put the pieces together, Danai said, "It means we can put this thing to bed a lot sooner than I feared."

CHAPTER 24

THIRD CAPELLAN CHARGERS FOB
OUTSIDE RAINSPIRE
SHERATAN
17 DECEMBER 3150

Danai stood behind her minuscule desk, poring over a plethora of reports from Rossetti's intel people, when a knock sounded on her door.

"Yes?"

The door opened, revealing Rossetti himself, looking uncomfortable and wary. "You asked for me?"

"Ross. Come in." Danai sat down as he entered and closed the hatch behind him. "Tell me, what covert assets are in place in Rainspire proper?"

"Two Masks I'm aware of, with several more spread around different parts of the continent. Of course, there could be more in Rainspire, and I'd never know it. You know how the Mask is."

Danai tapped some of the paperwork on her desk. "Maskirovka or otherwise, is there anyone with access to the insurgent leadership?"

Ross paused. "Why?"

"Because if there is a diplomatic way through this thing, then I want to find it."

"Begging your pardon, *Sang-shao*, but diplomacy failed quite a ways back."

"I want to meet with the insurgent leader."

"Begging your—"

"Ross, stop begging my pardon and just speak."

Rossetti cleared his throat. "*Sang-shao*, you meeting in person with any leader we could identify is a tactically disadvantageous plan. It puts you at great risk, for one thing, plus it's been attempted multiple times prior to your arrival."

"The arrival of the Chancellor's sister? No, this has *not* been attempted yet."

Ross squirmed. "Very well, but also, we even don't know who their leader *is*. We've tried to find out. These sons of bitches are a virus—there's no head of the snake to chop off."

"These *people*," Danai said, emphasizing the word, "thought of themselves as independent not long ago. Their entire history is fraught with rebellions, whether against the Confederation or the Republic. In other words, Ross, this is not their first fight. Someone is calling the shots, and I want to know who."

She stood to indicate an end to the meeting. Ross hurried to rise with her.

"Make it happen," she said. "Whatever it takes. Use my name, use the weight of the Chancellor, of the entire Capellan military if need be. Just get the word out."

"Yes, *Sang-shao*."

"Ross, one more thing."

Her fellow *sang-shao* hesitated, one hand already on the door.

"Look," Danai said, aiming for a collegial tone. "No *sang-shao* takes their job lightly. I know how you must be feeling after all this time. But you haven't been fully forthright with the Strategios lately. I think you've gotten away with it because the Chancellor has them busy on other fronts, with bigger battles, but our intel has to be frank and complete."

Ross' jaw worked behind closed lips, but he didn't speak.

"I need you to send a full report ASAP, all right? But don't worry about the Strategios. I'll handle them if it becomes necessary."

To her shock, Ross sneered. "I don't need protection."

So be it, Danai thought, and changed her own tone as well. "Good," she snapped. "Then do your job. Dismissed."

The word popped out of her mouth from force of habit, or so she tried to tell herself. Ross caught the insinuation immediately—that they were not of equal rank—and shot back, "Oh. I thought we were *sang-shao* to *sang-shao.*"

She stepped nearer. "*You* asked *me* here, Ross. I'm not here for a pissing contest. You decide, right now, what role you want me to play. Because I am just as happy to take this ship right back to my duchy and watch you lose this world and then explain it yourself to the Chancellor."

Their eyes locked.

Danai watched Ross cycle through several responses. She didn't envy his position, but she would not have made his simple mistakes. He might not have been doctoring or lying about his losses to the Strategios, but neither had he been fully transparent. As a result, he'd kept an entire regiment locked up with a paltry—if aggravating—insurgency when the Third Chargers should have been helping to take Procyon or Keid, or some other critical world in the path Daoshen was building toward Terra.

Slowly, Ross' expression lost some of its fire. "I'm sorry," he said at last. "I was out of line. But let's be honest, *sang-shaos* have been killed for smaller indiscretions."

"Not anymore," Danai said. "Not on my watch. Just follow the Zahn Doctrine. Send accurate reports, down to the last autocannon shell, and we'll take it from there."

"All right. Thank you, Danai."

She nodded. "Let's end this thing."

Ross nodded back, and let himself out of her small quarters.

Danai sank into her chair. The old headache she'd had prior to her stay in Castrovia had returned. She allowed herself a full minute to gripe internally about it, then went back to work, preparing to meet whoever was leading the Rainspire insurgency.

**THE HACKER PUB
RAINSPIRE
SHERATAN
20 DECEMBER 3150**

Jack's heart rate increased, but he kept his face neutral as Hemitt told him the news. The others around the table took pains to look busy, lifting pints, examining fingernails, gazing at the lighting fixtures overhead. If the news were different, Jack might have chided them for looking so damn obviously up to something.

But this news—this news *was* different.

"Danai Centrella-Liao," he repeated softly when Hemitt finished his report.

"That's right."

"And it's been confirmed."

"Someone fitting her last known description is for sure walking around their base with a McCarron's patch," Hemitt said. "I can confirm that much. And we did have confirmation of a DropShip landing. Just the one. I think this is credible."

"Credible," Jack said with a faint smile.

Danai Centrella-Liao. Sister to Chancellor Daoshen Liao, and recently named his successor if the old bastard ever kicked off. Jack knew her by her reputation on Solaris primarily, but had heard tales of her exploits on real battlefields as well. Drove the notorious *Yen-Lo-Wang*. He wondered if the shield-wielding BattleMech was on-planet now, and if he might get a crack at it. That would be frosting on this delicious cake.

Hemitt sat back in his chair, eyes wide. "You're not seriously considering it."

"Considering? Hell, no. I've already decided. Of course I'll meet with her."

The crowd at the table gave up any pretense of pretending they weren't paying attention.

"Are you suicidal?" a brown-skinned woman named Dyanne asked, gray hair falling from the bun on top of her head. She brushed the hair aside, her expression irritated.

Jack shook his head. "We mustn't be shortsighted. This is a big step. After so long, the tree is taking root."

"What tree?" Hemitt demanded.

Jack smiled the question away. He'd never told them his father's parable. "The appearance of so noble a personage as Danai Liao means this time it's different. We've been at this for three months. We've lost people. But so have they. Our patience is winning, while theirs is fraying. When we defeat *the* Danai Centrella-Liao, our compatriots in Daggaknott, Jaynesville...even Gellen's Heights will rally. Yes, I'll meet with her, because meeting with her puts us one step closer to getting what we want."

No one at the table looked convinced. Jack didn't bother trying to push. Too many words clouded objectives. They'd followed him this far; they'd follow the rest of the way.

They'd watered the tree and kept it alive in a drought.

He turned to Hemitt. "In the clearing, noon tomorrow. Let them know. You do your thing, I'll do mine."

"Just me?" Hemitt said.

"Just you."

Hemitt—and Dyanne, and the others—all scowled as if given a cue.

They also nodded.

CHAPTER 25

Noah Capshaw made his dislike of the meeting place known more times than Danai could count. She finally had to resort to ordering him not to bring it up again. He then insisted on being at the meeting, as he had been on Castrovia while meeting with the White Moon founder, and to this, Danai agreed.

She'd been given coordinates from Ross, who had received them from a Maskirovka agent. The location turned out to be a small clearing in the woods several kilometers from the FOB. Not quite flat, the space measured roughly 50 meters square, far too modest for a DropShip landing. Tall conifer trees stretched into the sky around them, while yellow scrub grass and short green bushes dotted the clearing here and there, too small to conceal an ambush.

The surrounding woods, however, were another story. Rossetti had already dispatched clearing teams through the woods to ensure Danai's safety, but like Noah, he disliked her going.

Danai didn't share their fear. She wore her reputation and status like armor. She didn't love her brother; he didn't love her, either. That said, anyone taking a potshot at the Chancellor's sister was liable to face an orbital bombardment the likes of which hadn't been seen since the Jihad.

"They'd have to be fools to hurt me," Danai explained to Noah as they walked to the meeting place, flanked by six infantry. The forest was too thick to allow for vehicles.

"They're insurrectionists against Capellan authority, they're already foolish," he argued.

"Fair enough. But they're smart enough to know how to wage a long-term campaign with few casualties. Killing me will end their quest in an instant, and, knowing my brother, likely end all life on Sheratan for the foreseeable future."

"I thought you wished to preserve civilian life."

"If they take me out, that decision will be Daoshen's. He does not currently operate under *my* rules of engagement."

They were less than a hundred meters from the spot. "Thank you for at least wearing a flak jacket."

"You're welcome." The protective suit under Danai's fatigues could stop most ballistics or lasers, at least long enough for her detail to get her to safety. A head shot, though—well, that would end things pretty quickly for everyone. She wore no helmet.

Woven between the aroma of pine and loam, Danai thought she smelled another, richer odor. In a few more steps, she realized it was cigar smoke wafting through the trees.

"There he is," Noah said as they came around a large tree trunk.

Danai nodded, keeping her eyes on the two figures sitting in the middle of the clearing.

As her team neared, Danai saw a man smoking a cigar as thick as her thumb. He wore civilian clothes that had seen better days. A bushy, brown-gray beard concealed half his face. A military-style gray cap covered his head. Even from 20 meters out, she could see his grin.

Seated beside him was a little girl.

"The hell?" Noah whispered as they broke through to the clearing.

Danai said nothing, though the same words ran through her mind as well. The girl's long, golden hair was worn in twin, braided pigtails. For as clear as the man's grin was, the girl's formidable scowl came across even more clearly—almost telepathic in her hatred.

"I don't like this," Noah whispered.

"Noted," Danai said. "Now be quiet."

She and Noah approached the pair, with Danai motioning for her guard detail to stay back a bit. They did, though not nearly as far as she would've liked. She understood. None of them wanted to be the one who failed to protect the Duchess of Castrovia, heir apparent to all Capellan space.

The man and child had brought thin folding chairs and a collapsible card table. The table was bare. Currently, the man rocked back on two legs of his chair like an impertinent student, while the girl sat with her back straight and chin lifted high in defiance. Something in her posture reminded Danai of herself at that age, just before she left the care of her Aunt Erde, who'd done most of her rearing until that point.

Danai and Capshaw reached the table, and stayed standing.

"I am *Sang-shao* Danai Centrella-Liao, Commanding Officer of the Second McCarron's Armored Cavalry and Duchess of Castrovia. With whom do I have the honor of speaking?"

The man yawned. "Jack Cade."

Danai offered a mild smirk. "Mr. Cade. And the young—"

"Colonel Jack Cade, technically," Jack added.

"Of the RAF, I presume."

"Sure, why not?"

Danai forced a chuckle. "Oh, this will be entertaining. And the young lady?"

The *young lady* stood and jutted her chin out with pride. "Major Cordelia Norfolk, and I am pleased to accept your surrender."

Incredulous, Danai met Cade's eyes.

The older man barely shrugged. "She's the brains of the outfit."

"I'm terribly sorry," Danai said, sighing. "When I extended the invitation to peace talks, I assumed such an offer would be taken seriously."

"'What, drawn and talk of peace?'" Cade said. "No no no, Your Grace. The major is correct. We're here to accept your unconditional surrender. Nothing less."

Danai said nothing. She kept her gaze squarely on the old man, who, despite his advanced age, gave her the impression of an upstart student of the type who occupied the back row in classrooms. Either he was not intimidated in the least, or he was a fine actor at it.

The girl, though. She was piss and vinegar through and through. Danai recognized the hatred in her eyes. That wasn't the sort of thing people could put on.

Danai moved gracefully to the chair and sat, back straight. Noah stayed on his feet, just behind her and to her right. "Very well. What are your terms?"

Cade reacted to her words, but only just barely. He covered the reaction by spreading his hands out before him. A line of smoke from his cigar wavered in the air between them.

"Easy. Take yourself and all your Capellans off this planet. Don't come back. Ever. Are we done here?"

"You know that's not going to happen."

"Then I'll settle for being a pain in your ass."

"No matter how many lives of your own citizens it costs."

"Or how many of yours, nope."

Danai laced her fingers together. "Colonel. *Major*. A Liao regiment occupies this world, with a second en route."

A bluff, but certainly possible; Danai was already mentally preparing to get Wu and the Second on-world as soon as possible. Cade didn't need to know how soon that would be.

She went on: "The Republic Armed Forces, whatever may be left of them, are off-world and unlikely to return any time soon. Your insurgency will collapse—one way or the other."

"Funny, isn't it, Major Norfolk?" Cade said, keeping his eyes steady on Danai. "This apparently weak and collapsing insurgency called for not one, but two regiments to contain it."

"Gimme a month!" declared the diminutive soldier, her braids swinging as she spoke. "It'll be three regiments. And we'll kill them, too."

Danai resisted a snort of admiration for her. Her youth reminded her of Tiko back on Castrovia. He had the same spirit. Danai's admiration quickly soured, though, as she unintentionally imagined the little girl blown apart by shrapnel. A fate entirely possible if the insurgency continued. Peace or escalation were the only two outcomes of this meeting.

"Colonel," Danai said calmly, "may I ask the nature of your relationship to the major?"

"We fight together!" Cordelia exclaimed.

Cade only gestured to her as if to agree. He puffed on his cigar.

Danai leaned forward 5 centimeters. "I can see you're a warrior, Colonel. You know the path we tread. Whoever she is to you, don't put her through this inevitable loss."

Taking on the first serious expression she'd seen him wear, Cade matched her lean forward. "Why would *your* inevitable loss harm *her*, *Sang-shao*?"

Danai shifted her gaze to Cordelia. She looked the child in the eyes while addressing Cade. "She'll die. Horribly."

"No other way in war!" Cordelia said.

"Then stop this absurd rebellion before that happens, *Major*."

Cade spoke softly. "How...*dare* you blame the major's death on me. I'm not pulling the trigger, Your Grace. That would be the two Capellan regiments you've threatened us with."

Incredulous again, Danai looked at him.

Cade's own eyes were frigid. "Now, Major Norfolk has already stated our business here. Get off this planet and out of our system, or we have nothing more to talk about."

"Right!" Cordelia chirped.

Danai sighed, sat back in her chair, and rubbed her chin thoughtfully between her thumb and forefinger. "I understand your desire for what you think of as your independence," she said carefully. "But I am not sure you fully grasp the benefits of Sheratan being a productive member of the Confederation."

Cade shook his head slowly even as she continued. "Not long ago, I visited a hydroelectric dam built by Capellan hands. It was an engineering marvel. But more marvelous was the pride the workers took in building and maintaining it, and in the benefits that accrued to their families for their efforts."

"Ah, yes, the Republic of the Sphere is known for its idle hands," Cade said, rolling his eyes. "So your proposal to us is, what—a job offer of menial labor for the Chancellor? How *tempting*."

"Not at all," Danai countered swiftly. "What I offer is peace, prosperity, and—" Here she glanced at Cordelia. "—long and productive life. For everyone on this world."

Cade wiped his forehead with his entire right hand before checking it as if for sweat. "Major, I don't think Her Grace has heard a word we've said."

"No," Cordelia said, with a look of such abject contempt Danai felt taken aback.

Danai glanced back at her security team. "I could have you arrested right now, take you back to our base, interrogate you both to death myself."

Cade leaned over the table. "Oh, and for sure I haven't made any contingency plans for just such an occasion, right? Lady, you don't show up to a meeting with a Capellan without having already put your affairs in order."

Danai bristled internally—and respected the honesty. After all, he wasn't wrong.

"Many years ago," he continued, his voice level, "you Caps allowed RAF fighters to leave Liao unmolested. So, I'll offer you that same opportunity now. Take your troops and go, and we won't blast you out of the sky. It's that simple."

Danai blinked slowly. "And if I don't?"

"Your regiments will never walk again. First we'll cripple you. Then we'll kill you. And we'll keep at it until you stop showing up."

Danai idly scanned the surrounding forest. She felt no more in danger now than she had upon arriving, knowing that the first hint of accosting her would result in Jack Cade's immediate death. She did, however, feel her patience running low, and even caught herself evaluating the value of killing Cade right now. Danai didn't doubt he was ready to die; insurgent leaders knew their likely fate from the get-go. If killing Cade would end the insurgency, she wouldn't hesitate.

But it wasn't what she wanted. She'd proven her ability to negotiate with the White Moon, with Mayor Olatunde on Hall. She loved a good stand-up fight, but this wasn't Solaris. This little girl's life was on the line just as much—in one way of thinking—as little Tiko's.

"This insurgency of yours is costing resources and materiel you cannot replace," Danai said at last. "Soon it will run out, and when it does, the people of this world will suffer."

Cade shook his head with a smile. "There you go again, blaming me for your invasion."

"It's not an invasion," Danai snapped, hating her loss of control. "This is our world."

Cade's lips popped off the butt of his cigar. "So you say."

"What can I offer you, Cade?"

"Offer me? Ha! You ever clean your ears, Your Highness? Get. Off. My. World."

"That's not going to happen, and you know that. What can I do for you? For your family? Your children?"

His face fell stoic. "Do not threaten my kids, Louie." He glanced at Cordelia, who sat still and hateful. "And they're *all* my kids."

With some difficulty, Danai let the epithet pass. To be called a Cap was one thing; a Louie, however, was meant to incite.

"I would never," she said, carefully. "Not yours or any other. I asked what I could offer, and that question remains."

Danai stood.

"Take stock of your situation, Colonel. One way or another, in time, your life as you knew it is over. You know that. I could have you killed. I could kill you myself. But I don't want that. I could hurt you, or threaten to hurt you. I don't want that, either. But I believe you are the person I'm speaking with because you can prevent further violence. Do so, and I can make things very comfortable for you, for Rainspire—for the whole of Sheratan. All you have to do is call off the raids. The bombings, the ambushes. I'd offer you money and title, but I doubt you'd take it."

Cade laughed. "Perceptive!"

"Then we are at an—"

Cordelia leaped up so quickly, her thin metal chair flew back. In a heartbeat, Danai perceived Noah reaching for his sidearm, and her security team raising their rifles.

"You killed my Papa!" she screamed.

The security team's training paid off by letting the girl live. Danai wondered if the child understood just how closely she'd come to death in that moment.

As her words hung in the air, Danai paused, assessing the scenario, letting everyone cool off before speaking. "Cordelia— Major—I am sorry to hear about the loss of your father."

"Yeah, you look it," Cade said under his breath—and quite clearly.

"And," Danai went on over him, "I want for nothing more than to prevent anyone else from getting hurt. You understand that, right?"

Cordelia turned, snatched her collapsed chair, set it back up, and sat. "You killed my Papa," she said, staring into Danai's eyes. "He taught school, and you killed him."

Danai took a breath. She always tried not to imagine the script everyone would follow at meetings such as these, but she always gave in and imagined anyway. The script never matched the reality, and this meeting was a prime example among many.

"You mean a Capellan killed him."

"Damn right!" the girl said.

Danai considered her responses. None seemed to further her cause. She did note, however, that Cade's gaze had hardened. *He knew Cordelia's father,* she realized. *May be related to him.*

She tried to find a way to use this theory to her advantage, but nothing came to mind. The looks in their eyes spoke volumes.

They were committed.

"This is pointless," she said quietly, almost to herself.

Cade puffed on his cigar. "Agreed."

"Why did you even agree to meet with me if you were not prepared to negotiate in good faith?"

Cade shrugged. "Same reason as you. To get a bead on my enemy. How's that working for you, by the way? Got me figured out?"

This man is no Aria Skyeler, she thought. "Colonel Cade, if it were up to me—"

"Isn't it? *Duchess?*"

Danai blinked. "No. It is not."

Cade blew his lips out. "Man. Tough gig. Here you are, badass MechWarrior, big ol' duchess, sister to the Chancellor of the Capellan Confederation, and what good's any of it doing you?"

"If it were up to me," Danai repeated, lowering her tone as anger at his perceptiveness flared inside her, "perhaps an agreement could be made—"

"Unless that agreement is you not being here anymore, the answer would still be no."

"Certainly you don't speak for this entire planet."

Cade took a sarcastic look around the field. "I don't see anyone stopping me. *Certainly*—" he spat the word sarcastically back at her, "—you've noticed that."

Danai tried one final tack. Perhaps speaking in more military terms would work. "There are far bigger things at stake here, colonel. This world is crucial to the Confederation."

"I bet it is. Two jumps from here to Terra, am I right? Yeah. Sheratan is important to the Confederation's need to subjugate every world in the Inner Sphere."

"No!"

"No? *No?* Are you kidding me, lady? Let me ask you something: How come when you come to my world and tell me I have to do what you say, and I don't, I'm a rebel. But when you land regiments of BattleMechs on worlds, you're a liberator. How's that work? How is it I'm not a liberator for *my* people?"

Danai laced her fingers together in front of her waist. "Because believe me when I assure you that the Confederation is not the enemy you should fear. I'm somewhat stunned at your ignorance, to be frank. You've shown your intelligence about the current state of the Inner Sphere, yet you think the Confederation is the monster in the closet? The Republic of the Sphere just left, how was life under their boot heel? The last time Sheratan was independent, it was plagued by pirates and civil war between rival factions. The Clans have but one goal. The Draconis Combine has a certain history with conquered peoples. Joining the Confederation—peaceably, which I believe you could do—is the best-case scenario for Sheratan. I think you must know that."

"So," Cade said thoughtfully, "roll over for you so you can protect us from the bullies? You're our least-worst option? Quite a sales pitch."

"Colonel Cade, to be honest, the Republic was a noble endeavor, one my cousin Kai gave his life to defend. That Republic is gone. It failed its citizens. It failed to prevent the Blackout. It put up a Wall, and left you on the outside. Wolves and falcons are at your doorstep. I know these are just words. Let me show you that there's a better path, one that doesn't end at the tip of a Clan sword."

"Duchess," Cade said, "our path won't end at the tip of anyone's sword."

Danai straightened her blouse. "Fine. I don't care what we are to you anymore. I came here to meet with you and see how to prevent further loss of life. You're not interested in that—"

"Not by your rules."

"—and so now I am disinterested. You want a fight, Mr. Cade, then you shall have one."

Cordelia Norfolk narrowed her eyes, utterly uncowed. "Fine by me."

Cade gave the girl a brief glance and proud smile. "Here's something people like you Capellans just don't understand," he said, not bothering to look at Danai. "We're not fighting to beat you."

"Then why are you?"

"The day you figure that out, it'll make both our lives a whole lot easier."

Cade rose from his seat, slowly enough to not make any of Danai's people shoot him down. "Thanks, Duchess. This has been great. Oh, and before I forget...thanks for not taking the sniper shot."

He mimicked Danai's earlier exact chin gesture.

Damn, Danai thought, but kept her face impassive.

Cade grinned as if reading her thoughts. "You can thank me for not taking mine anytime." With great deliberation, he wiped his dry forehead again.

Danai was unable to keep from clenching her teeth. *Damn, damn. You've lost your edge, Duchess. If you're not careful, it's going to cost you.*

"You ever change your mind," Cade said as Cordelia stood up beside him, "just say the word. Till then...well. I'll see ya out there." He snapped his fingers. "Hey, I don't suppose you have *Yen-Lo-Wang* with you? Because, wow. I'd love a shot at *that* title."

Danai, unthinking, grasped at his comment. "Would you consider a one-on-one? Clan-style, a Trial of Possession, to end this insurgency?"

Cade considered this offer—and genuinely seemed to consider it—before saying, "Naw, I can't do that." He winked. "But it's the most tempting offer you've made so far. See ya 'round, Duchess."

He and Cordelia turned and walked in the opposite direction from where Danai and Capshaw had entered the clearing.

"Take them?" Noah whispered, his lips barely moving.

"No. Nothing to be gained by it."

He moved to stand beside her, in Danai's periphery. "I don't understand. He had you in a sniper's crosshairs and didn't take the shot? Are you not valuable enough?"

"He assumes if he'd ordered the shot, the Chancellor would retaliate by bringing the entire might of the Capellan military down on this world."

"Which he would...right?"

"It's the sort of thing he'd do, yes. Not that I'd be around to object." She turned and marched away from the table, the way they'd come. "I want the Second MAC here. Now."

Noah fell in beside her. "That'll probably be a few weeks."

"I know. Start the process immediately."

"Got a plan?"

Danai stepped past the tree line with her guard detail in front and behind. "Maybe. Just tell Wu to make sure to land at night. I want everyone in Rainspire to see them coming. And I want dossiers immediately on Jack Cade and Cordelia Norfolk."

"Copy that. You weren't serious about a one-on-one, were you, ma'am?"

Danai said nothing. She kept a mean pace the entire way back to the FOB.

CHAPTER 26

"*This* is Jack Cade?"

Danai frowned at her noteputer.

Noah nodded, mimicking her frown.

The open file on Danai's tablet contained the insurgent's name, and nothing more. A completely empty field.

"Nothing, ma'am," Noah said. "Absolutely and literally nothing. The man's a ghost. Has to be a false identity. You're the first person to even get a name attached to a possible leader of the insurgency, which has the Mask in a snit."

Ghost, Danai thought, only half-listening. *A ghost...*

"No," she said. "He's a man. He's just a man. Brazen. Clever. Not opposed to taking risks. Understands the purpose and value of pawns on the board." She tapped the screen, asking, "What about the girl?"

"That's her real name. Born and raised in Rainspire. Mother died of illness when she was three. Her father taught literature, just as—"

"Shakespeare!" Danai blurted. "That's what Cade quoted yesterday. 'Drawn and talk of peace,' that's William Shakespeare. I recognized it, but couldn't place it at the time. I'll bet you anything Jack Cade is Cordelia Norfolk's uncle, or perhaps a cousin. They're related, the three of them, I'm sure of it."

"What's that mean, then?"

Danai looked up at him. Noah hadn't sat down, standing instead by the closed door to her cabin. "You have family, Noah?"

She knew the answer, but wanted him to say it. "My mother and father, and an older sister."

"And you'd be willing to do what if someone hurt them?"

Noah said nothing, only nodded shallowly as his eyes blazed.

"You were right," Danai went on. "Whether Cade is actually the insurgent leader or not, this is just the cult of personality you said. But it's not as simple as that. They'll follow him into Hell."

"What's that mean for us, ma'am?"

"It means Wu and the Second McCarron's Armored Cav are en route," Danai said, sighing. "And we're going to have to do this the hard way."

"Copy that. Ross wants to know what you want the Third to be doing until Second MAC drops."

"Given how many resources he's lost, let's have them keep the status quo. When there's a raid, chase them down, but pull back before going into the woods whenever possible. Let's let Cade fall into a rhythm, into a pattern. We'll lull him. A couple weeks from now, when Wu lands, then we'll shake things up."

"Understood, ma'am. I'll let Ross know."

"Plus one more thing. Let the Mask know I am open to hearing from Cade that he'll end the insurgency, right up to the last minute. I don't think he'll take it, but leave that line open."

"Yes, ma'am."

Noah braced, and let himself out of the cabin. Danai tilted back in her chair, gazing at the ID photo of Cordelia Norfolk on her tablet screen. In it, the girl smiled brightly, teeth white and braided hair 10 or more centimeters shorter.

This picture was taken before her father was killed, Danai thought, and suddenly realized: Cordelia said a Capellan had killed her father, but did not say when or where. Presumably Rainspire, and presumably recently.

Danai opened a small drawer and picked up the queen figurine Tiko had given to her. She put herself in his position, and imagined someone she loved being killed by a soldier. What lengths would she have gone to—even at eight, or twelve, or fourteen—to avenge that death?

She did not want to put Cordelia Norfolk to that test.

CELESTIAL PALACE
CHANG-AN
LIAO
7 JANUARY 3151

Robie listened intently that morning as Daoshen's military council gave their daily briefs. She'd learned a lot about the Strategios already during her time within the palace.

And even more about the Chancellor.

The council largely consisted of people dedicated to the Chancellor. Precious few, in Robie's opinion, were as dedicated to lesser members of House Liao. She recognized some of her classroom lessons playing out in real time here in Daoshen's large conference room, with its circular wooden table and overhead skylight.

One man, a dour-faced general named Volkov, ended his brief with bad news. Robie watched both his delivery and Daoshen's reaction with keen interest.

"Procyon, Keid, Epsilon Indi...all have suffered sabotage and theft over the last few weeks," Volkov reported. His entire face seemed to have been dragged down by invisible, clutching fingers.

"What is the nature of the sabotage?" Daoshen asked, his voice cool.

Volkov flicked through screens on his noteputer. "Shaped charges on BattleMech actuators and on vehicles. Tools gone missing en masse. One entire DropShip is currently waylaid thanks to a ship-wide bout of gastritis that has been linked to improperly prepared food...or poison. We do not know yet because the analysts can't leave their washrooms!"

Robie noted, with some admiration, that Volkov aimed his increasingly aggravated tone at the report, not the Chancellor. A finely tuned dance step, indeed.

The room fell silent, all eyes on Daoshen. The Chancellor sat quietly, unhurried, as his council waited for a response.

At last, Daoshen turned his head slightly left to address a pale, nameless member of the Maskirovka, a woman with black hair trimmed into a severe bob. "What of Sheratan and Liberty?"

"The Second McCarron's is en route to join *Sang-shao* Centrella-Liao on Sheratan," the agent replied. "With expectations of quelling the rebellion there in short order. Liberty is expected to return to our control in mere days."

Sheratan? Robie thought. *Why is the duchess there?*

If Daoshen was surprised to hear his sister being located on a world undergoing an insurgency, but without her Second MAC regiment, he did not show it. Instead he spread his arms wide, as if welcoming his council into a warm embrace.

"You see?" he said, unperturbed. "All is as planned. The most our enemies can muster against us are minor inconveniences, soon crushed."

"Do you not fear Devlin Stone?" Volkov said.

Daoshen's head snapped toward the officer like a snake. The Chancellor quickly recovered, however, letting his hands with their gold-enameled nails float gently back to his lap.

"We fear no one, Volkov," Daoshen said. "We are Liao."

No one moved until Volkov inclined his head. Daoshen recentered his gaze to address the table at large.

"Of course," he said, "caution should be exercised so close to our objective. Continue your focus on Sirius and Caph. If Liberty and Sheratan require additional aid, send it. And prepare Keid for our official visit."

Those around the table were visibly shocked. Daoshen had not informed them previously.

"Keid, Your Grace?" Volkov spoke for the group. "Is that safe?"

"I trust our Strategios and Maskirovka will make it so." Here, Daoshen looked aside to Robie, and offered a slight nod and smile, which Robie obediently returned.

Turning back to the group, he added, "There are many cards yet to play in our great endeavor. The Inner Sphere will see soon enough that shaped charges and stomach aches will not deter our destiny."

The group chuckled dutifully. Daoshen basked in the response for a moment before gesturing to the main doors. The Strategios stood and bowed to him before heading to the double doors opened by Daoshen's personal servants.

Robie approached the Chancellor when the doors closed. "Your Grace, I am duty-bound to advise you against this plan to go to Keid."

Daoshen turned to her. Smiling without showing his teeth, he took one of her hands and traced one of his golden nails along her palm. The sensation tickled intensely, but Robie gave no indication of it, keeping her demeanor professional. Kamer had warned her what her duties may entail, and Robie had accepted the Celestial Wisdom's attentions for the sake of the Confederation.

"Why is that, Robie?"

"It is simply not safe. We have not held the world long enough. You are much better protected here in Chang-an. In fact, I still recommend Sian, to be perfectly honest, Chancellor."

"A fact our enemies no doubt know, and thus a weakness to exploit. This is the other side of war, Robie. When they see the Capellan Chancellor enthroned on their conquered world, so close to Terra, this will shatter their will much more readily than their food poisoning and paltry insurgencies could ever break our own."

Still holding her hand, Daoshen rose majestically, his robes flowing. "I entrust my life to your hands, Robie, as I entrusted Kamer for so many loyal years. Coordinate with the Death Commandos to take whatever precautions you feel are necessary, but we will travel to Keid soon."

"Yes, Your Grace. May I ask a question?"

"Of course."

"You said there are cards yet to play. What cards, Your Grace?"

Daoshen released her hand, and slid the backs of his fingers along her left cheek.

"The Fortress Wall around Terra presents a technological challenge for the time being," he said softly. "But some technologies never lose their edge."

Robie inclined her head in acquiescence, even as something cold wrapped around her guts.

She did not know what Daoshen was referring to...and, for the moment, did not want to.

CHAPTER 27

Danai understood her goal on Sheratan now. She did not like it.

The worst part was that she was here not by some act of failure, but by acts of success. If Hall and Liberty hadn't gone so well—to outside observers, anyway—then Rossetti might not have asked for her help, and she wouldn't now be standing beside Noah Capshaw a kilometer away from the Second MAC's DropShip landing zone.

The Second came in hot and at night, as Danai had requested. One after another, the enormous ships hung suspended like fiery holiday decorations in the dark sky outside Rainspire before landing in a field. The field had once housed a generous stock of alfalfa, until Danai ordered Ross' armor division to affix blades and scrape the ground clean. The razing of the healthy field was one small shot across Cade's bow: *This is a taste of what I'm willing to do.*

Thanks to the white-hot burning exhaust jets, Danai knew there would be no doubt in Rainspire what was happening. Everyone in the town would either see it for themselves at a distance, or hear about it very quickly: Capellan reinforcements—a lot of them—had just made landfall a few klicks outside town.

Once the Second's ships had landed, cooled, and begun opening hatches, Danai and Noah started the trek over to the command ship.

"I'm sorry, Feng," she said grimly to *Zhong-shao* Wu Feng as her XO walked down a ramp to the soft earth.

"Eh?" Wu said. "Sorry for what, *Sang-shao*?"

Danai and he traded grins and handshakes. "For us succeeding on Liberty and Hall. If we hadn't done that, maybe we wouldn't be thrown into another insurgency situation."

Wu Feng smiled. "You can't help but win, boss. It's in your blood."

She grimaced good-naturedly in response. She didn't feel like a winner. Mina had been gone two years. In those intervening months since losing her, the rare person Danai had come to trust in a short period of time, Danai's rage had only grown more impotent, with nowhere to direct it. Many warriors had died on Hall and Liberty under her command, and she regretted each one in the way of most military commanders. They had been soldiers, though. People who'd volunteered to fight and die for the Confederation.

Mina hadn't been a soldier. Not even a diplomat, per se. Yet she still became a victim of an insurgency that hadn't known their people were under the protection of House Liao.

Danai feared more of the same on Sheratan. Even in the weeks since ordering Second MAC to join her here, Cade's insurgents had continued making raids, and two more soldiers had died. Ross' people dropped a *Locust* and its MechWarrior on the battlefield in response, but the loss of life weighed on her. She'd put in requisitions for new remote sensors and mines in addition to deploying them from her own stores, but the additional equipment was still inbound. Danai wondered if there was a production issue, given how stretched the CCAF seemed to be.

"I want this thing put to bed," she said abruptly as her thoughts turned dark. She, Noah, and Wu stood in a triangle together near the DropShip. "This Colonel Cade, as he calls himself, has been playing a long game, and it needs to end now."

"Yes, *Sang-shao*," Wu said. "I couldn't agree more."

Danai looked past his shoulder, watching BattleMechs disembark beneath enormous spotlights mounted on the sides of the DropShip. A *Marauder*, a *Vindicator*, a *Dola*, and another *Black Knight* like her own were the first to walk out of their berths and to the 'Mech-sized bay doors. The enormous war machines made the ground tremble with each step, a vibration Danai rarely noticed anymore. BattleMech combat had a way of desensitizing legs and feet to such tremors.

"Here's what we're going to do," she said, still watching the 'Mechs disembark. "We've extended the perimeter as best we can with our own supply of sensors and mines. Meanwhile, BattleMechs aren't the easiest things to hide. The insurgent 'Mechs are out there somewhere, somewhere close, and we are going to find them. My guess is a tunnel or cave network not too far from here, and Ross just hasn't pulled off the necessary grid-sweep to find them. I want three eight-hour shifts, around the clock, scouring these woods, Rainspire, everywhere, until we find those 'Mechs. Engage every target. If it doesn't have a Capellan transponder, blow it away. That'll do for a start."

"Yes, ma'am," Wu said.

"That begins as soon as possible," Danai went on. "I'll leave that choice up to you, *Zhong-shao*. Whenever you feel the Second is ready to roll."

Wu glanced at the DropShip, nodding. "Give 'em a few hours to bunk up, get acclimated. What time is it now? I'd say... first patrol by the dawn's early light, if that's all right with you."

"Perfect," Danai said. "Thank you."

Wu turned his attention back to Danai. "And how are you doing, *Sang-shao*? If I may ask."

Danai raised an eyebrow and looked to Noah, nodding at the younger man. "If memory serves," she said, "why don't you ask him?"

She turned on her heel and walked toward the Third's FOB. Smiling.

RAINSPIRE FOREST
OUTSIDE RAINSPIRE
SHERATAN
14 JANUARY 3151

"Contact!" Noah broadcast over the comm. "*Locust*, two o'clock."

Danai brought *Julian* to a halt and scanned her monitors to ascertain the target's position.

Her plan for round-the-clock patrolling missions through and around the local forest had met with some success, though less than she'd hoped. The Second MAC had routed a couple lances total so far, with minimal damage to the scouting parties. The work had been so relatively easy that Danai wondered why Rossetti hadn't tried it...or if the insurgents were lulling them into something bigger.

At the same time, her frustration continued to grow. Rossetti's AARs had indicated dozens of enemy 'Mechs, and Danai agreed with his assessments that there were likely more. So far they'd captured transponder signals from a total of seventeen machines; seventeen BattleMechs they could confirm did not belong to the Third Chargers or Second McCarron's. Those did not include the AgroMech MODs the insurgency had thrown into the mix. These machines had been counted "by hand," so to speak, via simple visual recognition and cataloging.

The one thing the Chargers and MAC had confirmed: The 'Mechs previously belonged to the Republic of the Sphere. Neither Danai nor Ross believed the MechWarriors crewing the 'Mechs were Rotters, though—the Republic insignia on each 'Mech had been painted over with a simple, arrow-like tree design over a blue circle. Danai took this to be the symbol of the Rainspire insurgency. Republic loyalists wouldn't have desecrated the insignia on their BattleMechs.

Noah opened fire on the *Locust* just as four additional targets appeared, then bobbed and wove on Danai's screen, disappearing and reappearing from behind tree trunks.

"Weapons free," Danai ordered the lance. "Take them out."

Her four companions from the Second MAC operated with smooth efficiency, breaking right and left to flank the insurgent light 'Mechs. The insurgents, apparently seeing that the five heavier MAC units were indeed attacking to kill, dodged around trees and fired blindly behind themselves whenever possible.

Danai got a bead on a fleeing *Stinger* and let loose with her two large lasers. The beams blew chunks off two different trees, scattering wooden shrapnel, but missing her target entirely.

Grimacing, she moved the heavy BattleMech closer as the *Stinger* attempted to juke left and right. *Nice piloting,* Danai admitted, and fired the twin lasers again. Both beams found their target this time, drilling into one of the *Stinger*'s hips. The actuator there gave way almost instantly, sending the bipedal BattleMech careening into a tree. *But not nice enough.*

The other four insurgent 'Mechs bounded off through the woods. The MAC MechWarriors chipped off armor, but nothing more. One MAC pilot saw the downed *Stinger* and took aim with their 'Mech's Gauss rifle.

"Hold your fire!" Danai called across the comm. "Noah, you're with me. The rest of you track down the runners if you can. Go!"

She took her *Black Knight* over to the fallen *Stinger* and pointed her PPC at the head as the other three warriors followed her order, blasting missiles and shells at the fleeing enemy.

Activating her loudspeaker, Danai spoke clearly to the pilot of the *Stinger*: "Attention. This is *Sang-shao* Danai Centrella-Liao. Exit your BattleMech or I will destroy you. This is your only warning."

She waited, keeping her hands off the weapons controls. No reason to be on a hair-trigger level of alert. About thirty seconds later, the cockpit hatch opened and a pale man with short black hair exited the 'Mech, raising his hands in the air.

Danai grinned.

"Noah," she said over the comm. "Would you be so kind as to have Ross send an infantry unit to this position to take our new friend into custody? He is to be treated well, and if I hear otherwise, there will be hell to pay."

"Copy that," Noah replied.

Over her loudspeaker, Danai addressed her new prisoner of war. "Thank you. Have a seat. We're going to bring you back to our base for questioning now. You will be treated well. Please follow instructions as they are given to you. Am I understood?"

The prisoner glared up at her cockpit glass and nodded before taking a slow, deliberate seat in the dirt, his back against the smoking hull of his *Stinger.*

A good day's work, Danai thought. *Very good indeed.*

Danai walked briskly to the DropShip brig, where doors and gates were opened for her by armed guards. She carried a noteputer and wore clean utility fatigues with her rank insignia polished and gleaming on her blouse. Noah, also changed into fresh utilities, met her at the prisoner's cell door. Danai nodded to him. Noah nodded back and unlocked the heavy steel door leading to an interrogation room.

The prisoner, per Danai's orders, was not shackled. He sat in a straight chair on one side of a simple table. Only one other chair was available, which Danai took as Noah positioned himself by the door, his hand dangling near his sidearm. Danai was not visibly armed, but her twin knives were concealed within easy reach in her boots.

"Hello," Danai said, setting the tablet on the table. "I'm Danai. And you are?"

"Not saying anything to you."

Danai appraised him. The prisoner clearly knew how to run a fast 'Mech through woods, but she didn't see any of the telltale signs of prolonged warfare in his eyes or on his skin. She guessed his age at roughly forty, and he bore no scars on his face or hands, which lay relaxed on the tabletop.

She smiled, utterly mirthless. "All right. Let's assess your situation. You're a prisoner of war of the Capellan Confederation Armed Forces. And your life, whatever it was before this moment, is now over. Wholly and completely. In a matter of days, I can have you shipped off to the Brazen Heart penal moon, where you will live a long and productive life in the mines, if you're lucky. I'm willing to bet that doesn't appeal to you. I'm willing to bet there is someone in Rainspire who'd hate to see that happen."

The prisoner's eyes darted side to side. Briefly, but clearly. She'd hit the right nerve.

"It doesn't have to go that way," Danai went on. "I can make your life very comfortable. I can make the lives of anyone you love very comfortable. Do you have children? Do you want them to have the best education? I can do that. Do you have ill or injured family, someone who requires long-term or serious care? I can do that, too. Or maybe you just don't feel like fighting a losing battle anymore, and would like to spend your days relaxing on a lovely world like Castrovia. That, too, is within my power to offer."

She leaned forward.

"But you're going to have to help me. Just tell me what you want, and I'll put those wheels in motion as soon as you answer a few questions. Starting with your name, if you please."

He tapped a finger on the table for a moment before grunting, "Kelsey."

"Kelsey. Very good. Where'd you learn to drive a 'Mech like that, Kelsey? You were amazing out in those woods."

Kelsey met her eyes. "Originally? LCMA."

Danai blinked. "The Liao Conservatory? When did you graduate?"

"Didn't. Survived it, more like. Came here. Started a family. Did pretty well with the Republic off-world. Then you all came along."

"When did you come to Sheratan?"

"'35, '36. Thereabouts."

"And on whose side did you fight during the riots at the Conservatory?"

"Didn't say I did."

It had been seventeen years, but the altercations and riot at the Liao Conservatory of Military Arts on Liao—in Chang-an, the capital city—were well-known lore in the CCAF. For a long time, the academy had taught warfare to bright, promising Capellan students. Liao fell to Republic forces in 3084, who took control of the school until Daoshen was able to wrest

Liao back into Capellan hands, where it belonged. During the Republic's years of domination, though, the academy tore itself apart along loyalty lines, Capellan versus Republic. A massive riot had broken out in Chang-an, and students on both sides were killed. Ultimately, students were folded into the defense force that kicked the Republic off-world.

But he didn't call it the Republic Conservatory, Danai thought, the name given the school late in the Republic's dominion. *So he was probably Capellan. Why leave?*

With genuine curiosity, she gazed into Kelsey's eyes and asked gently, "Why are you fighting us?"

"Because this world doesn't belong to you. It belongs to me and the other people who live and work and die here. So, with all due respect, *Sang-shao* Colonel Danai Centrella-Liao... bugger right the hell off."

"You know Jack Cade?"

"I do."

"Where is he now?"

"Couldn't tell ya."

"Could you find him?"

"Sure."

"Would you?"

"Nope."

Danai shifted in her chair. "Under promise of wealth or on pain of death?"

"Nope and nope."

"Why."

Kelsey smiled, ever so slightly. "And that's what makes you a Cap. Isn't it? Because you don't know why, and you never will."

Some internal organ of Danai's twitched. She prayed Kelsey hadn't seen it.

The prisoner eased back in his chair. "I'm done talking now. You do whatever you want to me, but I'm not giving you anything else. Neither will anyone in Rainspire, or probably the whole planet. You see, we hate you. With the fiery passion of our very sun. And nothing will ever stop that. No money, no pain, no death. You can try and take this planet, but we will fight you. Every. Single. Day."

Kelsey closed his mouth and breathed deep through his nose, his eyes not leaving Danai's. In them, she saw the same defiance she'd seen in Cade. In "Major" Cordelia Norfolk. She knew her people could go to work on him, make him give up something of some value with the vast array of pain they could inflict. But he'd never break entirely. Never give up anything that would actually turn the tide of the insurgency.

"Noah," she said, quietly, refusing to look away from Kelsey's eyes as much as he refused to look away from hers.

Capshaw stepped forward. "Yes, ma'am."

"I'd like you to take the prisoner to the main gate, and release him, unharmed."

She saw Kelsey's eyes flicker, and felt Noah's uncertainty. A tense moment of silence followed, which Noah finally broke by muttering, "Yes, ma'am."

Sitting statue-still, Danai addressed Kelsey: "When you see Jack Cade, give him my regards. And tell him plainly that Sheratan is now and forever a beloved world in the Capellan Confederation. Be sure to use those words, Kelsey. And tell Jack Cade that from this day forward, any person taking arms against a Capellan civilian or military unit will be summarily destroyed. There will be no more meetings, no treaties, no ceasefires, and no mercy. Sheratan is a protectorate of House Liao. Ergo, I am here to protect its people, and I will, by any means necessary."

She stood. Jaw clenched, Kelsey watched her.

Danai tugged on the hem of her tunic to straighten it. "What happens next is up to you."

She turned and marched to the door, which opened for her as if by magic, and closed again with a clang that rattled the veins in her arms.

She marched steadily through the DropShip until reaching the first officer she came across, a young woman with the lower rank of *sao-wei* on her uniform. Danai grabbed her arm to stop her. "You know who I am?"

"Y-Yes, *Sang-shao*!"

"Find *Sang-shao* Rossetti and *Zhong-shao* Wu immediately, and have them meet in my quarters. Interrupt whatever they are doing, on my orders."

"Yes, *Sang-shao*!"

The woman spun and raced back the way she'd come. Danai watched her for a moment, her mind spinning with war plans, before heading for a lift and going straight to her cabin.

She meant every word she'd said to Kelsey. The time for talking was over.

CHAPTER 28

**SECOND MAC FORWARD OPERATING BASE
OUTSIDE RAINSPIRE
SHERATAN
31 JANUARY 3151**

Noah approached Danai as she stood on a observation deck near the top of her DropShip. She held binoculars to her eyes and scanned as far as the electronics-enhanced machine would allow.

"Ma'am?" he said, standing beside her.

"Nothing," Danai said. "Two weeks, and not a peep since we let Kelsey go."

"Maybe Cade took it to heart, called it all off."

"No."

Noah sighed. "All due respect, ma'am...that's what it looks like. That's what the boots on the ground are starting to say."

Danai lowered the binoculars and turned to him, questioning.

Noah nodded. "Even the MAC is wondering what they're doing here. They're laughing it up, calling you the 'Killer with Kindness.'"

Danai arched an eyebrow.

He cleared his throat. "It's not, uh...not a very clever nickname. Ma'am."

Grinning mildly, Danai turned her attention back to the view. "They can say whatever they want, so long as every one of them is on high alert and ready to go."

Noah held his hand up to shade his eyes from the rising sun. "The only activity we saw yesterday was some farmers starting to harvest their alfalfa crops. Most of them are using tractors but there's a few Agros in the mix. When we stopped them for inspection, they didn't show a single sign of having been weaponized."

Frowning now, Danai used her binoculars again. "They're not all out there harvesting. Look out that way, the fields closest to us. Still green."

Noah looked, and agreed. "It could be," he mused, "that not all the farms have machinery. Considering how many AgroMechs Rossetti has reported, the locals might have to share equipment."

Danai dropped the binoculars again and shook her head. "It's coming, Noah. Right now, Cade is getting his soldiers into position. And they're going to hit hard."

Noah crossed his arms. "Permission to speak freely, ma'am?"

"Of course."

"How do you know? All the intel we have so far suggests the insurgency is over. No attacks in Rainspire, no raids on the FOB. Danai, maybe you did it. Maybe your presence and your words and a nice big stick called Second MAC was enough."

After releasing MechWarrior Kelsey outside the FOB's makeshift gate, he'd walked unhurriedly to the nearest road and begun following it until out of sight. Sans communication with Cade's forces, she guessed he would either seek help at a local farmhouse, or else walk the entire 30 klicks to Rainspire and give Jack Cade a full report once Kelsey could be sure he wasn't followed or monitored in some way.

Wu had been the first to suggest planting a tracker on Kelsey, when he met with Danai and Rossetti in Danai's cabin after she'd ordered Kelsey's release.

Danai had shot him down. "Cade will find it. Even if he didn't, I have no doubt everyone directly involved in the insurgency has been trained to act as though they do have trackers. Anyplace he went could be a decoy. Or ambush. I appreciate the thought, *Zhong-shao*, but it's not worth the effort."

Instead, Danai explained, they would send more units out to take a semi-circular flanking skirmish position. The rest would wait, openly, near the FOB gate and await the attack she was sure Cade would be mounting.

"Jack Cade will never give up," she said. "Double-check the rosters, make sure everyone, and I mean *everyone*, is ready to roll in a heartbeat."

"...Yes, ma'am."

Noah whisked silently away, back into the ship to follow his orders.

Danai glared at the countryside. "Whenever you're ready, Cade..."

UNDISCLOSED LOCATION
OUTSIDE RAINSPIRE
SHERATAN
2 FEBRUARY 3151

The temperature in Tai's underground hangar grew to an uncomfortable level as BattleMech after BattleMech fired up its engine. Jack found himself missing his old cooling vest, wanting to strip down to damn near nothing to bleed off some of the heat.

Sweat beaded at his hairline, and dripped in regular intervals down his face. He wiped some of it away, but some of it he let gather and fall. The sensation reminded him so clearly of MechWarrior combat that the minor irritation served as a sort of empathy with his pilots.

Just kids, some of them. Nineteen, twenty. One young woman gave up a plum job in finance to learn how to do all this, and had acquitted herself admirably already during some of the raids against the Louie FOB. Not a few old guys were in those machines, too, guys who should be rolling bocce or shooting pool at the Hacker instead of spinning up 'Mechs for assured combat with a stronger force.

And yet, that's what it was all about, wasn't it? Freedom from interference.

And revenge, Jack thought. *Don't forget revenge, old man. Today's the day, brother. Today's the day. You stayed patient, just like you were taught before you were Jack Cade, and now it's time to see it pay off.*

Hemitt approached from the central tunnel, radio in hand, headphones secure over his head. "All clear!" he shouted near Jack's ear. "The Louies still aren't sweeping. We've got a 10-square kilometer perimeter clean of them, probably more. They're staying close to home. They've kept up their skirmish line about a klick away from the crater, but that's it. Those're stationary."

Jack nodded. Ever since Kelsey had been able to touch base after his capture, the Caps had ceased running their all-day, all-night patrols into the Rainspire woods. The shift in tactics pleased Jack—they were waiting for him. They knew he was coming.

"Let 'em loose," he said.

Hemitt spoke into his hand-held radio. Within moments, the first of the insurgent BattleMechs stepped toward the tunnel systems, headed for the forests all around Rainspire.

Jack adjusted the noise-canceling headphones over his ears. The sound of dozens of 'Mechs walking in tandem was tangible; the weight of their shockwaves trembled through his body.

And it made him smile.

Jack leaned close to Hemitt to shout in his friend's ear. "I'm heading out! Meet you at the rendezvous!"

Hemitt shouted back, "Roger that! You sure you don't wanna hop into one of these? Last chance!"

Jack thumped Hemitt on the shoulder. "No," he said, "this won't be my last chance at all! See you on the field!"

Giving the marching war machines a wide berth, he headed for the stairs.

An hour from now, the Louies and their arrogant boss lady were going to get exactly what they'd been wanting.

Jack just hoped he had enough cigars to get him through the morning.

CHAPTER 29

Danai looked up as a klaxon blared in her cabin. The ship's captain announced over the loudspeakers, "Enemy contact, enemy contact. All personnel report to battle stations."

She'd heard the words many times since landing on Sheratan. This morning, she detected a harder edge to the captain's voice.

So this was it. Just as she'd expected.

Danai stood and took a deep breath. "All right, Cade. See you out there."

She leaped from her quarters.

The Third Chargers and Second McCarron's were ready when the assault came.

Combat began in the woods on the east side of the FOB. Reports flowed in quickly from Capellan MechWarriors of small engagements against the skirmish line—light 'Mechs taking potshots at the Second MAC and Third Chargers mediums stationed around the crater base.

Strapping into her *Black Knight*, Danai quickly responded, "Fire at will, but do not send reinforcements yet. Hold fast. QRF, stand ready."

Her orders were received, and single combat continued.

When *Julian* was spun up and ready to roll, Danai said into her comm, "Is the enemy retreating?"

"Negative," came a reply. "They're moving fast, but not retreating."

"It's a feint," Danai said across an open channel. She could easily picture her warriors engaging in a fight not unlike those she'd been in herself on Solaris: single opponent versus single opponent in some type of fabricated environment.

If this *were* Solaris, her money'd be on her Capellan warriors.

"Contact west, contact south," Noah reported. "Sounds like more of the same. One-on-one engagements."

"How we doing?"

"So far, so good. Hard to hit them, but we're holding up."

"How many of our 'Mechs are currently engaged?"

A short pause. "Fifteen, *Sang-shao*."

Fifteen, Danai thought, moving *Julian* toward the gate. *You have a lot more than fifteen, we know that. So what's next? What're you up to?*

Cade wouldn't assault the FOB directly, she was sure. The dozens of DropShips simply had too much firepower. Thinking back to her experiences on Liberty and Hall, Danai wasn't ready to be cocksure about that assessment, but still felt confident. No, Cade would want the fight to be in the woods, where his maneuverability and familiarity with the terrrain would be assets.

"Echo five, contact two, contact two," one of her warriors reported from the east. "There's more of them coming!"

Similar reports piled up from the south and the west. More light insurgent 'Mechs were appearing at the skirmish line.

That made roughly thirty insurgent BattleMechs engaging the Capellan skirmishers. *How many do you have, Cade?*

"Contact north!" Noah relayed. "Here they come."

Danai's HUD lit up with enemy wireframes and triangular carets. BattleMechs and hovercraft appeared on the horizon, still well out of effective range, but closing in.

Danai's military mind quickly assessed her teams. She had multiple lances stationed around the crater to act as quick-reaction forces to the skirmishers if needed. The bulk of her combined forces were northward, ready to pour out of the gate and engage a frontal assault.

This attack from the north did not surprise her. Cade had clearly hoped the engagements around the rim of the crater would pull more forces in those directions. Danai, however, trusted her old veterans to hold the line in the woods.

Instead, the frontal attack would be met with nearly everything the Second MAC and Third Chargers could muster.

Before giving the order she was itching to give, Danai radioed Ross. "When was the last perimeter check?"

"Last check, fifteen minutes," Ross replied over the comm. "No units found."

"Copy that," she said, then opened her wide channel to give a single, simple order: "Go."

Light, medium, heavy, and assault BattleMechs charged out of the FOB, moving to intercept the incoming insurgents. Danai hoped Cade was in one of the 'Mechs; a toe-to-toe with the old man would be a great way to conclude her stay on Sheratan.

Because after today, she was sure, she and the Second MAC wouldn't be needed here anymore.

NORTH OF SECOND MAC FOB

"They're coming out," Hemitt reported.

"Copy," Jack said. "Stick to the plan. This will work if everyone keeps cool."

"I'll send the reminder," Hemitt said.

Jack switched channels on his communicator. "Bravo Team, warm up, the blessed Capellans are coming to save you all."

A few of his warriors chuckled over the comm.

"Just sit tight and wait for the signal," Jack added. "You got this."

The MechWarriors replied with various affirmations.

Jack squinted toward the horizon, waiting for the battle to begin. In the meantime...

He lit a cigar.

OUTSIDE SECOND MAC FOB

Danai could not help a somewhat wicked laugh as the insurgent forces hesitated in their march forward. Hovercraft "skidded" to a stop on cushions of air. BattleMechs ceased moving forward.

"Do not let up," Danai said over the open channel. "Move fast, fire at will. Lights, stay close to your mediums."

The majority of two battalions of Capellan military might thundered north toward their enemy. Longer-range laser beams fired from the line of enemy combatants, but the insurgent units moved laterally or backward now. None stepped forward to close the distance.

Danai's teams immediately answered with their own longer-range weapons. LRMs cut smoke trails in the air, and electric charges of PPC fire arced across the fields of tall green crops. White and red lasers beamed over the roofs of farmhouses, seeking enemies.

When the first Capellan missiles caught their targets, the insurgent line broke. Danai imagined she could hear the panic in their cockpits as the hovercraft spun in quick circles and headed back the way they'd come. BattleMechs scattered left, right, and backward, firing their own weapons back at the Capellans, but to little effect.

"Chase them down!" Danai barked. "They go into the woods, you follow. No one escapes. Hit them with everything you've got, let's *end* this now!"

Her many lances spread out, picking out fleeing targets as they raced to the tree lines east and west, or further north into the farmland toward Rainspire.

Danai noticed in the ensuing action that the insurgents, previously showing great care to avoid the fields of crops, no longer cared about their fellow Sheratan farmers. Their 'Mechs stomped across green fields, heedless of their neighbors' livelihoods.

Because that's always how it goes, she thought with some smugness. *People like Cade talk a good game about freedom for their people, right up until it's their own ass on the line.*

She disliked giving her next order, but knew it had to be done. Cade and Kelsey had ensured it. When this nonsense of an insurgency was over, she would ensure the Confederation would take care of all material losses, with her own vast funds if necessary.

"MechWarriors," Danai said, her voice smooth, "movement protocols are now off, I say again, you are movement-free as needed."

Immediately, the Capellan force gave up trying to stay on the roadways the way Rossetti and Danai had both ordered previously. Like their enemies, the Capellan force now moved readily through the crop fields to get to their targets.

The Capellan lances rushed headlong toward their targets. The lighter insurgent 'Mechs backpedaled or outright sprinted away. White-hot slugs pierced the air, finding targets. Lasers burned off plates of armor. Missiles tore away BattleMech limbs.

Danai walked *Julian* almost casually into the fray, firing her extended-range PPC at targets in the distance, as if for practice. Based on her HUD, the Capellans were wrecking Cade's lighter 'Mechs and the dozens of hovercraft he'd thrown at them.

She entered a field of partially harvested alfalfa, firing her twin extended-range large lasers at a cluster of *Javelins* breaking hard for the tree line. She peered curiously at the narrow paths cut into the crops.

That's an odd way to do harvesting, Danai thought as she chased down her next target. *Those are just...rows.* Granted, her knowledge of agriculture was next to none. She knew this year-round temperate zone made feed crops possible for most of Sheratan's seasons, but that was book knowledge gleaned while she and Noah had been shipping here.

From the height of her BattleMech, Danai could now see that, for at least half a kilometer ahead and to the sides, possibly further, these narrow paths had been cut into the vegetation, creating columns of rough squares, around 30 by 30 meters each. The designs on the ground reminded Danai of children's blocks organized atop one another.

Or grid lines on a map.

A map...wait...

In that moment, Danai realized she'd marched her warriors directly into a trap Cade had set for them. One that just might work on a duchess whose desire was to get off this world as quickly as possible; on a colonel whose time on the lavish world of Castrovia had dulled her instincts more than she wanted to admit.

Her heart thudded. What was the trap? How would it spring?

No time to find out. Danai activated her radio: "All units—!"

An explosion at the front of the Capellan BattleMech line snapped Danai's attention to her screen. A solid hit from one of the retreating enemy vehicles, presumably.

A light Third Chargers 'Mech fell to the ground, its right leg shorn off.

"No!" Danai barked.

She'd seen no shot from an insurgent unit. The trap was sprung. She just didn't yet know what kind.

NEAR SECOND MAC FOB

Leaning with his back against a tree some 300 meters from the field and another hundred up a hill, Jack lit another cigar. He watched his warriors sprint across Dickson's alfalfa field, firing lasers blindly backward at the pursuing Capellan BattleMechs.

Hemitt, standing beside him, alternated his gaze between the portable signal module in his hands and the Capellan force.

"That's it," he announced as the last Rainspire 'Mech crossed an invisible threshold on the field. "We're clear. Who do you wanna hit first?"

Jack puffed on his cigar, eyes picking out each of the enemy 'Mechs. He had no real tactical preference; today was dealer's choice. With the Louies so far deep into his grid, though, he figured they'd start with the closest units and then chase them south when the Louies fell back. Which, he was sure, they would.

Clenching the cigar in his teeth to free his hand, Jack pointed at a *Sojourner*. "That one."

"Yes, sir," Hemitt said, smiling, and tapped the module.

CHAPTER 30

Another explosion to the left of Danai's 'Mech. A third to the right.

Her years of training and combat fluttered through her brain, trying to make sense of what she was seeing, to grasp the exact nature of Cade's plan.

Two more MAC 'Mechs were down. Both had suffered total destruction of their feet or legs. Dirt and crop remnants hung in the air, floating back to the earth.

Like Liberty! Danai thought. *Dammit, I knew it, they* do *have artillery...*

Wildly, she looked around for telltale signs of shelling, but neither heard nor saw anything out her cockpit or on her sensors to indicate artillery batteries. Quickly scanning the virtual crater caused by the explosion, she realized the blast had come from *beneath* the 'Mechs.

"God*damn*!" Danai shouted as the reality of the odd paths the farmers had cut through their crops finally became clear.

Grids.

She spun *Julian* halfway around to take in the entire landscape.

Grid after grid extended for hundreds of meters all around.

To the west, Danai saw one of the grids explode with two of her team inside. One 'Mech stumbled, then fell; the other staggered backward as if in shock, only to have another grid behind it explode and drop the BattleMech to the ground, its weaker rear armor decimated.

She imagined what the battlefield would look like from above.

Target grids.

The Confederation was known for its development of anti-'Mech land mines. As arguably the Inner Sphere's biggest military of the last hundred years, the deployment of the weapons seemed all but inevitable. Land mines were a cheap and effective means of disabling all sorts of machines, provided the military had time to place them properly...

And lead an enemy into them.

As a lifelong student of the Capellan military apparatus, Danai knew well the capabilities of land mines. Some were designed to activate as jumping units passed overhead, some set fire instantly to BattleMechs and caused a shutdown, or a retreat in fear of one. Other types existed as well, some field-tested, some still in the conceptual phase of development.

Danai had not heard that the RAF—much less a ragtag insurgency—had mines in their possession. Improvised explosives, yes; not mines.

Thirty meters to her left, another Capellan 'Mech's legs exploded beneath it. The model, a *Yao Lien*, was heavier and took the blow in stride, but Danai could visually see it had precious little armor remaining below its torso.

Target grids...no weight limit trigger...

"Comm det..." Danai whispered.

Traditionally mines were pressure-detonated, while specialized vibramines could be set for particular weights of BattleMechs. None had gone off beneath the insurgent force as they entered the crop fields, though, which meant these were command-detonated mines.

Somewhere, not too far off, someone was setting off the land mine grids at will as Capellan 'Mechs entered them.

"*Halt!*" Danai shouted into her radio. "All units, stop the advance!"

Only in exploded grids were her MechWarriors safe from the mines; she needed them to break off their movement. It took a precious few seconds for her words to reach all the BattleMechs and for their MechWarriors to follow the order. In that time, three more units suffered catastrophic explosions underfoot.

The MechWarriors went motionless, breaking a cardinal rule of 'Mech combat.

"Are we at ceasefire?" Wu all but demanded over her headset.

Her troops couldn't just stand still. Movement equaled life. Or did, unless surrounded by land mines...

"Incoming!" someone shrieked over the comm.

Danai spun *Julian*'s torso to the north in time to see innumerable volleys of LRM slicing through the sky and landing on her BattleMechs like miniature meteors. The volleys came from no less than a dozen small 'Mechs far afield to the north—her HUD identified a *Cougar* variant and handful of *Vixen*s. Each mounted only LRM-5 racks, but those racks were being burned through at a prodigious rate. Even in the chaos of her failure to discern the minefield she'd marched her soldiers into, Danai guessed the light 'Mechs had been turned into missile boats exclusively. With the Capellans pinned in the middle of this vast minefield, the insurgent BattleMechs could fire themselves empty and use their superior speed to retreat to safety.

Possibly, Danai realized, *to re-arm and come back to pick off stragglers. If there are any left...*

She knew instinctively that the first insurgent lances that had feigned retreat to draw the Capellans into the minefield were just inside the tree line, awaiting an order to re-enter the field and attack the damaged Capellans in the chaos.

"All units retreat!" she ordered. "LRM fire, clear a lane back to the FOB."

Her units seemed happy to comply. Those equipped with long-range missiles fired at the ground ahead of themselves to clear mines out of the way. The tactic worked eventually, but the insurgents went on setting off one grid after another until each of Danai's 'Mechs had taken some damage. Meanwhile, insurgent LRMs fell freely from the sky, like some giant child casting handfuls of sand overhead, and letting the grains fall where they may.

Ross said the perimeter was clear, Danai thought furiously as she moved *Julian* to hopefully safer places. *Our patrols picked up nothing.*

So maybe old Jack Cade's a bit more than you gave him credit for, Duchess. That's on you.

Some of Danai's 'Mechs were still ambulatory and reached the relative safety of the roads. Others were not so fortunate, taking the brunt of enormous amounts of explosive shrapnel. Danai saw two medium-class *Vindicators* each lose a leg entirely, and topple uselessly to the ground.

She did not bother to give the next order she gave herself— she moved deliberately toward any grid that had already been detonated. There weren't many. Cade's people had done an excellent job baiting them—*Baiting me*, Danai thought bitterly—deep into the minefield, such that movement in any direction would result in further damage. Her lances figured out the wisdom of her flight path for themselves, and tried to maneuver through exploded patches of earth.

A grid went off on her left. *Julian* rocked to the right. Alarms blared. Danai opted to roll with the motion, stumbling the big 'Mech for several long strides before regaining balance.

Upright still, Danai urged the 'Mech forward—then stopped as she glanced to her left to see how much damage she'd taken.

What she saw was Noah Capshaw's *Sojourner*. Face-down in a shallow crater.

Danai froze, ice filling the burning-hot cockpit.

She opened her link to him. "Noah?"

More explosions behind her, to the sides. She didn't so much as glance at them.

"Noah, come in!"

A small shower of sparks burst from the *Sojourner*'s back. That was all.

"*Noah...!*"

Something rammed into the *Black Knight*'s back. Danai whirled the machine, only to find herself facing Wu in his

Prefect. The *Prefect*'s right shoulder baffle was missing. The PPC in its left arm was mangled beyond repair. Dozens of smaller, smoking holes dotted the 'Mech's torso.

"I got him," Wu growled over the comm. "You have to go, *Sang-shao*."

Danai's first urge was to argue, to order Wu away, to leap from *Julian*'s cockpit and see to Noah herself. She had the range; she could provide cover for Wu while he saw to Noah; offer rear guard protection for them like a Solaris arena team.

Mina Liao's voice whispered quietly in her mind, though— the reassuring and empathic voice of reason that told her that, like it or not, she was too important to get hurt or killed. That she must act as a colonel, not a squad commander.

Clenching her jaw in fury, Danai forced herself to take a safe path out of the line of fire. The enemy kept up their volleys of LRMs as she and the survivors headed south toward the FOB, cracking bits of armor off the fleeing Second MAC. She felt several of the missiles explode against *Julian*'s rear armor.

The fleeing MAC, Danai thought grimly. *Not a phrase I've often heard.*

And then:

Please be all right, Noah.

The wounded lances limped for home.

Danai could barely see straight as she aimed *Julian* for the front gate. How quickly everything had gone to hell.

By the time she crossed the gate threshold, she'd received reports that the insurgent 'Mechs encircling the FOB had retreated and escaped through the woods. The Third Charger and Second MAC 'Mechs charged with holding the skirmish line had taken severe damage, but none had fallen. That seemed to be the only good news. At least they were mobile. How many legless or damaged 'Mechs still lay in the fields to the north?

Danai pulled her BattleMech to one side of the gate to allow others to pass her by. She didn't feel like getting out of the cockpit.

"Wu. Update."

"I'm bringing Noah home, *Sang-shao*."

"...Alive?"

"Uh...for the moment."

Danai squeezed her eyes shut. "The insurgents?"

"Gone, ma'am. They've run off."

"Very well," she whispered, and clicked off, unsure and uncaring if he heard her.

All right, she thought, trying to slow her breathing. *You got your ass handed to you, Duchess. Get your bearings, take your time, and*—

The earth rumbled.

Danai snapped up as if awakened from a nap. Tremors ran up *Julian*'s legs and into her own. The deep, bass note of a massive explosion sent a shockwave through her body.

What now?!

In the distance, the easternmost DropShip—one of Rossetti's—seemed to sink into the ground. Danai watched, horrified, as the enormous ship slowly tipped to its left, picking up momentum, until it finally crashed to its side. Danai winced in apprehension, anticipating the ship would explode. But even after a full minute of dull, horrified silence, the ship remained intact.

Utterly useless as a space-faring vessel, and with who-knew-what kind of damage to personnel within. But intact.

The trained soldiers of the Capellan Confederation Armed Forces reacted quickly. Like ants toward a fallen treat, the soldiers raced for the DropShip, shouting for fire response teams and medics.

Drawn by the unreal sight, Danai opened her canopy and stood on her command couch, surveying the scene. A quick assessment even from this distance indicated the ground had blown up under the ship. As if Cade's insurgency had constructed and planted a land mine of unfathomable size beneath the ship.

How? How in the world...?

When the most likely answer came to her, Danai's mouth dried.

She sank into her command couch and opened a channel to Rossetti's war room. "Ross. Initiate an emergency full-scale liftoff. Do it now."

Ross' voice was perplexed. "*Sang-shao?* Could you say that again?"

"They're *underneath* us. Cade is underneath the LZ. Get as many people as you can off this crater immediately and to the closest reserve landing zone."

"That's outside Daggaknott, Danai. We'll be—"

"Do it," Danai said lifelessly. "Before another DropShip falls into a pit."

Ross hesitated before hastily muttering, "Yes, ma'am."

One minute later, warning klaxons tore through the mid-morning sky, and confused soldiers stumbled around, trying to board their vessels.

Sang-shao Danai Centrella-Liao, Duchess of Castrovia, watched it all from the cockpit of her BattleMech, and tried to think of a way out.

Her mind remained nauseatingly blank.

THE HACKER
RAINSPIRE
SHERATAN
2 FEBRUARY 3151

"CADE! CADE! CADE! CADE!"

Everyone in the bar chanted his name as Jack sat in his usual chair at his usual table with his usual friends.

He took in the adulation humbly, not really caring to be a hero, but caring only that his brother—Cordelia's father—was seeing it all in whatever heaven old literature teachers went to after being gunned down by overzealous occupying soldiers. So what if Cade wasn't his real name? It was the name they knew him by, that's all that mattered.

Eventually the cheers abated, and Cade offered a humble wave to the denizens of the Hacker. Only after everyone was through shaking his hand or slapping him on the back did Hemitt lean in and speak quietly, "I gotta say, I'm surprised it all worked."

Cade grinned. "Same here."

"Ah, knock it off. You executed perfectly. But now I gotta ask...what's next?"

Cade shrugged. "We'll soon know."

Hemitt was immune to the laugher and celebration around them. He leaned closer. "Stop it, Jack. I'm serious. What happens now?"

Jack sighed. "They won't leave. They can't. We knew that. But they'll talk again. Oh, yes, they'll chat us up very soon. We'll argue, we'll debate. And then we'll reach an agreement: the Caps can have some unused property on the far side of the continent. Everyone on Sheratan gets to run their own lives without Louie interference. That'll buy us a few years. And while they're out there building, we'll be building too. We'll be ready."

The group cheered. Everyone but Hemitt, who met his eyes over the table. They spoke only with their eyes.

Hemitt knew the truth as well as Jack did. At two jumps from Terra, Sheratan was a target for every military determined to take humanity's homeworld. Their war would never end.

But tonight...tonight they'd won. Tonight the tree had grown.

Hemitt sat back and took a drink of his mead. After wiping his mouth with the back of his hand, he said, "Sounds great. I hope you're right."

Jack shrugged and lit his cigar. He looked forward to telling Cordelia all about their battle after school.

CHAPTER 31

Danai entered the medical bay slowly, feeling as though her feet were being sucked down into mud and blood. Apart from soft beeping, the bay was eerily silent.

She walked to Noah Capshaw's bedside, the muscles in her face strained. She struggled not to turn away.

She could smell him.

Smell his blood, his lymph, the faint odor of electrical smoke. Danai Centrella-Liao had fought a lot of battles, taken many lives, and considered herself used to the horrors of war.

The smells, though; very few people got used to the smells.

Noah lay mercifully unconscious. Pristine white bandages swathed the left side of his face and both arms, which lay atop a gray blanket. The blanket was pulled up to his armpits, but Danai could tell from the lumpy texture that thick bandages covered his torso.

He seemed to be breathing on his own, with only supplemental oxygen in his nose; Danai hoped that was a good sign. But Noah's breathing was shallow, barely registering. His heart rate monitor showed a slow but steady beat.

"I'm sorry," she whispered.

For no good reason at all, standing there beside her confidante, Danai realized she'd come to think of Noah as immune from such harm. A ridiculous—a *silly*—notion. This was war, and there were casualties. She could barely grasp the idea she'd allowed herself to have any feelings for Noah.

She reached for him, then pulled away. He was not comatose, according to the lead physician. Danai was loathe to risk waking him.

"I'm going to burn them down," she said to Noah's unconscious form. "And salt the earth."

No, you won't, she thought right on the heels of her words. *Because you know Cade is counting on that.*

What she wanted to do was unleash hell on the whole of Rainspire, the whole of Sheratan if that's what it took. After all, wasn't that what House Liao had been known for since the Night of Screams?

Danai grimaced, her gaze still focused on Noah, but her thoughts now roaming to military concerns. She knew it was true: the Republic of the Sphere had often made House Liao out to be "city burners," showing no concern for civilian life, relying on all sorts of fire to do its military work during the Capellan Crusades. On Hall and Liberty, Danai had taken deliberate steps to disallow that sort of combat or retribution, no matter what the insurgents came at them with.

When Mina had been killed, firebombing the town had crossed her mind, yes. Here in the quiet med bay, alone, Danai could admit that much to herself. But she hadn't ordered it, hadn't allowed it. The people of those worlds were, after all, Capellan—whether they knew it or not.

Taking a deep breath to calm her racing thoughts, her nose twitching away from the faint odor of char coming from Noah's body, Danai pressed herself harder on the issue: how to best handle this current situation with Rainspire, if not by fire?

Cade had proved crafty, but Danai wasn't convinced his craftiness equated cunning. Certainly he was egocentric, overconfident. Then again, after months of running circles around Ross and his Third Chargers, he had a reason to be.

But it's not a game to him, Danai thought. *He's ruthless. The way he baited us into that minefield...*

Well, that's on you, Duchess, she thought angrily. *You're the one who fell for it.*

A final report wouldn't come in for several more days at best, but at first glance, it appeared the insurgency had been digging at least one massive tunnel beneath the Third's crater landing zone, then used an enormous stockpile of agricultural chemicals—fertilizers and such—to blow a catastrophic hole.

This accounted for why the raids against the FOB had included AgroMech MODs but no MiningMechs; they had all been hard at work beneath the LZ. This plan also accounted for the raids themselves, which were designed to do little more than distract the Third Chargers, allowing the sound and tremor of battle to mask the digging going on right beneath their feet. In an odd twist, this initial report indicated such distraction may not have been necessary. The IndustrialMechs were deep enough that no one in the crater would likely have noticed the drilling and carving out of the earth.

As for the crater, what was now called LZ Alpha, no secondary blast had followed the first. Engineers couldn't promise there weren't other tunnels, not yet, but thus far, the crater had remained stable since the battle across the Rainspire farmland. Currently, all the other DropShips—Third Chargers and Second MAC alike—occupied an arid field outside the larger town of Daggaknott. Danai had forbidden any excursions beyond the LZ by any member of the Third Chargers or Second MAC. Whether they stayed here in the field or took the DropShips back to the crater to be near Rainspire, she had not decided.

Danai at last allowed her fingertips to rest lightly and briefly on Noah's unbandaged shoulder. "I'll come back when I can. But just know I'm going to finish this and get you back to Liao."

She reached for a bit of Noah's white hair to brush it off his forehead—completely unaware she had done so.

The door to the med bay slid open. Danai turned to find Wu walking over, his face sad and determined in one grim expression. "You haven't been answering your comm," he said quietly as he moved to stand on the other side of Noah's bed. "Figured I'd find you here. How is he?"

Danai said nothing.

"Got some news," Wu went on after giving her a few moments. "We found more tunnels."

Danai's eyes jerked to his.

Wu nodded as if she'd spoken. "I've got teams down there now. There was a BattleMech hangar underground, Republic-built. Empty now. One of the tunnels opened into the forest, well beyond our skirmish line. Looks like they've been marching their units in and out at will."

Danai spoke through clenched teeth. "How did Ross miss that?"

"He didn't raze the forest, for starters. But even if he had, the entrance was quite a ways out. Based on what happened in those fields, I figure they had boots on the ground, making sure we weren't anywhere nearby any time they exited or entered." Wu shook his head. "Hell of a thing to miss."

"Noah said all Rossetti did was chase down the raiders," Danai said, eyes drifting back to her *sang-wei's* bandaged face. "The Third was the wrong choice for the job." She shook her head as Wu started to reply. "Doesn't matter. What's done is done. All that matters is what comes next."

Wu crossed his arms. "And what's that?"

"I don't know," Danai said, suppressing a chill. "I need another day to think. Are we secure here, in this LZ?"

"Yep. Everything looks good so far. Daggaknott's been hopping, but no one's come out to say hello."

She arched an eyebrow. "Hopping?"

Wu scowled. "Partying."

"Celebrating," Danai corrected as the truth of it occurred to her. "Cheering our loss."

"Afraid so."

"And the heroic myth of Colonel Jack Cade grows."

Danai appreciated that Wu didn't bother to respond. He knew, too.

"This time tomorrow," she said. "Meet me outside my DropShip, by the 'Mech bays. Until then, keep everyone busy. Light work, but still work. Unless there's a direct assault on us here, you're in charge. I don't want to be disturbed."

"Copy that, *Sang-shao*." Wu gave a crisp brace before leaving the room.

Danai risked laying a couple of fingers on Noah's arm. "I'm going to get you home," she said to his unconscious form. "As soon as possible. And I'll make Cade pay, Noah. I swear it."

Feeling her eyes begin to sting, Danai turned quickly and left the medical bay.

Plans were needed.

SECOND MAC LANDING ZONE BRAVO
OUTSIDE DAGGAKNOTT
SHERATAN
5 FEBRUARY 3151

Danai insisted on meeting Wu outside. Her cramped DropShip cabin had begun to grate on her nerves.

At least, that's what she chose to blame for her short temper. Mask agents had confirmed Daggaknott had taken to the streets in celebration of the Capellan rout outside Rainspire. The city showed no overt signs of organizing to join Cade's insurgency, or fomenting one of their own, but Danai knew her battalions were on borrowed time. Blood often followed parties.

Wu joined her on a slow walk around the field where the Second MAC and Third Chargers had relocated. Everywhere, the LZ buzzed with activity. Until ordered otherwise, the soldiers were busy erecting barriers, deploying remaining mines and remote sensors, and preparing for assaults that Danai, for one, was sure would never come. Still—it was best to be cautious, and to keep idle soldiers' hands busy. She'd ordered round-the-clock reinforced patrols as well, close to the LZ perimeter.

She was not immune to the looks her soldiers gave her. Moreso from members of the Third than from her own Second MAC. They were angry glances, though she sensed the anger was not directed at her. They were expressions that clearly read *When are we going back and getting those bastards for what they did?*

"Bottom line," Wu reported as they walked under a cloudless sky, "we don't know how many of those mines they have. Which means we now have to watch every literal step we take. Maybe they're surrounding the whole of Rainspire, or maybe they planted every mine they had out in those fields. We just can't say. But that hangar we found was pretty big. It could have contained a whole lotta gear, *Sang-shao*."

None of which Danai didn't already know, but she let Wu get it out of his system. She knew the feeling. Saying a thing out loud sometimes helped. She knew one cadet during her training, Lydia Chen, who'd bounce a ball alone in their quarters for hours on end while talking to herself, coming up with new ways to defeat their opponents. She was now a *zhong-shao* and served in the Fifth MAC.

"How many 'Mechs did we lose?"

"Seven for scrap. That includes the MechWarriors. Twelve injured and out for recovery, including Noah. It's taking time to recover the salvage, as we're having to blow safe lanes to the wreckage."

Danai wanted to punch something. "If we accept for the moment that Cade's not being supplied from outside forces, and his weapons have come from a cache, then the same is likely true for the mines. Which he hasn't used until now. Like he was waiting. Like he's using the whole damn planet as a honey trap. He wanted more of our forces on-world. He knew it would eventually happen if he could keep up pressure on the Third Chargers. And once more of us landed, he was going to pummel the lot of us."

"All right," Wu said slowly. "But then he also has to know we could call in the *Aleisha Kris* and just erase his city from orbit. Especially after this beating we just took."

"But we wouldn't," Danai pointed out. "That sort of thing isn't in the playbook."

Wu raised an eyebrow. "Yours, maybe. I'd hesitate to speak so quickly about the Strategios or—" He snapped his mouth shut.

Danai smiled grimly. "You can say his name," she said. "But you also don't have to."

Wu released a breath and opted to reply with, "Thank you, *Sang-shao*. Now, here's what I really don't like about your theory."

Danai crossed her arms as they walked, waiting for him to say his piece.

"How far out has he gamed this?" Wu said, his expression darkening. "If you're right, and he intended to bring more of us to the surface, then how many more does he think he can handle? And how? What cards has he not shown us yet?"

"It could be he's shown us all his cards, but wants us to think he hasn't," Danai mused. Before Wu could argue, she dropped her arms. "But that's not something we can bank on, of course."

She rubbed her forehead. "Listen to me go," she grumbled. "He's got me going around in circles, and I still don't know who he is. I'm sure he's related to his little bodyguard Cordelia, but there's no record of that, still no record of Jack Cade anywhere. *Anywhere.* The man's a phantom. *And* he's kicking my ass. *And* I don't like it."

They paused at the crest of a short hill, watching wire fencing get laid out.

"What are your orders, *Sang-shao?*"

"Jack Cade took away our ability to move," Danai said, rubbing a hand across her chin. "Just like he told me he would. Maybe he really was a colonel somewhere."

"An insurgent colonel," Wu pointed out.

"He took away our ability to move freely," Danai said again, slowly. She lifted her gaze. "So we are going to take away his."

She clenched her hands. "Send me Draco."

Wu appeared to quite nearly take a stunned step back. "Danai—"

"Do it. Before we lose anyone else."

Wu swallowed visibly, and stared at her a moment before executing a crisp about-face and hurrying toward their command ship.

Danai didn't like it any more than he did.

But then, you never told Draco and their group to get out of the Second MAC, either, did you? she thought. *You and Xavier and all the other* sang-shaos *of McCarron's.*

You keep them around because you need them for just such an occasion.

Danai closed her eyes and tried to clear her head for the ensuing meeting. She had never met the person code-named Draco, and she had never wanted to. She simply saw no alternative.

The Third and the Second were in relative tatters. Cade would never mount a frontal assault; even now, the MAC and Chargers vastly outgunned any massed force the insurgents could field. If he had had that kind of power at his disposal, he would have smashed the Chargers months ago and never let them call for help in the first place. Danai guessed the insurgency's current silence was Cade awaiting word from her—

Not "word," Danai corrected herself. *He wants me to beg. He'll have a long wait.*

—awaiting a message from her to parley again. Doubtless he had a military engagement planned and ready to execute as well, but right now...no. He expected the defeated Capellan army to come to the table and hope for scraps from his oh-so-mighty insurgency.

And that is why she sent for Draco.

Because Jack Cade, Danai thought, *has underestimated just how Capellan I really am.*

CHAPTER 32

SECOND MAC LZ BRAVO
OUTSIDE DAGGAKNOTT
SHERATAN
6 FEBRUARY 3151

Draco turned out to be a tall, lean woman who reminded Danai of a junkyard dog—hungry, mangy, and ready to eat the face off any living thing if it meant surviving one more day. The special forces operator carried an air of mystique, of implied danger. Even as she stood before Danai, she appeared unarmed, yet Danai knew she'd already planned five ways to kill the duchess if need be.

"Here at your request, Your Grace," Draco said.

Her voice had the texture of pumice. Danai hated that her own heart rate picked up at the sound of it. She would face any comer in a BattleMech, but one on one, in person, she could feel the weight of the other woman's kills, and fear her. Draco wore plain utility fatigues with a nametape reading "*Li*," and the rank of *san-ben-bing*, or corporal. Danai assumed neither the rank nor name was true, but one could never be sure.

It didn't matter. While they spoke, she would merely be recognized as Draco, just as the previous contact had been. The code name was passed from soldier to soldier.

"So you are part of the Prizrak?" Danai began.

"If I were, I wouldn't admit it, would I, ma'am?" Draco's face remained utterly impassive.

"No. I suppose you wouldn't."

All regimental COs were privy to the code name of one person attached to their regiment who spoke for a secret, elite group known as the Prizrak, or Ghost Squad. Beyond knowing the code name, no one but the squad themselves knew who was in the unit. It kept politics out, and let the operators work unimpeded by red tape. Ghost squads were known to form their own interpersonal families, as bonded as a parent and children. They would never give each other up, they would never leave a brother or sister behind.

And they never, ever gave up once given a mission.

That sort of unrivaled dedication came at a price, one most were never able to pay. Inclusion into the Prizrak wasn't the sort of thing a soldier applied for; extant squad members chose one or two potential candidates at a time and clandestinely tested them for suitability based on a wide array of factors observed by the squad in passing. Prizrak membership was by invitation only. Prizrak membership did not exist on any CCAF records.

Jack Cade wanted to be a ghost? She'd fight him right back with a ghost.

"I have a job for your team," Danai said with all the command demeanor she could muster.

Draco's expression didn't change at all as she replied, "Clearing mines isn't something my unit's tasked with."

If that had been Danai's intent, Draco was explicitly refusing to follow orders. But Draco wasn't blustering. She was indeed incapable of ego, from all Danai knew of the Prizrak. Draco spoke Prizrak's truth, even to her *sang-shao*, and that was the end of it. Danai was free to try and punish her all she wished, but a Prizrak would never break, never capitulate.

"Not clearing," Danai said. "Avenging."

"What are your orders?"

"I've tried diplomacy. I've tried a square, stand-up fight. The man ostensibly running the insurgency has shown contempt for both. He wants a street fight, so you will give it to him."

Draco's face remained inscrutable. If the idea appealed to her, she didn't show it.

Danai leaned over the desk, fingers splayed across its surface. "Before the end of this month, report back to me and me alone when you've accomplished the mission. Make them suffer. Make them afraid to step outside."

"By any means necessary?" Draco asked. Her voice had dropped two octaves.

Danai stood straight, lifting her chin, ready—she hoped—to accept the burden of her order. "Not any means. Limited targeting. Root them out of their rat holes, destroy caches. Grab some prisoners for interrogation. Be seen doing it."

Draco offered a brief nod. "As you wish, Your Grace." She let herself out of the small quarters without bracing.

Danai collapsed into her chair. *Well, now you've done it*, she thought. *You let the dog off the leash, and whatever happens next is on you. For better or for worse.*

It was the kind of work she would rather have had the Death Commandos do, but those merciless special operators worked exclusively under the discretion of her "brother," the Chancellor. More to the point, they'd largely been deployed forward in Daoshen's push for Terra.

The Prizrak, on the other hand, were a relatively new creation of the MAC, initiated not long before Danai's birth. Prizrak operators were seeded out to different regiments around McCarron's. Sometimes two, sometimes ten, never more than a dozen, Prizrak agents—ghost agents—went about their daily work routines like any other MechWarrior, supply chain sergeant, or cook's assistant. Only when called upon by the highest echelons of their regiment did they band together for a specified purpose, upon completion of which they melted back into the ranks. Neither the Death Commandos nor Maskirovka were fans of the unit, but given MAC's relative autonomy, they were grudgingly tolerated.

The shorthand of it: Death Commandos had an emblem. The Prizrak did not. They did not exist.

Another difference: the Death Commandos were a front-line regiment, with wide latitude in fulfilling their orders. Their power extended to include the authority to execute Capellan soldiers...or even nobility, if circumstances indicated such action.

The Prizrak had no such latitude. They did not act unilaterally; they took and followed orders, full stop. They did not create policy, they enforced it, and only when all other public-facing means had been tried.

If there was dirty work to be done, the Prizrak would do it.

And this was dirty work.

Danai sighed. She could have sent the entire regiment stampeding into Rainspire. That would "work." Such a ploy would also read badly on Liao, not only to the public, but also to the Strategios. There was still such a thing as decorum and honor.

Also, there were her own rules of engagement to consider. In Danai's mind, the House you didn't bomb with nuclear weapons today might be the House who didn't bomb you with biological agents tomorrow. Under her rules, urban combat was out of bounds, with BattleMechs engaging only in uninhabited wilderness. While this did not always play out in practice, Danai—like generals throughout the centuries— knew engaging in door-to-door campaigns rarely went well for either side of a conflict.

I wonder what she's capable of, Danai thought idly.

And then answered herself: *If you truly wanted to know that, you wouldn't have sent for her, Duchess.*

CELESTIAL PALACE
CHANG-AN
LIAO
19 FEBRUARY 3151

"Celestial Wisdom!" said an excited officer as he raced into Daoshen's conference room, where he was currently conducting a meeting with his Strategios. "They've done it!"

Robie watched the uniformed man rush to the Chancellor's throne. She slid a step nearer, disliking his lack of self-control.

"It's the Second Liao Guards," the officer went on, handing Daoshen a tablet. "They've taken Sirius. Congratulations on an effective campaign, Your Grace!"

Robie fought a sneer of disgust. Proper respect for the office of the Chancellor was one thing; fawning, entirely another.

She noticed Daoshen's calm expression did not change as he took the tablet and scanned its contents. The table of Strategios sat still, waiting for their leader to speak.

"This is indeed welcome news," he said at last, handing the tablet back to the officer. "Unfortunately, this meeting is about our recent losses on Procyon."

The glee on the officer's face fell instantly. He turned to the table of Strategios. "Procyon? What...?"

"We have just learned that surviving elements of the Republic of the Sphere have hit the Fourth Liao Guards, which took significant losses," Daoshen said. His voice sounded even, but Robie detected a slight strain. "As a result, as of the sending of this message two weeks ago, Procyon is no longer fully in our control. We now await word on whether the Guards were able to fend off the attack and hold the planet or not."

Daoshen let this news sink in to the officer, who bowed and slowly walked away from the Celestial Wisdom, who turned his attention back to the table. From Robie's perspective, he seemed to meet each officer's gaze in turn as he spoke.

"Procyon. Liberty. Hall. Sirius. Sheratan. Keid. Epsilon Indi. Caph. These worlds are the stepping stones to our proper place at the head of the Inner Sphere. We lead the greatest liberation force ever known, yet insurgencies and sabotage keep us from our destiny. How can we free Greater Humanity when an invisible wall and a scant few resisters stop us in our tracks?"

Robie had her own thoughts on Daoshen's question, but knew better than to offer them. Likewise, the Strategios around the table traded glances, but did not dare speak. Daoshen was correct in his assessment of the worlds he listed. They were crucial to create a stable corridor leading straight to Terra. Robie knew that while many of the worlds had been liberated by the CCAF fairly quickly, that very quickness had caused Daoshen some alarm, and triggered many meetings like this one.

Why had some of these worlds given up without much of a fight? In the Chancellor's opinion, it was because their current chief adversary, the Republic of the Sphere, was laying a trap for the Capellans. Privately, Robie knew Daoshen fumed over his military's inability to detect and undo the trap. For her part, Robie felt unconvinced such a trap existed.

Daoshen rose. He gestured vaguely to the officer who'd brought the report on Sirius.

"We thank you for your bright spot of good news about Sirius. There remains, however, much more to be done, and done soon. Take whatever measures are necessary to reclaim Procyon from these rebels and to welcome our newly freed worlds back into our Confederation."

The assembled officers murmured their understanding. Daoshen turned to one of the Strategios, sliding his hands into the sleeves of his crimson robe.

"Now, what news of my sister on Sheratan?"

CHAPTER 33

SECOND MAC LZ BRAVO
OUTSIDE RAINSPIRE
SHERATAN
20 FEBRUARY 3151

Danai studied at Rossetti's report critically. He was doing well in establishing this new base of operations, but gaps remained.

Base of operations, she thought with grim anger. *It's not even a forward operating base because we're not "forward operating" on much of anything.*

Ross' engineers reported no further tunneling in the prior LZ. That was good news; Danai could move both regiments back to the crater if necessary. But that one word, *necessary*, plagued her.

There'd been no movement on Cade's part since the battle of the minefield. For the life of her, Danai could not guess his next move. She knew only on gut instinct that he was far from finished. Winners didn't melt away into the shadows.

Not unless they are particularly well trained and disciplined, she thought. *Dammit, Cade. Who are you?*

A certain tension had taken over the new LZ. All the Chargers and Second MAC were working well, establishing a strong perimeter and rebuilding what equipment they could in good time. It would take special gear shipped in to re-right the fallen DropShip, but the ship could be saved. Two deaths had been reported from its toppling, and dozens of injuries from minor to major, but overall, it could have been a lot worse. The tension Danai sensed on the ground, though, didn't come from the DropShip situation, or even their beating on the minefield.

It came, she was sure, from the unknown.

The insurgency's sudden quiet in the past weeks had unsettled the people on the ground. Danai felt it too. That there was yet some bigger gambit in the wings.

That generalized anxiety of Cade's next move only grew when Wu pounded on the door to her quarters. *"Sang-shao!"*

"Yes, Wu, come in."

The short man burst in, holding a holovid cube. Danai couldn't read his exact expression—anger? Fear?

"You need to see this." He placed the cube on her tiny, cluttered desk and activated it.

The image beaming up from the cube offered a slow, panning view of smoking ruins and rubble.

Danai frowned. "What am I looking at?"

"Rainspire," Wu said. "What's left of it."

Her initial reaction was confusion. The holovid's projection showed the urban remains of what appeared to be an orbital bombardment, and she had not requested any such action.

That initial confusion suddenly vanished as Danai realized she *had* in fact requested action, just not in the form she stared at now on her desk.

Draco. The Prizrak.

Danai knew her regiment's loadout well. She had a firm grasp on the Third Chargers' as well. What she hadn't considered was that the BattleMechs in her regiment would be appropriated by Draco and her ghost squad.

Even as the holovid revealed them, Danai scarcely grasped was she was witnessing: two 100-ton BattleMechs, the pinnacle of Liao technology. "The *Pillager*s..."

"Yes, *Sang-shao.*"

*Pillager*s were among the largest BattleMech ever fielded, designed expressly to assault urban centers and hardened fortifications.

Danai slowly rose, hands flat on the desk, looking down on the holovid image now as if such an angle would reduce the carnage it displayed. Block after block, buildings were reduced to rubble. Vehicles burned on streets littered with trash and bodies.

"Survivors?"

"We can look, but this is at least a full square kilometer of damage—"

In a rare loss of control, Danai swiped the cube from her desk and smashed it to the floor. "Then *look!* I want every available body kitted up and ready to roll to Rainspire in five minutes. And every medic, every doctor, every engineer. Food, water, blankets, everything."

Wu blinked. "Yes, *Sang-shao.*"

"Where is Draco now?"

"On their way back."

"Radio ahead, stop them immediately. What's the fastest way from here to Rainspire?"

"Fastest?" Wu repeated. "We have fast hovers, but traveling overland by BattleMech is safer and more direct. But—"

"Then that's how we're going. Vehicles can bring up the rear. Get going."

Wu braced quickly, and left the small room with all haste.

Danai stared at the holovid, still projecting from the floor. The vid had not yet started over. The roving camera which had recorded the vid still moved through Rainspire's streets, capturing its destruction.

Chest aching with fury, Danai snapped off the vid and lurched from her cabin to get to *Julian.*

She had to see for herself.

RAINSPIRE
SHERATAN
20 FEBRUARY 3151

This was not Danai's first battlefield, and it would not be her last, but the ruins of these city blocks in Rainspire made her stomach tighten.

Smoke rose in thick columns, billowing into the sunny morning sky. Distant moans and screams of the dying and their beloved echoed through the tall rubble like banshee wails. Buildings lay crumbled into jagged pieces of ferrocrete and rebar. She smelled the charred odor of a dozen different types of fires.

What have you done? Danai thought, but couldn't say which *who* she was referring to.

She'd arrived first, with only Wu and a lance of guardian 'Mechs coming along as she smashed through woods to reach Rainspire. Behind her by perhaps twenty minutes, nearly a regiment's worth of additional 'Mechs were following her trail-blazed path, while tracked, wheeled, and hovercraft vehicles were being loaded with supplies, and would soon also be on the roads toward the city.

For now, Danai was first on-scene. *Julian* stood parked just at the city limits. On her distracted order, two light 'Mechs and her security detail followed behind her by about a hundred meters as she picked her way through the rubble. Wu, also on her order, stayed behind to organize the incoming 'Mechs and vehicles into search and rescue teams.

She hadn't found Draco yet, nor any sign of the *Pillager*s. Wu had said they were on their way back to LZ Bravo, but currently, Draco and whoever was with her were on radio silence.

Danai's heart felt frozen in her chest. Not only was this destruction far from what she had intended and ordered...she now began to accept the truth of what must have happened.

This had to be the work of the Maskirovka.

At least two members of the Prizrak had willfully gone against her explicit instructions. Bad enough. That they'd walked 200 tons of devastating BattleMech machinery straight out of the LZ and perpetrated this scorched-earth assault on Rainspire? That required an endless litany of notifications, and therefore, coverups.

Enough such that she, *sang-shao* of Second MAC, had not heard a whisper about it until it was over. Not her, not Wu, not Ross.

But the Mask did not act unilaterally. They also followed orders. What confluence of the Prizrak, Mask, and House Liao had conspired to perpetrate this destruction, Danai didn't know. Not now, and—she realized with growing rage—maybe not ever.

Danai walked slowly down a side road, her steps muffled by scraps of paper and torn sheets of cloth. Curtains, perhaps, or clothing. Her guard detail stayed close, but not too close, as if sensing her mood. She walked for twenty minutes, aimless, stunned by the amount of damage done to this large corner of the town.

She did not stop until reaching a four-way intersection, at the center of which stood a tall pine tree. The tree was surrounded by a short brick wall of the sort that might host afternoon family lunches while children played beneath the boughs.

And it was on fire.

Despite having passed multiple blazes to reach the tree, one woman stood near it with a garden hose tapped into a nearby building, spraying the tree down with water.

As she watched, awed, Danai saw other townspeople arriving with tall ladders and buckets. An absurd brigade began, with old and young alike doing everything in their power to quench the flames. None of them seemed to notice her, none of them realized she wore the uniform of their enemy. The civilians were far too intent on saving the tree rooted in this intersection.

Danai backed away, leaving them to their fight. When she turned the nearest corner, she broke into a run.

She didn't stop until she reached her *Black Knight*. Most of the Third Chargers and Second MAC 'Mechs had arrived, with a few slower, heavier models trickling in. She scanned the assembled war machines before her gaze landed on one of the two *Pillager*s tasked to Ross' regiment.

Standing at its feet, leaning against the leg, was Draco.

Danai stalked to the woman, fingers itching to curl and throw a punch. Draco seemed to catch the intensity in Danai's march, and pushed herself off the leg of her BattleMech.

She also turned her body slightly, as if preparing for a brawl.

Somehow Danai kept her hands to herself as she raced up the Prizrak agent, almost nose-to-nose. "You leveled this city." She barely recognized her own voice.

"As ordered," Draco said in a neutral tone, eyes locked on Danai's.

"I never ordered you to reduce an entire city to rubble!"

Draco kept her voice low. "Pardon, Your Grace, but you were quite clear. 'Make them pay.' They have paid. Moreover, they've lost resources, hiding places, caches, personnel—"

"*Personnel?* Those are civilians we'll find buried there! *Liao* civilians. Those people were *Capellan.*"

For the first time since she'd met the operator, Danai saw an actual expression flit across Draco's eyes. Shockingly, it may have been pity.

"No, Your Grace," she said slowly. "You may wish to think they were, but they weren't. They were Sheratans. And they will stay Sheratans or die. I assumed you understood that point."

"You deliberately broke my rules of engagement!" Danai said between clenched teeth. "'No battle shall be waged in an urban area except under extreme circumstances. If the military objective of an assault lies in a city center, attacking troops must ensure that any hostile action taken causes the least possible amount of collateral damage. No attack may be made against any civilian target, for any reason.' Which part of those rules did you misunderstand?"

Draco met Danai's eyes impassively. Even now, despite her rage, the arctic glint in them chilled even Danai's veteran blood.

"I was given an order by my commanding officer, *Sang-shao* Danai Centrella-Liao," Draco said calmly, "'make them suffer.' I followed it."

"I did *not* tell you *to lay waste to this city!*"

"All due respect, ma'am...you wanted revenge. I've given it to you. To speak freely, I've done what *Sang-shao* Rossetti should have done from the outset."

Danai stepped even closer into Draco's face. Her voice dropped to a fearful pitch. "I did not give you permission to speak freely, and I *did not* order the destruction of this town.

Take your ghosts and go back to your ship and damn well stay there until relieved."

If confinement to quarters—never mind Danai's tone—had any impact on Draco, the young woman didn't show it. It was all just another glorious day in the corps. She said, "Yes, ma'am," before executing a razor-sharp Capellan about-face and marching down the nearest road out of Rainspire.

Faintly, she heard Wu urging a gathering crowd to move along. Danai fought an urge to run her hands over her pulled-back hair. Such a gesture would have publicly shown more frustration than she wished, so with an effort, she kept her hands at her sides.

She did allow herself a few deep breaths to get centered before turning and calling to Wu.

He raced up to her.

"Wu," she said, as steadily as she could muster, "gather everyone over there. Beneath *Julian*. I wish to speak to them."

Wu nodded and bolted.

Danai hiked carefully up *Julian*'s chain-link ladder as Wu sent orders to the troops. By the time she had reached the cockpit and stood upon the command couch, the canopy open, Wu had assembled most of the regiment below.

Hundreds of warriors stood looking up at their leader, awaiting her orders.

"Third Chargers," she called to the assembled Capellans. "Second MAC. Listen up. I want twenty-four-hour work crews. Every person here is on a twelve-hour shift starting now. Including me. This is our mess. We are cleaning it up. I want triage up immediately, and all wounded are to be accorded full care and protection as Capellan citizens."

She nearly added, *Is that understood?* But her mood was so foul she decided anyone not following these simple instructions would simply pay a price later. Based on their expressions, there was no misunderstanding.

Instead, she merely barked, "Go!" and her people scattered to work.

Danai lifted her gaze to again face the destruction of what had been Rainspire. Small fires sent plumes of gray smoke into the humid air. Not far away, someone cried for help.

From this height, she could see the entire town was not wasted; the Prizrak had decimated perhaps 20 or 30 percent of it.

She's right, you know, Danai thought as her soldiers got organized beneath her. *This is your mess, Danai. Clean it up.*

Danai Centrella-Liao, Duchess of Castrovia, climbed down from her improvised dais and literally rolled up her sleeves as she marched into what remained of Rainspire to start digging through rubble.

Two hours later, she found Colonel Jack Cade cradling what was left of Major Cordelia Norfolk in his arms.

CHAPTER 34

RAINSPIRE
SHERATAN
20 FEBRUARY 3151

Jack Cade was unarmed, so far as Danai could see. He wore no sidearm, at any rate, and she saw no rifle, blade, or other weapon within arm's reach.

Neither was the little girl in his arms wearing any visible weaponry. Beneath the concrete dust blanketing her body, Cordelia wore a red dress and black leggings. Only after another moment did Danai realize her leggings were not leggings at all, but the child's blackened skin.

One of her blond braids had been scorched clean off, the ragged end burned black near her ear. Cade appeared to have just found the little girl's body. Danai could not tell what the building had once been; perhaps a pub. He sat cross-legged, with Cordelia held in his arms, staring down at her closed eyes.

Swallowing something bitter in her throat, Danai said, "Cade."

The man didn't move. He didn't speak. Danai wrestled with an apology, yet all the variations were insipid and wrong. This was a war, after all. And standing there looking down at Cade, at Cordelia, she knew what had to happen now.

Danai was forced to clear her throat before she spoke again. "We have an accounting of every BattleMech of yours we've encountered so far. Signatures for each one. You will bring them here, right here, all of them, in the next six hours—"

She licked her lips, and tasted dust.

"Or we'll return and finish the job."

Cade shook his head slowly before she'd even finished. "No."

"You'll lose."

"We'll fight. I've already lost."

"Cade."

At last, he looked at her. She knew the expression all too well.

Danai unholstered her sidearm and let it dangle heavily at her thigh. "I'm going to say this for the last time, and then I'm giving the order. Surrender everything, absolutely everything, in the next six hours, or I will burn the rest of this city to the ground."

This time Cade hesitated.

Only, though, for a moment.

"No."

The silence between them hung heavier than sharpened steel. Danai stared into the man's eyes, searching for some scrap of weakness in his resolve. Anything to change her mind.

She saw only darkness. Darkness, and hopelessness. Cade wasn't afraid to die; he was afraid to quit. So he would not. None of them would.

In the silence, Danai's military mind began to whisper, and she at last listened. To end the insurgency—the destruction—required a new tactic. The very one she was still loathe to pursue, and yet...

"Understood," she stated.

Danai shot Cade in the forehead.

His eyes remained open and fixed as a tremor rocketed through his body just before he fell atop Cordelia. There was little blood.

Danai looked down at her holster as she'd been drilled so many years—eons—ago. According to her trainers, *If there's so much happening that you can't stop to look at your holster, the battle ain't over.*

She put the weapon away, turned on her heel, and walked to her stunned security entourage. "Tell the Mask agents to send armed teams to let the city know that in thirty minutes, every BattleMech in these two regiments will lay waste to every building in sight. Energy weapons only, save your ammunition. Thirty minutes to pack up and get the hell out of here and live. If they want. Otherwise, they're welcome to stay here and die."

Sang-shao Danai Centrella-Liao gave the smoldering city one glance over her shoulder. Her chest ached deep within as, keeping her expression steady, she added:

"Raze it."

CHAPTER 35

SECOND MAC LZ ALPHA
OUTSIDE RAINSPIRE
SHERATAN
17 MARCH 3151

Danai sat on the edge of her fold-out cot, hands clasped between her knees, head bowed, hair loose and hanging free. She couldn't remember the last time she'd wept, and the knowledge made her want to. She welcomed it, wished for it, yearned for the cleanse that came with honest-to-god, stomach-heaving tears.

None came.

She also—if she'd been paying attention—didn't know how long it'd been since she blinked. Danai's gaze was soft and unfocused, a bit of boot smudge on the floor acting as a focal point.

What, she thought over and over and over again, *the hell am I doing?*

She fought mightily to ignore the constant response: *Winning.*

Winning the wars, she thought. *Doing what is right for the nation, for the Capellan people. Protecting them. Providing them security to live their lives.*

Sheratan had been well in-hand until Jack Cade whipped up a furor to satisfy his own pride.

Hell, I would have hired him and all his people as mercs if given a chance.

Outside her own DropShip, which with the rest of the Third Chargers and Second MAC had relocated back to the crater, work continued to raise the fallen DropShip from the hole in the ground blown open by Cade's insurgents. Insurgents who now, to the best of Danai's or anyone else's knowledge, no longer existed. Either they were dead in the *Pillager* attack, dead in the decimation that followed, or had left Rainspire in time to save their own lives—and probably not much else.

In the near-month since the destruction of Rainspire, there'd been no further raids, no attacks of any kind. The full might of the Third Chargers and Second MAC had followed orders and leveled the entire town. The celebrations in Daggaknott came to an abrupt end, and talk of rebellion ceased. During the assault on Rainspire, the Capellans had uncovered numerous caches of weapons and equipment. In the days following, patrols found most, if not all of Cade's 'Mechs, in groups of two or three here and there, camouflaged in the forests. Danai and the Maskirovka agents attached to Sheratan still had no clear idea who their MechWarriors had been; smart money was on Republic of the Sphere veterans, but Danai had misgivings about that theory. The Rotters had occupied Sheratan until they fled back behind their Wall. She didn't think Cade was among their ranks. He hadn't behaved like an RAF soldier.

She didn't care anymore. Her job had once again slowed to an ongoing crush of paperwork and briefings.

Then there was the Mask itself, and the Prizrak. She'd managed to confirm Draco was the source of forged orders and misdirected tasks that led to the initial attack on Rainspire, such that most of the people involved were not willing cogs in an insubordinate shadow command subverting her authority. That's what passed for good news lately. Where Draco had gotten the "idea"—or orders—to attack, Danai did not yet know.

A delightful fact that often kept sleep at bay.

Guilt and simmering rage shared her thoughts equally in the ensuing weeks since the assault. She'd never wanted to bring this sort of destruction to Sheraton; but in order to end the insurgency, she had to make her point to the locals.

Well, they understand now, Danai thought with equal parts shame and resignation. *Sheratan is ours.*

She longed for Castrovia. Wanted to see how Tiko was doing. With things now quiet here, she knew she could send herself right back to her swanky palace and put the destruction of Rainspire behind her.

But she couldn't bring her herself to go without Noah, and she didn't want to face Tiko. Noah, still unresponsive, had been transported back to Liao for proper care weeks ago. He'd be there for some time, doctors told her. When one of the physicians had gently offered the option of letting him go, peacefully, Danai's hateful glare had sent him scurrying.

Meanwhile, the thought of trying to play with a child like Tiko made Danai's stomach curdle. She had, of course, done necessarily horrible things prior to meeting the little boy. Somehow, though, the fresh blood of Sheratan, particularly that of the defiant "Major" Cordelia, made her feel tainted. Not the sort of person who ought to be playing football with a bunch of kids.

So Danai stayed on Sheratan, gave orders, and watched the Capellan army do its job with its usual professionalism.

One more world for the Celestial Wisdom, she thought, and scrubbed her fingertips through her hair.

Someone knocked on her door.

"Who is it?"

"Wu."

"Oh. Come in."

Wu opened the door, but rather than step inside, he merely reached out to set a holovid cube on her desk and quickly pulled himself back past the threshold again. "Message from the Chancellor," he said, and briskly closed the door.

Daoshen? Danai thought. She hadn't heard directly from him in...well, that was a good question. She couldn't recall. Her officers routinely sent briefs back to Liao as transports allowed, and she received intelligence briefs on the state of the Confederation military machine.

But a direct message from Daoshen? That had been a long, long while. September...last year? No, 3149. So almost a year and a half since she'd been in his presence.

Hating how nervous she'd become at Wu's mere reference to Daoshen, Danai flicked on the cube.

"My dear sister," the electric image of Daoshen said, seated on a throne Danai did not recognize. *"Congratulations on your work on Sheratan. We are most pleased. In fact, I would like to extend my thanks to you personally, here on Keid."*

Keid? Danai thought. *What is he doing there?*

"Your continued excellence on the battlefield will be of great use here," Daoshen's recording went on. *"And I have a gift for you as well. Upon receiving this message, make all haste for our headquarters on Keid. Keep your garrison on Sheratan for the moment. They will have further orders soon enough.*

"I look forward to seeing you, Danai."

The recording stopped.

Danai stared at the blank face of the holovid cube, eyes narrowing. *What are you up to now, Daoshen? What?*

Keid had fallen to the Capellans just over a year ago, and of late, it had suffered a variety of acts of sabotage, along with several other worlds. That should have been reason enough for Daoshen to stay put on Liao, if not Sian, ensconced in his most secure buildings.

Arrogance, then, she thought bitterly. *He wants the Republic to know he's unafraid of them, unafraid to move closer to the front line.*

And perhaps with good reason, Danai's military mind suggested. Despite the difficult days she and the Second MAC had experienced on Liberty, Hall, and Sheratan, the lines on the map didn't lie. House Liao had made great gains in the past few years, while the Republic of the Sphere had steadily lost worlds. The closer House Liao got to Terra, the closer Daoshen would want to be to issue commands that could reach the army with much more speed.

Restless now, Danai flung the cube into her desk drawer, slapping it shut. She pulled one of her blades from its sheath and began drawing her sharpening stone against it.

She vividly recalled her last face-to-face meeting with Xavier McCarron, nearly two years ago. The theory he voiced then, in private with her, was now a common idea among the Strategios: Republic Forces were marshaling on Terra. The Republic Navy, dozens of potential regiments...whatever the RAF was building, the Capellans could only guess.

A last stand, Danai imagined. Daoshen had made clear the resources still ensconced on Terra would tip the balance of any house who held it. Cutting-edge technology, natural resources, caches of armaments, massive manufacturing capability—a treasure trove for any military. Xavier had even said as much to her on Liao: "The riches to be found among the corpses of the Star League and the Word of Blake and the Republic are worth claiming."

She hadn't disagreed with him.

Now, as she'd had time to ponder the point, Danai's way of thinking carried the goal of the conquest of Terra to another, deeper motivation. Xavier had spoken true, perhaps, but the spoils of Terra were dwarfed by the thing that really started and carried on any warfare:

Spirit.

Another word might be ego, but Danai dismissed it. Not that the people responsible for these battles near Terra weren't egocentric; of course they were. You had to have a touch of arrogance to be a MechWarrior, never mind the leader of people.

Or duchess, she reminded herself.

But no, possessing Terra was not about ego or even pride. The desire for Terra spoke to something more primal. A calling of sorts to the birthplace of all humanity, the precious and small blue world responsible for every lofty achievement and every hellish degradation the known universe had experienced.

Danai could admit—if only to herself—it was a heady notion. She understood and appreciated Terra's military value, but it was the system's very essence that drew warriors to its conquest.

Daoshen, the Republic, the Clans.

They thirsted for Terra...*because it was Terra.*

That lust, however, was not a battle plan. Desire fueled a great many achievements, but a BattleMech regiment could readily quench desire. Just ask Jack Cade.

Yes, Danai thought, *Terra is the goal, and it is a worthy goal. But not at the cost of the entire Confederation.*

Warriors across millennia had fought for the spirit of a place. In the name of a person, or for the sake of a plot of land otherwise worthless. To fight, bleed, and die on soil of no resourceful value was folly, yet it had doomed trillions over eons of humanity's history.

Terra was no different.

Danai ran the sharpening stone across her knife. She was a MechWarrior, and like all her warrior siblings across the Inner Sphere, she savored battle and relished victory.

Dying for someone's arrogant dream, however, was not an idea she cherished. Nor would she risk the lives of her subordinates in pursuit of it.

Even when the order comes from the Celestial Wisdom himself, as it's sure to do?

Well, some bridges were best crossed upon arrival. Whatever Daoshen's motives, there was no denying the order.

Danai summoned Wu back to her quarters to begin her preparation for leaving for Liao and gave the sharpening stone one last flourish against the blade.

Its razor edge gleamed.

PART 3

CHAPTER 36

NORMANDY
KEID
CAPELLAN CONFEDERATION
17 MARCH 3151

Robie admired *Jiang-jun* Tianzhu Liu. The commander of the Death Commandos came to his position naturally, as a calculating man of impeccable tactical prowess. The Death Commandos served as the CCAF's most elite troops, excelling in all aspects of warfare, from intelligence and counterintelligence to small-unit tactics and large-scale invasions.

As the commander entered the chamber, Robie took note of the excellence of his appearance. Not that Capellan soldiers of any rank or mission were prone to mistakes in dress uniforms, certainly not, but something in Liu's bearing gave his green uniform an impeccable crispness she'd rarely seen in other soldiers.

Attention to detail, she thought. *This man is a professional among professionals. Elite among elite. Watch him closely.*

Liu bowed to Daoshen. The Chancellor gestured gracefully toward the conference table, and Liu took a seat.

Daoshen's hands disappeared into the drooping sleeves of his golden robe. Robie stood still near an onyx pillar, hands behind her back, but not at parade rest. She willed herself into a state of being utterly inconspicuous. The general, she noted, had not so much as flicked an eye in her direction. Mission accomplished.

"*Sang-shao* Centrella-Liao has experienced considerable success on the battlefield," Daoshen said.

Robie heard the testing notes in his voice. He wanted to see what Liu thought. *Or rather, no—not what he thinks, but how he would respond.*

Liu's response came immediately. "Yes, I agree, Celestial Wisdom. Her gains have been impressive, and I must say, unsurprising."

Robie reviewed her known information about Danai Centrella-Liao. Liu was right; Danai's reputation as a MechWarrior and battlefield commander was well-earned.

So why was Daoshen talking about her to Liu? The Duchess of Castrovia was due to arrive soon, ferried here by the fastest means available. Though for what express purpose, Robie could not yet say—to herself or her superiors in the Maskirovka, a fact they disliked.

Daoshen, rather than sitting on his throne, paced softly around the conference table. "It is time her tactical prowess is put to use on a broader scale."

Liu nodded once, slowly. Robie could tell he was trying to assess where this meeting was headed. He didn't seem to realize the duchess was on her way here.

She shared his curiosity.

"Do you feel she is capable of such a task?" Daoshen asked. "Is my sister prepared to take a larger role in our campaign for the liberation of Terra?"

"Certainly," Liu replied cautiously. "Though I am curious what larger role or broader scale the Celestial Wisdom is referring to, precisely."

"Would you say," Daoshen said, coming to a stop at the far end of the table from Liu, "that Danai has the full support of her Second MAC regiment?"

"Yes, I would. Her people are fanatically loyal."

"And what of the rest of McCarron's Armored Cavalry? How do those regiments view my sister?"

Liu took a moment. Robie watched him processing the conversation. Daoshen watched him as well, his expression its normal inscrutable blank.

Robie mentally hurried to put the puzzle pieces into their proper place. Daoshen needed no human's approval for anything at all. He reigned supreme over all Capellan space. To a limited degree—perhaps a cosmetic degree—he was beholden to the House of Scions. That body of royal title-holders was largely decorative of late. With the might of the CCAF, the Death Commandos, and McCarron's Armored Cavalry, of which his sister Danai ran the Second regiment, Daoshen was unassailable in his control over the entire, vast Confederation. A Confederation growing larger almost by the day with the successful liberations of worlds like Liberty, Keid, Procyon, Hall, Epsilon Indi...

Why, then, bring in his Death Commando leader for a chit-chat about Danai that sounded suspiciously close to asking the *jiang-jun*'s permission?

"I think it is safe to say Danai has the full support and admiration of the entire McCarron's Armored Cavalry, Celestial Wisdom," Liu answered.

Robie noted the shift in Liu's posture. The old veteran had tensed. The movement was slight, nearly imperceptible, but she'd been trained by the very best to see such shifts.

Liu was growing uncomfortable. Robie had seen this in every person who stood before the Chancellor—a small but visible tension, a discomfort suggesting incipient nausea.

Robie herself had never experienced the sensation.

True, she had been somewhat awed to be in Daoshen's presence when she first met him. But the awe had passed quickly. Her training had been thorough. She was there to protect the office of the Chancellor, and the entire people of the Capellan Confederation. There was neither time nor need to be put off by the power radiating from Daoshen's presence.

"McCarron's has recently suffered many upsets," Daoshen said, resuming his leisurely walk around the table. He did not look at anyone in the room; rather, he seemed to be lost in thought, musing.

Robie didn't believe it. He was not making this conversation up as he went.

She caught Liu shifting again in his plush leather seat.

"As a result," Daoshen continued, "we fear the entire MAC may be less than effective in the battles yet to come. A fighting force of such size, power, and prestige requires...a loyal, guiding hand."

Liu offered another slow nod, clearly buying time. "Yes, Chancellor."

"I have decided we will name Danai as *Jiang-jun* of McCarron's Armored Cavalry."

Liu seemed to take this announcement in stride. Robie detected no additional tension in the man. "A wise choice, Chancellor. Though, the MAC has never before had a *jiang-jun*."

Liu's statement was correct: while Xavier McCarron had been the de facto leader of the unit named after his ancestor, he had not actually held a rank bestowing command over every element of the five extant regiments. With the rank and title of *jiang-jun*, Danai would be on equal footing with Liu—a general, ranking above Xavier McCarron himself.

Robie couldn't see why Liu would have any problem with this, and clearly, the general gave no indication that he disagreed with the Chancellor's decree in any way. Xavier, on the other hand, would not take this pronouncement in stride. Might he even threaten to leave the CCAF and return his troops to mercenary status? Perhaps, but the entire MAC had formally joined the CCAF ages ago. Legally, breaking the MAC away from the Confederation would be mutiny. The risk of mutiny was death.

Unless, Robie thought, admiring Daoshen's political prowess, *installing a respected leader from the ranks of MAC, like Danai, would quell any mutinous element before it began.*

"When Danai arrives," Daoshen said, "she will need assistance getting accustomed to her new role. We ask for your aid in this transition period, and to keep us apprised of any difficulties she may encounter."

Ah, Robie thought. *And now the truth is laid bare.*

Daoshen wanted Danai close at hand.

Or perhaps a better way to put it: under his heel.

As *jiang-jun*, she would no longer be on the battlefield. She would be here, not far from Daoshen's very presence, whether on Keid, Liao—or Terra. But while the Chancellor had the authority to merely order her to Liao and keep her there indefinitely, Robie understood there were protocols—optics— that needed tending to. Simply ordering his sister to stay on Liao and out of combat would raise eyebrows. Promoting her to general and bringing her closer into the large-scale planning of war operations would make perfect sense to any Capellan, from the lowest servitor to Liu himself.

Robie also parsed the meaning of Daoshen's request: Liu would now function as a spy. The Chancellor wanted tabs kept on his sister, and a like-ranked officer would have access to Danai in ways no other trusted Capellan would.

Daoshen and Danai are at odds, Robie thought. *Which, all things considered, makes perfect sense. And Daoshen has been Chancellor long enough to understand one of the oldest maxims of warfare: Keep your friends close and your enemies closer.*

Thus, to Daoshen's way of thinking, Robie realized, *Danai Centrella-Liao, Duchess of Castrovia, is his* enemy*?*

Robie again admired Liu as he spoke, "I'm sure the *jiang-jun* will have no problem adapting to her new role."

Daoshen turned his face to the general. The eyes of the Celestial Wisdom narrowed only slightly.

Silence crept through the conference room on dangerous feet. The two men let it grow until Liu finally capitulated by mildly clearing his throat.

"Of course," he added, as if there had not just been a monumental pause, "I will do everything in my power to ease her transition, and will immediately report any difficulties directly to...you, Chancellor?"

"Yes," Daoshen said, and the tightness around his eyes eased. Liu had placated him.

"When will the announcement be made public, Your Grace?" Liu asked, rising from his seat.

Daoshen returned to his dais throne, similar to the one he'd left back on Liao. He sat upon it like a great bird of prey. "Not until after the executions."

Robie tensed.

Liu also reacted visibly. "Executions, Your Grace?"

Daoshen turned to one of his servants, who stood as silent and invisible as Robie herself. The tall man with the facial scar, Guanken, hurried to a side door and opened it with a bow.

Two members of the Maskirovka entered swiftly and stood at attention near the conference table.

"Report," Daoshen said, as if bored.

"He is in custody on Liao," the shorter of the two agents said.

"Who is in custody?" Liu blurted, the first loss of composure Robie had seen him exhibit.

Daoshen took a slow, deep breath and let his gaze drift to the ceiling. Golden veins wove through the white marble, and Robie wondered if he missed the enormous skylight of his prime conference room on Liao. He seemed for all the world to be looking right through the marble.

"The failures of the Fourth and Fifth MAC on Northwind are inexcusable," Daoshen replied. "They have cost us precious lives, matériel, and perhaps worst of all, time. Xavier McCarron has been removed from command and imprisoned to await trial for his failures on Northwind and Liberty."

The two Mask agents bowed and exited the room as quickly as they had entered it. Guanken closed the door behind them and returned silently to his post against the far wall.

Liu's expression shifted to one of stunned dismay. "Xavier McCarron? Your Grace, I—"

"*Jiang-jun* Liu," Daoshen interrupted easily. "See to it in your own ranks that anyone dissenting of this action or supporting Xavier McCarron will suffer his fate."

Robie ticked off no more than two seconds before Liu replied, "Yes, Your Grace. I should also see to *Jiang-jun* Centrella-Liao's arrival."

"Good," Daoshen said, and seemed to settle further into his throne. "Good."

CHAPTER 37

Danai sat with her legs crossed, one elbow on the armrest to her left, gazing out the window of the maglev train transporting her and her entourage to Normandy. She kept a loose fist in front of her mouth to conceal how her jaw clenched, though no one sat with her in the luxury cabin.

Keid—or this part of it, at any rate—was not a particularly beautiful world. Pollution from mining and agricultural concerns seemed to dim an otherwise bright blue sky, though she guessed that might've been her imagination, influenced by her mood. Outside the window, the environment was fairly flat and nondescript, with occasional fields reminding her of Sheratan, and making her look away to study the high-end trappings of her luxury train cabin instead. These trappings—small fine art, silk cushions, a crystal chandelier—aggravated her too, so she would turn to look back out the window again.

Normandy looked like many other cities she'd visited during her tenure in the Capellan military. Even the presence of so many military vehicles on the roads came as nothing new. Capellan worlds or otherwise, they all had a similarity to them. Decoratively they differed, but humans tended to build up. Large cities like this were dominated by skyscrapers, which Danai could see in the distance, and which grew larger as the maglev approached downtown.

She'd been in this cycle of alternating her gaze out the window to the inside of the cabin for ten minutes when a soft chime rang.

"Enter."

It was Wu. Her XO entered the cabin under the watchful eye of guards not her own, dressed in the royal green of Daoshen's personal body detail. Her own detail was in the same train car, but further away than those assigned by Daoshen.

"Why do I feel like I'm under guard?" Danai said, not concealing her irritation—but waiting until Wu closed the door to speak.

Wu didn't seem to hear. He sat down on a couch opposite her and reached out with a tablet in his hand. "I hope Noah gets better soon, because I'm beginning to not like this job."

Danai took the pad, giving Wu a questioning glance. He was joking, but his words carried a heavy weight. She kept tabs on Noah Capshaw's progress, and while he'd regained consciousness, he was largely confined to bed, and would soon begin physical therapy.

She looked at the screen. Read its contents. Blinked, read them again. Then shot a sharp look at her XO. "This can't be right."

Wu nodded. "I thought the same, but no. It's true. Hasn't hit the public yet through the official channels, but it will soon."

Danai turned back to the tablet, scanning the report, her amazement and disquiet growing with each word she read.

Xavier McCarron was dead.

"Executed..." Danai breathed as she read the internal missive.

Sang-shao McCarron, blood relation to the founder of McCarron's Armored Cavalry, had been put to death by order of the Capellan Chancellor, Celestial Wisdom Daoshen Liao, for military failures—dereliction of duty, according to the missive. Not only that, *Sang-shao* Gwendolyn Vaughan of the Fifth MAC had spoken out against the sentence, and been summarily arrested, tried, and executed as well.

Danai pressed one palm against her forehead. She had a sudden headache.

"Xavier and Gwen," she said, as if Wu had not read the report already. "Over Northwind?"

"That's the official word, ma'am. And the loss of Liberty after we liberated it. It's since been retaken, but..."

Danai noted the deliberately neutral tone Wu opted to use. She looked at him. "And if *I'd* lost Liberty? What then?"

"Forgive me, but I'm not about to conjecture on that, ma'am."

Danai slapped the tablet down on the cushion beside her. "This is about Terra. This is about the *messaging* over Terra. Xavier didn't agree with Daoshen's intent to take it. Daoshen needed an example set. A big one, but not one that might cripple or slow the Strategios. He couldn't make an example of one of those Strategios officers—plus, they're aligned with his way of thinking. I doubt any have voiced disagreement over his plans."

Wu raised an eyebrow. "You didn't finish the report, ma'am."

Scowling, Danai fetched the tablet back. "What else?" It took another half-minute of reading to see what Wu meant. When she read it, she lifted her eyes to his as her mouth slowly fell open. "I don't believe it..."

"That explains the shift in guard detail," Wu said, gesturing to the closed cabin door. "I suppose I should say congratulations?"

Danai's stomach lurched sideways as the reality of her promotion sank in. "*Jiang-jun*," she muttered. "Senior General of the entire McCarron's Armored Cavalry."

"I don't recall you ever having such lofty aspirations," Wu said.

Danai only shook her head as she mentally scrambled to sort out Daoshen's goal. The timing of her orders to Keid... Daoshen's abrupt and public shaming of Xavier...his execution and her promotion...

Unbidden, Danai's brain did the math for her: *Daoshen knew.*

He knew exactly what he was going to do long before he did it. As always. He'd brought her back because he'd known he was going to promote her, known he was going to remove McCarron.

Xavier McCarron was dead long before his execution.

Danai crumpled against the couch, holding her abdomen as if gut-shot.

Is Daoshen really as angry as he appears to be over Northwind? Her mind whirled. *Yes, it was a terrible loss to House Liao, I don't deny that, but...what if Northwind had been a success? Would there have been some other imaginary slight that would have gotten McCarron killed and me made* jiang-jun?

She brought her free hand to her mouth.

No one is safe from Daoshen. And that means all of House Liao is at risk.

The failure at Northwind, while disruptive, did not call for the killing of a CCAF officer of Xavier's standing. Daoshen simply wanted no dissension among the ranks during his reckless quest for Terra.

Is that because, Danai wondered, *he has further plans that might raise such dissension?*

"We're slowing," Wu said, almost startling her. "We must nearly be in the city center. Is there anything I can do for you, *Jiang-jun?*"

Danai snapped her eyes back to his again. Wu offered the mildest of shrugs.

"You must get used to it," he stated. *"Jiang-jun."*

"Do you want Second MAC?" Danai asked suddenly, before she'd even thought to consider the question.

"Yes," Wu said immediately, and added, "but also, I'm not so sure. Not right now."

Danai nodded her understanding. The rank of *sang-shao* would put him one step closer to the Chancellor's office. Wu, while an outstanding warrior, leader, and officer, was not a politician.

Danai didn't begrudge his hesitancy.

As the maglev gently slowed beneath them, she said, "Think about it. There's no one better to take over."

"If you order me, I'll do it," Wu said. "But maybe we'd better wait a bit, see how all this plays out."

"Right," Danai said. "How it all plays out..."

She was curious about that herself.

Wu stood. "May I speak plainly?"

Danai nodded once.

"I'm scared, ma'am," Wu stated, emotionless. "There's something in the wind. Do you feel it?"

Danai nodded again, more slowly this time.

Yes. She felt it deeply.

CHAPTER 38

Zhong-shao Lydia Chen stood with her hands clasped behind her back, looking through her kitchen windows down the short hill at the farmland below. She loved the view, loved this part of Liao. She felt no superiority over the workers harvesting grain down in the field. They were servitors, with a love for the Confederation as deep as Lydia's own.

As deep as it had been until last week, at any rate.

The door to her small home opened without the entrant knocking or announcing their presence. Reflected in the window, she recognized *Sao-wei* Dante Holland, her executive officer, and the closest thing to a friend outside her two older siblings on Sian.

Dante closed the door and walked across Lydia's silk carpets to join her at the windows. She could sense the tension in him without looking.

"So it's over," he said. "The news just went public."

Lydia made no move nor sound.

"We should have stopped it," Dante added. "We should have stopped both."

"Then we would be at war with the entire Capellan Confederation, with no means of support."

"Fine," Dante snarled. "We were mercenaries once, we can be again."

A faint, sad smile touched Lydia's thin, unpainted lips. She could see strands of gray in her black hair in her reflection. "No house in all the Inner Sphere would trust such a shift for McCarron's Armored Cavalry. We may as well make for Solaris and seek our fortunes there."

"That's not the worst idea either, after this."

Lydia turned and used only her steel gaze to gesture to the comfortable appointments in her small house atop the hill. Always of a spartan mindset, Lydia's home consisted of her bedroom and an office, a tiled kitchen and informal dining area, and a small but comfortable area for entertainment, all in an open floorplan. The tiles were marble and exquisite, the carpets silk and tasteful in their colors. Art from well-regarded Capellan fine artists hung on the walls, gifts from superiors in the Strategios.

"Look around, Dante. Look at our lives. We are feared on all battlefields as much as we are cared for here on Liao. Our people were loyal to McCarron, yes, but they are also loyal to their own families. Leaving the Confederation now would risk a lifetime of discomfort few of our number have ever lived. No. No, we will remain the loyal servants, as we always have. For now."

"Have they asked you to assume his place?"

Lydia smirked. "No, nor will they. I feel they have someone else in mind. Someone with stronger ties to the Celestial Wisdom."

"Danai."

Lydia nodded once, slowly, and turned to look down at the field workers once more.

Dante folded his arms and shared her gaze. "She won't accept."

"She will."

Dante took this assertion stoically for a long moment before mimicking Lydia's slow nod. "I would fight for Danai."

"So would we all. And the Celestial Wisdom knows it."

"That doesn't change what his holy damned eminence has just done, Lydia. He killed Xavier and Gwen, recorded it, and sent it by courier to every Capellan world. It's not just the execution—"

"Murder," Lydia corrected softly.

"—Yes, murder. It's not just that, as if that weren't enough, but it was the humiliation. We can't let that stand."

"Dante."

"What."

"You are speaking sedition."

From the corner of her eye, she saw Dante blinking rapidly. "I—well, I...Lydia!"

Hands still clasped, Lydia spun on one heel to face him directly. She stood about 5 centimeters taller, boots or no.

"We belong to House Liao, and to them we have pledged our lives. That is the beginning and the end. Am I understood?"

Dante struggled momentarily before mumbling, "Yes, *Zhong-shao.*"

"Return to your post. We will likely have a lot of paperwork to do very soon when our new general assumes her role."

"You don't think it might be McCarron's son? Cyrus? He might be more suitable than Danai in a lot of ways."

Lydia had a more than passing familiarity with Cyrus McCarron. Not the worst MechWarrior on the field, to be sure, but unsuited to life in court. She believed the Celestial Wisdom would share that conclusion. "I'm sure Cyrus thinks so, but no. It won't be Cyrus. Now go."

Dante frowned, but tipped her a short bow. "Yes, *Zhong-shao.*"

"Dante?"

He paused.

Lydia stepped in closer, close enough that their dress uniform medals touched. She whispered into his ear.

Dante listened carefully, his eyes widening.

Lydia stepped back. Her voice was cool. "Dismissed, *Sao-wei.*"

Her *sao-wei* gaped at her openly, as if forgetting his place. Lydia arched a finely sculpted eyebrow. The gesture seemed to give Dante a shiver, after which he allowed a half grin.

"Understood, *Zhong-shao.*"

He bowed again, deeper this time, and let himself out of her home.

Lydia resumed her scan of the fields, heart thumping madly, as if in the heat of battle.

"For the good of the state," she whispered.

CHAPTER 39

**THE STATE ROOM
CELESTIAL PALACE (TEMPORARY)
NORMANDY
KEID
25 MARCH 3151**

Robie knocked on the door of the Celestial Wisdom's favorite room in the palace of Keid's former planetary governor. Daoshen referred to it as the State Room, a finely dressed space like a banquet hall, with a tall ceiling crisscrossed with fine latticework and stained-glass windows of intricate design where he preferred to conduct most of his official affairs.

Robie didn't like it.

The palace had security in place, of course, but the building lacked certain defenses, countermeasures, and fallbacks afforded the Chancellor in Chang-an. Further, she didn't like the unnecessary expense and risk of moving Daoshen from Liao to Keid in the first place. The move was ego, nothing more. Robie had elected, however, to keep her worries to herself, and focused instead on making Daoshen's travel and accommodations as safe as possible.

When he did not respond to her knocking, Robie let herself in. The armed guards on either side of the tall doors watched her dispassionately. They knew her on sight, and besides, she'd already passed all the identification stations further up the long, ebony-wooded hallway.

But the guards did not know who she was, exactly, which told them everything they needed to know. There were soldiers on the battlefield who wore combat uniforms with no insignia nor rank, and who shoved their way to the front of chow lines. Smart soldiers said nothing of this intrusion. If you were a person who had no identifying marks, you were a person best left alone by the rank and file.

So when they guessed, silently—never spoken or shared with another—that Robie was Maskirovka, chances were excellent they were right.

Robie wore a crimson gown over fitted black tactical pants, cleaned and pressed to mimic having come straight from the shelf. Her straight, red hair was pulled up and held in place with a decorative comb that matched the gold thread inlays of the gown. Her shoes were stout black leather boots with soft soles that made little sound when she walked normally, and none whenever she so chose.

"Celestial Wisdom," she said after closing the door behind her.

Daoshen was alone in the State Room but for Guanken, his personal servant, who stood against a far wall as usual, his gaze slightly averted.

The supreme leader of all Capellan space stood before a three-dimensional holographic rendering of Terra. Robie recognized its blue oceans and distinct continents immediately.

Daoshen gestured her nearer.

"Beautiful," he commented.

Robie bowed. "Exquisite, Your Grace."

"It belongs to House Liao."

"Agreed, Your Grace."

"There can be no dissension on this point, Robie."

"Yes, Your Grace."

"Have you heard any such dissension?"

She did not hesitate. "No, Your Grace. The people are with you."

Daoshen raised his eyebrows, as if neither agreeing nor disagreeing. "A Chancellor's life is always in peril. To lose a Chancellor when we are so close to our dream could be crippling to the Confederation. To the people of Liao, whom you have sworn to serve."

Robie lifted her chin. "I will die to protect this office, Chancellor."

Daoshen offered a mild smile. "Yet you would rather we were not on Keid."

"I will not deny that, Chancellor. Chang-an has greater security, fewer unknowns. All the more so on Sian."

"I had faith in your predecessor, Kamer, and now I have faith in you."

"Thank you, Your Grace."

Daoshen tapped on a keyboard. The image of Terra shifted to one of the world of Hall. "You lost friends on Hall," he murmured. "When Danai was there."

Robie lowered her gaze. "Yes, Celestial Wisdom. Brothers and sisters, of a sort. We in the Mask are quite close."

"An unacceptable loss."

Robie said nothing.

An entire detachment of her fellow Maskirovka agents had been aboard a DropShip on Hall when the landing party was attacked. Their ship had been utterly destroyed. No survivors. It was a dark day for the Liao intelligence community, and one not soon forgotten. Indeed, many plans were already being enacted to extract proper justice for the assault.

Robie was keen to be part of them, but her duty to the office of the Chancellor came first.

"Normally," Daoshen said, gazing at the projected image, "there is no room for base vengeance on the battlefield. But in war, such opportunities sometimes present themselves."

"Indeed, Your Grace."

Daoshen faced her. "I shall soon present you a gift, Robie, for your excellent service. I hope you will like it."

Robie kept her suspicious reaction masked behind a calm smile. "I know I will, Your Grace." She could not fathom what sort of gift he was referring to, but the glint in his eye unnerved her.

Daoshen clicked off the image. "Danai has arrived by train. I would like you to see to her security and comfort personally."

"Begging Your Grace's pardon, my place is at your side. The *jiang-jun* has ample security."

"Who I do not know or trust, not as I trust you. You may return to my side when you are satisfied with her safety."

Robie bowed again. "Yes, Your Grace."

"I will send for her as time permits," Daoshen added, as though just arriving at the thought.

Robie knew better, but pretended otherwise. "I will inform her, Your Grace."

CELESTIAL PALACE (TEMPORARY)
NORMANDY
KEID
28 MARCH 3151

Danai tried to contain her anger, but lately, it was getting harder to do.

She thought she'd grown accustomed to Daoshen's whims and the way he manipulated her time. He wanted to speak with her? Great—but not today. And not tomorrow. Perhaps next week? Perhaps the week after...it all depended.

After all, the Chancellor had a vast kingdom to run and war to execute. Never mind that his blood relation—no matter how tainted—and recently promoted general also had responsibilities to attend to. Oh, no no, her job was to merely wait for his royal summons.

There were many things Danai disliked about Daoshen, but at the moment, this ranked first.

She had been on Keid for three days before finally receiving word that Daoshen was ready to receive her. He'd sent one of his Red Lancers to beckon her from a security briefing at her quarters, a comfortable, single-story home in a tony neighborhood. The home had belonged to a Republic of the Sphere officer who had disappeared, leaving behind a trove of military memorabilia and antiques Danai appreciated.

Danai left Wu behind to finish the briefing. The news was mostly good for the Capellans: Sirius and Caph had both been liberated and returned to the protection of House Liao.

Sheratan remained quiet. More invasions were forthcoming, that much was clear. Danai could not resist a certain pride in the taking of these additional worlds, but that pride came tempered with anxiety.

Daoshen's nonstop push toward Terra continued to worry her. The recent Capellan victories came at the cost of leaving behind garrisons of Home Guard units drawn from the Confederation's rimward territories. As Sheratan so recently proved, even a garrison might not be enough to hold off insurgents, never mind organized invaders. In theory, there were no major powers near enough or powerful enough to invade...but Danai knew better than to trust in theories.

Daoshen Liao had taken up residence in a palatial building once belonging to the former planetary governor. Danai did not ask about the noble's fate; she did not care. But whoever they had been, they'd had excellent taste.

The mansion—now palace—stood on a grassy hill. As her state car pulled up in front of it, a ray of sunlight shone upon the roof as if the universe bestowed its blessing on the Celestial Wisdom.

The sun ray also illuminated armed guards on the rooftop. Three BattleMechs stood at the ready, one each on the right, left, and rear flanks of the house. Additional guards in powered armor lingered on the ground surrounding the three-story mansion.

Danai let herself out when the vehicle stopped. She and the Mask agent assigned to fetch her approached the double white main doors, were checked for clearance by a trio of uniformed Capellan soldiers, and admitted.

Inside, a broad staircase led up into two wings of the house. Additional uniformed guards stood attentive at chokepoints while silk-draped servants swished silently past, headed to whatever tasks they were assigned.

"How long have you been with Daoshen?" Danai asked her primary escort, the Mask agent named Robie Anjing, as they walked briskly down a long corridor toward Danai's meeting with the Chancellor.

"Fifteen months," Robie replied. She kept her gaze focused square ahead at the two guards clearing the way of random Capellan military and office workers.

"How have you found the work?"

"Rewarding."

"Good. That's—good. Daoshen can be—"

Robie glanced at her.

"—demanding," Danai said, and nearly laughed. That wasn't at all the right term, but her relative was not easily summed up in one word.

"*Jiang-jun,*" Robie said after passing a security checkpoint, "when your schedule permits, I would appreciate a private meeting with you. Your insights into the Celestial Wisdom could be very useful to his protection."

They came to a halt outside Daoshen's State Room doors. The guards at the front of the procession stepped aside, pressing their backs into the wall to make room for Danai.

Danai appraised the younger woman. "All right," she said after a pause. "If you think it will help."

"Thank you, *Jiang-jun,*" Robie said, inclining her head. "I'll be here after your appointment to take you home."

Danai nodded. She moved toward the double doors, which were opened for her by the guards, and closed behind her after she passed through. She quickly scanned the large room. Nicely appointed, but not as grandiose as Daoshen's prime conference room on Liao.

The Celestial Wisdom sat on a throne at the head of a large oval table, the throne itself elevated on a short dais. Daoshen wore green robes that shone with an inner light.

"Danai," he called as she approached. "It is good to see you after so long."

She dove in before even reaching the nearest chair. "Could have been three days ago, Your Grace. Alas, I was not summoned."

She scored a point; Daoshen's left eye twitched, ever so slightly.

The game's afoot, Danai thought, and dropped herself into a chair. She noticed they were not alone. Three servants lined one wall, perhaps 20 meters away. Danai ignored them. In Daoshen's world, such servants were accoutrements.

Danai plunged ahead. "I've just come from a briefing," she said, resisting an urge to add, *"Which you interrupted."* "Wolf and Jade Falcon Clans began massing near Terra late last year. I assume you know as much."

"Indeed," Daoshen said.

"And doesn't that worry you even the slightest bit?"

"It does not."

"Why?"

Daoshen activated a holovid. The colorful lights showed a star map of Capellan space, one Danai knew well.

"The Wall may be down," he said with a vague smirk.

"*May* be," Danai emphasized. "We don't know that."

"We will soon enough."

"You're going to test the Wall?"

"Naturally."

Danai narrowed her eyes. "What's changed in the year since the last test?"

"As you say," Daoshen replied. "The Jade Falcon and Wolf Clans were massing near Terra. For what reason? The Wall is down."

"That's conjecture."

"Born of evidence."

"Not of intelligence."

Daoshen's façade cracked at those words, but he quickly recovered. Danai realized it was because he'd mistaken the word *intelligence* to mean his own intellect, not military information.

The thought nearly made her grin.

"Daoshen—" Danai began.

"Your Grace, or Celestial Wisdom," he corrected softly, but unmistakably firmly.

Danai clenched her jaw. "...*Your Grace*...as a sitting *jiang-jun* serving the Capellan people, it is my duty to advise against another test of the Wall at this time."

"*Jiang-jun*," Daoshen said thoughtfully. "We have received no thanks for this promotion."

Goddamn you, Danai thought. "My duties have unfortunately kept me away from my stationery," she said. "I will be sure to send my formal thanks as soon as possible. Please accept my verbal thanks now. *Your Grace*."

With a pleased look, Daoshen nodded, and gestured for her to continue.

His interruption had succeeded in throwing off her thoughts; Danai now hurried to regain her thinking. She elected to speak more carefully. This was too important to get lost in a sparring match with her brother.

Father.

"Your Grace," she said again, mustering a calm tone, "you have reclaimed many worlds rightfully belonging to the Confederation. But with each stepping-stone toward Terra, our army is necessarily reduced. If Jade Falcon and Wolf do attack Terra, we would face two Clans on top of whatever forces the Republic has marshaled for Terra's defense. Yet the bulk of our army would be strung out behind us in a long line of garrisons, insufficient to take, much less hold, Terra."

"Xavier McCarron once said such things."

Danai openly gaped at the Chancellor. The threat needed no embellishment.

Daoshen let the words hang between them for a long moment before pointing to the holovid map. "We are unassailable, Danai. Our victories mount, one atop the other."

"Like Northwind?" she hissed.

Daoshen did not rise to the bait. "Northwind will be taken in due time. Like Sheratan. Like Hall. Liberty. Keid. The mighty Danai Centrella-Liao now heads an armored cavalry unparalleled in the Inner Sphere, so I have confidence in Northwind's embrace of House Liao."

"McCarron's is indeed powerful," Danai said, deliberately using the MAC's surname. "And you do sit at the head of the largest army in the Inner Sphere, Your Grace. But all projections and wargaming to this point underscores certain defeat if you attempt to take and hold Terra, which I do not believe to be possible."

The edges of Daoshen's eyes tightened. Danai felt the fury emanating from him.

She pushed ahead: "Let's pretend for the moment that you take Terra. Do you anticipate the Wolves and Falcons will lay down their arms for you? They will both come at us, likely at the same time."

"With the riches of Terra in our hands, they are welcome to try."

Danai had to force herself not gape again at her father's smug expression and the certainty in his voice.

Before she could marshal a response, the Chancellor continued. "We will have all the worlds between here and Terra. Weapons, matériel, warriors, resources. Advanced manufacturing centers, Terra's factories, and natural resources are abundant. Terra does not hold the key to the Inner Sphere, Danai; Terra *is* the key. Whosoever possesses it possesses the explored universe."

He took a deep breath, as if pleased by the sound of his own voice. He slid his hands into the oversized sleeves of his robe. "And you forget one thing about the Clans, Danai."

She could barely speak above a whisper as she tried to digest the depth of his hubris. "What?"

Daoshen turned to her, his eyes half-closed in the manner of a man full of rich food and drink.

"They," he said softly, "are not gods."

Danai spent a full minute processing his words. She knew well her father's megalomania, and had witnessed it grow over his years in power. But this—surely he had not abandoned all rationale? Surely he did not think...

He was himself a *god*?

Discovering her mouth had gone dry as she looked into her father's eyes, Danai worked to get moisture across her tongue.

"And as such," he said, in a falsely calm voice, "I serve the will of my beloved people."

Danai did not move.

"There are other factors in play, *Jiang-jun*," Daoshen continued. "Factors you will be made aware of in due time. For now, you will continue to monitor the Cavalry and keep them on a ready alert. As for the Wall, I have dispatched ships coreward to see if this defense still stands."

"You already sent them," Danai said in disbelief.

"Of course."

"You can call them back, Daoshen—"

"These ships," he said, speaking over her, "will arrive at their testing sites in roughly two weeks. I invite you to join me as my personal guest aboard the *Aleisha Kris* to witness their success."

Danai slowly stood from her chair. Moving stiffly as if on autopilot, she offered a bow toward Daoshen. "It will be my honor, Celestial Wisdom."

When she recovered from her bow, she saw Daoshen smile like a sated snake. "Wonderful. I will see you then. Please, return to your briefings."

He gestured toward the doors. As if anticipating him, two of the silent servants already stood there, opening them in tandem.

Danai's heart clenched and unclenched in unsteady beats. Gripping the upper portion of her tunic in one hand, as if suffering a heart attack, she turned away from him and walked to the doors. Without a word, she marched out of the room.

Once the doors had closed behind her, Danai fell back against one wall in the hallway. Two guards on duty kept their eyes forward as she sank against the cool wood, bent at the waist to support herself with her free hand on one knee.

"Mad…" she whispered.

Even if the guards heard, they would not react—and did not. They were professionals, after all.

Abruptly Danai stood straight, her head swinging back and forth between them. Watching them intently, she then understood her stark reality.

Oddly, perhaps, it was not Daoshen's pronouncement that he was a god that shook her to the core. The actual cold terror came now, watching the two loyal guardsmen—two who would die to protect the Celestial Wisdom.

There were legions upon legions of troops just like them.

She stumbled away from the guards, walking backward. One of them, on her left, dared to raise an eyebrow about 3 millimeters; but otherwise, they were as stoic as ever. Over her years in service to the Confederation, she'd grown used to their presence. Had eventually, now that she thought of it, come to see them as little more than furniture, like Daoshen's servants. Trained and deadly furniture, true, but furniture nonetheless.

Staring at them now as she backed down the hall, Danai became acutely aware of her impossible situation.

Her brother—father—ruled the entire Confederation with no check. To many, he was not just a leader, but embodied the people himself, an incarnation of the will of all Capellans.

In his own mind, she saw now, he was also an incarnation of the will of *all people, everywhere.*

And as such…was indeed a god.

Danai turned, and, unable to help herself, ran from the palace.

Her personal guard detail leaped to follow her as Danai crossed a reception area. Robie, also present, likewise jumped and rushed to follow the fleeing general. *"Jiang-jun!"* she called.

Danai heard but ignored the younger woman. She didn't stop until she'd reached the outdoors, gulping in the warm air of Normandy.

Her four-man detail immediately took up positions in a diamond shape about 5 meters away from Danai. Robie went straight to her. "Are you all right? Are you hurt?" Already the young agent was scanning Danai's body as if looking for wounds.

"Fine, I'm fine," Danai gasped. She forced herself to stand straight, closing her mouth to make herself breathe through her nose. She took several such breaths until she was back in control.

"What is it, *Jiang-jun?*"

Following an instinct, Danai looked into Robie's eyes and stated, "He thinks he's a god."

Robie blinked in response. Danai waited. Why she'd said it came down to a simple urge to see for herself: how did rank and file Capellans feel about such a pronouncement?

When Robie said nothing, Danai pushed on, desperate for someone in the military apparatus to understand the problem with such a belief. "Did I mishear him? Did I misunderstand the Celestial Wisdom?"

Robie placed her hands behind the small of her back, gazing steadily at Danai.

"The Celestial Wisdom can only speak truth, Your Grace."

CHAPTER 40

CELESTIAL PALACE (TEMPORARY)
NORMANDY
KEID
2 APRIL 3151

Danai glowered over a report from Sheratan, and considered sending Wu back.

The planet remained mostly quiet, but sporadic bursts of sabotage had popped up in Daggaknott, a much larger city than Rainspire. Nothing seemed to be taking root; the damage caused was minimal, the perpetrators mostly young, and no one had been seriously injured.

Statements like that often ended in the word "yet."

She'd handed another regiment XO the reins to the Second MAC, wanting Wu to come with her to Keid, knowing she'd need some sort of steadying influence. And Wu had, as always, performed admirably in that capacity. But she also knew the Second would chafe under someone else's command—anyone's, really. It was probably time to send Wu back to handle the day-to-day operations.

Plus there was Daoshen's order to think about. Danai was under no illusion that the Second would remain on Sheratan for long. Wu could best prepare them for a quick egress to whatever new target Daoshen had in mind.

She had left the door to her makeshift office open. When Wu walked in, Danai was surprised to see her old comrade smiling. *"Jiang-jun,"* he said as he approached her desk. "Sorry for the interruption, but it's important that you see this."

He had no tablet nor papers in his hands. Danai scowled. "What?"

Wu half-turned toward the open door.

Through the doorway walked Noah Capshaw.

Danai stood immediately. "Noah!"

Noah grinned. His walk was more of a shuffle, but it was unaided—no walker and no nurse guided his steps.

He hadn't made it more than a meter before Danai had closed the distance and embraced him, heedless of any fragility. Suddenly realizing her breach in decorum, Danai parted from him. Happily, Noah did not seem particularly upset by the attention.

"I'll leave you two to catch up," Wu said discreetly, letting himself out of the office and closing the door on his way out.

Danai held Noah's arms by the sleeves of his fatigue tunic. "What are you doing here, why aren't you on Liao recovering?"

"I had to be with you," Noah said.

They locked eyes.

"...*Sang-shao*," he added hastily. "What I mean is, I wanted to be of as much help as I can, *Sang-shao*."

She did not notice Noah's use of her former rank at first. The office walls somehow grew closer while at the same time dissolving away as she looked at him.

"Danai," she said quietly.

Noah's expression softened. "Danai."

Danai squeezed her eyes closed. *What are you doing? There's work ahead, hard work. It's good Noah is back, now see if he's strong enough for what's to come. Whatever it may be.*

She opened her eyes and said, more clearly now, *"Jiang-jun."*

Noah frowned at the obvious question.

"Daoshen promoted me," Danai went on, releasing the sleeves of his tunic. "If you didn't know that, then there must be a lot you don't know."

She took a deliberate step back. Noah squared his shoulders. "That's true, *Jiang-jun*," he said. "Is now a good time to get caught up?"

Danai gestured to the chairs in front of her desk. "Please."

She hastened to take her own seat, and sat down before Noah had made it halfway across the room.

"Can I get you anything?" Danai said as he reached the chairs.

"No thank you, *Jiang-jun*."

Danai laced her fingers on the desktop. "You've got a long way to go to show me you're fit for duty."

Noah nodded, sighing slightly as he eased into the guest chair. "Restricted duty," he said. "No BattleMechs for me for a while."

In his eyes, Danai saw the possible truth: *he may not ever pilot a 'Mech again.*

Since he did not offer this, she let the observation go as Noah spoke.

"I was surprised to find you not on Liao," he said. "The doctors wanted me to wait, but believe me, I waited as long as I could in that hospital. A Mask agent helped me find you and work my way here. I want to help."

Danai smiled sadly. "There's a lot you need to know first. Let me get us some tea. And possibly wine. We'll need it."

BASTIAN-CLASS ORBITAL DOCKYARD STATION
   VICTOR'S BLADE
HIGH ORBIT, LIAO
2 APRIL 3151

Si-ben-bing Bishop, a man with pockmarked cheeks and scarred hands, scowled at the pad. "This can't be right."

The young delivery sergeant raised his palms. "I just load things onto pallets and put 'em where they belong, *Si*."

Bishop pointed a meaty finger at the younger man. "You stay right the hell there till I confirm this with the *sao-shao*."

"*Si-ben-bing*, listen, I gotta have you approve delivery of this stuff—"

"Stay. The hell. There."

The younger man gave up, and made as if to sit on the large black crate he'd brought in with a LoaderMech—then thought the better of it and stayed on his feet, grimacing at his cargo.

Si-ben-bing Bishop stalked to a hardwired phone mounted on a bulkhead. When the operator answered, he snapped, "This is Bishop in receiving. I need to speak to *Sao-shao* Jie right now."

He squeezed the black receiver hard in his hand, fearful the gathering sweat would let it slip from his grasp.

It took several minutes for Jie to respond.

"Sir, I have a strange order down here in receiving for some new warheads," Bishop said. "This can't possibly be right, sir, and I—"

He closed his mouth as the *sao-shao* replied.

"Yes, sir, I'm looking at it right now on the order, but this guy wants me to sign off on it and leave me with—"

The captain of the ship spoke again.

Muscle by muscle, Bishop's face lost all strength. His jaw loosed and fell open, his cheeks sagged. His heart seemed to cease beating.

"Yes, sir," he said after the *sao-shao* finished. "Understood."

He hung the phone back in its cradle and walked, dazed, back to the delivery sergeant.

"Print?" the younger man asked softly.

Moving as if asleep, Bishop pressed his thumb against the pad. It beeped at him.

The younger man had to take the pad away from him as Bishop stood there in stupor, his eyes fixed on the black box.

"Good luck, man," the delivery sergeant said, and moved out of the bay with a lot more quickness than was usual for him. He cast one last look at the crate on his way with an expression of revulsion.

Bishop heard none of the usual commotion around him as he stared unblinking at the new cargo. If not for his reptilian respiration system kicking in, he might have passed out from lack of breathing.

Still staring, he shouted, "Carney!"

A lanky man with greasy work gloves ambled over. "Yeah?"

"Get these warheads loaded. Right now. And do it alone. You hear me?"

"Alone?" Carney whimpered. "Aw, but—"

Bishop sprung to life, whirling and grabbing the collar of Carney's jumpsuit. "Do what I tell you! Do it now, and do it alone!"

"Yeah, yeah, okay," Carney babbled. "Sure thing, boss. All by myself."

Bishop shoved him away and stalked to his tiny office.

Once there, in its privacy, he leaned over his steel trash bucket and vomited.

CHAPTER 41

Noah had enjoyed perhaps half his tea when Danai started her briefing with him. By a couple of minutes in, he'd set the hot drink down on the edge of her desk on its delicate saucer and sat transfixed as Danai filled him in on recent developments.

She did not drink her own tea, either. Both cups sat and cooled as she talked.

When she finished, Noah, his eyes wide, gave only one response: "...Shit."

Danai smirked. "That sums it up nicely."

Noah pushed himself carefully out of the chair. Danai started to rise to stop him, but he held up a hand. "Just need to move around a bit."

He took a few cautious steps, circling the chair until he stood behind it, hands placed on the seat back. "First question," he said. "Are you worried about Lindsey?"

Danai re-secured her long, black hair into a ponytail so tight it lifted her eyebrows a centimeter. Lindsey Baxter was commander of the Fourth MAC, and had been present for the failed attack on Northwind. Briefings indicated she placed the blame on House Kurita failures; the Draconis Combine had previously agreed to Daoshen's offer of treaty and cooperation that would allow both Great Houses to pursue their own goals without interference from the other. A month ago, Daoshen had expelled the Combine's liaison from Liao.

Based on what Danai had read between the lines, she agreed with Lindsey's assessment: the Combine had failed them. Danai considered Lindsey Baxter both a friend and a reliable military operator. When Daoshen declared that any support for Xavier McCarron would result in immediate execution, Danai had been relieved that Lindsey had kept her mouth shut.

She also knew the CO well enough to guess remaining silent in the face of Xavier's and Gwen's executions might have been Lindsey's most difficult mission. She'd resigned her commission only days later, and no one seemed to know her whereabouts ever since.

"Worried about her?" Danai echoed. "No. Her loyalty to the Confederation is not in question, not to me. She did the right thing by stepping down after what happened to McCarron and Vaughn. If I know Lindsey, she'll find herself a nice mercenary unit on the far side of the Inner Sphere."

Noah frowned. "Isn't that a betrayal? If you're right, we may end up fighting her ourselves someday."

"One day at a time, Noah. And no, betrayal is always personal. It's the knife you don't see coming. Lindsey hasn't betrayed the Big MAC or the Confederation, not in my eyes."

Noah nodded. "Have you gamed out what happens if the Chancellor's gambit to test the Wall fails—or succeeds?"

Danai leaned back in her chair, grimacing. "You would think a general would be privy to such war games. Alas."

"You don't know the Strategios' plans?"

"I'll find them out, eventually. Honestly, it's as if there used to be an HPG connecting me to my own brother, and it's been destroyed with the rest of them. Happily," she added with unconcealed sarcasm, "I've been invited to join Daoshen on his ship to watch the test personally."

Noah straightened. "I'd like to join you."

Danai eyed him critically. Noah seemed pale, and the shocking white of his hair struck her as dimmed now, more gray than white, for a man his age. He'd lost much of the muscle Wu had helped him gain. But his eyes were bright, and during their discussion, she'd detected no slip in his mental acuity. He was clearly tired, and clearly weak, but ready to regain his place at her service.

"Yes," she decided. "I've been wanting to send Wu back to the Second, this would be a good time. I'll send him back right away, and...oh, what the hell. I'll just promote you both."

The surprise in Noah's expression made her chuckle as he stuttered, "I'm sorry, *Jiang-jun*, that was not at all my intent, I—"

She waved him off. "Shut up, Noah. It's done. Congratulations, *Zhong-shao* Capshaw."

Danai watched as he took a moment to let this new title sink in, then gave a perfectly crisp bracing salute. "Thank you, *Jiang-jun.*"

"It's not a favor. You've earned it. Go get some rest, we'll meet again soon to plan our little outing with the Chancellor."

Noah braced again, smiled, and slowly shuffled out of her office.

Danai watched him go. His musculature was mending fine, but she recognized his slow gait as stemming from neurological damage often sustained from the sort of concussive blow he'd received on Sheratan. She hoped he'd be able to get back into a BattleMech cockpit again soon.

BattleMechs, she thought idly. *That's what I could use right now.*

She faced her noteputer and began the tedious electronic paperwork needed to promote Noah to *zhong-shao* and Wu to *sang-shao*, as well as Wu's orders to Sheratan. Upon completing this, she scheduled herself time in the nearest BattleMech simulator at the earliest opportunity.

FENG-HUANG-CLASS WARSHIP *ALEISHA KRIS*
ZENITH JUMP POINT
KEID SYSTEM
16 APRIL 3151

The JumpShip armada assembled far beyond the *Aleisha Kris* gave even *Jiang-jun* Danai Centrella-Liao pause. Safely nestled within the Combat Information Center, with one of the *Kris'* two grav decks providing comfortable stability, she could not see the actual vessels, but the green carets representing the ships on various screens were numerous.

Zhong-shao Noah Capshaw articulated her concern, whispering as he stood at her shoulder, "He's sending them *all*?"

On a massive holovid at the front of the CIC, at least a dozen Capellan JumpShips hovered in the vast space surrounding the *Kris*, one of the CCAF's remaining WarShips, assigned to the duty of taking the Chancellor and his entourage near the jump point where this armada would test the Fortress Wall protecting Terra and other nearby systems using LF batteries to double-jump: one in...and ideally, one out.

The CIC had a full complement of twelve crew at various operations consoles, each wearing serious and professional expressions as they executed their missions. At the door to the rear of the bridge, six of Daoshen's bodyguards stood looking relaxed, but wholly alert.

The Chancellor stood within the holotank, as if to reach out and touch the three-dimensional images if he so wished. Just behind him and to his right stood Robie Anjing, hands folded in front of her, observing the room with cool detachment.

Danai and Noah were further back, near the captain, *Sang-wei* Novar. Danai appreciated the tension she detected in Novar's otherwise stoic expression as he quietly issued orders to his team.

He didn't like being here, either.

"*Sang-wei*," Daoshen said without turning, "you may execute when ready."

"Aye, Your Grace," Novar said. Danai heard no shake in his voice.

Novar spoke to his crew. "All ships, mission is go. I say again, mission is go. Godspeed."

Danai noticed Daoshen's head twitch ever so slightly at the sendoff. Appraising Novar, she saw he did not regret using the last word.

On the holovid, one by one, the JumpShips, filled with volunteers no doubt eager to please the Chancellor and their own direct superiors, disappeared from space. Each ship was headed to a Republic world previously guarded by the Fortress Wall.

Including Terra.

Danai wondered at the theatrics of it all. She'd learned Daoshen knew the Wall around the other worlds near Sol had been down for at least the past two years, so why this large-scale "test" now? Maybe it served as camouflage for the real test: Terra itself.

When all the electronic blue carets that indicated JumpShips had vanished, Daoshen turned his back to the holovid and addressed the crew.

"All of you here are witness to the liberation of humanity's homeworld this day," he orated. "With this test complete, the Confederation will have demonstrated to our enemies our power and our resolve. Soon, my friends, we will walk under the sunlight of Sol itself!"

The speech was met with cheers and applause. Danai joined in, but studied each crew member in turn, gauging their authenticity. It was hard to tell. Some wore the awestruck expressions she'd seen before in those who'd never met the Chancellor in person. Several, she was sure, were *performing* their enthusiasm, just as much as she was.

Novar's expression remained neutral, but he too applauded.

"Contact!" shouted one of the crewmembers.

Everyone fell silent. The crew instantly turned back to their consoles.

"JumpShip Alpha," the crewmember went on, her eyes unblinking as she leaned over her array after the Alpha double-jumped. "Target, New Earth. Jump complete...jump successful!"

The crew burst into more applause.

Danai watched Daoshen. The Chancellor's faint smile was so smug, she had a sudden urge to smack it off his face.

Other reports came in. The energy in the room felt electric as one after another, the JumpShips returned in perfect working order, all souls accounted for.

All but one.

One missing ship.

Novar shook his head, scowling at his own personal monitor, then said, "Wait—"

The caret indicating the JumpShip bound for Terra reappeared, the last of the armada to do so. The little electronic triangle glowed red.

Someone on the bridge gasped. Silence dropped like a cloak over the entire crew.

Daoshen, basking in the crew's adulation, was the last to catch on to the quiet. He turned to face the holovid.

The final JumpShip, the *Crimson Cat,* had returned, but was not returning hails.

"Send a quick response boat," Novar said. "Now. Live feed, directly to the screen."

Off to one side of the holovid projection, an enormous flat screen slowly dropped from the ceiling.

"QRB away," someone reported. "Time to intercept, ten minutes."

"Continue hails," Novar said, and met Danai's eyes. She read the expression in them instantly. *Don't get your hopes up.*

Danai turned to watch the screen.

Nine minutes later, the screen glowed to life as the small quick-response rescue ship approached the jump point.

"*Crimson Cat*, this is *Aleisha Kris*," an operator said. "Respond, please. Resp—"

"Oh my god..." Novar muttered.

The rescue ship reached visual range of what remained of the *Crimson Cat*. The formerly needle-shaped JumpShip looked like nothing so much as a sheet of paper crumpled between the hands of a vengeful deity, half the size it should have been. Occasional crackles of blue electricity flared across its warped surface.

"*Kris*, this is *Hollis*," reported the rescue ship, piped into the *Kris* CIC. "Uh...we have visual contact, are you seeing this?"

"We see it," Novar said, his voice grim.

"We're on approach," the *Hollis* commander said back over the comm. "How do you want us to—ugh!"

Several of the console operators in the CIC gasped as the *Hollis* shifted its video capture to real-time. Half a human head, split lengthwise, bumped soundlessly into the camera. The remaining eye was wide open, as if staring in horror.

"Uh, *Kris?*" the *Hollis* said after a moment as it circled the mangled wreckage of the JumpShip. "There's no salvage here. What do you want us to do? Survivors don't seem likely at this time."

Novar faced Danai. Danai faced Daoshen.

The Chancellor stood motionless, eyes fixated on the flatscreen. Danai saw his hands clenched into fists at his sides.

No one moved.

After a terminally long pause, in which even the crew on the rescue boat seemed to intuit to not break in over comms, Daoshen tucked his clenched fists into the sleeves of his robe.

"*Jiang-jun,*" he said to Danai. "Please join me in my quarters. *Sang-wei?*"

Novar stood from his seat. "Yes, Your Grace."

"Begin preparations for our return to Liao."

The captain visibly restrained a confused frown. "Right now, Your Grace?"

"Immediately."

Daoshen approached the exit. His security detail surrounded him as he walked. Robie Anjing brought up the rear, trading a quick glance with Danai as she passed.

Once the Chancellor and his team had left, activity resumed in the CIC. Capshaw moved to stand in front of Danai. "What now?" he murmured.

Danai, eyes locked on the flatscreen as the *Hollis* continued to maneuver around the wreckage, could only shake her head. "Let's go find out."

CHAPTER 42

FENG-HUANG-CLASS WARSHIP ALEISHA KRIS
ZENITH JUMP POINT
KEID SYSTEM
16 APRIL 3151

With Daoshen's permission, Noah was allowed to join Danai in Daoshen's office suite aboard the *Kris'* grav deck. Robie Anjing stood nearby, as always.

Daoshen's office quarters were luxurious compared to the rest of the ship, and was probably the biggest room on board, not counting hangars, cargo areas, and perhaps the bridge. A low wooden table bolted to the floor took up most of the space, with comfortable chairs surrounding it. At the head sat Daoshen, in a scaled-down version of his dragon throne on Liao.

"All is as I have foreseen," he began as Danai and Capshaw took seats near the throne.

Danai almost blurted a laugh of disbelief. *Foreseen?*

Her expression must have betrayed her, for Daoshen arched an eyebrow at her. "Yes," he went on as if she had spoken. "It comes as little surprise that the Wall remains in place around the jewel of the known universe. But the Republic knows it cannot hold her forever, and knows our recent routs of its worlds preface their ultimate destruction."

"Chancellor," Danai said, in as professional a tone as she could muster, "we just lost an entire JumpShip."

"Our military remains the most formidable in the Inner Sphere," Daoshen said. "Do you believe I would have risked so many of our assets to test the Wall without knowing the potential for loss?"

"Of course not," Danai said with forced deference.

"The test was merely phase one of my plan," Daoshen said. "With these proven results, we will now engage phase two— the near-complete encirclement of Terra."

He touched a button on the table. A holovid sprang up from the center.

"New Earth," he narrated as the holovid showed a pre-programmed set of system maps. "Talitha, Van Diemen, Pollux—"

"Eight more worlds?" Danai said.

The Celestial Wisdom nodded. "Followed by more than a dozen."

Aghast, forgetting to use a proper title among subordinates, Danai said, "Daoshen, we do *not* have the resources to take and hold them all right now."

Robie gazed at her. "Incorrect. The vast majority of our regiments report they are at 80 percent strength or higher."

"And at least eight of them report they're at 70 percent or less!" Danai exclaimed.

"More than enough to liberate these worlds," Daoshen said, gesturing absently at the glowing system map. The Celestial Wisdom dropped his hand to tap on a keyboard set below the level of the table. The holovid shifted to show a current map of Confederation holdings. "This is all of Capellan space as of this moment. The largest territory House Liao has ruled in centuries. Your lack of confidence surprises me, sister."

"Chancellor," Danai said, trying to calm her rising emotion. "Let us say, for the sake of argument, that these eight worlds represent only a degree of difficulty equal to those we have faced thus far. We lost a lot of resources on Hall and Sheratan. We failed to take Northwind—"

"*McCarron* failed to take Northwind," Daoshen corrected, eyes narrowing.

Danai took a breath. "We had to fight twice for Liberty. You know as well as I do the Republic is falling back to prepare for the very assault on Terra you are building toward. The Wolves and Jade Falcons are still out there, with their eyes on the same prize, and they won't sit back and watch you pick off every world surrounding Terra. We'll have to add the Combine to our list of opponents if you intend to encircle Terra. The Davions, too. Chancellor...you invited me here to speak of conquest for the people of Liao, and it is on those terms I must urge you to reconsider these invasions."

Daoshen laughed. It was an uncommon expression for him, one that made Danai blink and sit back in surprise.

The derision in his voice boiled her blood. "Danai, Danai. Your concern is noted, and dismissed. I invited you here as a courtesy before speaking to the Strategios, who already have plans in place for these operations, and only await my word to carry them out. The Confederation has...an array of resources we have yet to bring to the battlefield. I assure you, these resources are being fielded even as we speak. You'll see."

He tapped the holovid off.

"You will order the Second MAC to return to Hall," Daoshen said. "And keep the rest of the MAC at a ready level. That is all for now. Oh...perhaps one more thing, Danai."

Danai clenched her teeth, waiting.

"The MAC is no longer, in fact, headed by McCarron," Daoshen said. "You should submit a formal name change as soon as possible. Perhaps 'Danai's Dashers,' or..." He waved a hand dismissively, not even bothering to finish the thought.

Danai stood up slowly, afraid her legs would give out, even in the grav deck's slight downward pull. "Of course. I will see to it. Thank you, Your Grace." She offered a shallow bow. Noah stood and braced before falling in behind her and leaving the Chancellor's office.

As soon as the door had closed, Noah said, "I have to renew my question, *Jiang-jun*," he said quietly as they left the gravity of Daoshen's chambers and pulled themselves along the hall. "What now?"

"What now?" Danai repeated. "I'm sending Wu and the Second to Hall, as ordered. I want the rest of the MAC on alert, ready to move, also as ordered."

"And the name change?"

"Must have slipped my mind," Danai said through gritted teeth. "*Your* job is to find out what I don't know."

Noah glanced questioningly at her.

"These 'resources' he mentioned," Danai told Capshaw. "I want to know what they are and where they're going."

"I'll do my best, *Jiang-jun*. And you?"

"I'll be crafting messages to the lead officers in the MAC," Danai said. "I need to know where they stand."

CELESTIAL PALACE
CHANG-AN
LIAO
CAPELLAN CONFEDERATION
8 MAY 3151

Weeks after the failed Fortress Wall test, Danai fought a headache during one of Daoshen's frequent briefings upon their return to Liao. She tried to console herself with the notion that at least she'd been invited this time.

"When were you last at the palace, Your Grace?" Robie Anjing asked as she and Danai left the briefing with Daoshen and the Strategios in Daoshen's conference room.

"A year," Danai said. "Almost two. Something like that."

"Was your visit long?"

"No. Not particularly. I had a meeting with Xavier McCarron, then Daoshen. Frankly, I left as quickly as I was able after that. Why are you walking with me?"

"I have been tasked with interrogating you."

Danai stopped and stared at the younger woman. Robie grinned. "Those were not the Celestial Wisdom's exact words," she admitted. "But it is what he meant. He wants me to gauge you, see where you stand on the current efforts."

"He could have asked me."

"Would you have answered honestly?"

"Would he have cared if I did?"

Robie gestured down the hallway for them to continue walking. "No. But I would still appreciate your...let's say, unfettered opinions."

Danai glanced meaningfully at their escorts ahead of and behind them.

"Not here and now, of course," Robie added quickly. "As you are Duchess of Castrovia, I would like to give you an updated tour of the palace and grounds, so you can be familiar with our current security protocols."

"Because our enemies may end up here on our doorstep," Danai murmured. *And speaking of enemies, they are who we keep closer. Isn't that the old adage? So which are you, Robie? Friend or enemy?*

Robie shrugged. "As unlikely as that may be, it is my job to protect the office of the Chancellor, an office which you are now one heartbeat away from assuming. I must prepare for all contingencies."

Danai said nothing. *One heartbeat away.* She'd made a point to keep that truth out of her conscious mind ever since Daoshen had named her duchess. She wasn't ready to face that looming, yet abstract, future.

"You're assuming," she said, "that the Chancellor has a heartbeat."

Robie laughed. Danai did not believe its authenticity. Robie was good, but young. It took time to develop a convincing laugh for court. Danai knew her own still needed work.

"May I show you around now?" Robie said as they reached a four-way intersection in the palace. "I would like to have you caught up as soon as possible."

Danai considered. Nothing but logistics reports to catch up on. And maybe tea with Noah, time permitting. Nothing that couldn't wait.

She sighed. "Sure. Let's go."

Robie gestured to a side corridor. "This way, Your Grace."

The young Maskirovka agent started the tour on the lowest level of the palace, deep underground. The bottom of the palace served as a bunker, with a backup CIC and war room in the event of an attack on Chang-an itself, which, Robie hastened to point out, was extraordinarily unlikely in the current state of the war.

"This entire level can withstand an air-burst nuclear explosion directly over the palace," she said with some degree of pride.

"No one would dare use a nuke in-atmosphere these days," Danai said. "Not since the Jihad."

"Correct. But the bunker was built when times were less sure."

"You think they are sure now?" Danai asked.

"I suppose nothing is sure in war, Your Grace."

Danai nodded faintly.

Robie walked her through escape protocols, most of which Danai already knew, though there were some new changes. The tour took more than two hours, at the end of which Danai found herself standing outside the main public entrance of the palace with Robie, scanning the perimeter.

The public portion of the towering crimson palace had the look of a civic business office, with a two-story beige building backed by the ornate cathedral domes of the palace proper. Outside its doors, unpolished flagstones extended to a two-lane public street. The view was unobstructed, except for short birch trees in enormous, decorative concrete pots near the doors.

"Despite myself and several agents before me trying to change his mind, the Chancellor has not allowed us to push civilian traffic further away," Robie remarked, nodding at the busy street less than 50 meters from the six sets of double glass doors leading into the palace.

"Of course," Danai said, smirking. "We are one big happy Liao family."

"Exactly. Those decorative stone bollards along the sidewalk conceal ferrocrete posts, so no wheeled vehicle is getting close, and the bollards are too high for hovercraft."

"And if any BattleMechs stomped those bollards and walked up to the front doors?" Danai asked, eying twin pairs of SecurityMechs stationed at either corner of the palace building.

"Security operates command-detonated mines under the flagstones."

Danai flinched at the mere mention of the weapons. She nodded quickly to conceal her reaction.

"For what it's worth," Robie said, "I do wish the Chancellor would reside on Sian, in the Forbidden City palace. We are fairly secure here, but that building and those lands are the most secure in the Confederation."

"I agree," Danai said.

"Perhaps the next Chancellor will see fit to reside there."

Danai gave her a sharp look. Robie's face was—unironically—a blank mask.

"That's the rough outline," she said after a moment, folding her arms. "I'm sorry it was not as thorough as—"

"Where are deliveries taken?" Danai asked, keenly watching a vehicle over Robie's shoulder.

Her eyes had narrowed dangerously as a white six-wheeled delivery truck rolled to a stop along the northbound street—almost right up onto the sidewalk, only a couple of meters from the line of bollards.

Robie followed her gaze.

Around her, Danai felt time cease, as if all were frozen. With the instant and crystal clarity of a combat veteran's tunnel vision, she counted ten armed and uniformed Capellan guards at the doors and the four *Guard* SecurityMechs. She saw civilian workers and families walking the sidewalk, many casting admiring looks at the crimson palace looming behind Danai. She smelled cherry blossoms and exhaust. She felt a single drop of sweat release from her left armpit and slide down her body.

Then time sped up.

"Go!" she barked at Robie.

But the agent was already racing back to the glass doors as she screamed, *"Lockdown!"*

Danai bolted for one of the armed guards, each of whom carried an assault laser rifle in hand and a sidearm strapped to their waist.

The attack began just as she reached the surprised guard and yanked his sidearm out of his holster.

CHAPTER 43

CELESTIAL PALACE
CHANG-AN
LIAO
CAPELLAN CONFEDERATION
8 MAY 3151

Robie arrived at the private staircase in the palace lobby when the first explosion went off outside.

The public doors, made of the same transparent armor as BattleMech canopies, held despite the concussive blast. Civilian workers in the lobby screamed as the blast shook the ground.

Robie didn't so much as glance back. Her entire focus went to and stayed on Daoshen Liao.

The Chancellor's various meeting rooms were on the second floor of the palace. Robie dashed up the stairs and bolted from the stairwell, passing Capellan guards.

She grabbed one by the arm as she raced for the conference room. "The Chancellor?"

The guard pointed.

Robie released him and ran for the conference room.

The guards on duty gripped their rifles pensively. Robie smelled anxiety on them.

She booted one of the double doors to the conference room open. "Chancellor!"

The conference room struck her as comically calm. Guanken, Daoshen's ever-present servant, stood near the throne. Several uniformed Strategios around the table were on their feet, looking right at Robie.

Daoshen Liao sat on his throne, faintly smiling.

Robie rushed toward the throne. "We need to move you, now!"

Daoshen lifted a hand. Half his fingers were utterly relaxed, as if he couldn't be bothered to extend them all. "No."

Robie felt as if she hit a wall. She stopped abruptly, still halfway to the throne. Likewise, the heads of every Strategio around the table whipped around to stare at their Celestial Wisdom.

"Chancellor," Robie said carefully, resuming her movement toward the throne, but now in measured steps, "I have to get you to safety. The palace is under attack."

"Indeed," Daoshen said. "I appreciate your dedication, Robie, but we will be perfectly safe here." He gestured at one of the officers in attendance. "*Sang-shao*? Continue."

"But, Y-Your Grace..." the *sang-shao* stuttered.

Robie reached the side of the Chancellor's throne. Guanken dutifully took a step back.

"Chancellor," Robie whispered. "I beg you, come with me to a secure location, *now*."

Daoshen leaned closer to her. Dropping his voice to a tone so soft as to not carry to those gathered at the table, he said directly to her: "The Chancellor of the Capellan Confederation will not race through these halls for protection. I...cannot...be harmed."

Chest heaving from her run up the stairs, Robie could only stare at the Chancellor's profile. She moved to position herself between Daoshen and the table, so that she faced him directly, her back to the Strategios. Guanken stood still a meter beyond the throne.

"Chancellor," she said as quietly as she could, "you are not a god."

Daoshen reached out and ran the backs of his fingers along her cheek, a gesture he'd been more and more prone to as her time went on in the palace.

He smiled.

"You may return to your position," he said, gesturing to one side with his eyes.

Robie stepped away, braced, and walked stiffly to the nearest pillar, which she stood with her back against.

"*Sang-shao?*" Daoshen repeated to the officer who'd spoken. "We were discussing the assault on New Home? Continue."

Robie resisted an urge to lick her lips, and hoped all was as well downstairs as the Celestial Wisdom believed.

A squad of battle armor deployed from the back of the white panel truck, pointed weapons at the lobby doors, and opened fire.

Danai dove for cover behind a decorative concrete pot and returned fire. The guards and four *Guard* SecurityMechs followed suit a heartbeat later, firing lasers and machine guns at the attackers. Civilians scattered for cover or raced away from the palace, screaming.

Their battle-armored opponents moved swiftly away from the truck, concentrating fire on the lance of SecurityMechs now marching closer. Danai held her own fire for a moment to assess the scenario.

The attackers had made clear beelines away from the large-wheeled truck. Pedestrians cleared the street, crying out in terror—but only one, a young man with brown hair, looked back specifically at the motionless truck as he ran.

Dammit.

This was all Danai had time to think as she realized what the man's instinctive backward glance meant.

The truck exploded.

She pulled back behind her cover as shrapnel flew across the flat plaza in front of the palace doors. Her ears felt filled with damp cotton. Chunks of metal cracked into the doors, which held, but spiderwebbed. Additional shots would bring them down—removing the first obstacle toward Chancellor Daoshen Liao.

The five attackers were well out of the blast radius, and continued firing as the Capellan force tried to recover from the sudden shockwave.

Danai peered around the planter. The five suits moved quickly, but in a lumbering fashion reminding Danai of great apes on Terra. *Simians*, she realized. Each suit had articulated hands and what appeared to be a modular weapon on its right arm. A spotlight—useless in the mid-morning sun—was mounted beside their main weapon system. Smooth, helmet-like headpieces jutted over their torsos, leering.

A Capellan guard fell beside Danai, his chest ripped open and charred by laser fire. Danai grabbed his laser rifle and nestled the stock against her shoulder before popping up from behind cover and shooting at the nearest battle armor.

Her shots landed on the attacker's torso. The armored fighter pivoted on its heel toward her. Danai's chest tightened, as if feeling the enemy's targeting reticle land on her. She fell back, firing as she retreated, as her opponent triggered jump jets and rocketed toward her position.

Every instinct screamed at her to break contact, to run, as 1000 kilograms of weaponry landed within kicking distance. Her legs almost went out from beneath her from the tremor.

Instead, with a cry of rage and heedless of her important place in Capellan society, Danai leaped forward. She jammed the barrel of the rifle beneath the protruding head of the battle armor and depressed the trigger.

The laser cut a vertical slit through the battle armor. Even through her temporary near-deafness and the cacophony of battle out on the flagstones, Danai heard the battle armor pilot scream, then fall silent as the laser split their head in half.

Melted armor poured off the battle armor. Danai moved the angle of her rifle to avoid the drops, which sizzled against the concrete. She fell back, swinging the rifle in a wide arc, seeking her next target. The battle armor in front of her stayed motionless, arms dangling, emitting the odor of burnt metal and flesh.

With one battle armor suit down, the SecurityMechs were able to meet their adversaries one-on-one. Six of the ten guards were dead, but reinforcements now appeared from around the palace corners and landed from jumps off the roof. Realizing her vulnerable position, Danai crouched behind the next nearest planter and waited for the combat to end.

The war had come to Chang-an after all.

She was not surprised.

The chime at her apartment door sounded. Danai, wearing a green silk robe, walked to the door and opened it, knowing any visitors would have to have high clearance to get past three imposing security checkpoints to reach her private apartment.

Earlier in the day, there'd been only one such checkpoint. Robie Anjing had instituted rapid changes in the wake of the attack.

Danai hoped the person outside her door was Noah.

Instead, it was Robie. "Your Grace."

"Robie," Danai replied, hiding her disappointment. "Hello."

"My shift just ended. I wanted to see how you were doing."

Danai blinked slowly. In truth, she felt exhausted. In the hours since helping repel the attack, she'd found her body aching and her heart longing for Castrovia.

Surprised to discover she held Tiko's queen sculpture in her hand, and rather than express her desires to the Maskirovka, Danai pocketed the trinket and said, "I'm fine. How is my brother?"

Robie held her gaze for an uncomfortable moment before replying, "Perfectly well. In fact, planning an impromptu speech in the Great Courtyard first thing in the morning."

The Great Courtyard near the palace served as an outdoor venue for many official state activities. "Shall I attend?"

"He has not asked for you to be there, Your Grace."

"Good." Danai pulled her shoulders back, trying to work out a knot in her upper back. "Is there anything else?"

"Yes," Robie said. "Who else knows he is your father?"

Danai felt an invisible fist punch her sternum. Quickly, she grabbed the agent by the lapel and yanked the younger woman into her apartment, even as she felt certain Robie could have resisted had she wanted to.

She slammed the door shut and got into the young woman's face. "Where did you hear that?"

"It's my job to protect the office of the Chancellor," Robie said, unperturbed. "As such, it's my business to know everything *about* the Chancellor."

Danai stared hard into her eyes, jaw clenching as she raced through what to do with her. The two women—the older twice the age of the younger—held each other's stares. Danai could feel the fire smoldering in her own, while Robie's return gaze was merely curious, as if wondering what the second-most-powerful person in the Confederation might do next.

Danai's first impulse was to take the whelp's life.

And who would stop her? Who would even accuse her? And if they did, what of it? She had the power of the Confederation in her hand. But for Daoshen, she was the law. *One heartbeat away*, after all.

Yet this impulse died as quickly as it arose. As she looked deeper into Robie's eyes, she detected no guile, no *quid pro quo*. The young agent did not seem to be after something.

But then why make the comment at all?

Danai spun away and went to her living room area, sitting on a soft white leather sofa where she'd been sipping green tea and reading reports of the attack, until restlessly getting up to wander the apartment. She realized that's when Tiko's gift must have ended up in her hand—as she paced aimlessly around the rooms.

Her aimlessness was over now as she sat and stared at Robie. "I'm listening."

Robie stayed in place near the door. "Your Grace, I have nothing more to say."

"But you know. I suppose the entire Maskirovka does. I guess that was inevitable. How long has it been known?"

"Your Grace," Robie said carefully, eyes darting back and forth as if searching for proper etiquette. "If I have offended you, I beg your forgiveness."

Danai brushed the apology aside before the agent had even finished speaking. "Just tell me what you know. Here. Sit down. Tell me everything."

Robi pursed her lips, hesitated, then came to join Danai, sitting on a matching armchair. "The Maskirovka tries to deal in facts whenever possible. Of course, that is harder than not, most times. I have no facts, Your Grace. Just an instinct and a...a way of observing relationships, if I may be so bold. I've watched how you interact with the Chancellor at briefings, and watched some of your dealings from security recordings. Something was amiss."

Danai nodded. "I see."

"And if you will permit one more indiscretion...?"

Intrigued, Danai gestured for her to go on.

Robie leaned nearer over the low birch coffee table. "I was raised on Liao to one day be in the Maskirovka, and when I was of age, I *chose* the Maskirovka. We all do. We are not forced. We are free to choose another path should we wish. But I chose this. There is no higher honor for me than to live, and die if necessary, in the service of the Capellan Confederation."

She scooted forward to the edge of the cushion, holding Danai's gaze.

"The only other thing more important," she said, very quietly, "is to be trusted by those I serve. I am here to be used as needed, Your Grace. I can simply listen, if it is beneficial, because any secrets revealed in my hearing will die with me."

Robie sat back.

"I say this to you now because your father is getting older. He is healthy, but he will not be Chancellor forever, if you'll pardon my bluntness. You are much younger than he, and I much younger than you. Kamer served for thirty years. I expect to do the same or more. I hope that starting our relationship now will help me serve you better when the inevitable occurs."

The inevitable, Danai thought, and got momentarily dizzy. *The inevitable. In other words, my inevitable ascension to the throne.*

Maybe I'll get lucky and die in a BattleMech before then.

Danai considered the young agent carefully. This child had not seen the things she'd seen, done the things she'd done. Robie Anjing was so, so young, yet her dedication felt immutable.

Of all the sins Danai carried in her soul, it was not her own that weighed the most. It was the sins of her father and her mother.

Might it not lighten the load to at last share it aloud with the one person who was born to be trusted? And if death on the battlefield was not forthcoming—given her new position in the military, such a fate seemed much further away lately—Robie had a point about their relationship. All the same, Danai knew that confiding honestly with a spy was not likely to serve her well. Especially not one who seemed to have more interest in a successor than in her current protectee.

"Perhaps," she said slowly, feigning trust, "the day will come when I will avail myself of that listening ear."

Robie dipped her head. "It would be an honor, Your Grace."

Danai gave herself a shake. "Until then—back to work. I'm sure the Chancellor has...*need* of you. Which reminds me."

Robie cocked her head. The gesture reminded Danai of a sparrow.

"I, too, can be trusted with secrets, Robie. If *anyone* were to mistreat you, for instance, even if in the service of your duties, I am someone who would understand. I, too, make observations."

A flash of something passed across Robie's face. Guilt? Fear? Rage? Danai could not tell. It had come and gone too fast. She was a good little Mask, for sure, but not yet experienced enough to conceal her thoughts entirely.

Robie stood. "Thank you, Your Grace. I will remember that."

"By the way, how is the investigation into the attack going?"

"Early, but we have leads. Currently the Republic of the Sphere seems most likely. The battle armor is of their design, though the fact there were five units of battle armor has some wondering if there is possible Clan involvement."

"Mm-hmm."

Robie cocked her head again. "Is there a problem, Your Grace?"

"No," Danai said. "No problem. I just hope it was indeed the Rotters, and not someone closer to home."

"A Liao citizen?"

"Even that would be a relief." Danai rubbed her forehead, which had begun to ache. "Robie...I know you got your position by being the best choice for it. I knew Kamer. He was a good agent and a good protector. So I trust you will follow in his footsteps and consider every possible angle of this attack. Including the potential that it may have been Capellan military."

Danai saw the girl's face register a moment of shock.

"Yes," she said, as if Robie had spoken. "Because if that is the case...House Liao is in much greater danger than ever. My broth—" Danai stopped, snorted a disgusted laugh, and went on: "My father's life is in your hands. Assume nothing, and trust no one."

Robie's shock had already passed. "Even you, Your Grace?"

Rather than take offense, Danai slowly nodded.

"Yes," she said. "Especially me."

CHAPTER 44

TOWER PARK
CHANG-AN
LIAO
9 MAY 3151

Dante Holland and Lydia Chen met in one of Chang-an's beautiful public parks, far from the palace. The day was warm for the season, and Lydia elected to stand at the edge of a human-made lake, eyes concealed by reflective sunglasses. She stood, unconsciously, at parade rest as Dante stood beside her. They did not look at one another.

"The distraction failed completely," Dante said quietly. "The agent didn't have a chance to get near Daoshen. He wasn't even evacuated the way we'd expected."

Lydia Chen nodded slowly.

"So now security will be heightened," Dante continued. "I'm so sorry, *Zhong-shao*. This failure is my responsibility."

Lydia smirked. "Not a complete failure, *Sao-wei*. I have learned more about our beloved Chancellor as a result, and that knowledge may prove useful. Whether to us or to another."

"What is it?" Dante asked, pretending to be interested in a Liao eagle soaring overhead as it searched for a meal.

"That there is no limit to his hubris," Lydia replied. "That he genuinely believes himself to be untouchable. And that will be his undoing. Internally or externally, someone will turn that delusion against him, and then this foolishness will finally end."

Dante frowned. "We won't make another attempt?"

"We cannot. Not now. They may yet trace the attack back to us as it is. Fortunately, you and I are bound for Epsilon Indi in less than two days, on the next stepping stone toward Terra."

Sighing, Dante said, "He will have us killed if they do figure it out. I guess that goes without saying."

"He'll try," Lydia said, her smile now blooming. "And I welcome the attempt."

Dante regarded her with pride and awe. "*Zhong-shao...?*"

Lydia turned to him. "We are the McCarron's Armored Cavalry, Dante. And the McCarron's Armored Cavalry we shall remain."

LOTUS FLOWER APARTMENT BUILDING
CHANG-AN
20 MAY 3151

Kamer sat with his legs crossed, arms crossed, expression—cross. He watched the video multiple times, losing count after viewing number four.

The recording provided via Daoshen's chief attendant, Guanken, did not offer the audio he hoped for. All the same, Kamer could read Robie and Daoshen's body language clearly enough. His Maskirovka protégé was attempting to move the Chancellor to more secure quarters, and Daoshen was refusing. Even the Strategios barely concealed their concern while an assassination attempt carried on just one floor down.

Reckless? Kamer wondered in his small, dark office. No. Daoshen had never been *that. Arrogant, though—yes.* Dangerous, yes, from the moment he assumed the throne.

His obvious response to Robie in this footage seemed to Kamer an encapsulation of Daoshen's entire strategy against the Republic of the Sphere: hubris. A sense of invulnerability, even as the Chancellor lost entire JumpShips, DropShips, and regiments to testing that blasted Fortress Wall, or to clever insurgents, or to ongoing acts of sabotage.

Which we still cannot prove is the Republic, Kamer reminded himself. The alternative was an inside job of some sort, a possibility Daoshen apparently did not lend credence to. What the Chancellor seemed to ignore was how coordinated the sabotage attacks had been, even if they seemed unrelated. The fact that they all began within days of one another suggested to Kamer—and others in the Maskirovka—that the order had come from some central location, and not been the work of radical elements of the Republic acting on their own to disrupt Capellan operations.

That said, Kamer doubted Daoshen would care. The sabotage wouldn't stop him.

He turned off the video, and hoped Robie was still up to doing her job. She was needed now more than ever.

CHAPTER 45

Danai paced briskly down a dimly lit corridor to Daoshen's primary war room in the palace. She wore her full MechWarrior kit, having been summoned from a relaxing training session in a simulator. At one point in the mock battle against Noah in an adjacent sim, she had to fight a compulsion to quit and go visit her *Black Knight* in its berth, to see for herself that the machine was fit and ready for duty.

"Well, this sounds big," Noah said as he walked beside her.

Danai didn't respond. Her mind flooded with possibilities for the purpose behind the summons. Obviously something had happened militarily. Given how stretched thin the CCAF and its assorted subsidiary units were at the moment, those possibilities seemed endless.

They reached a checkpoint and were swiftly admitted.

The CIC was more brightly lit than the outer hallway, and Danai blinked against the sudden glare. The room was smaller than Daoshen's favorite conference room, and lacked his usual throne. Multiple monitors and holovids lined three of the four walls. A central table, littered with paper, teacups, and sweaty steel water cups dominated the room. Smaller desks peppered the perimeter.

Danai checked each of the monitors in quick succession. The gathering of murmuring Strategios provided a backdrop hum, making it impossible for her to hear any one piece of useful information.

Her gaze settled on Daoshen, wearing a crimson robe, standing at the head of the table. His expression was inscrutable. Nearby stood Robie, who caught Danai's eye. She nodded at the largest screen at the head of the room.

Danai pushed past several colonels and other generals to get a closer look at the screen before asking loudly, "Well? What the hell happened?"

A younger officer looked at her, startled. "We just got word. Alaric is the ilKhan."

Danai and Capshaw exchanged a glance before she turned her attention to Daoshen. "IlKhan?"

The ambient noise quieted somewhat as Daoshen spoke. "We now know that Clan Wolf, Clan Jade Falcon, and forces from the Republic of the Sphere have clashed on Terra. Alaric and his Wolves have crushed the Republic and defeated the Jade Falcons in a Clan Trial. Devlin Stone has disbanded the Republic, and Alaric has been named ilKhan, and the Wolves as ilClan."

The Celestial Wisdom smiled.

"You seem pleased," Danai said cautiously.

"Our forces have already launched for their targets," Daoshen said, gesturing to one of the wall-mounted monitors. "Holdfast Guard to New Earth, Laurel's Legion to Rigil Kentaurus—"

"I can read," Danai snapped.

The room silenced.

"What I don't understand," she went on, heedless of the *faux pas* of interrupting the Celestial Wisdom, "is why any of you think this is good news."

"We continue to encounter Republic forces," Daoshen said, his tone cool. "But they are weak and ill-motivated. Now that they know Devlin has surrendered, their resistance will be token at best. This will allow us to close our grip around Terra."

"A world that now boasts two unified Clans under one leader!" Danai said.

Daoshen scanned the attendees of the meeting, smiling proudly, and raised his voice. "It is amazing, is it not, what unified worlds under one leader can accomplish."

Danai wanted to scream at the smirk in her father's voice. "Their Wall still remains," she said instead. "You can't blockade Terra into submission, their resources are—"

"Their resources are what will make Liao the sole and proper leader of the Inner Sphere."

Danai walked back to the Celestial Wisdom's side. "Daoshen," she said, lowering her voice once the room resumed its previous buzz. "This is not the great news you believe it is."

"If it is great news you seek, the advance scouts we deployed in March have captured or destroyed many Wolf JumpShips," Daoshen said. "The Wolves are not the threat we feared so many years ago."

"Look," Danai said, picking out a monitor showing current Capellan deployments using a nearby console to take control of it. "You can't just watch the lines on a map. They don't tell the whole story. Zoom in. We are stretched to a breaking point, and are now relying on the good will of our allies and neighbors. Do you really trust the Draconis Combine to uphold its agreement with us?"

"I do not fear the Combine, sister. Our second wave is preparing to launch in mere weeks, and upon completion, our enemies on Terra will have nowhere to run."

"Backing a wolf into a corner doesn't strike me as a healthy idea, Your Grace."

Daoshen tilted his head. "I named you Duchess of Castrovia, Danai. I named you *jiang-jun* of the MAC. Now I wonder if you have the confidence needed to liberate the Inner Sphere and provide for Liao. Have I miscalculated?"

Oh, you have miscalculated, Danai thought. *But not in the way you mean.*

"No, Your Grace," she answered, forcing herself to assume a neutral tone. "I'm only doing my job under both titles. It's important you have all opinions. Isn't it?"

Daoshen smiled mildly, and turned away.

Danai took a step back. "I should get back. Logistics for the entire McCarron's is somewhat time-consuming, Your Grace."

"Which brings up an interesting point," Daoshen said, looking at a monitor and decidedly not at Danai. "It is still not McCarron's anymore. I have been waiting to see the official designation change submitted, yet so far, nothing. Make that a priority, *Jiang-jun*."

Danai gave him a silent Capellan brace salute rather than reply. She had no intention of changing the name. Daoshen would forget about it eventually.

She turned on her heel and went for the exit, with Noah at her back.

CELESTIAL PALACE
CHANG-AN
LIAO
12 JULY 3151

Danai exited the BattleMech simulator drenched in sweat and anger. While she'd defeated her digital enemies, the victory did not improve her mood.

Life in the Celestial Palace was not going well.

After her performance in the palace CIC the previous month, and despite her rank and title, Danai had been quietly excluded from Strategios briefings, instead receiving only written reports, and then often a day or more later than the meeting. She had not seen Daoshen since last month. In some ways she counted this as a blessing, but she didn't like being kept in the cold. She'd put in numerous requests for meetings with him, all denied under the excuse of his being overwhelmed by the work of overseeing the war.

Danai snatched a red towel from a table nearby and wiped her face and head. The simulator battles helped, but only for a time, and then not always. Like today.

Why am I a general, and why am I duchess? she thought, scrubbing her hair. *Daoshen knows he's wasting me by keeping me here. At least put me on a battlefield somewhere where I can do some good.*

The door to the simulator room opened, and Noah stepped in. *"Jiang-jun?"*

"Over here, Noah."

Noah walked to her sim pod. Danai noticed his gait had improved. That was good news, anyway. She wanted him at full capacity.

"Latest briefing," he said, offering a pad.

She waved it off, unzipping her pilot's kit to let air circulate across her sweltering skin. "Tell me. And how old is it?"

"Two days ago."

"Dammit. Go ahead."

"We haven't heard a single thing from the Holdfast Guard since they headed to New Earth," he reported. "It's like they were wiped out of the Inner Sphere entirely."

"Any theories?"

"Eighteen thousand," he joked. "In other words, no, nothing concrete yet."

"What else?"

Noah tapped the pad. "Third Sian Dragoons have been ordered out of New Home to go investigate. That in itself isn't surprising, but you should know the Chancellor is sending a major naval detachment along with them."

Despite her dismissal a moment ago, Danai grabbed the tablet from Noah and looked at its screen herself. "He's sending the Second Raventhir Cuirassiers to New Earth as well," she read aloud. "And all these combat DropShips...this is far more than is needed."

She looked at Noah for insight, but he only shook his head. "I agree," he said. "And look—he's got JumpShips headed for Chara, Devil's Rock, and Pollux as well."

"The Wall still holds," Danai said, not quite a question.

"To the best of my knowledge, yes."

"And while this is more than is needed for New Earth, it's not nearly enough for Terra..."

"Agreed."

Danai raised the tablet as if to smash it against the table, but stopped herself. "Dammit, what is he up to?"

"Danai..." Noah began, then hesitated, looking aside.

She handed him the tablet. "Go ahead. What?"

"It's just...what are we doing here? The entire MAC is dispersed around various systems, and they're all just sitting there. Shouldn't we be engaging someplace?"

"We're here," Danai said, throwing the towel back to the table, "because Daoshen Liao wants it that way. Listen, Noah, and while I don't know who else has pieced this together, keep it to yourself."

He edged closer.

"Daoshen promoted me to *jiang-jun* before ordering McCarron's execution. He knew he was going to do it. Northwind might have been a failure, but I believe Daoshen would have found any excuse. He killed the one publicly vocal opponent of his quest for Terra. I'm about the only other person in the system who would even consider making a similar move, so he wants me close at hand."

"You would never publicly question him—would you?"

"No. It would only further destabilize an already unstable situation. So here we are, and here we stay, until the Celestial Wisdom sees fit to deploy us in a forward position...or garrison some conquered world while he expends the rest of the CCAF on attacking Terra."

"Danai, where does this end?"

"I don't know. I don't. Any word back from any of the MAC commanders?"

"Not yet. Your message went out as ordered, but—" Noah gestured with the tablet, "—with all the forward-moving logistics, getting responses will take a while."

"Naturally. We wouldn't want the MAC *jiang-jun* to have fast access to her regiments, after all."

Noah gave her a sick grin of agreement.

Danai pointed to the exit. "Join me for lunch?"

"Thank you, yes."

Side by side, they walked out of the simulation room.

Robie watched General Volkov rise from his seat at the conference table and face Daoshen. The Chancellor sat upon his throne swathed in white robes, his face calm.

"Chancellor," Volkov began his report as the other assembled Strategios watched him and, in Robie's opinion, tried to conceal their gratitude that they had not been tasked with giving the report. "We believe we have determined the fate of the Holdfast Guard. They used a pirate jump point, and mis-jumped. They are lost."

The entire regiment? Robie thought, and darted her gaze to Daoshen to see his response.

The Chancellor's calm expression seemed to freeze. Only her proximity allowed her to see the change, though; Robie was sure the Strategios did not notice.

Though they could probably guess at it.

"Then," Daoshen said as Volkov took his seat, "that will be the last such loss. From this point forward, order your regiments that the use of pirate jump points is forbidden."

The Strategios murmured their affirmatives.

"Despite this terrible loss," Daoshen continued, "there is a benefit."

The Strategios collectively shifted in their chairs.

"We can now assume that when word reaches our enemies, they too will cease the use of pirate jump points," Daoshen said. "It will no longer be necessary to keep any of our reserves close to strategic worlds with near-orbit pirate points. Those reserves and garrisons are now free to use as we advance our front."

Robie saw the generals and colonels trade glances, begging one another to be the one to speak. Volkov, to his credit, took the burden. "Your Grace," he said, "such a shift in doctrine may be...inadvisable. If our enemies decided to risk a pirate jump point—"

"Then they would suffer the fate of the Holdfast Guard."

"Perhaps, but perhaps not. We cannot guarantee that any jumps will result in the loss of ships."

"Nor can our enemies guarantee they will not." Daoshen sighed and stood. "Unlike our Confederation, they lack the significant military resources to risk such a jump. Losing the Holdfast Guard, while tragic, does not hinder our goal."

"Your Grace?" asked a *sang-shao*. Robie recognized her as representing the Third Tikonov Guards on Keid. "May I ask, why the concentration of ships to New Earth now? Why marshal so many to New Earth after the disappearance of the Holdfast Guard?"

At the question, Daoshen's placid grin grew slightly. Scanning the assembly, Robie noted that most of the Strategios were looking at the colonel as if sharing her question. Several others, however, kept their eyes on the Chancellor, their expressions blank.

Each of these watching Daoshen, Robie noted further, were also Maskirovka.

The calculus of these responses formed rapidly in her mind: The gathered agents already knew the answer. What they did not know was how Daoshen would respond.

"New Earth houses industrial plants needed to further our effort," said the Chancellor. "It will fall quickly, and perhaps quietly. With our superiority on the ground, production will ramp up in a number of factories. This will give us an extreme advantage when the time comes to liberate Terra."

Some members of the assembly shifted, as if preparing to ask more questions. Daoshen silenced them with a mere glance.

"Furthermore," he went on, "and perhaps more important-ly...New Earth is of great psychological benefit in our battles against the Wolves and Jade Falcons. The land and its history are of great value, a value that will be evident soon enough."

In a swirl of robes, the Chancellor retook his throne. "Services for the Holdfast Guard will be kept private. Immediately send the order to your fleets and soldiers regarding the forbidden use of pirate points. That is all."

The Strategios stood as one and offered deep bows. Guanken and his fellow servants hurried to open the double doors at the end of the room.

Robie left her position by one of the colossal pillars to approach Daoshen. "They are uneasy."

He nodded slightly. "Perhaps. But they are loyal. They see the great prize for what it is."

"*Jiang-jun* Centrella-Liao has not been present of late."

"The duchess has other responsibilities at the moment. Have your meetings with her yielded any great insights?"

"No. She is wise, and cautious. She has no reason to trust me, Your Grace. Are you certain this is the best use of my time? I should ever be at your side."

Daoshen lifted his right hand to press it against the small of Robie's back. "You *are* ever at my side, Robie. Continue your meetings with Danai. It is crucial we know her mind."

"Do you trust her?"

Daoshen smiled. "It is not her trust I require." His hand slid further down. "Yours, however, is paramount."

CHAPTER 46

Over the next few months, Robie felt the Celestial Wisdom's trust growing in her abilities and her devotion. Her own personal network of contacts within the palace had developed considerably as well, making it easier to best serve the office of the Chancellor.

On this day, Robie took a private elevator down to the palace communication center to file her daily report. While she had no real friends—her sole focus was on Daoshen—she had a friendly relationship with one of the comms experts, a woman her age named Sara.

Sara was on duty at her cubicle when she came in, and greeted the young Mask agent warmly. "How is palace life treating you?"

"It beats sitting at a desk all day," Robie said, smiling. She'd been developing Sara as an asset for some time. "What's new?"

"Uh...I flagged this one for you," Sara said, handing her a printout. "I didn't see it on any of the official schedules, which seems kind of odd."

Robie studied the report quickly. "She is coming here? Now?"

"On her way. Courier reported it just an hour ago. Does the Chancellor know?"

Robie allowed her eyes to lose focus as she connected all the strands of this news she could summon in her mind. "I don't think so."

Sara looked perplexed. "The Chancellor doesn't know of a state visit?"

"Maybe it's not a state visit. Scramble ships to be prepared to intercept."

Sara went to work on her keyboard. "You mean 'escort.' Right?"

"Just do it."

Sara continued typing. "Given her current vectors, we don't have much time to prepare a proper ceremony."

Robie ignored the comment, eyes focusing again on the printout. "She will be planet-side sooner than I'd like...Sara, can you send the absolute latest intelligence on the MOC to my drive right away?"

"Consider it done. Everything all right?"

"We're at war," Robie muttered. "Nothing is ever all right."

She skipped filing her daily report—it would take up to an hour—and went instead back to her quarters near Daoshen's and sent a message to Kamer.

CAFÉ MORPHEUS
CHANG-AN
16 NOVEMBER 3151

Robie met her handler at the same café where he'd given her the assignment to the Chancellor's office. Kamer looked good, if puffy; his broad shoulders sagged a bit, and his tunic concealed a visibly growing paunch. Additional wrinkles pulled at his eyes, but his hairline remained intact.

"You look good," Robie said after their meal arrived. It was a light affair—fruit and biscuits with tea.

"And you are a liar," Kamer replied, grinning. "But thank you."

Robie sipped her green tea. "Is your 'retirement' treating you well?"

"As well as expected." Kamer savored a piece of melon. "How is he treating you?"

Robie remained pointedly silent, focusing on her meal for the moment. Kamer frowned. "I'm sorry," he said in a low tone.

Robie shrugged. "For the good of the state."

"Yes. For the good of the state. So tell me. How close are we?"

Robie chewed and swallowed a bite of her biscuit, chasing it with water, weighing her answer. She'd been weighing it for months. Now was no different. "Closer than I'd hoped."

"Mmm."

"Not everyone is getting all the same intelligence at the same time," Robie went on, keeping her voice light but quiet, mindful of eavesdroppers. No one seemed to be in earshot or paying attention—nor paying so much inattention as to reveal themselves as a spy. "He is keeping his hands firmly on every lever of the military. Even *Qipao* is being kept out of the loop."

Kamer raised an eyebrow at the code name, but continued with his meal. "I see."

Robie paused to dab her mouth with a napkin and again assess their security, knowing Kamer, with his decades of experience, was doing the same as they spoke. For the moment, all seemed well. It would be best to finish quickly, though.

"An unscheduled visit is also coming soon," Robie added.

"I got word last night of that. Worrying."

"I agree. Hence my call. Should I expect a change in plans?"

Kamer ate several bites before replying, "No. Carry on. Protect the office at all costs. Is there anything else?"

"I don't think I'm making any progress with *Qipao*."

Kamer grinned once more as he chewed and swallowed more melon. "Don't worry about her. You'll be there when it becomes necessary, that's all that matters. I realize you already know this, but don't take anything personally."

"Of course."

"I should go," Kamer said, draping his napkin over his half-eaten meal. "It was good to see you, Robie. But let's not make it a habit. You have your orders. All of the Capellan Confederation is counting on you to see to them."

"I will."

"I know." Kamer stood and pushed in his wicker chair. He stepped toward her on the way to the exit, pausing to lay a palm on her shoulder. "When this is over...I will ensure you are taken care of."

"That's not why I do it," Robie whispered.

Kamer squeezed her shoulder. "Which is why you were the right choice. Take care, Robie."

The older man left the café. Robie stayed behind to finish her meal before leaving for the palace, using a circuitous route and watching for surveillance along the way. She spotted none.

CHAPTER 47

BEI SPACEPORT
OUTSIDE CHANG-AN
LIAO
CAPELLAN CONFEDERATION
30 DECEMEBER 3151

The Great Courtyard, as it was known in Chang-an, hosted cultural events throughout the year, and served as the official greeting area of visiting dignitaries after they landed in the city. Hundreds of meters square, it boasted its own private landing pad for DropShips and shuttles up to a certain size, in an area of land kept clear of all structures.

The courtyard itself was tiled with gleaming black marble. Five great crimson pillars marched down the middle of the flat space, holding at their pinnacles statues of the great Liao leaders: Franco Martell, Aleisha, Romano, Sun-Tzu, and of course, Daoshen himself. Candle *farolitos* were lit by hand every night on the short brick wall surrounding the courtyard, while powerful white spotlights hung from towers just outside the walls to light the interior like a sporting arena when needed.

Ilsa was familiar with the landing pad and the courtyard, which made her all the more confused at first as to why her ship was not landing there.

Instead, as she gazed out a porthole window, secure in her landing seat, she realized her ship had descended at a small commercial spaceport just outside Chang-an.

Don't act so surprised, she told herself with a grimace. *Daoshen knows this game too well.*

The DropShip landed. Ilsa stayed in her seat, clenching her teeth against the pain in her hips. Through the window, she saw a small crowd of Capellans waving and cheering at the ship as it prepared for disembarkation. Balloons juggled in the hands of children, hand-painted signs read variations on "*Welcome, Ilsa!*"

Ilsa snorted. She recognized at least three of the signs from her last visit. The office responsible for state visits must have brought them out of storage and passed them out to the paid servitors who mingled with the legitimate fans of the Magestrix—themselves likely transplants or descendants of the Magistracy.

The crowd stretched on either side of a grand red carpet being rolled out along a colonnade. At the far end of it, a waiting limousine idled, with uniformed agents at its four corners.

I see, she thought. *Short and sweet official state greeting? So be it.*

The DropShip captain indicated all well for passengers to disembark. Ilsa went to the main exit doors, flanked by her entourage. She smoothed her immaculate red gown, and met eyes with Zandra Thao, who wore her dress uniform. Thao gave her a brief nod of encouragement; the military aide saw what Ilsa saw, and instantly grasped the insult.

Daoshen wasn't going to give the Magestrix a microphone. Certainly not on Liao.

The door cranked open, and Ilsa conjured a political smile as she strode down the extended ramp to the red carpet. She badly wanted a cane. The pain in her hips intensified as she walked, but she kept the smile up as she waved and blew kisses to the gathered admirers—both paid and legitimate.

With each gesture, she thought, *Damn you, Daoshen. Damn you.*

She took her time on the carpet, slowing her walk for more than one reason. First, it gave her more screen time—many cameras tracked her every move and broadcast it throughout Liao, and on into Capellan territory at the speed of light, or to be bundled into physical storage for transport to outer worlds. Every added second in front of the people and the cameras would annoy Daoshen.

Second, for her true supporters in the crowd, it gave the appearance of consideration. And she did love them, her admirers and supporters, in her own way. They were the people she worked for, after all.

Finally…taking more time to wave or shake a hand gave her aching body a break.

Ilsa managed to wring ten full minutes from her walk down the carpet before ending at the limo. There, she turned, smiling brightly all the while, and waved both hands at the crowd before being guided carefully into the back seat by one of the Liao security team.

Thao joined her on the other side, while the rest of her entourage got into luxury vehicles ahead of and behind the limo.

Once the door was closed and the car was moving, Ilsa let the smile drop. She assessed the young woman sitting in a jump seat opposite her.

"Your Grace," the woman said, and Ilsa instantly recognized the bearing of a Maskirovka agent. The girl was young, though. Quite young, with red hair shorn close to her scalp. "Welcome to Chang-an. I am Robie Anjing, personal guard to the Celestial Wisdom."

"Though we are not actually in Chang-an just yet, are we?" Ilsa said. She gestured. "Zandra Thao, my personal aide."

Robie Anjing shook hands with Thao. "We'll be traveling straight to the palace, where the Celestial Wisdom waits to meet with you."

"So soon?" Ilsa said lightly. "And without the pomp and circumstance? Tell me, Robie Anjing, personal guard to the Celestial Wisdom…is there some compelling security reason we did not disembark at the Great Courtyard?"

"There is," Robie replied. "There was an attempt on the Chancellor's life several months ago, and the ringleaders are still at large. Your safety is the Chancellor's prime concern."

Ilsa laughed, and turned her head away as the reaction gripped the pain in her bones. "You're delightful, Robie Anjing," she said, and coughed. "The perfect Mask."

Robie said nothing, and gave no indication of having taken offense.

The ride was swift, with Liao security on two-wheelers clearing the roads ahead. Ilsa fell silent, watching Chang-an outside her armored window.

A shiny, rotten apple, she thought. The populace appeared well-fed, the streets and buildings clean. *But inside, you are corrupt to the core. My dear brother would have you fighting over scraps if his ambition goes unchecked. Will you smile so big when the Clans take this world from you?*

The limo slowed and stopped at a rear entrance to Liao Palace. Ilsa only smirked at the realization, far beyond being surprised at Daoshen's treatment of her. The limo and cars emptied, and Robie led the entire group to private elevators that took them to the Chancellor's suite of offices.

Robie directed most of the attendants to comfortable waiting areas outside an ornate wooden door, flanked by armed officers. She permitted Thao to join Ilsa, but no others.

At last, Robie opened the door and stood aside for Ilsa and Thao to enter.

Daoshen had chosen a windowless room that Ilsa felt was soundproofed the moment she crossed the threshold. The sensation in her ears reminded her of days gone by as a child, swimming deep in ponds and pools. Dimly lit, the room boasted only floor lamps, no overhead lighting. A low, rectangular table of dark wood sat in the middle, surrounded by four plush black leather seats—one of which sat slightly higher than the others.

In this chair sat the Celestial Wisdom, dressed in a loose green silk suit. He smiled as the group entered and Robie closed the door behind them. "Sister," he said. "I am so glad to see you arrived safely. Please. Sit. May I offer you something?"

"Brother," Ilsa replied, her voice equally as saccharine as Daoshen's. "Some water would be lovely, thank you."

Ilsa noticed only then another person in the room, an elderly servant with a long scar down one side of his jawline.

This servant disappeared through a well-concealed door, and returned before Ilsa had even taken her seat. He placed a tall glass of water on the table before her and slipped away.

Thao took the seat nearest Ilsa, while Robie remained on her feet, a few meters behind the Chancellor.

"You took great pains to come for a visit," Daoshen said. He had no drink nor other refreshment, and did not seem to even notice Thao's presence. "I understand you commandeered a command circuit to make your way here."

"All the sooner to meet with you, Chancellor."

"As you know," Daoshen said, "we are quite busy with fighting a war with the Republic of the Sphere, so I am afraid our time may be rather limited."

"Then let's get to our business," Ilsa said. "You—"

The door opened. All eyes went to it.

Danai Centrella-Liao took a cautious step inside, then paused.

"Ilsa," she said.

The Magestrix thought she detected a slight tremor in Danai's voice. "My dear Danai! Come in, won't you? We have so much to discuss with our brother..."

CHAPTER 48

Danai tugged her tunic straight and strode into the room. She sat in the only free seat, between Daoshen and a woman whom she seemed to recall served as Ilsa's military advisor.

Ilsa confirmed as much when she made introductions. "And now," she said after Thao and Danai traded nods, "Zandra, I must ask you to give us our privacy for the moment. Daoshen? Would you dismiss your servants and guardians?"

Daoshen eyed her for a long moment before waving his fingers in the air. Robie Anjing, his servant Guanken, and Thao all bowed and left the room, leaving the Liaos alone.

"Well, now," Ilsa said brightly. "Isn't this lovely. Our family all together."

"What's going on?" Danai asked.

"First, Danai," Ilsa said with what Danai supposed passed for tenderness, "I believe you have not yet heard—Erde is gone."

Danai gripped the arms of her chair. "Aunty Erde's dead?"

"A stroke. In August. I'm so sorry."

Danai's vision swam momentarily. Erde Centrella-Liao, Ilsa's regent in the Magistracy of Canopus, had filled the role of mother when Ilsa seemed uninterested in the job.

She refocused her gaze on Daoshen. "How long have you known?"

"It seemed best to have you focused on your current duties," Daoshen said.

Fire bloomed in Danai's gut. She leaped up from her seat. "Duties? My *duties* here may as well include sweeping the floor! How *dare* you keep this from me!"

"As a soldier, you know our military affairs of state must take precedence, sister."

"Don't call me that," Danai growled. "The both of you...you—"

Ilsa glowered. "Consider your next words carefully, Danai."

"Or *what*?" Danai snarled back.

Ilsa pursed her lips, readjusted in her seat, and spoke again: "We can be civil here. I wanted to bring you the news in person, Danai, a gesture I'd hoped you would find loving."

"Loving," Danai repeated, mostly to herself. "Is that what we are, Mother? Loving?"

She briefly savored the flash of anger and possibly guilt that crossed Ilsa's face.

Still standing, Danai crossed her arms. "What am I doing here? This little chit-chat has nothing to do with family."

"It has *everything* to do with family," Ilsa said darkly.

"Defined how?"

Daoshen broke in. "Defined as the Capellan Confederation and its citizens. You are Duchess of Castrovia, heir to the Capellan throne—"

"A subject we will return to momentarily," Ilsa put in.

"—and one of the highest-ranking soldiers in the entire Capellan military," Daoshen continued, with a withering glance at his sister.

"The same high-ranking soldier who is kept in the dark until deemed convenient by the Chancellor," Danai spat back. "Including this very visit from the Magistracy."

"For the good of the state," Daoshen said.

Ilsa tapped her fingertips together in her lap. "Which brings me to my first discussion point. Danai? Please, my dear. Join us." She gestured to Danai's chair.

Danai swiveled her gaze between them, unsure. A mix of emotions she was unaccustomed to juggling made her sweat inside her uniform. They were her parents—that relationship could not be denied, not when it was just the three of them.

Yet there was no love here, not between any combination of them, not in any direction.

All the same, the CCAF remained the largest military force in the Inner Sphere at the moment, and the Magistracy Armed Forces, while smaller, remained formidable. The Canopians remained allied with House Liao—at least for the moment—so staying here would doubtless reveal some actionable intelligence she'd not been privy to of late.

Danai sat.

Ilsa offered her a bland, manufactured smile, and turned to her brother. "Daoshen. It is important we discuss your use of MAF troops."

"I do not command the Magistracy Armed Forces," Daoshen said with his usual dismissive smirk.

Ilsa's manufactured smile froze on her face. "You used MAF troops to protect your most valuable worlds while you waste the CCAF on abandoned Republic worlds."

"The Republic does not abandon worlds until forced to do so by the CCAF," Daoshen countered.

"They were undefended, Daoshen!"

"Your intelligence, as always, is lacking, sister."

From Danai's point of view, Ilsa's entire face appeared to tremble with wrath.

"Our first duty is always to the state," Daoshen went on. "Liberating Capellan worlds stolen from us, and our extension of protection to neighboring systems, *such as* those in the Magistracy, ensures that these systems do not fall victim to the predations of the ilClan."

"The ilClan is on Terra," Danai said.

"Not any longer," Daoshen said. "We now have reports that several Clan Wolf Galaxies are besieging Capellan systems. We will defeat them, of course, but they are no longer confined to Terra."

While Danai gaped at this colossal news, the Chancellor faced Ilsa. "And so, sister, yes—I will use all available resources to defend us."

Ilsa struggled to regain her composure. "You're overstepping yourself, Daoshen."

"Clan Wolf has begun a counterattack on New Earth," Daoshen said. "This is but the first volley of their inevitable spread to the rest of the Inner Sphere. They will stop at nothing to resurrect the Star League, and only I can prevent it."

"And what will you stop at nothing to achieve, Chancellor?" Danai said.

He faced her, eyes narrowing. "Whatever is best for the people and subjects of House Liao."

Danai carefully rose to her feet once more, and again straightened her uniform tunic. "How long have you known about this counterattack on New Earth?"

"Only recently. The Wolves made their first foray three weeks ago. Naturally, without the HPG system, time lags in our communication remain our greatest weakness."

Danai met his eyes evenly, unafraid, and read between the lines of his statement. Daoshen was right, of course; with the HPG systems down across the Inner Sphere, communication lagged between the Chancellor and his forces by as much as two weeks, and often longer. War, she knew well, moved much, much faster.

The fact of delayed communications wasn't what unnerved her about Daoshen's words. Danai heard the subtext as clearly as if he'd spoken it: *I will give orders weeks or months in advance, heedless of the situation on the ground.*

More to the point, she realized as she stared into his dark eyes: *I have already given orders not easily rescinded.*

"What did you do?" Danai said in a quiet voice.

"Do?" Daoshen tilted his head, birdlike. "I do what is right for House Liao, *Jiang-jun*, as I know you will as well."

Danai swallowed bitterness at the back of her throat and took a step back from the table. "I have...there are some things I must attend to. For the good of the state. Ilsa, thank you for the news of Erde's passing. I will send a public message of condolence immediately. Chancellor..."

She had nothing to add after that. Instead, Danai bowed slightly, and walked swiftly to the double doors without looking back.

Opening the doors herself, Danai swept into the adjacent waiting room, where Robie leaped to her feet and Thao rose as well. Guanken had not taken a seat.

"Jiang-jun," Robie said. "Are you all right?"

"Perfectly. You may go back in, I'm sure the Celestial Wisdom will appreciate your presence."

Based on Robie's expression, her sarcasm landed perfectly. She pushed past the Mask agent as Guanken hurried to return to his post in the small meeting room. Turning a corner, Danai saw Robie enter as well, closing the doors gently behind herself.

Danai marched down corridors and up flights of stairs until reaching Noah Capshaw's small but tidy office, with a window that overlooked the front courtyard. All signs of the battle there from months ago were long since sanitized and erased, as if no assault on the Chancellor of the Capellan Confederation had ever taken place.

Noah looked up at her abrupt entrance and struggled to get quickly to his feet. *"Jiang-jun?"*

Danai closed the door to his office and pressed her back against it. "Something bad is happening, Noah."

Concern twisted his expression. "What is it, what can I do?"

"I don't know," Danai said. "That's just it. I don't know what it is, or when it's going to happen. But trust me, Noah…"

She used both palms to smooth her pulled-back hair, drying them of sweat. "Something's coming."

Robie stayed discreetly away from the table, but met Guanken's eyes briefly. She realized the elderly, scarred servant could teach her much about the art of being invisible while remaining in plain sight. For now, though, standing still and keeping her eyes on Ilsa Centrella would have to suffice.

"Well," Ilsa began, shooting Robie a narrow glance. "Alone again at last, brother."

"This discussion will be brief," Daoshen said, and Robie noted there was a disconcerting shift in his tone of voice. He sounded—human.

"Brief?" Ilsa echoed with a sharp barking laugh. "I suppose there are important affairs of state to keep Your Grace busy. Very well. I *will* be brief. Your exploits on Joppa are—"

"My exploits, as you call them, are the province of this office, and not to be questioned by lesser states. But if you wish to speak of exploits, what of Sadurni? That world is under the stewardship of House Liao, and you have deliberately undermined that stewardship."

Ilsa arched an eyebrow. "Your own Capellan garrison welcomed me on Sadurni when I arrived to quell the uprising there. Now answer for Joppa."

Robie recalled what she knew of Joppa's recent history. In March, unrest in the form of protests had roiled the planet after Capellan citizens landed in the world's sole colony while the Confederation upgraded Joppa's lunar station, Specula. Overwhelmed by the new citizens, resources on Joppa were soon depleted. Thanks to the actions of a popular religious leader, a food catastrophe was averted, but large numbers of Joppa's colony—Canopian citizens—took their outrage to the streets. The protests were nonviolent at first, but ultimately, Capellan military forces were engaged, and thirteen Canopian citizens were killed.

"The incident at Joppa is put to rest," Daoshen said, blinking lazily. "The Capellan Confederation did what your people failed to do."

"So you take responsibility for the actions of your troops," Ilsa marveled. "I don't know whether to be impressed or appalled. Is the Celestial Wisdom aware that, strangely enough, the murder of Canopian citizens by Capellan military forces put our pact at risk? My people are openly questioning our agreement, Daoshen."

"A situation which *Erde* handled quite capably," he replied, seasoning the deceased regent's name.

Robie sensed tension in Ilsa's frame. The Magestrix's knuckles whitened as they lay clasped in her lap.

"Indeed," Daoshen went on, with the tone of a man holding only high cards in a poker game, "the Maskirovka reports to me that many Canopians—*your* people, Ilsa—are upset at your travel so soon after losing Erde. Better that you should attend to the affairs in your own backyard."

"You left me no choice," Ilsa snapped, and Robie was surprised to see her façade of composure crack. "I wouldn't have had to sprint through space to see you in person if you'd returned my messages personally rather than sending that lackey Fisk. I sent you a message myself, and you dispatch Fisk to respond to me? To *me*? Why such an insult, Daoshen?"

"Ha! You speak to me of insult. The buildup of assets in Andurien must cease immediately. Your plotting with Humphrys without consulting me is the insult here."

"My 'plotting' is strengthening both our nations, yours and mine."

"It was *I* who joined our three nations!" Daoshen snapped, in a rare display of emotion. "Without my aid, there would be no agreements between you and the Duchy of Andurien. Ari Humphreys would be your mortal enemy instead of your 'beloved' husband. And what of Sadurni? It is a Capellan world that you seem compelled to wrest from House Liao."

Ilsa answered smoothly. "It's a Capellan world that desires to be Andurien. Let them have it, Daoshen. You need the garrison to join your quest for Terra."

"Do not tell me of my needs, Ilsa."

"Daoshen...do not let your quest blind you. Think! Ari is an old man who cannot long sit on the throne. He is an aging duke whose passing will disrupt all of Andurien. With no other claimant, the Duchy of Andurien will be mine. Yes, some elements within the duchy will doubtless scream from its rooftops, but our combined forces will prevent them from rebelling against my accession. When that happens, Daoshen, we will share Andurien. You and I, the Magistracy and the Confederation. That border will be secure, and you will have more resources to add to your...war effort."

Daoshen steepled his fingers. "You will, of course, thus inherit Andurien's military and enlarge your own."

Ilsa looked legitimately shocked. "Of course!" she said. "To better crush the Free Worlds League."

"Ah," Daoshen said, and Robie heard the sarcasm layered deep within his voice. "To grow my empire, no doubt."

Ilsa frowned, appearing at a loss for words.

Daoshen rose from his seat and strode thoughtfully to a suspended viewscreen. There, he brought up a map displaying the whole of Capellan, Andurien, and Canopus space.

The Chancellor studied this colorful image for some time in silence. Robie's gaze darted between him and his sister, as Ilsa sipped her glass of water. Robie wasn't sure, but it seemed the old woman's hand shook ever so slightly.

"Ilsa," Daoshen said at last, still facing the screen. "It pains me to discover this day that you have forgotten where your obligation lies. Your ambition to allegedly grow both the Confederation and Canopus is laudable, but misplaced. It is you who have been blinded to your first duty as a Liao. And you have misunderstood the greatest threat to us both."

Ilsa slowly rose from her seat, using the armrests to push herself. Thao instantly stood also, as if prepared to catch the elderly woman. "Daoshen," she said in a low voice. "Do not try to say that Terra—"

Daoshen whirled, the hem of his tunic flapping. To Robie, it seemed his eyes were on fire.

"Yes! *Terra!*" the Chancellor roared, clenching a fist and shaking it. "It is the Wolves who must be eliminated! It is Terra that must be seized! They are the threat, sister, they and no other! Our responsibility—*your* responsibility—is to this House and its people! With Alaric and his ilClan in possession of it, the entire Inner Sphere could fall! All Liao must meet this threat, and that includes Ilsa Centrella-Liao!"

"Even if," Ilsa said quietly, with something akin to fear in her eyes, "the entire Inner Sphere must fall to Daoshen Liao first."

Robie heard the Chancellor inhale deeply through his nose. His voice and body slowly calmed.

"We will reclaim all Confederation worlds on our way to liberate Terra," he said, as if this negated Ilsa's charge. Robie, still growing in her study of politics, knew his words were not a denial. "All other concerns apart from Terra are secondary. Including yours. Sister."

Also clearly forcing herself into a calmer demeanor, Ilsa swept the sides of her robes into her hands and took measured steps toward her brother.

"And what of Danai? The Duchess of Castrovia, whom you appointed? You are not the god you told me you were, Daoshen. You too will die, like our father before us. Clearly you mean for Danai to rule the Confederation on that day. She is my heir as well, heir to the Magistracy. Her empire can include all of Andurien, as well as Sian and Canopus...if you will only listen to reason."

Daoshen gave the Magestrix a pitying look as she drew closer. "Danai will serve the Confederation as she always has. The Magistracy's succession issues are its own. And yours."

Ilsa ceased her approach. Her face betrayed a barely harnessed rage, such that Robie slightly angled her own body to intercept a possible attack on the Chancellor.

The room hummed with tension. Robie saw Thao swallow and twitch her fingers near her thigh, as if seeking a sidearm that was not there.

Ilsa gazed unblinking at the Chancellor, lips tight together. Daoshen—as if enjoying the standoff—grinned mildly and slid his hands into the sleeves of his gown.

Robie had an intrusive thought: *What must their childhoods have been like?* Amusing—but distracting. She quickly dismissed the image.

Daoshen was the first to speak. He turned with great deliberation to the viewscreen as if to assess troop movements. "You may go."

Ilsa held her blistering gaze for another few moments... then spun and marched so quickly toward the doors that Guanken nearly missed opening it for her. Thao leaped to follow, casting Robie a worried glance before disappearing.

Guanken closed the door quietly and resumed his post. Robie stood still, eyes on Daoshen, waiting for his next order of business.

It came quickly.

"Robie," he said, with a jovial note to his tone. "Please ensure that the Magestrix reaches her ship safely and quickly, and that her entire entourage makes it off Liao."

He turned his head slightly toward her.

"And out of Confederation space."

Robie bowed her head. "At once, Your Grace."

CHAPTER 49

CELESTIAL PALACE
CHANG-AN
LIAO
3 FEBRUARY 3152

The bureaucracy Danai ran into may as well have been solid plates of ferro-fibrous BattleMech armor. Daoshen had all but disappeared in the weeks since Ilsa's visit, Danai's access to him curtailed by a never-ending series of secretaries, guards, and even Robie herself, the few times Danai got close enough to even see the young agent.

Today, after an endless series of put-offs by Daoshen's underlings, Danai returned to her office with Noah in tow and slammed the door, recognizing the unusually immature reaction in herself.

"He's sidelining me again," she growled, walking behind her desk and glaring at the smooth surface. The lighting here was too bright and unnatural. She had a window, but it was square and utilitarian, nothing like her suite on Castrovia. She wondered, as a passing thought, how Tiko was doing; his queen figure was the only decoration on the windowsill.

"I agree," Noah said, standing behind one of the guest chairs, one hand resting atop its back for support. "What I'm not so sure of is why."

"Oh, I'm his favorite pet," Danai snarled. "He likes having me on his short little leash. Noah, send a message to Wu.

We're coming back to the Second MAC and offering ourselves out as mercenaries to the highest bidder."

He frowned. "Um...really?"

Danai threw herself into her chair. "No. But much more of Daoshen's hiding and I'll start thinking seriously about it."

She tapped her computer console on and scowled at the steady stream of updates scrolling along the left side of her screen. One of them made her sit up and pause the feed. "Dammit!"

"What now?" Noah asked.

"Two Andurien regiments attacked Wallacia in January. They were met by the Capellan Home Guard and some local merc units, but..."

"Has Wallacia fallen?"

Danai re-read the bulletin from the Strategios. "Uncertain at this time. And this information is weeks old. Anything could have happened by now." She covered her mouth with one hand and frowned at the update, filling in blanks as best she could.

Duke Ari Humphreys of the Duchy of Andurien was technically a relation to her. In the public's eye, with Ilsa as Danai's sister, Ilsa's marriage to Humphreys made him brother-in-law to both herself and Daoshen. Suspicions over the Duchy's military buildup had been growing among the Strategios for some time, but common theory was Humphreys would assault systems in the Free Worlds League. His marriage with and union to Ilsa's Magistracy—and her long-time border with Daoshen's Capellan Confederation—suggested there was no reason to fear an Andurien assault.

Yet here we are, Danai thought.

She considered the chessboard in play across the entire Inner Sphere. What did Humphreys have to gain by wading into Capellan space during House Liao's march toward Terra?

Danai might have laughed as the pieces on the board came together in her mind, except there was nothing remotely amusing about this report. "Ilsa."

Noah raised an eyebrow.

"Ari Humphreys has nothing to gain by attacking us, not with the FWL right next door. This is Ilsa's doing. She knows Daoshen has stretched us too thin. She needs us on her border, and knows if his gambit for Terra fails, so too might the Magistracy."

"So she's..."

"She's knocking Daoshen upside the head," Danai finished for him.

"I assume that's conjecture on your part, not in the report, correct?"

"Right."

"Then the Chancellor will know it's her as well."

Danai spun her chair to look out the office window. "Maybe. But maybe not. It's a bold move, even for Ilsa. Given how quickly she left here after her visit, I wouldn't be surprised if Daoshen believes he's cowed her into submission. This is Ilsa, I'd wager on that, but I'd also wager Daoshen won't believe it."

"So now we face another front," Noah said from behind her. She heard him sit in the guest chair with a heavy sigh. "That's not what we need right now."

"And Ilsa knows that."

"Wallacia is not too far from Sian," Noah said, his voice dropping to a wary tone.

"And Castrovia," Danai muttered. Hearing Noah and herself say the systems out loud dumped another shot of adrenaline into her blood.

When news of this attack on Wallacia reached the public, as it inevitably would, people quickly draw the straight line from Wallacia to Sian, at a time when the bulk of the CCAF was driving pell-mell coreward toward Terra. Even the *Zang shu sheng*, the official Capellan state propagandists, would have its hands full trying to downplay this assault on Wallacia.

That same straight line between Wallacia and Sian could as easily be drawn from Wallacia to Castrovia, which lay within just a few jumps of Wallacia.

Danai's gut tightened. Her perceived kinship with Castrovia had grown quickly during her time there, time that now seemed forever and a day away. Tiko would be...good Lord, ten years old now? Moving into more advanced training, no doubt. She thought of their games together, and of the populace's regard for her. She kept tabs on the activities of the White Moon, which of late had indeed split into two factions, one of which was building a settlement on the land offered by Danai. Castrovia was in good hands, and under Yunhai's watchful eye.

She longed to return now more than ever.

Danai turned her chair back to Noah. Returning to Castrovia was out of the question; for as much as Daoshen wanted her nearby where he could exert more control over her, she wanted to be near him as well, to more quickly assess his maneuvering. If it was taking days and weeks to catch up with Daoshen's machinations here, it would take months if she were to leave Liao.

"Ilsa or Ari, it doesn't matter," she said. "They're too close to Castrovia, too close to Sian, and too big a distraction. I don't agree with the push for Terra, but I'll damn well not sit around and let anyone creep up behind us with a big stick."

As Noah watched, Danai reached out and activated a holovid recorder attached to her computer system. Once on, she leaned forward, lacing her fingers and placing her hands atop the desk.

"Magestrix," she began. "I'm sure you're aware of the recent assault on Wallacia, a Confederation world, by factions identified with the Duchy of Andurien. Given your unique place in Andurien society, I send this request to you, as a *jiang-jun* of the Capellan Confederation Armed Forces and Duchess of Castrovia, and heir to both the Magistracy of Canopus and the Capellan Confederation:

"Please take pains to end any ongoing hostilities on Wallacia, and withdraw any Andurien forces there. I ask that this be done with all haste, and evidence of the Andurien withdrawal provided immediately."

Danai paused, took a breath, and centered herself.

"Ilsa...neither of us needs this distraction. The stakes for both our nations are far too high. I am doing and will continue to do my best to restrain our 'brother' and his ambitions, but I cannot do so when once-friendly allies now seem to threaten my own world. I ask you, please...take whatever measures are needed to prevent further Andurien incursions.

"Thank you, Magestrix. I await your response."

Danai turned off the recorder, waited a moment for it to save, then lifted the holocube toward Noah. "Send that immediately," she said as he rose to his feet. "Fastest means possible."

Noah took the cube. "Shall I send a copy to the Strategios?"

Danai's lip curled. "They're so good at keeping tabs on things, let them find out when they find out."

**CELESTIAL PALACE
CHANG-AN
LIAO
29 FEBRUARY 3152**

Danai's headache grew with each word spoken by her mother. The three-dimensional image of Ilsa Centrella-Liao somehow managed to glare directly into Danai's eyes.

"Wallacia is home to a Capellan garrison threatening the Duchy of Andurien, young Danai—"

Danai bristled at the dismissal.

"—and Ari Humphreys is well within his rights to protect his people. I am amazed to find that you believe I have any sort of authority over Duke Humphreys' military engagements. If you have diplomatic desires, address your concerns to the duke, not I. Good-bye, Danai."

That was it. The holovid ended. As cold and terse a response as any Danai could have dreamed from her mother.

"What now?" Noah asked from across her desk. He'd been asking that a lot lately.

Danai shook her head slowly, teeth grinding. "I don't know. I don't know who else..." She straightened abruptly in her chair. "Nikol."

Noah frowned. "I imagine Nikol is...busy."

"Yes," Danai said, with a little more snap in her voice than she preferred when speaking with Noah. "But I am rapidly running out of options."

Nikol wasn't Capellan, but was for all intents and purposes the person Danai trusted most in the Inner Sphere. A distant part of her brain suggested that someday, perhaps she would entrust Noah Capshaw with some of the secrets she kept. Certainly she trusted him with her life on the battlefield, and with her safety on Liao, and even her misgivings about the Chancellor. It would be nice to trust him with more...

Danai squeezed her eyes shut to push the thought away. Now was not the time to idly muse about such matters.

"Nikol has her hands full dealing with the Wolf Empire," she said, not because Noah didn't know this, but because she needed the sound of her own voice to bring her back to focus. "But we go back a long way. I just need her to make some inquiries, perhaps hint at a show of force nearer than any I can muster right now. Daoshen has built a house of children's toy blocks, and one wrong nudge will bring the whole structure down. The Anduriens invading Wallacia is just such a nudge. I'm going to record a message right now. Noah, find out where she is likely to be and how quickly I can get the message to her."

Noah stood. The movement was more fluid now; his physical therapy sessions seemed to be helping his recovery. "Right away, ma'am. I'll use a military courier. But, you understand, it's not going to be fast."

Danai nodded. "Do your best."

Noah returned the nod and left the office. Danai exhaled heavily and rocked back in her chair, considering. If Nikol was unwilling or unable to help, what then? How to best protect Castrovia and Liao from further incursions?

She shut her eyes against the throb in her temples and tried to think.

CHAPTER 50

Robie studied the three-dimensional map as carefully as the assembled generals and colonels that made up Daoshen's immediate Strategios war cabinet were. She also noted several empty chairs around the table. Doubtless the missing Strategios were embarked on missions critical to Capellan security. She was sure that was Daoshen's assumption.

It was not her own. She had theories about the missing Strategios and, as in all things, kept these thoughts to herself.

"Wolf units have left Terra, and are en route to Rigil Kentarus and Alula Australis," said General Volkov.

"They have landed on these worlds?" Daoshen inquired.

Volkov cleared his throat. "Negative, Chancellor. But that is our belief as of now. Unless they use pirate jump points, in which case we can't know where—"

"No one will risk a pirate jump point after our recent loss to one," Daoshen interrupted. "They are far too risky. Has there been a single report of the use of such a jump since then?"

A few Strategios shook their heads, and no one spoke up. Robie knew there must be cases of pirate point usage, but tellingly, every Strategios in the room maintained a stony silence.

Daoshen rose from his throne. The others began to rise as well, but the Chancellor waved them back to their seats. He took a long, slow lap around the conference room, as if admiring the tall pillars and searching the gleaming marble floor for scratches or scuff marks. No one spoke. Above the conference table, the map image flickered, as if uncertain of what it was showing.

"What of New Earth?" Daoshen asked at last, as he neared the carved throne.

"Celestial Wisdom," Volkov said, "the shortest answer I can give you is 'meat grinder.' We are significantly delaying the Wolf advance on the surface. We enjoy aerospace superiority. But we are most definitely taking casualties. Also, Your Grace... Warrior House Hiritsu has fallen to Clan Wolf."

Robie felt a wave of tension ripple through the room. Warrior House Hiritsu gone? They were among the Chancellor's most prized battalions.

The Chancellor himself seemed frozen for a long moment before quietly asking, "Andurien?"

"Last report was similar to New Earth, though we are holding the Duchy's forces in place on Wallacia. It's a slog, Your Grace."

The Chancellor twitched his eyebrows, as if only mildly concerned about the news. Robie felt sure she was not the only person who saw past his façade. "Our momentum seems to have been temporarily blunted. Perhaps our army would benefit from a show of support and strength from the Capellan people."

No one answered. Robie saw clearly that no one wanted to.

"The Third Sian Dragoons are on New Earth, as well as other auxiliary forces," Daoshen continued after the leaden silence from his war council. "The Anduriens on Wallacia are, as you say, held in place by the Capellan Home Guard for the time being. We must trust our CCAF on Rigil Kentarus and Alula Australis to counter any attempt by Clan Wolf, if they are, in fact, the Wolves' destination. The movement you've reported may be a feint."

Volkov shifted uncomfortably in his seat, but went motionless again after a slight glance from the Chancellor.

"Evacuate all our forces from New Earth," Daoshen abruptly declared. "Have Sian Commonality forces regroup and prepare to buttress Wallacia as needed. All other forces are to remain on their current mission."

Volkov looked around at the other generals, as if for support, before turning to Daoshen once more. "Your forgiveness, Celestial Wisdom," he said, "but...how is this a show of strength?"

In an unusual response—as far as Robie's experience went—Daoshen Liao laughed. The sound was so abrasive and shocking, she couldn't tell if he'd manufactured it, or if it truly came from a source of amusement.

She could not see anything amusing in Volkov's question.

"Instruct the Dragoons to leave a gift for the Wolf Clan," the Chancellor said, smiling. "They will understand."

Robie watched Volkov try to formulate his next query. The older man seemed at a loss for words before managing to say: "May I ask...?"

Daoshen resumed his throne. "This is the will of the Capellan people. Send the orders immediately."

The gathered council waited for several seconds to see if more was forthcoming from the Chancellor. When the silence dragged on, they finally stood almost as one, as if seeing some invisible cue.

Each of the Strategios bowed and thanked the Chancellor before exiting out the double doors opened for them by Guanken and another servant. Only after the last of them were gone and the doors firmly closed once more did Robie approach the table and squint at the holovid map. "Your Grace...may I ask a tactical question?"

Daoshen looked toward her, amusement still on his face. "Why, yes, Robie. By all means."

"The Third Sian Dragoons...where would you have them retreat to?"

"I do not recall using the word 'retreat.'"

Robie looked to the map. "Then where?"

Daoshen sighed. Dramatically. "Robie, there are weights that only a Chancellor must bear. You will come to understand the will of the Capellan people soon enough. And if you recall,

I promised you a gift, a small token to help alleviate the pain you endured when your fellow agents were lost on Liberty. That gift is on its way now."

Robie glanced at him. Daoshen had his eyes, too, fixed on the map, and his smile remained.

She did not believe him. Not for a moment. Daoshen was a consummate actor in his role as Chancellor, but she'd taken enough tactical courses to see what was plain on the current map.

The Capellan Confederation Armed Forces were, at last, showing the deleterious effects of Daoshen's relentless plunge toward Terra.

He has to know, Robie thought. *He had to keep up the appearance of control before the Strategios...or, rather, he* felt *he had to keep up the appearance.* For her part, Robie thought the best course of action at this point was to ask the war council for their thoughts, advice, and strategy, rather than simply dictate action from his giant throne.

The assault on Wallacia had come as a surprise. Even her contacts in the Maskirovka had been taken aback by it. Further, it was two entire regiments—the kind of force expecting to come in, take a world, and hold it for some time. Luck, some well-paid mercenaries, and the sheer fortitude of the Capellan Home Guard had prevented that fate so far, though Robie knew the stalemate could not and would not hold forever...

Yet another factor Daoshen must know, yet refuses to acknowledge, even to his generals. So he is readjusting his front lines, she concluded. *Which is smart. But would they need to be adjusted had he taken a more measured approach to his conquest in the first place?*

Eyeing the Chancellor more closely now, Robie searched for any sign of this "weight" he claimed to bear. She saw none.

What she saw was a man of such certainty and ambition that he would risk his entire nation for the sake of one singular goal.

CHAPTER 51

UNION-CLASS WARSHIP **AUTUMN RAIN**
HIGH ORBIT, NEW EARTH
STAR LEAGUE PROTECTORATE
10 APRIL 3152

Sang-shao Hao Jie, or "Bent" to his colleagues, sat in his command chair in the *Autumn Rain*'s CIC, watching multiple screens lighting up with interstellar combat. His feet were sweating inside the magnetic boots he wore to stay seated and steady.

"Sir, we're in position alpha," reported one of his sub-ordinates.

"Copy," Bent said.

His heart beat madly, drying his mouth. It was a sensation he was accustomed to after so many years in space, fighting battles that should have taken his life more than once. He'd lost a lot of good people, and their memories haunted him.

But this. This mission would haunt him all the way to hell.

For months, the Victoria Commonality's flagship CCS *Czernobog*, the Sian Commonality's CCS *Capella Prime* and CCS *Sword of Sian*, along with several *Lung Wang*-class ships and assault DropShips, had prevented Clan Wolf's Wolf Hussars from overrunning the outnumbered Third Sian Dragoons and other Capellan ground forces on New Earth. Bent's vessel for this mission, the *Union*-class WarShip *Autumn Rain*, slipped in and among these other ships, specially guarded by a detachment of aerospace fighters, but both the *Autumn*

Rain and its escorts maintained a low profile, observing and maneuvering more than engaging in actual combat.

Bent would have preferred a stand-up fight. But that was not the mission.

For several hours now, the fleet regiments—the *Overlord* A32-class *Czernobog* in particular—had been pummeling the Wolves' primary encampment on New Earth with capital missiles. The results of these strikes were as predicted, and, as it turned out, necessary; several Clan Wolf aerospace fighters had taken off from the planet and engaged with the Capellan navy ships directly.

"Embarkation status," Bent said to his crew. The Capellan forces on the surface had been ordered to flee New Earth two days ago. Now all Bent's crew had to do was wait until they were all accounted for, and proceed with their own orbital assault.

"Transport DropShips are outbound," came the reply from Deck Officer Marjory Hinton. "They'll be off-world in five minutes."

"All of them?"

"That's the report, sir. There were some stragglers, but they're accounted for and headed off-world, too."

"Good." Bent took a deep breath, and repeated to himself, "Good."

He watched the pitched battle in space on his screens. So far, the Wolves weren't paying any attention to the *Autumn Rain*, focused instead trying to take *Czernobog* out of the black sky. *Czernobog*, for its part, continued to rain hell on the surface below.

"All DropShips away," said Hinton.

"To all ships, covering action," Bent ordered.

The order went out over comms. Quickly, the Capellan flotilla maneuvered into new positions as it fought off the Wolf aerospace fighters.

Another three minutes into the battle, Hinton broke in again. "Sir, *Czernobog* reports a hit on the nose weapon array. They're asking if it's time to withdraw."

Bent scanned his personal monitors as well as the combat outside the *Autumn Rain*. From external cameras mounted on the DropShip, piped into several CIC screens, flashes of silent explosions popped here and there like popcorn kernels in blooms of red, yellow, and white.

"Yes," he said. "All units fall back, covering fire. Make sure the transports are protected, and keep up the barrage against the Gamma camp. Helm?"

"Sir."

"Get us to position Bravo. It's time."

The CIC of a *Union* DropShip was never silent nor warm. The atmosphere in the room after Bent's words, however, quieted and chilled.

"Sir," the helm replied after a brief hesitation.

The *Autumn Rain* moved swiftly to a new position around New Earth while the rest of the Capellan navy staged a fighting retreat away from the planet. Wolf aerospace fighters gave chase, perhaps emboldened by the damage the *Czernobog* suffered.

In mere moments, the *Autumn Rain* eased into a new orbit around the planet. Bent felt the crew holding its collective breath.

"Prepare to launch the White Shark."

The CIC burst into additional activity. Bent called upon all his strength to keep his face neutral, his body still. Beneath his skin, though, wicked electricity snapped from joint to joint.

"Ready, sir," someone said.

Bent could barely hear it. He waited for the comms to come to life, for some Capellan Strategio to reach out and call off the mission.

The call did not come.

Bent took in a slow, steadying breath before saying the word.

"Fire."

No alarms went off. He heard a series of additional soft beeps at someone's terminal, that was all.

"Payload released," Hinton said, and Bent was grateful to recognize the voice this time. "Detonation, thirty seconds."

"White Shark missile confirmed on target," someone else said.

Someone else swore softly. Bent didn't bother to seek out the offender.

"Four," Hinton counted. "Three, two, one."

Unable to stop himself now, Bent rose from his command seat and stared at one screen that showed a real-time camera angle pointed at New Earth, such that the screen was the next-best thing to an actual window. He wondered suddenly if the rest of his skeleton crew were watching through actual portholes in the DropShip.

Then:

A small, eldritch white light exploded on the surface of New Earth, a bright pupil against a sea of brown earth.

"Detonation confirmed," Hinton said. Her voice was neutral, but strained.

Detonation confirmed. The words echoed not just in Bent's ears, but in the marrow of his bones.

That land, he thought, *will be uninhabitable for generations.*

He was one of only a few who knew just how big and bad the weapon he'd just deployed really was, how it was salted with cobalt and sodium to ensure maximum destruction and maximum fallout.

Nor was he ignorant to the Chancellor's choice of targets. This attack was an affront to every descendant of Nicholas Kerensky and his Clans. The Wolves on New Earth would take the brunt of the damage, but all the Clans would feel the hit. They'd feel it far deeper than the mere physical.

Their retribution, in whatever form it took, would be swift and unforgiving.

We just punched a very hungry wolf, Bent thought. *We just punched an entire menagerie of foxes wolves, falcons...God help the Confederation.*

Standing now, Bent turned to face his crew. All of them were already looking at him, apparently expecting him to speak.

"I know what you all are feeling right now," he said. "I feel the same way. Remember what we have done is in service to the people of the Capellan Confederation. Our families, our friends. The soldier to the right and left of us. This was a decision deemed necessary by the Celestial Wisdom himself.

We will let history be the judge. For now, we've done our duty, but we are still on a combat footing. We still have jobs to do. So carry on. Helm—get us out of here."

He expected no applause, and got none. The *Autumn Rain* maneuvered in space, then fired its fusion drive to propel it away from New Earth.

It would never be fast enough, Bent knew. New Earth would be a fist around his heart for the rest of his life.

CELESTIAL PALACE
CHANG-AN
LIAO
5 MAY 3152

A *Phoenix Hawk* BattleMech exploded on Danai's sim screen. The dazzling white and yellow burst gave her a short jolt of pleasure, but it didn't last. She'd been using the simulators more and more lately, almost—she knew—to the point of neglecting other responsibilities.

No one seemed to care.

She didn't like leaving Noah to clean up any of her business, but the *zhong-shao* did so with speed and accuracy. She'd be lost without him.

Danai manipulated her controls to spin her simulated *Black Knight* to target a *Locust* and opened fire, just as a blue indicator light flashed incessantly in the cockpit. She glanced at it. A quiet indicator siren went off.

The simulator screens went dark, and the sim pod canopy opened without her command. Someone outside the pod had initiated a shutdown.

Danai looked up, squinting against the overhead lights in the sim room as a figure stepped near, silhouetted. Even in shadow, though, she recognized Noah's outline.

"Noah? What is it?"

"Sorry to interrupt." His voice reminded Danai of desert sand. She took off her neurohelmet and stood, her combat cooling uniform she always wore in the simulator clinging tightly to her body.

"What the hell, Noah? What's going on?"

Noah placed a palm against his abdomen as if to prevent vomiting.

"Danai...we nuked New Earth."

CHAPTER 52

CELESTIAL PALACE
CHANG-AN
LIAO
5 MAY 3152

Still wearing her full BattleMech kit, complete with twin Ceres knives sheathed on her calves, Danai sat at her office desk in awe, reading the complete eyes-only report from the Strategios.

Noah stood near the door, his expression the gravest she'd ever seen. The weight of this new reality seemed to push down on his body from above.

New Earth, still known by some as Tau Ceti, had been the first planet outside the Sol system human beings had stepped foot upon. Clans Wolf and Snow Raven had jumped to New Earth when coming out from behind the Fortress Wall. They'd also done so, Danai now realized, on the anniversary of humankind's landing on New Earth.

Apart from Terra herself, New Earth carried enormous significance to the Clans. Wolf, Jade Falcon, Snow Raven, Sea Fox—the planet had almost religious symbolism to them all.

"How many killed?" Danai whispered, scanning the report again.

"Unknown," Noah answered, barely above a whisper himself. "It's not thought to be many. The bomb was aimed at Foundation Point, which is often under excavation, but the area around the site is largely uninhabited."

The heritage site, Danai thought. *Daoshen, what were you thinking?*

The target of the Capellan nuclear attack had been, centuries ago, the Star League Defense Force command center where the legendary Aleksandr Kerensky had planned the liberation of Terra from Amaris the Usurper. This attack was spitting in the face of the spawn of Kerensky—the Clans.

Danai leaned away from her screen. Daoshen's message would be crystal clear to the Clans, and to Alaric on Terra. Even if not a single human soul was lost in the attack, his temerity would be seen as the greatest possible insult. He cared nothing for the history of the Clans, and certainly did not fear them.

"According to the report," Noah said through the silence, "the weapon was seeded with cobalt and sodium. That will render the area unapproachable for years."

The very ground where Kerensky planned the Usurper's downfall, Danai thought. *Daoshen, you're not entirely foolhardy, after all. You knew* exactly *how Alaric would read this message.*

And I guarantee his response is already coming for us.

Eighty years ago, the Draconis Combine had used nuclear weapons against Clan Snow Raven on the world of Galedon. Snow Raven's response was decisive and merciless. City after city had been obliterated by a Star of WarShips. Had Daoshen forgotten his history? The Clans most certainly did not. They would not bear this insult lightly.

Danai stood up quickly, her chair smacking back against the wall. Noah visibly jumped. She stalked around the desk and threw the door open, all but running into the hall past her secretary, past her guards, and deeper into the palace.

Her subconscious registered that many people followed behind her now—bodyguards and probably Noah, but Danai didn't cease moving long enough to confirm. She didn't even wait for an elevator, opting instead to rush down the stairs to the second floor and crash through the door there, startling palace employees.

Someone called her name. Probably Noah. She didn't care.

Only by force of rank and station was Danai able to bypass the various security checkpoints on her race to Daoshen's conference room. No one offered even token resistance as she reached the double doors and seized their great bronze handles in both hands, tearing the doors open.

The Celestial Wisdom sat on his throne at the head of the table. Strategios *jiang-juns* sat around it, flanked by assistants and aides on their feet. Robie Anjing stood near one of the colossal crimson pillars, and moved nearer the Chancellor the instant her eyes met Danai's.

Two *sang-shaos* pushed their chairs out of the way at Danai's approach.

She leaned her body over the table, slamming her hands on the top of it. Papers scattered. A teacup went spinning.

"What have you done?!"

To his credit, Daoshen made no attempt to pretend to not know to what Danai was referring. "I have done what is necessary to protect the Confederation."

"You have lit a fuse that will end with all of us *dead*. The Confederation, *gone*. It wasn't enough to gamble our future on Terra? You had to bring the might of the united Clans down upon us?"

Daoshen slowly placed his palms on the arms of his throne. His fingers clutched the ends in sequence, like spider legs. As if moving through water, the Celestial Wisdom raised himself, now standing a quarter-meter higher than all in attendance.

His eyes blazed as he spoke, "Those dogs are not the inheritors of the Star League, and never will be. This Confederation will not bend to Alaric, nor the Republic, nor the Clans!"

Danai pulled herself back from the table and lifted her chin. "They will come. And they will rain fire."

Daoshen sneered. "Your mewling is unbecoming of a *jiang-jun* of the Confederation Armed Forces."

Danai's body took over. In the smooth motion of a trained and seasoned fighter, she lifted her right calf and swiped the Ceres blade from its scabbard.

Robie Anjing moved even before the knife had left its sheath. She put her own body in front of the Chancellor while shouting, *"Security!"*

With one looping, windmill motion, Danai slammed the blade into the tabletop. Its point sank centimeters into the

TOM LEVEEN   329

wood. She pointed to the weapon with one finger extending from a clenched fist. "*That* is our fate now."

Danai stepped back, away from the table. The Strategios barely moved, watching the theater play out before them.

Daoshen smirked over Robie's shoulder and said nothing.

Danai turned and stalked out of the room just as armed guards entered, weapons drawn. Their faces betrayed utter confusion as she walked past.

Noah had not entered. She passed him as well, waiting in the lounge just outside the conference room, but he quickly fell into step beside her, staying alongside the entire way back toward her office.

I almost threw it, Danai thought wildly as she walked away. *I really did. One more second and I would have thrown that knife straight into Daoshen's throat. Robie was right to interpose. She probably saw it in my eyes.*

"What are we going to do?" Noah asked as they marched.

Danai noted the nervousness in his voice, a quality she did not often hear when it came to discussions of a military nature.

She also wondered, briefly, which "we" he was referring to. The two of them? The CCAF? All of Capellan space? Humanity?

"This was a red line, and somehow, Daoshen doesn't see it," Danai said, her voice as brisk as her walk. "This is the beginning of the end of everything if we don't do something."

"Okay, but Danai—"

His hand on her arm stopped her. She whirled to face him.

"—what is that 'something?'"

Looking into Noah's earnest gray eyes gave Danai the centering she needed. She caught her breath, held it, released it slowly.

Think, dammit, she told herself. *Put the pieces together.*

"Second MAC," she said at last. "I'm sending Wu and the Second to Wallacia. That'll do for a start."

"All right. I'll put that into motion immediately. But to what end?"

Danai's military mind kicked into high gear.

Daoshen hadn't just decided to nuke New Earth on a whim. It took time to put such a plan into effect, particularly given how long the gaps were in communications across the Inner Sphere. He'd had this intent for a long time before he executed it.

Executed—just like Xavier McCarron, she thought grimly. *That was no whim, either.*

The Chancellor hadn't banked on his own sister and brother-in-law sneaking up behind the Confederation to attack Wallacia. And of course, that information was months old—like the light from a star that left eons ago, the intelligence about the Andurien invasion was intelligence from months gone by. They knew the Duchy had fielded two full regiments, and that the Home Guard regiments were performing admirably against them...but even the latest intel on that combat was weeks old.

The Duchy may have already taken the planet, for all we know. They may have moved on to another. They may be on their way to Sian, or Castrovia. We don't know.

Such a rapid advance seemed unlikely, but still possible. In any event, Daoshen could not have anticipated such an assault. Wallacia, coupled with news of the Wolves blasting off from Terra, had put a squeeze on his resources, the very squeeze Danai had seen coming. Worried about the Andurien invasion and other fronts opening up on his push for Terra probably was all it took for the Chancellor to bring such a barbaric weapon into the fight. He must have dusted off the warheads ages ago for just such an occasion.

Which meant he had probably dusted off more.

Now, will the rest of the Great Houses follow suit? Will the Clans? What's inside Pandora's box, Daoshen?

"Danai?" Noah asked gently.

Danai shook herself. "Back to basics. Boot camp 101, Noah. We can only tackle what's in front of us and what we can control, just like we were taught. Doesn't matter if it's underwater knot tying or executing a plan for Terra. What's in front of us and what we can tackle is the Anduriens on Wallacia. We'll overwhelm them and kick them back to the Duchy. That should at least help protect Sian and Liao and Castrovia."

Noah regarded her closely. "Is this about the boy? Tiko?"

Danai glared at her subordinate. His eyes did not leave hers.

"No," she said after a tense pause. "This is about keeping watch on the back door into the Confederation. Daoshen thinks his nuke will keep the Clans at bay, and he's wrong. So we have to protect as much of our borders with as much strength as we can."

Noah nodded briefly, accepting her logic and ready to move on.

"Get the word out to Wu and move the Second MAC, ASAP," she said. "Keep me posted on its whereabouts and when they can expect to arrive on Wallacia."

"Yes, ma'am. Danai..."

Noah paused, as if searching for words.

"The...knife."

Danai rubbed her forehead. "I wasn't thinking. Not the smartest move to make, I admit."

"No, it's that...except for Robie... No one else tried to stop you."

Danai stared at him. Noah met her gaze with some degree of trepidation, but also insistence.

"The Strategios are old," she said, but heard the lie in her voice. "That's all. Their reflexes aren't what they used to be."

Noah said nothing. They stood in silence as the import of his observation sank into them.

"Of course, ma'am," he said abruptly, and turned to go.

"Noah..."

The *zhong-shao* hesitated, looking back at her.

"I'm—just glad you're here for all of this. Thank you."

Noah held her gaze for a moment, then repeated his nod before heading off down the corridor.

Danai watched him go before going back into her office. She closed her door and stood with her back against it.

Daoshen, she thought. *Ilsa. You were handed the keys to the kingdom and between the two of you, you'll bring it all crashing down. So that leaves me, Danai. Duchess of Castrovia.* Jiang-jun *of McCarron's Armored Command. What will I do?*

What will I do?

CHAPTER 53

CELESTIAL PALACE
CHANG-AN
LIAO
15 JUNE 3152

"No response from Nikol Marik yet," Noah reported.

Danai stood facing her office window, watching the bustling town below, rubbing Tiko's queen carving absently in her hands, her head aching dully as Noah went through her morning briefing.

"No," she replied. "I'm not surprised. She won't. She can't."

"Rumor has it there's an all-out invasion of the Wolf Empire coming from her direction."

"That might be good for us. Keep the Wolves busy." Danai sighed. "Getting Nikol's help with Wallacia was a long shot. Have Wu and the Second made planetfall?"

When Noah did not reply instantly, she turned.

"Please don't throw the messenger out the window," he said with a dour expression. "But your orders were countermanded. Wu and the Second remain on Sheratan."

"Countermanded by who?" Danai demanded, then tossed up a hand to silence Noah even as he took a breath to answer. "Never mind. Daoshen."

"Yes, ma'am."

Danai faced the window again, feeling her shoulder sag. She hadn't felt well or right since last month, upon learning of Daoshen's nuclear attack on New Earth. Since then, the Third

Sian Dragoons—who she now knew were responsible for the actual launch—had landed on Liberty, taunting Clan Wolf. Wolf had risen to the bait, and last Danai knew, the two forces were in a brawl on the very planet she herself had liberated only two years ago.

"Mina died for nothing," she said suddenly.

"Ma'am?"

"On Hall. That will be the next battle, won't it? The Wolves will come for Hall, and possibly reclaim it, making all the work we did there pointless. Mina's death will be pointless. If it wasn't already. Daoshen won't let me send my own regiments to protect Wallacia, which might put Castrovia in the Anduriens' sights. My own moth—"

She paused.

"My own sister is probably behind that attack," she went on. "I've been handed five regiments, the entire McCarron's Armored Cavalry, and can't do a damn thing with it. My brother keeps me as a pet. And someday soon, the ilClan will arrive to take revenge for New Earth."

"Not here," Noah said cautiously. "Not Liao."

"No, probably not. But somewhere. I'm tired, Noah."

"You sound it, ma'am."

Danai turned again and took her chair. "Not that kind of tired. You know, I've never been cut out for court life. For politics. I thought I knew enough to keep up, but the truth is, I don't. Put me in a BattleMech against a lance, and I'll take it to them every time. But this..." She gestured vaguely around the office. "This isn't where I belong."

Her chest ached a bit as Noah's expression saddened. "I'm sorry, Danai," he said. "What else can I do to help?"

"Are there any McCarron's COs on Liao?"

"I believe Lydia Chen is on-world at the moment for planning sessions."

"Lydia. I know her. Good. I want to meet with her. And I need a message sent out to every CO of the MAC, under the radar. Can you do that?"

"I can. What's the message?"

Danai tapped the top of her desk. "That it's time I played politics."

CELESTIAL WISDOM PARK
CHANG AN
LIAO
20 JUNE 3152

Danai enjoyed the warm afternoon sunshine as she walked slowly around a man-made lake 10 kilometers from the palace. It reminded her somewhat of Castrovia and of Tiko—watching children play and families gathering while supporters and servitors snacked on skewers of meat and fish sold from vendors scattered around the long, narrow park.

She wore civilian clothes, and had asked Lydia Chen to do the same. Both women wore cheongsams and loose silk pants with slip-on shoes. Danai's security detachment, also in civilian outfits, roamed in a wide circle around them.

Today's meeting is the first step, she thought after having given her idea to Lydia. *When Daoshen discovers what I've done, there will be no turning back. As is right.*

For all the time that had passed since the destruction of Rainspire, and despite Sheratan's pacification since then, the weight of her choices there still nagged at Danai. Adding to it were Daoshen's reckless use of a nuclear weapon against the Clans and her own sense of powerlessness, despite her titles.

So now it's time to take responsibility of those titles and put them to work.

"Are you serious, *Jiang-jun*?" Lydia asked as they walked, keeping her eyes fixed ahead on the clean concrete path.

"I've already had the message sent to other commanding officers," Danai said.

"And...you'll pay for this yourself?"

"Turns out that as Duchess of Castrovia, I am a woman of some means," Danai said, smiling genuinely at the thought.

"I assume this has not been discussed at the highest levels, much less approved."

"The MAC is mine, Lydia. There is no higher level."

"We both know that's not entirely accurate."

Danai stopped her stroll. Lydia stopped alongside and faced her. "I thought you'd leap at this opportunity after everything the Chancellor has done."

"I am," Lydia said. "But I also need to know what I'm leaping into."

Danai stepped slightly closer to the *zhong-shao* of McCarron's Fifth. "No," she said. "You need to know what you're leaping *out* of. You're a good commander, Lydia. And I know your fealty to the Confederation is unflappable. You also know we are in dangerous times. McCarron's has been my home, and it has served the people well. It's time to let them return to what they were best at."

Lydia arched an eyebrow, but kept her lips pressed together.

Danai pivoted and resumed their walk. "The entire MAC will be cashiered. Each regiment and regimental CO will be free to do as they please. I offer full employment to any regiment, battalion, or individual who wishes to remain in the Confederation. Those who wish to seek employment elsewhere are free to do so."

"Returning the MAC to mercenary status," Lydia finished. "It's a bold move. Many battalions will, in fact, leave, you know."

"I assume. But many regiments will stay."

"You mean Wu."

"We will see. I trust Wu's judgment."

"And the first assignment for those who accept your payment?"

"Wallacia."

Lydia chuckled. "Of course. The Chancellor will not take kindly to this offer."

"Perhaps the Celestial Wisdom should have considered that earlier in his dealings with the Big MAC."

"Agreed. Now also tell me why."

Danai winced at an unbidden mental image of Jack Cade holding Cordelia Norfolk in the ruins of Rainspire. "Our destiny may well be Terra. The path to arrive there must be re-examined. The Celestial Wisdom and I...diverge on this point."

"Clearly," Lydia said quietly. "He'll be taken aback at this, to say the least."

"Do you accept the offer?"

"I do, *Jiang-jun*."

Danai stopped again. "Thank you, *Zhong-shao* Chen."

"Mmm...colonel, I think," Lydia said, grinning slyly. "That feels more appropriate."

Danai grinned back. *"Sang-shao."*

The two women shook hands. As they did so, Danai's attention was caught by a distant siren deeper in the city. Her brow furrowed.

Lydia appeared to see the shift in Danai's expression, and turned as if to see the source of the siren. "Air defense," she said. "Training exercise for another of Daoshen's ill-considered attacks?"

Danai didn't hear the insult layered into Lydia's choice of words or tone. Already the Chancellor was merely "Daoshen."

There were no trainings scheduled so close to Liao. And even if there were, they wouldn't be anywhere near the capital city. Danai watched as several kilometers away, a DropShip rose from its port. Farther, a second and third took to the sky.

"What on..." Lydia muttered just as several elements of aerospace fighters zoomed overhead, heading out of the atmosphere.

More sirens kicked on, nearer now. Pedestrians stopped and looked skyward, traded confused looks—then began to race for nearby buildings.

The reality of the situation dawned on Danai.

"Lydia," she snapped. "Get out of the city, now. *Go!*"

Lydia didn't hesitate. She broke into a run.

Danai ran the opposite direction, shouting at her detail. "Back to the palace, *now!*"

Her detail closed ranks around her, ensuring a clear path to her waiting armored vehicle and convoy. Noah stood just outside her vehicle, expression worried as Danai and six guards careened toward them.

"What's happening?" he said, instinctively opening the rear car door as Danai reached the vehicle.

Danai gripped Noah's arm, eyes wide.

"We have to get back to the palace. It's the Clans."

CHAPTER 54

**CELESTIAL PALACE
CHANG-AN
LIAO
20 JUNE 3152**

Danai leaped from the armored car almost before it had time to stop in its underground parking lot. One of the guards shouted to stop her, but she whirled and said, "Get everyone into the bunker, *now*! That's an order!"

She wasted no time to see if they obeyed or not. Instead, she raced for the staircase to get to Daoshen's floor. Her mind raced equally as fast. What was coming? A nuke? Several? Orbital bombardment? In minutes, at most, she and the rest of Chang-an would find out.

And how did they get so close? The answer hit Danai like a punch, and the irony would have otherwise made her laugh. *A pirate jump point. The very thing Daoshen assured none of our enemies would dare use. You fool.*

Noah, operating at almost his pre-injury capacity these days, stayed at her side. "You should come down," he said, huffing at her pace. "The Mask will take care of your brother."

Danai knew he was right, but couldn't make herself take the advice. She was operating on pure instinct, and her instinct was to protect the Chancellor of the Capellan Confederation, even if he happened to be Daoshen Liao.

They reached the second floor. Danai leaped through the stairwell door...and froze in shock.

Here, life carried on as normal.

People sat at desks, or walked leisurely into and out of meeting rooms. One man walked past her with a lunch bag of food. Two women in tidy beige skirts passed the other direction, laughing.

"We called," Danai said, standing in place, stupefied by the lack of concern. "From the car. We called…"

At her side, Noah said, "We did…I, I told them…"

"*Daoshen.*" Danai hissed the name. Dammit, he'd heard the sirens, and surely been told the news of planetary defenses scrambling—and dismissed it, like he dismissed anything not in line with his own personal narrative. Danai knew it in her gut.

She turned to Noah. "Get these people down to the bunker right now. Do *whatever* you have to. Save them. I'm going for Daoshen."

Noah nodded once and ran to the middle of the wide reception area that guarded the offices beyond. He waved his arms in the air. "Everyone! Eyes on me! Listen…!"

Danai raced ahead toward Daoshen's conference room. The guards on duty looked perplexed and doubtful, trading glances; clearly they'd gotten the warning she'd sent while on the way, but stood nervously now, unsure.

Danai stopped in front of one uniformed guard. "This building," she said to his face, "is about to burn. Get to safety downstairs. I'm getting the Chancellor."

She went abruptly forward, leaving the guards to determine their own fate.

Reaching the double doors, Danai pulled them open and rushed in.

The men and women in attendance were not Strategios, but members of the House of Scions. All were royalty, and dressed the part, but none looked happy to be seated around the table.

"Danai," Daoshen said as she burst in. "Have you come to deface more of my furniture? I had to replace the former one with something more sturdy after your temper tantrum."

He swept a hand across his of the table to indicate the heavy black iron that had taken the place of the previous wooden table.

Danai did, in fact, stand at the opposite end of the table, as she had the last time she was in the room. "Daoshen! You have to get into the bunker now! *The Clans are here.*"

"Perhaps," Daoshen said lackadaisically. "If so, we are well protected."

"Listen to me, damn you!" Danai shouted. "All of you! This is happening, and you must get into the shelter immediately before they attack the surface!"

"Anyone," Daoshen said over her, "leaving this room will be dealt with as a traitor."

Two of the members of the House of Scions who'd risen at Danai's words now sat back down.

"Daoshen, please—"

"I will not be swayed by those *animals*," Daoshen spat. "They cannot hurt me."

"They will *kill* you!"

Daoshen lifted his chin. "They will not—"

At that, the first explosion sounded.

Robie edged closer to Daoshen as Danai Centrella-Liao went on her tirade. She believed the duchess, but it would take more than words to get the Chancellor to move.

That opportunity came as a massive *boom* went off outside the palace walls, shaking the floor.

The House of Scions, cowed into their seats by Daoshen's threat, now stood up as one, shooting looks between the Chancellor and his sister as if for guidance.

Another explosion. Closer. Robie's knees almost buckled from the tremor.

Courtyard, she thought quickly. *That was the front door. The next will be on our heads.*

"Chancellor!" she said, striding to the throne. "We must go."

More explosions, deafening Robie momentarily. One of the columns supporting the roof cracked and rained white plaster down.

Daoshen jumped to his feet, and at first, Robie believed he'd had enough encouragement from the attack raining upon them. Instead, the elderly Chancellor bellowed over the noise, "We will stay! All of you! Do not be threatened by the barking of mere dogs!"

Danai stepped backward, away from the table. More explosions sounded outside the palace. Now Robie could make out screams coming from the reception area outside the conference room.

"That's an orbital assault. A nuke might be next. *Chancellor*!"

Daoshen's lips pulled away from his teeth. *"Never!"*

Robie watched as Danai stared at the Chancellor for a moment. "Then die here, you arrogant bastard."

She ran from the conference room.

At this, the assembled House of Scions broke their paralysis and fled en masse.

"No!" Daoshen raged.

Robie clutched the sleeve of his robe. "Chancellor, she is right. I have to get you to—"

"Let them come!" he scoffed, tearing his arm way from her.

Robie prepared to force the older man to her will, but at that moment, the very walls and ceiling fell.

Guanken cowered against the wall as tremendous thunder rocked the palace. One of his two co-servants, a younger man, grabbed at his tunic, crying in terror.

The Chancellor, Guanken thought. *I must protect the Celestial Wisdom.*

He shook off the weeping servant and strode toward the Chancellor even as the girl, Robie, reached him and tried to pull him off his throne dais.

Guanken made it only half the distance when a bone-chilling *crack* resounded through the room, a noise of such epic scale he thought his very skull had split.

A black crevasse, like obsidian lightning, skittered the length of the room along the ceiling. The pillars first jostled, then imploded as the ceiling collapsed.

"Daoshen!" Guanken cried, unthinking, unaware he would never have dared use the Celestial Wisdom's name aloud.

Then he was flat, crumpled beneath chunks of concrete.

Danai turned at the colossal sound from the conference room as the House of Scions members ran past her, chattering and screaming.

Across the distance between them, she found Daoshen's eyes.

Then the ceiling of the conference room came down in a rush of gray powder. Sparks exploded from torn wires overhead. Bodies and furniture from the third floor rained down atop the rubble, splitting open or smashing apart.

He's gone, she thought. *Move.*

Emotionless, Danai spun to head for the private staircase Robie had shown her, to get to the bunker. She got halfway across the open space when Noah appeared in a doorway, looking wildly around.

They spotted each other.

"Danai!" he shouted. "I got everyone out, they're headed—"

The wall behind Noah blew outward, tossing him 10 meters away.

Danai's body instinctively crouched. She felt the sting of small shrapnel against her face and hands. When she could move again, she immediately ran to Noah's side.

He'd landed in a heap against the far wall. Blood streamed from his ears and nose. Danai slid next to him on her knees. "Noah!"

She knew even before touching him.

Danai slid a hand under his shoulders, knowing the only safe place would be the downstairs bunker. But Noah flopped lifelessly in her arms, as if his bones had been ripped from his body.

"Noah...please..."

She checked his neck for a pulse—and found it faint.

Above, the ceiling rumbled.

You have to go, said a voice in her mind, and it sounded like Noah, or maybe Mina, perhaps Tiko. *You have to go, Danai.*

Fine. But Noah first.

"Help!" she shouted.

A man and woman in civilian attire seemed to realize who had called, and raced to Danai's side.

"Get him out of here," she ordered. "Then find me when this is over."

The two Capellans nodded and hurried to get Noah's limp form to safety.

Danai watched them go for two precious seconds before running fast for the stairwell, which she leaped into one heartbeat before the ceiling came crashing down.

Guanken could hear nothing and could move nothing, but he could still see.

The servant of Daoshen Liao blinked, and slowly discovered he was buried beneath rubble, but had a clear line of sight on the heavy new table Daoshen had put in to replace the one recently defaced by Danai Centrella-Liao.

The iron table, with its many thick legs and solid surface, was largely intact.

And beneath it, Guanken saw the white robes of the Celestial Wisdom.

Moving.

He was alive! He was safe! Praise to the Celestial Wisdom, who lived forever!

Someone else moved beside the Chancellor then, and through a growing haze of pain and shock, Guanken recognized the red hair of Robie Anjing.

She saved him, Guanken thought, giddy with joy and agony. *Bless you, Anjing...*

Guanken smiled even as the remaining breath in his crushed lungs left his body.

Eyes wide open, even in death, he gazed upon the Celestial Wisdom, and smiled with joy, having died while in service to the state.

Danai was the last to reach the bunker. Anyone left behind was horribly wounded or dead.

Though there were multiple rooms in this safe area, the main lobby seemed to be where everyone congregated. More crashing and catastrophic booms echoed above them. The lights flickered, prompting a scream from the civilians.

"Quiet!" Danai ordered.

Her voice somehow carried over the sounds of the assault above. It took another few moments for her to realize that the crowd did in fact go quiet...and that she could hear them going quiet.

The explosions had ceased.

She stood by the heavy steel door, breathing hard, tasting concrete dust and blood in her mouth. She wiped her chin, and her fingers came back red.

A uniformed guard stepped forward in the relative silence. "The Celestial Wisdom?" asked the guard. "Where...?"

Danai shook her head. "He's gone."

A collective gasp went up from the gathered survivors.

Licking his lips, the guard glanced back over his shoulder. Then he faced Danai, stood straight, and braced. "What are your orders, Chancellor?"

Danai Centrella-Liao lifted her eyes and stared at him for a very long time.

Robie clinically assessed her body. Right ankle—smashed, possibly flat. Right tibia—snapped. Right hip—out of socket, or perhaps shattered. Lungs—filled with dust and small debris, but functional. Hands and torso—functional.

She was alive. The conference table had protected them for the most part.

In front of her, on his back, the Celestial Wisdom moved. Coughed.

His head turned and he met her eyes.

And smiled.

"Robie," he said softly through the dust in the air around them. "You see? You see? They cannot touch me. I am eternal, Robie. House Liao stands!"

We barely made it under here, she thought as he rambled. *Danai saw us, thinks we're dead. Everyone else who was in the room must be dead, too.*

Robie pushed herself up, grateful for the shock that prevented the worst of her pain from registering. She slipped her hand into her tunic and pulled a slender blade about the width of a pencil from its pocket, where it had resided since the day she was given her assignment by Kamer.

There is always only one, he'd taught, *who must stand ready to do what is needed to protect the Confederation. You are that one, Robie. We serve a rare but crucial function.*

Robie pulled herself to Daoshen, and positioned herself over his prone body while the Celestial Wisdom laughed. "You see?" he said again. "Even with fire from the skies, they fail to stop me. I am *eternal*—"

Robie gazed into his eyes, propping herself on one arm like a lover looking down upon her beloved.

Then slid the sharp blade effortlessly into Daoshen's chest.

The dagger pierced his heart. Daoshen's smile fell away. He looked as if he were screaming now, yet not a single sound escaped his throat.

The Celestial Wisdom's mouth arched down in silent agony. His eyes reflected pure shock, utter dismay—and, Robie saw, a complete lack of acceptance.

Even now, as her cold steel punctured his flesh and stopped his heart, Daoshen Liao still believed he was immortal.

"You," said the assassin gently; said Robie; said the Maskirovka agent, "are not a god."

Daoshen shuddered, clutching her tunic. He struggled to speak. Blood hissed from the corners of his mouth.

Robie whispered into his ear, "For the good of the state."

And held him until he died.

BERSERKER
Assault—**100** tons

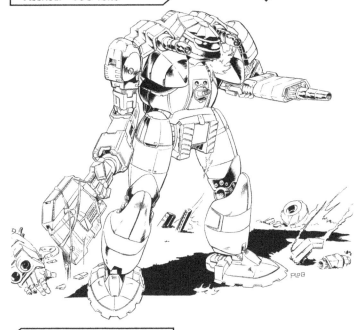

BLACK KNIGHT
Heavy—**75** tons

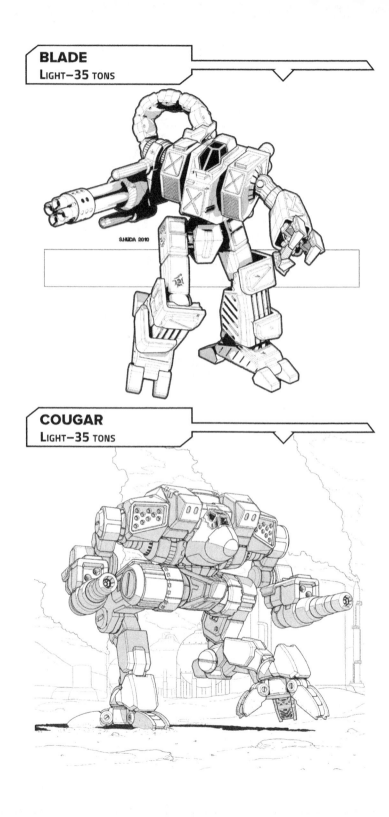

BLADE
LIGHT—35 TONS

S.HUDA 2010

COUGAR
LIGHT—35 TONS

DOLA
LIGHT—30 TONS

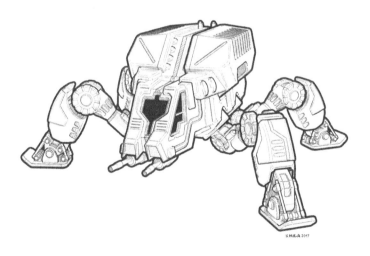

GUARD
ULTRALIGHT—15 TONS

KHEPER
MEDIUM—55 TONS

LOCUST
LIGHT—20 TONS

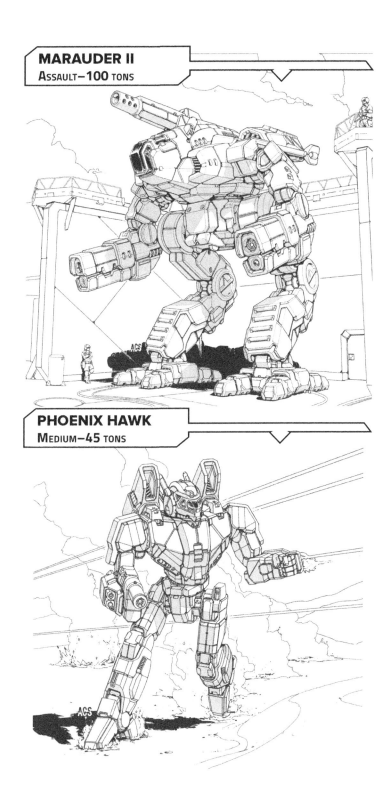

MARAUDER II
ASSAULT—**100** TONS

PHOENIX HAWK
MEDIUM—**45** TONS

PILLAGER
Assault—100 tons

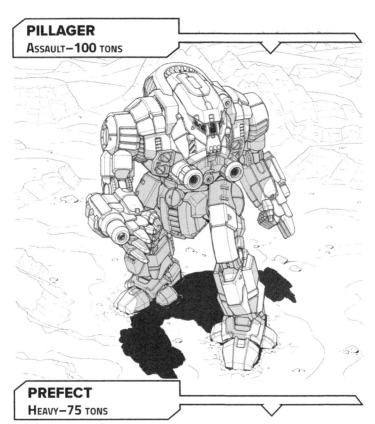

PREFECT
Heavy—75 tons

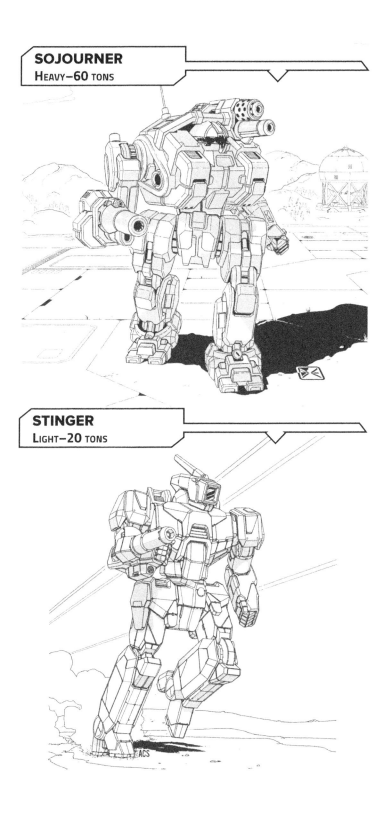

SOJOURNER
Heavy–60 tons

STINGER
Light–20 tons

VINDICATOR
MEDIUM—45 TONS

VIXEN (INCUBUS)
LIGHT—30 TONS

WARHAMMER
Heavy—70 tons

BATTLETECH GLOSSARY

Throughout this book, the Capellan officers are referred to by their ancient Chinese rank names. The equivalent ranks in English are:

Commissioned officers:
Sang-jiang-jun: Senior General
Jiang-jun: General
Sang-shao: Colonel
Zhong-shao: Lieutenant Colonel
Sao-shao: Major
Sang-wei: Captain
Sao-wei: Lieutenant

Enlisted Ranks:
Yi-si-ben-bing: Master Sergeant
Si-ben-bing: Sergeant
San-ben-bing: Corporal
Shia-ben-bing: Recruit

AUTOCANNON
A rapid-fire, auto-loading weapon. Light autocannons range from 30 to 90 millimeter (mm), and heavy autocannons may be from 80 to 120mm or more. They fire high-speed streams of high-explosive, armor-piercing shells.

BATTLEMECH
BattleMechs are the most powerful war machines ever built. First developed by Terran scientists and engineers, these huge vehicles are faster, more mobile, better-armored and more heavily armed than any twentieth-century tank. Ten to twelve meters tall and equipped with particle projection cannons, lasers, rapid-fire autocannon and missiles, they pack enough firepower to flatten anything but another BattleMech. A small fusion reactor provides virtually unlimited power, and BattleMechs can be adapted to fight in environments ranging from sun-baked deserts to subzero arctic ice fields.

DROPSHIP

Because interstellar JumpShips must avoid entering the heart of a solar system, they must "dock" in space at a considerable distance from a system's inhabited worlds. DropShips were developed for interplanetary travel. As the name implies, a DropShip is attached to hardpoints on the JumpShip's drive core, later to be dropped from the parent vessel after in-system entry. Though incapable of FTL travel, DropShips are highly maneuverable, well-armed and sufficiently aerodynamic to take off from and land on a planetary surface. The journey from the jump point to the inhabited worlds of a system usually requires a normal-space journey of several days or weeks, depending on the type of star.

FLAMER

A small but time-honored anti-infantry weapon. Whether fusion-based or fuel-based, flamers spew fire in a tight beam that "splashes" against a target, igniting almost anything it touches.

GAUSS RIFLE

This weapon uses magnetic coils to accelerate a solid nickel-ferrous slug about the size of a football at an enemy target, inflicting massive damage through sheer kinetic impact at long range and with little heat. However, the accelerator coils and the slug's supersonic speed mean that while the Gauss rifle is smokeless and lacks the flash of an autocannon, it has a much more potent report that can shatter glass.

JUMPSHIP

Interstellar travel is accomplished via JumpShips, first developed in the twenty-second century. These somewhat ungainly vessels consist of a long, thin drive core and a sail resembling an enormous parasol, which can extend up to a kilometer in width. The ship is named for its ability to "jump" instantaneously across vast distances of space. After making its jump, the ship cannot travel until it has recharged by gathering up more solar energy.

The JumpShip's enormous sail is constructed from a special metal that absorbs vast quantities of electromagnetic energy from the nearest star. When it has soaked up enough energy, the sail transfers it to the drive core, which converts it into a space-twisting field. An instant later, the ship arrives at the next jump point, a distance of up to thirty light-years. This field is known as hyperspace, and its discovery opened to mankind the gateway to the stars.

JumpShips never land on planets. Interplanetary travel is carried out by DropShips, vessels that are attached to the JumpShip until arrival at the jump point.

LASER

An acronym for "Light Amplification through Stimulated Emission of Radiation." When used as a weapon, the laser damages the target by concentrating extreme heat onto a small area. BattleMech lasers are designated as small, medium or large. Lasers are also available as shoulder-fired weapons operating from a portable backpack power unit. Certain range-finders and targeting equipment also employ low-level lasers.

LONG-RANGE MISSILE (LRM)

An indirect-fire missile with a high-explosive warhead.

MACHINE GUN

A small autocannon intended for anti-personnel assaults. Typically non-armor-penetrating, machine guns are often best used against infantry, as they can cover a large area with relatively inexpensive fire.

PARTICLE PROJECTION CANNON (PPC)

One of the most powerful and long-range energy weapons on the battlefield, a PPC fires a stream of charged particles that outwardly functions as a bright blue laser, but also throws off enough static discharge to resemble a bolt of manmade lightning. The kinetic and heat impact of a PPC is enough to cause the vaporization of armor and structure alike, and most PPCs have the power to kill a pilot in his machine through an armor-penetrating headshot.

SHORT-RANGE MISSILE (SRM)

A direct-trajectory missile with high-explosive or armor-piercing explosive warheads. It has a range of less than one kilometer, and is only reliably accurate at ranges of less than 300 meters. It is more powerful, however, than an LRM.

SUCCESSOR LORDS

After the fall of the first Star League, the remaining members of the High Council each asserted his or her right to become First Lord. Their star empires became known as the Successor States and the rulers as Successor Lords. The Clan Invasion temporarily interrupted centuries of warfare known as the Succession Wars, which first began in 2786.

BATTLETECH ERAS

The *BattleTech* universe is a living, vibrant entity that grows each year as more sourcebooks and fiction are published. A dynamic universe, its setting and characters evolve over time within a highly detailed continuity framework, bringing everything to life in a way a static game universe cannot match.

To help quickly and easily convey the timeline of the universe—and to allow a player to easily "plug in" a given novel or sourcebook—we've divided *BattleTech* into eight major eras.

STAR LEAGUE
(Present–2780)

Ian Cameron, ruler of the Terran Hegemony, concludes decades of tireless effort with the creation of the Star League, a political and military alliance between all Great Houses and the Hegemony. Star League armed forces immediately launch the Reunification War, forcing the Periphery realms to join. For the next two centuries, humanity experiences a golden age across the thousand light-years of human-occupied space known as the Inner Sphere. It also sees the creation of the most powerful military in human history.

(This era also covers the centuries before the founding of the Star League in 2571, most notably the Age of War.)

SUCCESSION WARS
(2781–3049)

Every last member of First Lord Richard Cameron's family is killed during a coup launched by Stefan Amaris. Following the thirteen-year war to unseat him, the rulers of each of the five Great Houses disband the Star League. General Aleksandr Kerensky departs with eighty percent of the Star League Defense Force beyond known space and the Inner Sphere collapses into centuries of warfare known as the Succession Wars that will eventually result in a massive loss of technology across most worlds.

CLAN INVASION
(3050–3061)

A mysterious invading force strikes the coreward region of the Inner Sphere. The invaders, called the Clans, are descendants of Kerensky's SLDF troops, forged into a society dedicated to becoming the greatest fighting force in history. With vastly superior technology and warriors, the Clans conquer world after world. Eventually this outside threat will forge a new Star League, something hundreds of years of warfare failed to accomplish. In addition, the Clans will act as a catalyst for a technological renaissance.

CIVIL WAR
(3062–3067)

The Clan threat is eventually lessened with the complete destruction of a Clan. With that massive external threat apparently neutralized, internal conflicts explode around the Inner Sphere. House Liao conquers its former Commonality, the St. Ives Compact; a rebellion of military units belonging to House Kurita sparks a war with their powerful border enemy, Clan Ghost Bear; the fabulously powerful Federated Commonwealth of House Steiner and House Davion collapses into five long years of bitter civil war.

JIHAD
(3067–3080)
Following the Federated Commonwealth Civil War, the leaders of the Great Houses meet and disband the new Star League, declaring it a sham. The pseudo-religious Word of Blake—a splinter group of ComStar, the protectors and controllers of interstellar communication— launch the Jihad: an interstellar war that pits every faction against each other and even against themselves, as weapons of mass destruction are used for the first time in centuries while new and frightening technologies are also unleashed.

DARK AGE
(3081-3150)
Under the guidance of Devlin Stone, the Republic of the Sphere is born at the heart of the Inner Sphere following the Jihad. One of the more extensive periods of peace begins to break out as the 32nd century dawns. The factions, to one degree or another, embrace disarmament, and the massive armies of the Succession Wars begin to fade. However, in 3132 eighty percent of interstellar communications collapses, throwing the universe into chaos. Wars erupt almost immediately, and the factions begin rebuilding their armies.

ILCLAN
(3151-present)
The once-invulnerable Republic of the Sphere lies in ruins, torn apart by the Great Houses and the Clans as they wage war against each other on a scale not seen in nearly a century. Mercenaries flourish once more, selling their might to the highest bidder. As Fortress Republic collapses, the Clans race toward Terra to claim their long-denied birthright and create a supreme authority that will fulfill the dream of Aleksandr Kerensky and rule the Inner Sphere by any means necessary: The ilClan.

CLAN HOMEWORLDS
(2786-present)
In 2784, General Aleksandr Kerensky launched Operation Exodus, and led most of the Star League Defense Force out of the Inner Sphere in a search for a new world, far away from the strife of the Great Houses. After more than two years and thousands of light years, they arrived at the Pentagon Worlds. Over the next two-and-a-half centuries, internal dissent and civil war led to the creation of a brutal new society—the Clans. And in 3049, they returned to the Inner Sphere with one goal—the complete conquest of the Great Houses.

LOOKING FOR MORE HARD HITTING BATTLETECH FICTION?

WE'LL GET YOU RIGHT BACK INTO THE BATTLE!

Catalyst Game Labs brings you the very best in *BattleTech* fiction, available at most ebook retailers, including Amazon, Apple Books, Kobo, Barnes & Noble, and more!

NOVELS

1. *Decision at Thunder Rift (The Gray Death Legion Saga, Book One)* by William H. Keith
2. *Mercenary's Star (The Gray Death Legion Saga, Book Two)* by William H. Keith
3. *The Price of Glory (The Gray Death Legion Saga, Book Three)* by William H. Keith
4. *Warrior: En Garde (The Warrior Trilogy, Book One)* by Michael A. Stackpole
5. *Warrior: Riposte (The Warrior Trilogy, Book Two)* by Michael A. Stackpole
6. *Warrior: Coupé (The Warrior Trilogy, Book Three)* by Michael A. Stackpole
7. *Wolves on the Border* by Robert N. Charrette
8. *Heir to the Dragon* by Robert N. Charrette
9. *Lethal Heritage (Blood of Kerensky Trilogy, Book One)* by Michael A. Stackpole
10. *Blood Legacy (Blood of Kerensky Trilogy, Book Two)* by Michael A. Stackpole
11. *Lost Destiny (Blood of Kerensky Trilogy, Book Three)* by Michael A. Stackpole
12. *Way of the Clans (Legend of the Jade Phoenix, Book One)* by Robert Thurston
13. *Bloodname (Legend of the Jade Phoenix, Book Two)* by Robert Thurston
14. *Falcon Guard (Legend of the Jade Phoenix, Book Three)* by Robert Thurston
15. *Wolf Pack* by Robert N. Charrette
16. *Natural Selection* by Michael A. Stackpole
17. *Ideal War* by Christopher Kubasik
18. *Main Event* by Jim Long
19. *Blood of Heroes* by Andrew Keith
20. *Assumption of Risk* by Michael A. Stackpole
21. *D.R.T.* by James D. Long
22. *Close Quarters* by Victor Milán
23. *Bred for War* by Michael A. Stackpole
24. *I Am Jade Falcon* by Robert Thurston
25. *Highlander Gambit* by Blaine Lee Pardoe
26. *Tactics of Duty* by William H. Keith
27. *Malicious Intent* by Michael A. Stackpole
28. *Hearts of Chaos* by Victor Milán
29. *Operation Excalibur* by William H. Keith
30. *Black Dragon* by Victor Milán
31. *Impetus of War* by Blaine Lee Pardoe
32. *Double-Blind* by Loren L. Coleman
33. *Binding Force* by Loren L. Coleman
34. *Exodus Road (Twilight of the Clans, Book One)* by Blaine Lee Pardoe
35. *Grave Covenant (Twilight of the Clans, Book Two)* by Michael A. Stackpole
36. *The Hunters (Twilight of the Clans, Book Three)* by Thomas S. Gressman
37. *Freebirth (Twilight of the Clans, Book Four)* by Robert Thurston
38. *Sword and Fire (Twilight of the Clans, Book Five)* by Thomas S. Gressman
39. *Shadows of War (Twilight of the Clans, Book Six)* by Thomas S. Gressman
40. *Prince of Havoc (Twilight of the Clans, Book Seven)* by Michael A. Stackpole
41. *Falcon Rising (Twilight of the Clans, Book Eight)* by Robert Thurston
42. *Threads of Ambition (The Capellan Solution, Book One)* by Loren L. Coleman
43. *The Killing Fields (The Capellan Solution, Book Two)* by Loren L. Coleman

98. *Honor's Gauntlet* by Bryan Young
99. *Icons of War* by Craig A. Reed, Jr.
100. *Children of Kerensky* by Blaine Lee Pardoe
101. *Hour of the Wolf* by Blaine Lee Pardoe
102. *Fall From Glory (Founding of the Clans, Book One)* by Randall N. Bills
103. *Paid in Blood (The Highlander Covenant, Book Two)* by Michael J. Ciaravella
104. *Blood Will Tell* by Jason Schmetzer
105. *Hunting Season* by Philip A. Lee
106. *A Rock and a Hard Place* by William H. Keith
107. *Visions of Rebirth (Founding of the Clans, Book Two)* by Randall N. Bills
108. *No Substitute for Victory* by Blaine Lee Pardoe
109. *Redemption Rites* by Jason Schmetzer
110. *Land of Dreams (Founding of the Clans, Book Three)* by Randall N. Bills
111. *A Question of Survival* by Bryan Young
112. *Jaguar's Leap* by Reed Bishop
113. *The Damocles Sanction* by Michael J. Ciaravella
114. *Escape from Jardine (Forgotten Worlds, Part Three)* by Herbert A. Beas II
115. *Elements of Treason: Honor* by Craig A. Reed, Jr.
116. *The Quest for Jardine (A Forgotten Worlds Collection)* by Herbert A. Beas II
117. *Without Question* by Bryan Young
118. *In the Shadow of the Dragon* by Craig A. Reed, Jr.
119. *Letter of the Law* by Philip A. Lee
120. *Trial of Birthright* by Michael J. Ciaravella
121. *VoidBreaker* by Bryan Young

YOUNG ADULT NOVELS
1. *The Nellus Academy Incident* by Jennifer Brozek
2. *Iron Dawn (The Rogue Academy Trilogy, Book One)* by Jennifer Brozek
3. *Ghost Hour (The Rogue Academy Trilogy, Book Two)* by Jennifer Brozek
4. *Crimson Night (The Rogue Academy Trilogy, Book Three)* by Jennifer Brozek

OMNIBUSES
1. *The Gray Death Legion Trilogy* (ebook box set) by William H. Keith
2. *The Blood of Kerensky Trilogy* (ebook box set) by Michael A. Stackpole
3. *The Legend of the Jade Phoenix Trilogy* (ebook box set) by Robert Thurston
4. *The Founding of the Clans Trilogy* (ebook box set) by Randall N. Bills

NOVELLAS/SHORT NOVELS
1. *Lion's Roar* by Steven Mohan, Jr.
2. *Sniper* by Jason Schmetzer
3. *Eclipse* by Jason Schmetzer
4. *Hector* by Jason Schmetzer
5. *The Frost Advances (Operation Ice Storm, Part One)* by Jason Schmetzer
6. *The Winds of Spring (Operation Ice Storm, Part Two)* by Jason Schmetzer
7. *Instrument of Destruction (Ghost Bear's Lament, Part One)* by Steven Mohan, Jr.
8. *The Fading Call of Glory (Ghost Bear's Lament, Part Two)* by Steven Mohan, Jr.
9. *Vengeance* by Jason Schmetzer
10. *A Splinter of Hope* by Philip A. Lee
11. *The Anvil* by Blaine Lee Pardoe
12. *A Splinter of Hope/The Anvil* (omnibus)
13. *Not the Way the Smart Money Bets (Kell Hounds Ascendant #1)* by Michael A. Stackpole
14. *A Tiny Spot of Rebellion (Kell Hounds Ascendant #2)* by Michael A. Stackpole
15. *A Clever Bit of Fiction (Kell Hounds Ascendant #3)* by Michael A. Stackpole
16. *Break-Away (Proliferation Cycle #1)* by Ilsa J. Bick

17. *Prometheus Unbound* (*Proliferation Cycle #2*) by Herbert A. Beas II
18. *Nothing Ventured* (*Proliferation Cycle #3*) by Christoffer Trossen
19. *Fall Down Seven Times, Get Up Eight* (*Proliferation Cycle #4*) by Randall N. Bills
20. *A Dish Served Cold* (*Proliferation Cycle #5*) by Chris Hartford and Jason M. Hardy
21. *The Spider Dances* (*Proliferation Cycle #6*) by Jason Schmetzer
22. *Shell Games* by Jason Schmetzer
23. *Divided We Fall* by Blaine Lee Pardoe
24. *The Hunt for Jardine* (*Forgotten Worlds, Part One*) by Herbert A. Beas II
25. *Rock of the Republic* by Blaine Lee Pardoe
26. *Finding Jardine* (*Forgotten Worlds, Part Two*) by Herbert A. Beas II
27. *The Trickster* (*Proliferation Cycle #7*) by Blaine Lee Pardoe
28. *The Price of Duty* by Jason Schmetzer
29. *Elements of Treason: Duty* by Craig A. Reed, Jr.
30. *Mercenary's Honor* by Jason Schmetzer
31. *Elements of Treason: Opportunity* by Craig A. Reed, Jr.
32. *Lethal Lessons* by Daniel Isberner
33. *If Auld Acquaintance Be Forgot...* (*Kell Hounds Ascendant #4*) by Michael A. Stackpole
34. *Giving up the Ghost* (*Fortunes of War #1*) by Bryan Young
35. *Blood Rage* (*Fortunes of War #2*) by Craig A. Reed, Jr.
36. *A Skulk of Foxes* (*Fortunes of War #3*) by Jason Hansa
37. *Let Slip the Dogs of War* by Bryan Young
38. *Hounds at Bay* (*Fortunes of War #4*) by Geoff Swift
39. *Heavy is the Head* (*Fortunes of War #5*) by Philip A. Lee
40. *A Night in the Woods* by Michael A. Stackpole

ANTHOLOGIES
1. *The Corps* (*BattleCorps Anthology, Volume 1*), edited by Loren. L. Coleman
2. *First Strike* (*BattleCorps Anthology, Volume 2*), edited by Loren L. Coleman
3. *Weapons Free* (*BattleCorps Anthology, Volume 3*), edited by Jason Schmetzer
4. *Onslaught: Tales from the Clan Invasion*, edited by Jason Schmetzer
5. *Edge of the Storm* by Jason Schmetzer
6. *Fire for Effect* (*BattleCorps Anthology, Volume 4*), edited by Jason Schmetzer
7. *Chaos Born* (*Chaos Irregulars, Book 1*) by Kevin Killiany
8. *Chaos Formed* (*Chaos Irregulars, Book 2*) by Kevin Killiany
9. *Counterattack* (*BattleCorps Anthology, Volume 5*), edited by Jason Schmetzer
10. *Front Lines* (*BattleCorps Anthology, Volume 6*), edited by Jason Schmetzer and Philip A. Lee
11. *Legacy*, edited by John Helfers and Philip A. Lee
12. *Kill Zone* (*BattleCorps Anthology, Volume 7*), edited by Philip A. Lee
13. *Gray Markets* (*A BattleCorps Anthology*), edited by Jason Schmetzer and Philip A. Lee
14. *Slack Tide* (*A BattleCorps Anthology*), edited by Jason Schmetzer and Philip A. Lee
15. *The Battle of Tukayyid*, edited by John Helfers
16. *The Mercenary Life* by Randall N. Bills.
17. *The Proliferation Cycle*, edited by John Helfers and Philip A. Lee
18. *No Greater Honor* (*The Complete Eridani Light Horse Chronicles*),
        edited by John Helfers and Philip A. Lee
19. *Kell Hounds Ascendant* by Michael A. Stackpole
20. *Marauder* by Lance Scarinci
21. *Fox Tales* by Bryan Young
22. *Gray Death Rising* by Jason Schmetzer
23. *Fortunes of War, Volume One* edited by John Helfers
24. *Fortunes of War, Volume Two* edited by John Helfers

MAGAZINES
1. *Shrapnel*, Issue #1–*Shrapnel*, Issue #20

The march of technology across BattleTech's eras is relentless...

Some BattleMech designs never die. Each installment of *Recognition Guide: IlClan*, currently a PDF-only series, not only includes a brand new BattleMech or OmniMech, but also details Classic 'Mech designs from both the Inner Sphere and the Clans, now fully rebuilt with Dark Age technology (3085 and beyond).

STORE.CATALYSTGAMELABS.COM

Made in United States
Orlando, FL
15 August 2025

63948770R00203